Rough Trade

DATE DUE

1 3 JUN 2003	- 4 FEB 2004	2 0 AUG 2010
- 4 AUG 2003	1 8 AUG 2004	- 1 DEC 2010
- 6 AUG 2003		1 4 APR 2011
	2 NOV 2004	
1 4 AUG 2003	2 0 DEC 2004	1 AUG 2011
2 SEP 2003	1 2 DEC 2005	2 4 AUG 2011
1 8 NOV 2003		0 5 JUL 2012
	1 9 MAY 2006	
- 8 DEC 2003		
	1 1 SEP 2006	
	3 0 APR 2007	
1 4 JAN 2004	1 4 MAR 2008	
2 7 JAN 2004	2 0 APR 2009	

2519/07/96

DOMINIQUE MANOTTI teaches nineteenth-century Economic History. *ROUGH TRADE*, her first novel, was awarded the top prize for the best thriller of the year by the French Crime Writers Association. Her other books include *Cop* and *To Our Horses!*

ROUGH TRADE

DOMINIQUE MANOTTI

translated from French by
Margaret Crosland and Elfreda Powell

A ARCADIA BOOKS
LONDON

Arcadia Books Ltd
15–16 Nassau Street
London w1w 7AB

www.arcadiabooks.co.uk

First published in the United Kingdom 2001
Second impression 2002
Originally published by Editions du Seuil, Paris, 1995
Copyright © Dominique Manotti 1995

This English translation from the French, *Sombre Sentier*
copyright © Margaret Crosland and Elfreda Powell 2001

Dominique Manotti has asserted her moral right to be identified as the author of this work in accordance with the Copyright, Designs and Patents Act, 1988.

A catalogue record for this book is available from the British Library.

ISBN 1–900850–46–x

Edited, designed and typeset by Discript, London WC2N 4BN
Printed in the United Kingdom by Bell & Bain Limited, Glasgow

Arcadia Books Ltd gratefully acknowledges the financial support of The Arts Council of England and of London Arts. This book is supported by the French Ministry for Foreign Affairs, as part of the Burgess Programme, headed for the French Embassy in London by the Institut Français du Royaume-Uni.

Arcadia Books distributors are as follows:

in the UK and elsewhere in Europe:
Turnaround Publishers Services
Unit 3, Olympia Trading Estate
Coburg Road
London N22 6TZ

in the USA and Canada:
Consortium Book Sales and Distribution, Inc.
1045 Westgate Drive
St Paul, MN 55114–1065

in Australia:
Tower Books
PO Box 213
Brookvale, NSW 2100

in New Zealand:
Addenda
Box 78224
Grey Lynn
Auckland

CONTENTS

Everything, or almost everything, has been invented in this story. The characters, plot and action are entirely fictitious: any resemblance to real events or personalities is therefore, as they say, entirely fortuitous. On the other hand, quotations from the press are accurate, as is the context in which they were written, in particular that of the Sentier in spring 1980 and the illegal workers' endeavours to obtain legal status.

Heroin is now entering from Iran, Pakistan and Afghanistan. Last year Iran harvested 1,500 tons of raw opium. It is in these countries that the opium is being refined – and particularly in Turkey – then transported by road into Western Europe. Note, however, that this heroin is 20 per cent pure, as opposed to only 3.5 per cent as produced in Mexico. In Germany last year there were 600 cases of overdosing as a direct result of this new heroin.

Libération, 15 January 1980

There's a girl, sitting naked on the edge of a vast white bed in the middle of a room, with mirrors all around. She's childlike yet already world-weary. In a corner is a Louis XV armchair; at the far end, a table-height fridge. On it are tumblers, flutes, goblets, an assortment of glasses. She's gently swinging her legs and singing to herself. A man comes in. He's also naked. She studies him, gives him the once-over. Around forty-five, bullneck, fat, small bum, thin legs, balding, but a real mat of ginger hair on his chest. She smiles and beckons, and he, with gluttonous face, sidles slowly towards the ice-box, opens it, pours himself a very generous whisky –'Want a drink, baby girl?' – he raises his glass to her. The gesture is rather too expansive: he sloshes the whisky on the thick white carpet. She shakes her head, says nothing, but has a constant smile. He drinks, lets the glass fall on the carpet, goes over to her, collapses on the bed, laughing.

She makes him lie face down, sits on the small of his back. Next to him, she's incredibly fragile. She begins massaging him, mewing softly to get herself into the rhythm. He lets her do it, groans with pleasure, encourages her. 'Give your little daddy a cuddle.' She lies on top of him, nibbles his neck, his ears. He stirs slowly, emits a few inaudible sounds, snatches at the carpet with his fingers. She turns him over on to his back. He looks pleased. She gently massages his dick. The man leans up on his elbows. He looks at this tiny body barely able to balance on his, turns towards the mirrors and smiles at them. He's humming. She solemnly applies herself to her task. Her face is more attentive, her smile fixed, her eyes watching the other person's reaction.

All at once the man senses he's being watched. He seems to be waking from a long sleep, but his eyes are glazed. The girl slowly raises her hands towards the man's nipples and starts pinching them gently. The humming transmutes to a long moan. He sits up and she falls on the bed. He's overcome with panicky fear. His eyes are dilated. He screams 'She's going to kill me'. He curls up, hands over eyes, and starts kicking out at the girl. 'Is it a game?' she asks, still smiling, but seems a little anxious. She avoids the kicks and tries to calm him by drawing him down on the bed, caressing his shoulders and nipples. 'Remember, I'm your baby.' But he screams again. 'Don't grow up, don't grow up.' Then he grabs her by the throat, shakes her, throws her down on the bed and squeezes, squeezes. 'You won't have me.' She struggles a bit, not much, she's completely crushed by the man's massive weight. She can't cry out any more. After one, two minutes she stops struggling altogether.

7 a.m. Sentier Metro station

A group of Turks, about fifteen in all, and five or six Frenchmen, are crowded together at the back of a café-tabac opposite the station. Everyone's drinking black coffee and the French are eating croissants. On a table are two huge piles of leaflets in salmon pink paper, typewritten then just roneoed, recto in French, verso in Turkish.

> The Defence Committee for Turks in France calls upon the Turkish workers of the Sentier district to stop working on Monday 3 March, and to assemble at the Sentier Metro station at midday. The purpose of this meeting is to get your papers legalized and have better working conditions.

They cluster around a map of Paris. Soleiman's forming small groups of five, made up of Turks with a Frenchman in charge. Each group receives a list of streets to cover, some are jotting down names on a bit of newspaper or cigarette pack. The scene has an air of Bolshevik Russia, pre-1917.

Everyone stands up – there's bedlam – and goes out into the square. It's going to be a beautiful day. Like plunging into the complete unknown, but that's too shaming to admit. You must look as though you know what you're doing.

Soleiman takes charge of a group and begins to tackle rue d'Aboukir, a female journalist from *Libération* in tow. He's tall, slim, very erect, even a bit rigid, with a longish face, high cheekbones, a thin prominent nose and huge blue eyes, a light brown mop of hair, dark complexion. The Turks listen to him, the girl looks on. Each building is to be gone into, the names read on the mailboxes, and any picked out that look Turkish or Yugoslav. They climb the stairs. In the old buildings the entrance halls are dark, staircases tortuous. On every floor the noise of sewing-machines can be heard. Soleiman knocks on the door. The boss opens up, or more often a worker. A discussion then ensues, either in Turkish or French. 'Good morning. We're the Defence Committee for Turks, we've come to talk to you about the strike and the rally to get legal papers for Turkish workers.' Whoever opens the door turns to the workshop: 'What d'you reckon? Shall we let him in?' 'Yes . . . sure . . .' Not a single door is shut on them the whole morning.

Cramped, ill-lit, overheated workrooms, smells of dressing. But a warm atmosphere. Enormous radio sets broadcast news and music from back home. There's talk, banter. From time to time a cousin drops by to say 'hallo' or a worker goes downstairs to play the pinball machine.

When Soleiman and his group enter, the machines stop, people jostle between the tables, coffee's passed around, the boss joining in the discussion. The idea seems remote. But will they come for the midday meeting in the Sentier? Maybe. Soleiman leaves a few leaflets. The group heads for the next floor up or the next building.

Boulevard Saint-Denis, then rue du Faubourg-Saint-Martin . . . the buildings become more spacious, the workrooms better lit, more airy. Behind the nineteenth-century façades, some of the courtyards are real factories, with tailoring on every floor and female workers living in the servants' quarters in the attics; women in headscarves and long skirts open the door. Soleiman doesn't know what to say to them. He must find it inappropriate for them to go down into the street.

The group works its way back up as a far as rue de Belleville. Really dilapidated buildings sometimes, seedy corridors, miserable workrooms, some even without a door, just a big cardboard box blocking the entrance, but the same welcome everywhere. The group's worn out, it's hot at this hour of the morning. More and more frequently they stop at bistros, and here workers are already coming to ask Soleiman for leaflets themselves (for here everyone knows everything). Now they must turn back in order to be at the Sentier Metro station at midday.

In the street running down towards the square, small groups of militants are joining forces, overexcited by the welcome they've received. They move out on to the square. No one's there. Of course, it's what you'd expect. Imagine opening the workroom door, listening, yes, going down to the street: they mustn't fantasize. But the militants have a fighting spirit and are used to being on their own. Soleiman puts the PA system in position. They unravel some rolls of red fabric to mark boundaries for their meeting place. That raw red is beautiful in the sun. Soleiman begins speaking in Turkish. He gives an account of what it's like to have illegal status, disguised as a tourist with a camera slung over his shoulder; the fear you have to overcome when you see a policeman on the street, the way you have to go on walking, the friskings, the nights in police stations, deportation orders. It's over. We want no more of it. We're here, we're working. We want residence permits, work permits. Dignity.

And then the nearest cafés, packed full, begin to empty on to the square. The men listen, discuss things among themselves, enter inside the red cloth boundaries.

Little groups come down from adjacent streets, in small prudent clusters, but there are more and more of them. By 1 p.m. more than 2,000 workers have assembled inside the boundaries; in rue Réaumur the traffic is brought to a standstill – but not a cop in sight. It's intoxicating. The illegal workers are occupying the street, and no one's coming to move them off. The men are shouting 'Yasasin grevi – Long live the strike. Residence permit, work permit'. The PA systems move about, everyone wants to put in a word. Soleiman is shivering in the sunshine. He has wanted this moment with every breath in his body, but he couldn't believe it – only now does he become aware that he never believed it – this heady moment when the masses begin to be real, and abstractions are left behind, this moment where everything becomes – perhaps – possible . . . when the world will erupt into change.

No one knows what to do with this huge, unexpected crowd. Even if the cops aren't here, they could still come. Staying in this one place makes them too vulnerable. But the men don't want to leave any more. Unobtrusively Soleiman moves the cloth boundaries forward towards the Bourse du Travail – the Trade Union Centre. Here they can get news on the negotiations taking place with the government: they must stick together. They'll be in a safe place too. The demonstration's running very smoothly, it's impressive seeing this really compact group of swarthy moustachioed men all in shades of grey, shouting slogans in Turkish without ever pausing for breath and clutching those long, silent red banners.

4 p.m. Police station. 10th Arrondissement

'Hallo. Police station, 10th arrondissement here.'

'Is that the police?' A strong foreign accent.

'Yes, *monsieur*.'

'Come quickly. I've found a body. A girl, in my workshop.'

Thomas and Santoni walked in through the porch of 43 rue du Faubourg-Saint-Martin. Left staircase. Third floor. No elevator of course. The entrance door was ajar. They knocked. Immediately, a man was there to meet them, obviously very upset.

'Local Squad. Was it you who just called the police?'

'Yes. Come in.'

And there in the dark entryway, twenty or so pairs of red linen gypsy pants were piled on the floor. The man picked them up. Underneath was the body of a very young woman, almost a child, of Asiatic origin: completely naked, lying on her back. Thomas went over to her and bent down. Death leaves no room for doubt. He tried lifting one of her arms. Must have happened more than twenty-four hours earlier. Bluish marks on her neck. Probably caused by strangulation. He looked a bit closer. With bare hands.

'Was it you who found her?'

'Yes.' Said nervously.

'Santoni, call Crime.'

Thomas took a look around the apartment. The entryway, cluttered with rolls of fabric and plastic. A corridor led into the two fairly light main rooms which overlooked the courtyard. Inside the two rooms, five big wooden tables fixed to the floor, spattered with different stains, twenty or so solid iron chairs, electric cables hanging here and there from the ceiling, huge neon striplights. And two old, somewhat dilapidated sewing-machines. On the other side of the corridor, a kitchen. White tiles. Sink, hot and cold water. Fridge, cooker. Formica table. Everything sparkling clean. Not a plate in sight. Seemingly absent-mindedly Thomas opened the fridge. It was full of vegetables, cheeses, drinks. Under the sink, the bin had been emptied and washed. Beyond the kitchen were two very dark recesses, perhaps an old bathroom, a small bedroom.

Then he concentrated his attention on the man who'd phoned them. His name was Bostic. He was Yugoslav, he rented the apartment and managed the workroom.

'When did you find the body?'

'When I opened the workroom, this afternoon.'

'Why not this morning?'

'There was the strike. I found the body, there, under the gypsy

6

pants. I sent the workers home and phoned the police. I haven't touched a thing.'

Thomas groaned.

*

Shortly afterwards, the officers from the Crime Squad arrived and took over. Specialists, the investigating magistrate,[*] photographs of the body, transport to the morgue... Thomas handed over the first statements made by Bostic, without comment.

'What should we do then, with him?'

'I'd like him to be held in custody with the Local Squad. That way, you have him at hand for further questioning tomorrow if you want. And we'd like to ask him a few questions ourselves on how his workroom's run. Working without work permits, I'm certain. Just one Yugoslav, that's not taking any risks.'

'OK. Can you think of anything else you want to tell us?'

Thomas glanced enquiringly at Santoni.

'Not me. You?'

'No, nothing.'

Once Bostic was in custody, Thomas turned to Santoni.

'What d'you think?'

'He found the body this morning when he opened his workshop.'

'Agreed.'

'That gave him almost eight hours to spare.'

'Just about.'

'Before phoning us, he sold his machines, so we couldn't seize them. It's a workroom for illegal immigrants.'

'Right again.'

'It's a normal sort of set-up for the Sentier, fairly grubby. But not the kitchen. Did you see how it was all spick and span? That's where the workers eat and drink all the time in sweatshops like that. Even when it's well run, it's never as clean as that.'

'So what shall we do?'

'We'll go back there, try to find what it was he cleaned up and threw away. And not a word to those smart alecs in Crime.'

*

The building had a concierge, apron over shapeless dress, and

---

[*] In France the investigating magistrate has wide responsibilities for investigating crimes, arresting suspects, and gathering evidence.

check carpet slippers. After two beers and a quarter of an hour's rambling conversation, Thomas and Santoni learned that in fact Bostic put the bags of rubbish out at 10 a.m. Two blue bags.

*

An old sheet was spread out on the ground in the yard, under the timed light. The two men took off their jackets, rolled up their sleeves and emptied the first of the building's three dustbins. They had to press the light switch every three minutes, open up the waste bags one after the other, sort out the household rubbish, bits of rag, newspapers, empty bottles. Everything had to be examined much more closely since they didn't know what they were looking for. Perhaps, for the best – when you knew what you were looking for, you risked making a judicial error, so my chief told me when I began in this business. No risk of that here.

The concierge arrived to cast an eye every now and again. First dustbin: nothing. All the jumble of rubbish had to be put back. Second bin: nothing. Third bin: contents which could have come from Bostic's kitchen, like the other sacks. Coffee grounds, paper plates, wrapping paper, stale bread. And two strong plastic bags of a good size, transparent, empty. Thomas stood up. Along the joints was a very fine white powder. Very carefully he took a speck on his index finger, and tasted it with the tip of his tongue. Smiled at Santoni. This was it. Heroin.

9 p.m. Villa des Artistes

It's already dark. Soleiman walks briskly down avenue Jean-Moulin, dives into a porch and enters the villa des Artistes, muttering. Third house on the right amidst a jumble of greenery, big studio window, white blinds lit from behind. An outside lantern glows above the entrance. He rings twice, pushes the door, enters and locks it behind him. A large spacious room, spotlights almost everywhere, leather, wood, a mezzanine in the shadows. A man is busy in a kitchenette at the back of the room behind a wooden counter. The kitchen's very modern, tiled in shades of ochre. The man's about thirty-five, rather handsome square face, well-built type once, a Rugby three-quarter, brown eyes and hair. In jeans and polo neck, bare feet.

'Ah, congratulations. Your meeting was a success, well beyond all your expectations. My chums weren't anticipating that – quite honestly, they didn't know what to do.'

'We said you didn't meddle in that sort of thing and you'd left me *carte blanche.*'

'But I didn't meddle, did I. Congratulations.'

'Leave off. I can manage without your congratulations.'

'OK, OK. let's get down to business. You've seen loads of people today. Now, do you have something for me?'

'Possibly. Rue du Faubourg-Saint-Martin, near the boulevard, on the left as you go up, there's a Turkish sandwich shop. A tiny little shop, with a counter right on the street. The Kurds say that that's where the Turks are peddling drugs.'

'I know where you mean. I'll put it under surveillance tomorrow morning. It may be our first lead, after a month of floundering around...' Going back to the kitchenette. 'It's ready. Lay the table.'

'I'm not staying for dinner. I've friends to see.'

'Soleiman. Stop messing me around. You can go and see whoever you want, but afterwards. You're dining with me, because I want to fuck you after I've eaten, not before.' And, with a big smile: 'And there's no need to look so grim all the time. It doesn't put me off; quite the reverse, it gives me the feeling I'm forcing you, and that I find exciting.'

8 a.m. Rue du Faubourg-Saint-Martin

Daquin had stopped off in a café right opposite the sandwich bar, which had just opened. The sandwich place was somewhat basic. Just a deep narrow passageway, with a counter all down one side and a cramped street frontage, completely open today as the weather was fine. No tables or chairs. Three men were busy behind the counter. At the back were a door and hatch through to the kitchen. Customers were forever coming and going – all Turkish, on first impression. Sandwiches, salads, coffees, teas, rakis, beers. No one seemed to stay for any length of time. A duff lead?

'Another coffee please.'

Once the early morning rush was over, the clientele quietened down. People standing at the counter chatted for longer. Every so often, someone went right to the back of the shop, passed behind the counter and from there into the kitchen, then came out again. Must check if there's any significance in this.

10 a.m. Passage du Désir

Daquin walked up to the Local Squad's headquarters in passage du Désir. It was there, on the third and final floor, of a small brick and stone building, jammed into a tiny scruffy street in the 10th arrondisssement, that Daquin and his team were installed: a meeting room had been turned into an office for the duration of their investigation. They were a small *ad hoc* team, whose remit from the head of the Drugs Squad was to explore any leads to an eventual 'Turkish trail', following tip-offs from the German police. Large bright room with sloping ceiling, two metal desks – one for Daquin, the other for his inspectors,* two upright armchairs, six chairs, an oval table, two typewriters, two telephones and a small sink, a stove, a coffee-machine. On one side two big windows overlooking the courtyard, on the other, a glass door on to a calm, light corridor. It was a makeshift den, but pleasant.

Daquin's two inspectors were waiting for him. On the surface Attali and Romero appeared much the same. They'd grown up

---

* In France an *inspector* is roughly equivalent to a detective or an American lieutenant.

together in a council block on the Belle-de-Mai estate in Marseilles. They were the same age – around twenty-five – and both wore bomber jackets, jeans and basketball boots. But Attali had been the good boy, top of his class, quickly passing his inspector's exam, so he could support his mother and sisters, who'd been having a hard time. He was serious, polite, boring. Romero's childhood and adolescence had teetered on delinquency. He was a handsome guy: regular features, jet-black hair. But he'd abused his physique. He'd passed his inspector's exam at the same time as Attali, purely as a challenge, and perhaps because of a secret wish to be up and off. It was the first time that, after three years in the business, they'd teamed up together under Daquin's leadership, as from a month ago. When Daquin came in, they were playing noughts and crosses.

He cast a disillusioned glance in their direction, made himself a coffee, then said: 'I've some work for you. A Turkish sandwich shop, at the bottom of rue du Faubourg-Saint-Martin, very near here. It's to be put under surveillance – with cameras. It's a lead from one of our snouts. No way you can use a vehicle. If you have to stay several days, you'll be spotted right away. Might be better, perhaps, to find a window in the building opposite. Take complete responsibility for mounting this operation. I want photos – not of all the customers of course, but all the ones who go right into the shop and pass behind the counter. See the Super at the 10th arrondissement: Meillant's his name. He's been told about our team. He's been in this neck of the woods at least twenty years. Knows everybody. He'll certainly be able to help you.'

*

Once the two inspectors had left, Daquin delved into the newspapers. He was convinced that part of the solution to the problem was back there, in the countries of origin, and he needed to understand what was going on there. With the Ayatollah Khomeini coming to power, always making trouble, US hostages in Tehran, the extreme right and extreme left slaughtering each other in Turkey at the rate twenty deaths a day, and now Soviet intervention in Afghanistan, reading the papers was a lengthy business.

10 a.m. Parish of Saint Bernard

It was here that the Defence Committee for Turks in France had found a base. A small windowless office in the basement of the parish hall next to the church.

Today, the day after the demo, it was like a tidal wave. The narrow dark corridors of the ground floor were swamped with Turks who wanted to join the Committee. Soleiman made each new member answer an anonymous questionnaire. How many hours a day d'you work at present? In the off-season? Wages? When, why did you change your job? Family? How long have you lived here? Lodgings? Who's the landlord? What rent d'you pay? Four packed pages of questions, in Turkish and French. Men were sitting around all over the place, in the corridors, the yard, assiduously filling in their questionnaire. And supposing, by some miracle, it might come in useful for something? Soleiman read through them all again, discussing items with each person, explaining or filling in gaps, if questions hadn't been understood properly. He was here for everyone, listening attentively. He'd never sat behind a sewing-machine himself, had lived on his wits, always, while he'd been in Paris, photographing tourists at the foot of the Eiffel Tower, selling popcorn, roast chestnuts, and here he was becoming a specialist on work problems in the rag trade.

There were rumours that a black market in membership cards had already started in the Sentier. Sold to the Committee at 16 francs, they were being sold on at 100 francs in workrooms where there were people unwilling, or too scared, to show their faces outside. For the Turks, these were the first official documents they'd had in France. It was said, and it was probably true, that some men had produced their card at an identity check in the Metro, and that the police had let them through.

Gradually, the wave of people reached the small windowless office. All the corridors on the ground floor stank of strong stale tobacco, the lino was spattered with fag ends and burn marks. So many people were milling around, they had to impose a one-way system with notices in Turkish. The lavatories were filthy and overflowing. The small, rather peaceful canteen was taken over and turned into a café open all hours, a smoking den. Priests and parishioners present in the building shut themselves away in their offices. Cohabitation was going to be difficult.

Negotiations with the office of the Secretary of State for Immigrant Workers would be opening the following day. The Committee was taking part. Brief confab. Soleiman was appointed, unanimously, to represent the Committee.

He could forget Daquin, breathe again. Soleiman left to chat up the girls on the boulevards.

7 p.m. Drugs Squad

'Our first leads at last, *patron*. But there're a few fairly significant points I'd like to talk to you about, which aren't in the written report.'

'I'm listening, Théo. I've all the time in the world. My wife's off skiing, and I'm a bachelor just like you. Whisky?'

'No thanks. I'd like a vodka though, if you have one. When you formed my team a month ago, we had a clear objective. It was to be a very limber, loose sort of group, set up to look for leads. You promised me you'd fill it out in due course as we progressed, or have the Paris Drugs Squad take up certain files. Does this still apply?'

'Sure.'

'Good. For nearly a whole month now we've found nothing. We checked the names and info the Germans supplied and they don't tally with anything of ours. Maybe the guys in question aren't in France, or more probably we haven't found any trace of their presence. Now Attali's gone through all the police files on overdosing there've been in the last three months in the Paris area, to try to find any abnormal overdosing compared with the usual scenario, so we can track down eventual dealers. Good idea. Loads of work. Complete dead end. What's more, our statistics don't yet show any rise in deaths through overdosing, as the Germans' do. It's probable that Turkish opium isn't yet operational. Our second line of attack was to nose around the Turkish communities in the area. Romero's been mooching round the Turkish workers at Citroën-Aulnay. They're very isolated – no contacts with the French, very confined. So, hardly likely there. I've kept the Sentier for myself. I wasn't familiar with it at all, but I had a good sense of the place: right in the heart of Paris, an expanding immigrant population, and not illiterate peasants, but totally uncontrolled – neither by our police, nor by the immigration services. At the same time, there's a move among the Turkish workers in the rag trade to get legal papers. I don't know if you've been following this item in the newspapers?'

His chief gave a vague wave of the hand, which could have meant absolutely anything, accompanied by a large swig of whisky. Daquin found himself wondering if the Old Man was interested in anything he was saying. He had to overcome his feeling of despondency and carry on.

'Seventeen Turks have been on hunger strike since last 11 February. The people behind this strike are extreme left-wing militants. According to our German colleagues, if you recall, the drugs are in the hands of the extreme right. I'm going to hang around on the strikers' side. I've had photos taken. I've asked our Turkish colleagues for reports on this whole community. And from their responses, I've chosen a guy who seems to me, let's say, "vulnerable". He's here without any papers, under a false name. In Turkey, he's labelled a militant in a very active ultra left-wing group. He's been wanted since '79 for the assassination of an extreme right-wing militant in Istanbul and close on the heels of that, for the murder of a cop who was chasing him. Not only that: between eighteen and twenty, he was arrested several times by the Istanbul police because he made a living as a prostitute in the tourist areas.'

His chief glanced over his glass. There, I've caught his interest, Daquin thought. He could swear that his eyes held a smile, but he chose to ignore both the smile and its innuendo.

'He seemed to me to correspond exactly to the profile I was looking for. We provoked a brawl in a bistro where he hung out, arrested twenty or so guys, and dispersed them among the police stations in the arrondissement. The following day, my young assassin was in my office. There I forced him to accept or refuse: either he stirred himself and got me leads on drugs in the Sentier, or I sent him straight back to Turkey. It didn't work right away. So, I threw in the bit about the drug network being controlled by the Turkish extreme right. If he gave me these tip-offs, I'd liquidate the extreme right, and then he could do what he liked with his mates: legalizing illegal workers, I don't give a toss. I added a couple of remarks about what the effect would be if his mates found out he'd been a prostitute. I told him the Turkish police had sent us photos – which wasn't true – but it worked. Yesterday, he gave me our first lead. But this morning two inspectors from the Local Squad in passage du Désir came to see me. Yesterday they found a body in a workroom in the Sentier, a girl of twelve or thirteen, a Thai, probably a prostitute. And, in the same workroom, two bags which had contained heroin – the purest sort – exactly what we're looking for. About a kilo's worth. Which could be the start of a second lead.'

'Brilliant job, my dear Théo, and when all's said and done, in record time. So, what is it you're asking for?'

'Well, first, I wanted to put you in the picture, as regards my snout, bearing in mind the current unrest among the Turkish workforce. Then, the body in the workroom. The workroom manager's in police custody, but time's running out for that, and the case belongs to Crime. I'd like to be able to keep the follow-up of the inquiry into this murder, since it's probably linked to drug trafficking, and for that augment my team with the two inspectors from the Local Squad who've let us take part in it, and who've already been very impressive. We've everything to gain by this.'

'It's a reasonable request. We'll extend police custody for your man, and I'll give you an official reply as to the rest tomorrow; but, for my part, I agree. I should also tell you that the Marseilles team has drawn a complete blank. In spite of the, let's say, "insistent" leads from the Americans. And in spite of promising beginnings. You remember that haul of six kilos of morphine-base found in the tyre of an Armenian's car last December? Since, then, nothing – impossible to find where the network starts. We've just folded up the team. Daquin, don't put your trust in appearances, don't believe I haven't listened to you with the utmost attention. I really like your approach to your work.'

8 a.m. Rue du Faubourg-Saint-Martin

Attali took the first surveillance shift – from when the sandwich shop opened. They were in an apartment belonging to a patrolman from the 10th arrondissment police station, retired for almost fifteen years. It was Meillant, the Superintendent from the 10th, who introduced them. Third floor, almost opposite the shop. Two tiny rooms, but with two big windows on the street, massive dark wood furniture, small kitchen, bog and so forth: every modern comfort. Attali had sunk into a large high-backed armchair by the window, the telephoto lens trained on the shop entrance, a truly comfortable situation. The old man wandered into the room, in slippers, with the red puffy face of an inveterate alcoholic. He was as happy as Larry to take up with the service again, he said. He'd prepared some café au lait and croissants. Then, without any breathing space, the first pastis. Attali tried vainly to be an honourable drinker, but right after the coffee the pastis was a bit startling. And already smells of sautéed mutton and haricot beans were coming from the kitchen.

He photographed people coming out of the long passageway which formed the shop interior. A waste of time photographing those standing in front, out in the street, where there was a permanent huddle.

The old man rambled on about the decadence of the neighbourhood. It was better before; now there were wogs everywhere, you couldn't understand what anybody was saying any more. The camera worked on steadily.

10 a.m. Rue Saint-Denis

If they had the chance to keep on the case, they would have to prove how efficient they were. A small Thai prostitute doesn't fall out of the sky naked and strangled into a workroom in the Sentier. The forensic surgeon's report said that the body had been moved after death. So, where had it come from?

A prostitute. Santoni knew the area well. He went into a porn shop which sold videos and various other accessories. A bespectacled pimply youth behind the counter didn't even look up from his paper. Some customers – all male – were wandering between the shelves – sidelong glances, flushed cheeks, hands in pockets, not really relaxed. Santoni brandished his warrant card, said 'Police' in a loud voice and walked towards the pimply youth, who jumped and looked at him stupefied. When he reached the counter, he turned round: all the customers had vanished.

'See. It's easy to ruin your turnover.'

'Why're you doing this, *monsieur*?'

'To set your brain ticking, scumbag. A Thai kid, twelve years old, a prostitute, was killed on Friday or Saturday, in this area.' He placed a photo of the dead girl on the counter. 'Thomas and I want to know who she is, and who did it. It's in your interest to find out: if not, we'll be obliged to search your premises. And you're going to see me here more often than you'd wish. Raids, arrests, interrogations. The big stuff. Not good for your customers. Get it?'

'I've never heard any mention of this girl, *inspecteur*.'

'That's not good enough. Understand? You'd better stir yourself. Keep the photo – that would help. You can meet me at lunchtime – Chez Mado.'

Santoni walked out without looking back. A bit further up the street, at the entrance to a narrow, dirty, very dark corridor, was a superb black woman: aged about twenty, in an extremely clinging short red skirt and tube top of the same colour – too short – you could see her navel. With the ghost of a smile, Santoni ran his hand up under her skirt, slipped it into her pants and gently pinched her fanny, as it's said grandfathers used to pinch their grandchildren's cheeks once upon a time.

'Hi, Snow White, where's your girlfriend?'

'Upstairs. Don't go up. She's busy.'

'Out of my way.'

He pushed her roughly aside and ran up the steep stairs, walked along the corridor, took a key from his pocket and without pausing opened the last door on the left. Small bed-sit, window on to the street, proper shower room to the left, big bed to the right, mirrors everywhere, on the ceiling and walls. A table at the foot of the bed on which a blonde lay outstretched, legs dangling. The client got to his feet, terrified.

'Police.' Santoni brandished his card. 'Get dressed and hop it.' The blonde sat up. A genuine blonde, a bit skinny, enormous breasts, pink rings round the nipples. 'You can get dressed too. I'm taking you in.'

The client had already gone. He must have been doing up his flies as he ran down the corridor.

'Wait. I might as well make the most of it. Play with me between your tits.'

And Santoni undid his trousers, standing in front of the door.

Once the girl had washed and dressed, Santoni passed her a photo of the little Thai girl and gave her some details.

'You've two hours to ask around. I'm having lunch at Chez Mado. If I don't have anything by the start of the afternoon, come this evening. I'm banging you up. Cold turkey for you. Understood?'

*

Thomas meanwhile, accompanied by five uniformed policemen, investigated one of the two Thai restaurants in the area. He made his presence known, brutally overturning tables, breaking a piece of china. A couple of smacks across the face for the owner, the staff lined up against the wall, the young cook (who had no papers) manhandled out of his hiding place under the kitchen table, hand-cuffed and attached to the coat rack by the entrance. Passers-by stared in, eyes popping.

'Know this girl?' Photo of the dead girl. 'A girl from your own country. We want to know who she is, where she comes from. Find me details, and I'll give you back your cook. Otherwise, he's deported tomorrow, and the tax inspectors for you.'

Thomas and Santoni called this tactic 'getting rid of the dead wood'.

12 a.m. Rue du Faubourg-Saint-Martin

After the fourth pastis, Attali ate the mutton sauté from a plate on his knees, and downed a bottle of Cahors with it, without leaving the window. At a rough guess, only Turks were going into the shop. Coffee and cognac. Attali caught himself hoping this cushy job wouldn't last too long. The old boy went to have his siesta. Attali was nodding off too. The old boy was back, he was interested in the technology, was looking about, asking questions. It made his head reel even more than the pastis, but he had to remain friendly.

'Why're you only taking photos of the sandwich shop?' the old boy asked.

'Because we're interested in the people working there. What else d'you think we should be photographing?'

'Well, the accessory shop next door to it. (Shuttles, bobbins, scissors, sewing-machine repairs.) It's owned by the same people. They're either in one shop or the other, it depends on the time of day.'

'How d'you know that?'

'They've been there several months now, and we've had time to watch them, me and the owner of the bistro down there. They go from one shop to the other through the yard at the back: there's a way through.'

Attali grouchily went on taking photos.

12 a.m. Rue de la Fidelité

Mado was an institution in the neighbourhood. An old prostitute, who'd moved over, with some style, into the restaurant business. Thomas went into the bar, behind which the ancient pimp and current husband sat enthroned, anaesthetized by alcohol fumes and abundant easy money. He'd served no useful purpose for a long time, but Mado was a woman of feeling and a faithful one at that.

Thomas greeted him politely, parted the thick red curtain which divided off the dining-room. Mado was there, her fifties all but faded away, a bottle blonde of Fellini proportions, tightly constricted in a tiny black skirt and pink angora top, and smothered in rings, bracelets and necklaces. With a Yorkshire terrier tucked between left forearm and bosom, she navigated her way between the tables to check they were properly laid.

Thomas placed his two hands on Mado's buttocks. They were immense and firm, a foretaste of bliss.

'Good morning, Big Boy. Table for later? Here, for two.'

She placed a small reservation card on it. Then led him by the arm towards the apartment just above the restaurant. Mado still slept with her 'serious' clients, but they no longer had to pay. After a bout of rumpy-pumpy she would automatically offer them a meal. Revenge? No one, in any case, would have dreamed of refusing.

And especially Thomas, who adored big blondes, and who, Mado had convinced him, was an extraordinary lover. She had talent and a trade, and thought it best to stay on good terms with the cops.

*

At 1 p.m. Thomas walked downstairs into the dining-room, where Santoni was waiting. They sat down.

Mado came to sit at their table for a few minutes. It was here that they talked business. She would not have allowed Thomas to do it in the bedroom earlier on. A Thai girl of twelve, a prostitute, killed on Friday night/Saturday morning and whose body had been found in a rag trade workroom in rue Faubourg-Saint-Martin: did that mean anything to her? No. On first impulse, absolutely nothing. You've already rung a few bells in this area this morning? Well, perhaps that's begun to have some effect. I'm going to see what I can pick up. A few swaying steps between the tables and Mado disappeared round by the bar.

She was an important person in local life. Everyone knew she talked to the police, but she stayed within the rules, within the accepted boundaries. She was recognized by everyone as an indispensable means of communication.

After a number of to-ings and fro-ings, Mado came back and signalled to the waiter: two coffees and two cognacs for these gentlemen.

'Nothing on the girl herself. But there are people in the neighbourhood who work with Thailand and who can't be totally legit. An agency which puts on shows, so-called. The Aratoff Ballets, in rue des Petites-Ecuries. As far as the shows are concerned, their main business seems to be organising a tour of the brothels in Bangkok through specialist travel agents.'

'Sort of unfair trading through relocation of employment? Thanks for the lead, Mado.'

'See you again some time, Big Boy.'

4 p.m. Rue du Faubourg-Saint-Martin

Romero arrived to change shifts. Attali was swaying slightly as he greeted him. Confab while the old boy, being discreet, went out to the kitchen. Decision taken to photograph anyone coming out of both shops: they would go over it with the Super tomorrow.

As he left, Attali passed under the porch and into the yard of the building. There were numerous tailoring workrooms on every floor, a hell of a racket. A bit of a chat with the concierge, a woman in her fifties, smiling, because she was so happy to be having a natter with a Frenchman, she missed it, you know. There were certainly two shops, with two names and two tenants, but they had a single letterbox and either one or the other picked up the mail. But you know I'd be amazed if their business was of any importance.

Attali went back into the street with a more assured step. He still felt very drunk. It was impossible to go home in this state. His mother would kick up such a fuss about it. He decided to take the photos to the lab, then go and see an old detective film in the Latin Quarter: it was a question of sleeping it off in peace.

8 a.m. Passage du Désir

Nerves on edge. It was always the same once an investigation got under way. Afterwards you managed the mountain of pressures and risks as best you could. On his desk Daquin found the packet of photos Attali had brought. Good work.

Thomas and Santoni arrived . . . introductions . . . handshakes . . . Daquin knew they were close colleagues of Meillant. Thomas and Meillant knew each other in the Resistance, and had joined the police together as patrolmen in 1945. But Thomas hadn't wanted to, or couldn't become a Super. He was, and would remain, a divisional inspector and he sensed a bitterness invading his whole personality. Santoni, whose career had taken a more classic course, had less ambition, was happy to play the role of faithful right-hand man. They both looked the same: in their fifties, paunch, moustache. Both looked typical cops: a combination of ease and pride. Daquin glanced into the small mirror over the sink. He had to keep the distinction between himself and them.

Now, the Yugoslav's ours. They exchanged information, established tactics for questioning. Simple. He has to crack. Go to it.

*

The Yugoslav was waiting in Thomas and Santoni's office handcuffed to the radiator pipe. He was sitting on the floor. Thomas got him up with a kick and manhandled him into a chair, his hands behind his back and attached to the chair's struts. He took off his belt and tied a leg to the chair-leg, then did the same for the other one with his colleague's belt. Daquin silently noted that both belts had been adapted with holes for this kind of operation. Obviously, it wasn't the two men's first attempt at this. They dragged their chairs up to sit very close to the Yugoslav. Daquin remained withdrawn, at arm's length – or leg's length away, behind a desk. Santoni signalled to him to open the top drawer. He did so and saw that, carefully tucked into their envelope, were the two plastic bags that had contained the heroin.

'Good. Now you're sitting comfortably, we can begin our chat. I just want to say, right away, so we don't waste time, that we don't believe a word of the statement you made yesterday. If you don't cough up all you know – and quick – you'll find yourself with charges of murder and sexual assault on a minor. If there comes a point when the cavalry's out of sight, your chances of coming out of this are slight. Understand?'

He nodded 'yes' with his head.

'When did you find the body on your premises yesterday?'

'About four.'

No time to finish, he got kicked twice in the shins and cried out. A punch in the face from the right. 'Don't cry. You'll ruin our reputation.' A blow from the left. 'Say "Yes, *monsieur l'inspecteur*", when my colleague speaks to you.' The Yugoslav was completely disorientated. When Crime had questioned him the day before it had been a whole lot less emotional and he'd not expected this sort of welcoming committee. He tried to twist his head round to see who the third man was in the background, but there wasn't time. Thomas caught him by the hair and pulled his head upright, while Santoni kicked him in the shins again.

'Look at us, you asshole. It's not polite not to look at people when they're talking to you. Now you'll give me a correct answer to my question: when did you find the body in your workroom?'

'Seven in the morning.'

A glance passed between the three cops: rapid, professional – this was not a hard case. It was decidedly better.

'So why didn't you phone the station right away? What were you doing between 7 a.m. and 4 p.m.?'

'I was selling the machines.'

'Why?'

'Because they'd be seized.'

'And why would they be seized?'

'Because I employ illegal immigrants and I thought the police would find out.'

Inspector Thomas stroked his chin, over and over again.

'It's good you respect the intellectual capacity of the police, it's rare nowadays.'

The Yugoslav looked as though he were about to cry.

The (still invisible) Super's voice: 'And you cleaned your kitchen.'

Said in a very calm, anodyne tone, and at the same time as he drew from his jacket pocket a large signet ring, which he calmly

23

put on his right hand. The Yugoslav said nothing. Santoni hit him again.

'Answer me. You cleaned your kitchen. Yes or crap?'

'No. I did not clean my kitchen.'

His field of vision was interrupted by the Super with a mighty backhander. The chair fell over backwards, the Yugoslav with it. He hit the desk as he fell and his right eyebrow streamed blood.

'Just listen to me, asshole. The police lab told us the kitchen was cleaned from top to bottom on Monday and it was you who were in the workroom. We've got witnesses.'

The Yugoslav was openly weeping now, still upturned on the floor, with the Super standing over him. Blood was pouring into his hair.

'Yes. Perhaps I did clean my kitchen. I don't remember very well.'

'Make an effort to remember. Why did you clean your kitchen?'

As he asked, the Super caught the Yugoslav by the shirt collar, and rather brutally brought the chair upright, and with his other hand shoved the two bags in their plastic envelope under his nose.

The Yugoslav groaned in terror. It was over, he wasn't really a hard case, all that was left to do was to record his confession.

It hadn't been his idea. It was one of his Turkish workers. He'd brought in the two packets yesterday morning at about six. They'd both gone into the workroom, without noticing anything out of the ordinary. The Turk must have opened the two packets in the kitchen and made up the small 50 gram doses, weighing out each one, and then sewn them into the pockets of the twenty pairs of red gypsy pants which were on top of the pile. And then they would have mixed the pants into a delivery that was to be made. It was when he went to load the rest of the heap of gypsy pants, that he'd discovered the body.

'And what about the delivery? How was that going to be made?'

He normally had stuff from five manufacturers to deliver. The Turk had made him a list, in a particular order that had to be followed, of twenty shops where he had to stop to deliver the gypsy pants containing the drugs.

'And you made this delivery before notifying us of the body?'

'Yes.'

A barely whispered yes. He waited for a fresh onslaught, which didn't happen. He still didn't understand all the rules of the game.

'Go on.'

'I went into the shop, with the red pants over my arm, so that they were easy to see. Someone was there, waiting for me. I said: "I've brought the design." He took the pants and said, "Thanks. I'll pay you later". That's all. And then I left.'

'You didn't handle any money?'

'No.'

'Who pays you then?'

'The Turk.'

'How much?'

'Five thousand francs.'

'I'd like the list of shops.'

The Yugoslav tried to remember, slowly coming up with twenty or so manufacturers' shops, one by one, scattered through the Sentier.

'And now the Turk's name and address?'

The Yugoslav gave his name, Celebi, an address of 25 rue du Faubourg-Saint-Martin, but pointed out these were probably false. He'd hired him two weeks ago at the Café Gymnase on the boulevard. That's the way Turks did things, round there, they drink coffee at the Gymnase, the workroom bosses go there, they chat, they do business. Then they give an address, but it's never a genuine one. In any case, they're always paid in cash.

'Could you recognize him?'

There was some hesitation. The Yugoslav wasn't sure. He said 'Yes', very uncertainly.

Santoni flipped through the photos that Attali and Romero had taken. Daquin watched him. One of the photos made him look up at Daquin. 'That's him.'

'Are you sure?'

'Certain.'

'Would you be willing to testify?' The Yugoslav was frightened. 'Listen to me hard. We'd only ask you to testify if we arrested the whole network. And then you wouldn't be the only witness, not even the most important, and they'd all be in the nick. There's nothing much to be afraid of. If you testify that this Turk prepared the sachets of heroin in your workroom kitchen on Monday 3 March, we wouldn't hold you to any drug trafficking charge. If you don't testify, we'll have to show that someone was responsible for the presence of heroin in your kitchen. You see what I'm getting at? So now that you've got my drift, I'm going to ask you again. Will you testify against this Turk when we ask you?'

'Yes, *monsieur le policier.*'

Daquin stroked his hair. It was so much better like that.

'Now to another matter. You're not French. Who's your manager?'

'I just head the workroom, I've no company. I work for Anna Beric. She's the one who gives me my orders, my invoices and payslips.'

'Who's this Anna Beric?'

'She was Yugoslav originally. A very distant relation of mine.'

'How long have you worked with her?'

'A very long time. At least five years.'

'Where can I find her?'

'She lives at 21 rue Raynouard, in Paris.'

Daquin signed to the cop waiting at the door.

'Take him away, and warn the nick he's agreed to testify so they must treat him properly.'

7 p.m. *Villa des Artistes*

Daquin's waiting for Soleiman, as he prepares a meal. Vegetable soup with Tomme cheese from the Savoy, a genuine low-fat Tomme, such a rarity in Paris he couldn't resist it. And salami. Not much in the mood for cooking tonight. Remember to ask Soleiman whether or not he eats pork.

He's listening to the news on the radio, only half concentrating. The chief of the Belgian drug squad has just been accused of drug trafficking. What a laugh. The American hostages in Tehran have been handed over to the Revolutionary Council. Good luck, comrades. Rain begins to fall against the window.

With the news finished, the doorbell rings twice. Soleiman comes in, closes the door behind him. He's standing stock still, looking grim, ill at ease, his hair streaming, soaked to the bone in his shabby pullover. He's even shivering with cold.

'Come on, you bloody fool. Go and have a hot bath; there are towels up there and my dressing-gown. And have a shave. You're a

26

disgrace with your two-day-old beard. Dinner's ready in a quarter of an hour.'

Soleiman goes upstairs. He hasn't uttered a word.

After a shower, he stands in front of the bathroom mirror in a splendid dressing-gown – it's blue with fine black stripes and much too big for him – looking at his reflection as he shaves.

He can see himself again, in Daquin's office, cornered, trapped, and his mind trying to function, but it isn't easy. If it really is the extreme right trafficking in drugs . . . and nothing else. He can still hear Daquin making a date at his place, and adding, 'Before you come, shave off your moustache, I don't like men with moustaches.' It had taken a few long seconds to realise the implications. He'd wanted to kill himself. And then he'd come to with a jolt: not now, not when the Sentier's beginning to move, not when people are beginning to trust him. After all, Daquin wouldn't be the first he'd gone to bed with. He must just close his eyes. Let it happen. Wait.

He gently rubs his lips. He has a frantic need for a smoke. But Daquin's made it clear: 'No cigarettes at my place. I can't stand the smell of stale tobacco in my house.'

At the table, Soleiman eats in silence. He always gives the impression he doesn't give a toss about what he's eating. Daquin watches him throughout the meal. He waits fairly patiently for Soleiman to tell him what he has to say. It's just before coffee that it comes out.

'Two days ago now, I was asked to represent the Committee on the negotiations team that's meeting at the Ministry.' Daquin says nothing and continues watching him. Is that all? No reaction?

'Listen, Sol. That's your business, not mine.'

'You're not going to phone them and tell them I'm a murderer?'

Daquin looks at him incredulously.

'What're you playing at? Frightening yourself? Come.' He stands up. 'We'll have coffee.' They sit side by side on the couch. On the low table is a packet of photos.

'Look at these photos carefully and tell me if you recognize anyone.'

'Where were they taken?'

'You'll see afterwards.'

One by one, the photos slowly pass through Soleiman's hands. Their quality varies.

'This guy here – he's one of the three in charge of the Association of Lighting Technicians.'

'Explain.'

Daquin puts the photo to one side. Soleiman explains the Grey Wolves Fascists in Turkey, the infiltration of Turkish immigrants... the murders of left-wing militants in Germany. Last November the association established a base here, near rue de Château d'Eau. They work with the CFT at Aulnay. Daquin writes it all down in his notebook.

'D'you know his name?'

'Yes. It's Hassan Yüçel.'

'Go on.'

Two further photos are added to the first. When Soleiman's looking at one of the photos, Daquin senses a sudden tension, an involuntary jolt. But Soleiman passes on. If this prick says nothing, I'll give him the boot, Daquin thinks. Three, four photos on, then Soleiman stops, goes back, picks up the photo he'd reacted to, points his finger at a rather blurred figure in the background.

'I'm not completely certain.'

Daquin heaves an inward sigh of relief. He would not have liked to kick him out.

'Can it be enlarged and made clearer?'

'Yes, it can be done tomorrow. But even so, let me know tonight. We can confirm it tomorrow.'

'I think it's Ali Ağça.'

'Fine. But that means absolutely nothing to me.'

Soleiman leans back on the couch, solemnly.

'I knew him in Istanbul. He's the same age as me, perhaps a year or two older. He was studying political science at the university I wanted to go to. He was a Grey Wolf, and a real professional killer.'

Smile. 'And weren't you a killer, not a real one, not a pro?' Soleiman frowns. 'Go on.'

'He killed several people, always using the same technique in the street, at point-blank range, right in the heart. He was arrested for the assassination of the editor in chief of *Milliyet*, a leftish newspaper, in 1979. Just at about the time I left Turkey, he escaped from gaol in Istanbul. If he's here, it's to kill and to kill people like me what's more.'

'Are you afraid?'

Soleiman stands up, exasperated. For years and years now he's lived with this fear in his gut. In his family, in his village, in Istanbul. Fear too when, that evening, he walked in Yeniçeriler Cadesi, with his gun in his pocket, to meet the man he was going to kill. How can a cop like Daquin understand something like that...

'A Fascist prick doesn't frighten me and you can go to hell.'

'Sit down. I'm being serious now. I've noted everything down. Look at the other photos.'

Soleiman shuffles through them distractedly. He'd been reliving the nightmare, the man crumpling to the ground, him starting to run, the cop barring his way, him aiming at the cop, firing at him twice, at random, running into the black night of winding streets of old Istanbul, for what seemed hours and hours. Daquin brings him a coffee.

'Make an effort and listen. These photos were taken from opposite the sandwich shop you told me about, not of the straightforward customers outside. A Yugoslav dealer we arrested has formally recognized a Turk who'd delivered drugs to him in this series. Look, it's this one.' Daquin takes out a photo from the packet. 'Goes by the name of Celebi. In this same series, you've recognized four people from the Grey Wolves. I draw two conclusions from this. First, your lead's a good one. There are drugs hanging about this particular shop. Secondly, it confirms that there's a close link between drugs and the extreme right. And as far as you're concerned, that's good news, isn't it? You can relax a bit.'

Soleiman leans back on the sofa, eyes closed.

'I'm bushed.'

'Sol. You're going to spend the night here. You can't leave in this rain – it isn't going to stop – not in the rags you're wearing. Tomorrow morning, I'll see what I can find you in the way of clothes. Come on. Let's go to bed.'

8 a.m Passage du Désir

All the photos taken in the last two days were spread out on the table. Daquin, Attali and Romero were carefully arranging them in two series: the sandwich bar and the accessory shop, in chronological order.

Enter a fair-haired young man, on the dumpy side, white shirt, dark suit, tie, brief-case and tortoiseshell rimmed spectacles. He introduced himself as Lavorel, of the Finance Squad.

'We were expecting you. My chief told us yesterday that you'd be coming. Coffee?'

'Yes, please.'

He looked surprised.

Daquin went over to the machine, made coffee for everyone. Then he began to re-examine the photos. The classification was finished.

'First shop: only Turks or similar. Second shop: much more mixed clientele. We speculate that the first shop is used as a rallying point for the supply network, and for the moment we won't discuss that. It's too serious and we haven't enough information. The second could be used for putting the drugs into circulation, which, *per se*, involves more French than Turks, and third- or fourth-rank roles. We're going to take soundings there. You two, you go and hang about in the area. Choose someone who comes out of the shop who might look like a dealer. Stop and search him – some distance away, and be as discreet as you can. If it's a dealer, bring him here. If you don't find any drugs, make your excuses. And, most important, don't make any mistakes. Good luck.'

*

Daquin and Lavorel were left on their own.

'You've read my report on Bostic?'

'Yes.'

'Are you familiar with the Sentier's professional underworld?'

'No way. For the last three years I've been in Finance, working on the misdemeanours of members of the Stock Exchange. My presence here, so I understand, is the result of some compromise among the high-ups. Some are absolutely for a clean-up in the

Sentier, so as not to leave the territory completely free for the people demanding the legalization of illegal immigrants. Others think it's bullshit, and we should let it stay as a sector that's working well and can't do so without illegal labour. So they agreed on designating someone, but they took on some naïve young guy who knows nothing, and who'll get himself tied up in knots, very likely. So, here I am.'

'And what's your opinion of the whole business?'

'That's what I'm here to find out. That's what I see my role of cop as, and I can tell you I'll bust a gut to get something out of this dungheap.'

'You've a curious way of expressing yourself for a suit-and-tie man.'

'I haven't always been one.'

'Ah, right. And what did you do before you were in Finance?'

'I was a hooligan.'

A moment's silence.

'I mean, what did you do in the police before you were in finance.'

'It was my first posting.'

'Would it be very indiscreet to ask why you're in Finance?'

'No, it's not indiscreet. I've always hated people you call suit-and-tie men. And I've no wish to go yob-bashing in high-rises.'

'Well, as you'll see in the Sentier, neither the workers nor bosses are exactly suit-and-tie men.'

'We'll see.'

'We've organized a small office for you, next to this one. I'd like you to keep me posted on your work every day. And pop in to say hallo. Let me know who owns those two shops at 5 rue du Faubourg-Saint-Martin.'

9 a.m. Rue des Petites-Ecuries

Early that morning Santoni parked a 4L van, converted into a surveillance vehicle, with two-way mirror side windows, just in front of the window of the Aratoff Ballets Company in rue des Petites-Ecuries, and set himself up more or less comfortably inside, with cigarettes and cans of beer close to hand. At nine o'clock precisely, a large woman opened up the agency office, went in and sat down behind a counter, at the back on the left. Santoni was unable to see what she was doing. Towards ten, a man and another woman were in the building. They hadn't gone through the street entrance. At twelve-thirty, the fat woman came out, locked the door behind her. There was no longer anyone in the offices. There hadn't been a single customer all morning.

Santoni unfolded himself carefully. He was stiff all over. And followed the woman. Not far – to a café-brasserie fifty metres away. She sat at a very small table on the terrace. Santoni went in and found a seat right next to her. She ordered steak and French fries and a glass of red wine. Santoni gave her the once-over. A big fat lump, well and truly past her fiftieth birthday, with short, permed, mousy hair, large breasts which sagged on to a big belly, swollen legs, feet bulging over the tops of her shoes. A small white blouse and navy-blue pleated skirt. And between her breasts a cross and a medallion of the Virgin of Lourdes jangled on a gold chain. She could have passed for a schoolgirl from Sainte-Marie de Neuilly who'd grown poor and ugly. At about one-thirty, the lump rose. A little saunter as far as Montholon Square. Santoni found it was a good idea.

12.25 p.m. Rue du Faubourg-Saint-Martin

Attali and Romero strolled past the accessory shop. From time to time, they paused at a café opposite. They also went up to say hallo to the old boy and promised to keep him posted on how the investigation was developing. They were just wondering how they would recognize a dealer. No kidding ... they'd already taken two hours and not reached any conclusion. It was already past midday. They would have to think about having some lunch. At that very moment there came into view a superb young woman, in her mid-twenties, no more, very slim, her mid-length hair blowing in the wind, almost dancing as she walked. Looks like a model, Romero said to himself. He knew little about that sort of thing, however. She was calmly walking down rue du Faubourg-Saint-Martin, confident she was the centre of attention, and neither caring, nor hesitating, nor slowing down, she walked straight into the accessory shop. Romero and Attali exchanged a single glance. They might not know how to recognize a dealer, but they knew how to appreciate a pretty girl. In any case, she'd be more fun to play with than some dead-beat junkie in his thirties. When she re-emerged ten minutes later they followed her at a distance, one on each pavement, most discreetly. She went back up the Faubourg, taking the direction she'd come, and, unhurriedly, turned left into passage Brady. It was a fine day. She was wearing a sporty beige raincoat over a skirt and sweater which were also beige. A large dark brown Vuitton bag swung on her shoulder. When they reached passage Brady, the two cops prudently kept their distance. She took rue d'Enghien.

The street was deserted at that hour and Romero judged they were far enough away from the shop to try something. He glanced round to check they were alone, went up to the young woman, passed his left hand under her elbow and with his right presented his warrant card. He pushed her under a porchway. Attali followed them.

'Police. We're running an investigation into drug peddling and you've been seen in the company of known peddlers. I'm obliged to search you, to check whether or not you have drugs in your possession.'

The young woman protested vehemently and fought vigorously. She kicked them in the shins to try to get away. Romero leant all his weight on her, and pushed her into the dirty dark entrance to a stairwell which gave on to the porch. Attali signalled to him that he was controlling access points.

While he held her face against the wall and her wrists behind her back, Romero undertook the search. First, the bag. The girl continued fighting energetically. Romero upturned the contents of the bag on the ground, a jumble of handkerchiefs, lipsticks, face powder, loose change ... Signalled to Attali, who quickly checked the contents of her wallet, purse and powder compact. Nothing. He put everything back in the bag, and took up a position at the entrance to the stairwell. A glance towards Romero, whom he sensed was about to make a monumental blunder, but said nothing.

Romero trapped the girl's wrists with one hand, and with the other he undertook a body search, all the time holding her squeezed against the wall with his shoulder and body weight. Nothing in the raincoat pockets. Nothing in the shoes. His hand felt up her legs, nothing in her tights. A lump under the elastic in her panties, between her buttocks. He tore at her knickers, and, lo

33

and behold, there was a sachet of white powder, about twenty grams' worth by the look of it. Excitement? Pleasure of the hunt? Contact with the girl? He got the distinct impression she was fighting less. Consenting? The stairwell was in darkness. And Attali could only find one thing to say: 'Hurry, hurry...' Romero leaned against her with all his weight, undid his flies with one hand and pulled up her skirt. Groans of pleasure. Attali was torn between envy and anxiety. The girl drew away.

'Right. Keep the sachet, but let me go. Otherwise I'll bring a charge of rape. You know I can prove it.'

Attali: 'Let's nick her, quickly. Don't hang about.'

'You'll regret this, you pig.'

With her hands handcuffed behind her back, and an inspector on either side, they quickly walked her back to passage du Désir. Romero and Attali exchanged not a single word.

1.25 p.m. Passage du Désir

Romero pushed the girl into Daquin's office, removed the handcuffs and made her sit down, while Attali placed the sachet of powder on the desk. Romero gave a quick report of what had happened, omitting all the 'details'. While he sat quite still, listening, Daquin looked at the violet bruising on the girl's wrists and scratches on her face.

She pulled herself up on her chair and said to Daquin: 'Your shitty cop raped me, on the pretext of searching me. He had me pinned against the wall, half broke my wrists and raped me. I want a medical examination.'

Daquin retorted in glacial tones: 'You wish to lodge a complaint, mademoiselle?' A few seconds' pause. 'Frankly, I'm not sure it's the best solution. When you play dangerous games the way you do, you can't honestly expect to be mingling with the upper crust the whole time. If you lodge a complaint against my inspector, which you're entitled to do, I'll immediately charge you with drug dealing. My inspector will be transferred, but you'll be banged up for at least four years.' He stared at her for a moment. 'And I'm even convinced that if Romero gave you a hundred francs, which isn't your usual rate, but in view of the circumstances, you'd agree to make him a special price.' The girl went scarlet, but said nothing.

'Romero, put a hundred francs in Mademoiselle's mack pocket. Now let's get down to serious matters. Attali, write it down. Your name, age?'

'Virginie Lamouroux, twenty-five.'

'Where d'you live?'

'With a girlfriend.'

'Would you mind speeding things up for everybody? When I ask a question, I want a precise answer, is that clear? Where do you live?

'With a girlfriend, Mademoiselle Sergent, at 10 rue de Belzunce.'

'Occupation?'

'Model.'

'Be specific.'

'I model for ready-to-wear. I work for a number of different employers – it varies from day to day.'

'Names? Dates?'

'In the last six months I've worked for all the big names in ready-to-wear, from NafNaf or René Dhéry to Julie La Tour or Jules & Julie.'

'And what does your job entail?'

'Mainly modelling clothes, by request, for an eventual wholesale purchaser. It's more important than the collections.'

'And the buyer keeps the model for the evening?'

'That's none of your bus – '

She didn't have time to finish her sentence before Daquin slapped her, without even standing to do it.

Shocked, she said: 'It can happen that way.'

'In which case, how much d'you make?'

'Why? Why are you so interested? It's not relevant.'

The second slap was harder. Daquin had taken the trouble to stand up this time. Virginie Lamouroux sniffed.

'Don't think about it, just give me an answer. How much d'you make on a date like that?'

'It doesn't happen like that. There aren't any rates. It's the kind of world where you sleep around. After the show, well, you're free. You spend the evening together. Can't you find yourself a girlfriend? ... Well, that's it. Those who want to, pay. Others pretend they thought we did it for fun. Girls who don't sleep around don't get the jobs, that's all there is to it.'

35

Daquin sat down again.

'OK. Let's move on to drugs. Romero, take a look at Mademoiselle Lamouroux's arms and ankles. I don't suppose you had time to do it just now. Any needle marks?'

'No, *commissaire*.'

'So, mademoiselle, what form are you taking them in?'

'Who told you I was taking drugs?'

Daquin stood up to his full, massive height. He was seriously angry. He came round the desk, caught her by the hair and forced her to look up at him.

'Just look at me, and stop behaving like a child. At twenty-five, you're a dealer and a tart and you take drugs. Which ones and how?'

'Heroin. I smoke it,' she said regretfully.

'Go on.'

'Powder. In a special silver cupel, you heat it with a candle. It goes like caramel and gives off smoke. You lean over it, with a scarf over your head, and inhale it very slowly and deeply. It makes you feel fabulous and it's not dangerous, it's not like using a needle. I've never injected myself. I'm frightened of injections.'

'It's a rather unusual way of taking it. Who taught you?'

She hesitated. Daquin moved closer to her.

'It comes from Iran, it was some Iranians, at parties. I don't know their names.'

'Parties?'

'Yes. In ready-to-wear, you meet lots of people. And very different sorts. At parties given by one lot or another.'

'And taking heroin happens quite frequently on such occasions?'

'Not frequently perhaps, but not infrequently either. Heroin and a load of other things.' She sat up in her chair. 'Don't tell me, *commissaire*, that you didn't know.'

'Who gave you the address in rue du Faubourg-Saint-Martin?'

'The addresses of the suppliers get passed around and change a lot. That address was given me a fortnight ago. It's the first time I've been there.'

'Who gave it to you? You haven't answered my question.'

'I don't remember any more.'

Daquin made a show of putting on his signet ring and raised his hand.

'Perhaps it was Lestiboudois, a businessman I went out with that evening. I haven't seen him since.'

Daquin paced up and down his office, saying nothing. Then: 'I'm going to release you. For the moment. You're going to sign a short statement. I ask you not to leave Paris, and to let me know if you change your address. And to report in at the 10th arrondissement police station every two days at 9 a.m. from Monday next.'

'And if I don't sign?'

'I'll lock you up for being caught in the act.'

A moment's reflection.

'I'll sign.'

'Romero. Take Mademoiselle Lamouroux back downstairs.'

The Super waited for him to come back, saying nothing, rocking in his chair.

*

'So, Romero, clear something up for me. Did you rape her before or after you found the drugs?'

'After, *commissaire.*'

'Are you aware that I've just got you off being transferred to some dead-end place in the sticks, or are you proud of yourself?'

'I'm not proud of myself, *commissaire.*'

'Right. Let's recap, Romero. You prepare a report for me on Virginie Lamouroux's arrest for tomorrow morning, omitting anything that could harm our team's reputation. I'll make a note on her cross-examination myself. You both keep the investigation into this girl. In my opinion she's rotten to the core and she hasn't given us anything she knows. Even if she doesn't know all that much probably. You can begin by locating her, which may not be all that easy, and lay on the pressure for me, since we haven't anything better we can do. Either she'll crack, or people in the network will take the initiative. We'll observe and gather information. So, get down to it. Try to be as efficient as you can and show a bit more restraint.'

2 p.m. Rue des Petites-Ecuries

Santoni returned to the van where Thomas was waiting for him. Thomas had paid a visit that morning to the syndicate which co-owned the property. There he'd found a detailed plan of the building

37

and the names of all the occupants, along with some comments. Thomas had taken notes. Santoni cast an eye over them.

'Monsieur and Madame Bernachon, alias Aratoff. Probably the ones I saw this morning. They live just above the agency. You take over here, you'll see. It's a bore. I'm going to take a walk inside the building.'

A very common type of building, in this area. A concierge's lodge, but no concierge at that hour. No elevator. Santoni took the stairs. Two apartments per floor. A red carpet up to the fifth. On the sixth, maids' rooms. WC on the landing. No one in the corridor. With plan in hand, Santoni tracked down the two rooms which belonged to the Bernachons. Strong, though not complicated, locks. Apparently no one in at the moment. He went downstairs to cast an eye over the cellars. Found the entrance easily. Two floors of vaults. Superb. It was badly lit and a bit grubby. Some cellars still had very ancient doors with openwork, others had reinforced ones. He checked the plan to see where Bernachon's cellar was. A new, solid, wooden door, same locks as on the maids' rooms. He went down to the lower basement level, and, since he was in no hurry, walked along the corridor and among all those disparate rooms, found one identical to the Bernachons'. New wooden door, same locks. Was there a meaning in this? He made a note of the cellar's number.

3 p.m. Rue Saint-Maur

Lavorel wanted quick results. A need to prove something? To whom?

A short conversation with Bostic yielded the names and addresses of two Yugoslav workers who'd worked with him for many years. The only two who had papers among the twenty he employed.

A building on rue Saint-Maur, full of Yugoslavs. A fairly grotty staircase. A small, very clean apartment on the second floor. A middle-aged woman in a headscarf.

'Madame Jentic?' She nodded. 'Is Monsieur Jentic in?'

She gestured with her hand: he wasn't in. She didn't speak a word of French, or feigned not to. Lavorel asked the neighbours, with no success. The baker, on the ground floor, finally agreed to act as interpreter.

'Police. I want to ask you a few questions, but you've nothing to fear, nor has your husband.' She only half believed him. 'Has your husband any payslips?' She signalled the affirmative. 'Can I see them?'

She held out a large packet in a strong envelope. Payslips for every month, for years, all of which seemed perfectly in order: name of the business, stamp, calculation of deductions, taxable total, everything was there. His wages were decidedly above the minimum. It was just that the name of the company changed every three months and was invariably followed by a note which read: 'Currently being registered with the Trade Register.'

Lavorel took notes. And three payslips on the sly, while Madame Jentic was looking the other way. He thanked her. 'Remember, you're not to worry, everything's completely in order.' He then left to check with the Trade Register. A new company registered every three months. Manager: Anna Beric.

Sandwich. Beer. Metro to the Social Security Office. None of these companies ever paid out a sou in national insurance. Neither on the part of the employers nor the wage-earners. Normally a company's allowed three months' delay in paying national insurance contributions. If, at the end of three months, it no longer exists ... If Jentic's payslips are anything to go by ... all this had been going on for a number of years. Friday afternoon, not worth continuing the tour of civil service offices – I wouldn't find anyone in.

4 p.m. 10th Arrondissement Police Station

Attali went to see the duty officer.

'From Monday morning next, a young woman should be coming here to register her whereabouts every two days. Virginie Lamouroux. A suspect in a heroin-dealing case.'

'Virginie Lamouroux? Hold on a minute. I have something on that name.' He delved into a large notebook. 'I knew it. Wednesday, 5 March, a Robert Sobesky, ready-to-wear manufacturer, living at 20 rue de Paradis, came in to notify us of the disappearance of Virginie Lamouroux, model, also residing at 20 rue de Paradis.'

39

8 a.m. 10 rue de Belzunce

Romero shook Attali who was dozing on the bottom steps of the staircase.

'VL's coming down. Our move. You take the girlfriend. I'll take VL.'

Attali slowly mounted the stairs. He passed Virginie Lamouroux on the first floor, gave her a silent nod and continued his ascent. She was surprised, stopped to say something, looked at her watch and continued walking downstairs. She came out of the building, and there, on the pavement just in front of the entrance, was met by Romero.

'Good morning, mademoiselle. Would you open your bag.' He pointed to the light travel bag she was wearing over her shoulder. 'I have to check you don't have drugs on you.'

VL was completely thrown. Does he have the right? she thought. What am I doing?

Romero had already put out his hand and in one brief movement had whipped the bag off her. No resistance. He began a systematic, not very discreet search. Passers-by gawped at the scene. The contents were standard for those of an elegant young woman taking a weekend break. He gave the bag back to her.

'Thank you, mademoiselle. See you soon.'

He went back into the building. VL stood rigid for a moment, then continued walking. Before she reached the street corner, she looked back. No one there. Turned. Waited. Still no one. Crossed the road, took a street on her left. No one. So she walked at a good pace towards the taxi rank in the square, on the corner of rue Lafayette and the church square of Saint-Vincent-de-Paul. Romero was already there, hiding. He saw her turn round one last time and jump into a taxi which took off and passed right in front of him. He noted the registration number, then went back up towards 10 rue de Belzunce.

Attali was by the front door.

'She arrived at her friend's last Friday. Before that, she'd been living with someone called Xavier Sobesky at 20 rue de Paradis. And she left to go on an unexpected trip on Saturday, 1 March, very early in the morning. Never said where she was going.'

*

While Romero was busy tracing Virginie Lamouroux's taxi, and locating her for the weekend, Attali was trying to discover where she'd been for the last five days. If she took the train or a car, it's impossible, he thought. If she took a plane, I've got a chance ... if she left under her own name ... if she didn't leave on a double booking at the last minute ... Begin with Orly. If I find something, I'll get home to Antony quicker. He checked the list of companies. Several hours of work: nothing. It was three in the afternoon. A shitty job. He tried Roissy. And after only a short time, there it was: Saturday, 7.43 a.m., Continental Airlines, destination New York, Virginie Lamouroux. Return journey: Wednesday, 8.17 p.m.

2 p.m. Passage du Désir

So Anna Beric was much more than a small manufacturer. The Social Security swindle she'd set up in the Sentier had been going on for years. Daquin closed Lavorel's report. Slumped in his armchair, with his feet on the table he sipped his coffee.

And in one of her workrooms there'd been a corpse and drugs. What should I do next? I can take the twenty or so names of manufacturers Bostic gave me and have them watched. I can put on file all the Turks who pass through the sandwich shop and have them followed. I can draw up a list of Anna Beric's workrooms and search them. Put all the manufacturers VL has talked about under surveillance. Dozens of cops, hundreds of hours of grind for pathetic results. The best that would come of it would be that we pick up a few small time dealers, almost by chance. The factory owners Bostic mentioned probably know nothing about the men hanging around in their shop, waiting for a delivery of red gypsy pants. The Turks may give up going to the sandwich shop from one day to the next and disappear into thin air. And VL could have spun me any old tale. I have to look at the problem totally differently. I must suppose there are links between the Turkish extreme right and drugs, and they're strong enough for the drug channels to be modelled on the political ones. The political channels are a known fact, so who can talk to me about them? He picked up the phone.

'Hallo. Lenglet? Daquin here. How you doing? I need you. Can you help me meet someone discreet who's really knowledgeable about the Turkish extreme right? Easy? Monday, one o'clock at Pierre's, place Gaillon. I've written it down.'

He looked at his watch. It was 3 p.m. Nothing to do till 8 that evening when he would have dinner with friends in square de l'Alboni.

But square de l'Alboni was right near rue Raynouard. He checked the map. A five-minute walk away. And it so happened he hadn't found anyone to watch Anna Beric's flat. The temptation was too strong to resist, and he'd never really tried to resist this kind of impulse. He dialled Anna Beric's number. There was an answerphone: Anna Beric isn't here at the moment. Leave a message after the bleep. He took a bunch of keys and picklocks from a desk drawer, pocketed them and was on his way: Metro as far as Passy.

He phoned again: still no one at Anna Beric's. He loitered around the block for a while. Very plush, very peaceful, a Saturday afternoon. He entered the building and went directly to the care-taker's lodge. Madame Beric please. Fifth left. The concierge didn't even look away from the TV to glance at him. Really easy. He walked up the stairs, slowly, to observe the rhythm of life in the building. Little movement, and people taking the elevator. He reached the fifth floor. In the apartment on the right, he heard a broadcast of a Five Nations Rugby Tournament match on TV. It was 4 p.m., so he had little chance of being disturbed by the neigh-bours on the landing. He took out his bunch of keys. In three minutes the door yielded. No one had taken the stairs; the elevator had gone up once to the sixth floor.

He went in, carefully closing the door behind him. His heart was thumping, all his senses on tenterhooks. Silence. Half shadow. First he made a rapid tour of the apartment, walking soundlessly. A big living-cum-dining-room with a study facing the front. A win-dowless bathroom, a bedroom and a kitchen on the street side. A back entrance in the kitchen, locked, but the key was above it. He must open it to give himself a safety exit if someone arrived. Visualize routes to this exit from all sorts of places in the building. And now to work.

Standing stock-still in the middle of the room, he tried to guess the personality of the woman who lived here and make the most of the moment: a rare and curious danger and pleasure, about which no one would ever know. He opened all the drawers and cupboards. There were quite a few. The clothes were carefully put away, there was a lot of silk, classic designs, frocks: certainly well dressed. One garment fascinated him: a crimson red sheath dress with a low square neck, of an extraordinary simplicity and power. A dress, he had the feeling, he knew. Must be a brunette to wear something like that. Hardly any slacks. Lingerie in abundance. Lots of silk here too. He gently ran his hand through the pile of slips. It was a slightly quaint thing to do. A strong subtle perfume he couldn't quite identify on all the lingerie. At the bottom of a cupboard, piles of shoe-boxes. About thirty. Some were empty. At the bottom of another cupboard, a closely woven wicker trunk, with leather corners and a brass clasp. Daquin passed his hand over the wickerwork. Lifted the lid: the trunk was empty. Perhaps it was used as a laundry basket. On the bed, very pretty sheets from Deschamps. Definitely a brunette, tall and slim. No doubt she was impeccably made up, took great care of her hair, for there was an armada of beauty products. And she had gone, he sensed it: some empty coat-hangers, no toothbrush in evidence in the bathroom...

Daquin passed into the living-room. The canvas blinds were lowered, but the shutters not closed. He guessed a stone balcony ran along the room and, beyond, a splendid view over the whole of the south of Paris. He stood rooted there, breathing in small intakes of breath, cautiously. There was a discrepancy he couldn't fathom between the apartment's location, her refined clothes and the way this living-room was furnished: it was tasteless and uninteresting. A large table in a light-coloured wood with chairs around, a fabric sofa, two assorted armchairs, a wooden coffee table, like the other – cheap furniture, no refinement. She didn't live in this room and entertained no one here.

He went into the study. Very welcoming. There, too, a french window, the balcony, Paris beyond. The three walls furnished with shelves in light wood, running from top to bottom, full of books. In the middle of the room, a huge English desk, with a green leather top, behind it a matching leather armchair, and in front of the window a small two-seater sofa in fawn leather. It must be really pleasant working here. He went to the bookcase: nineteenth-century novels, Russian, English, American. Classical Greek tragedies,

Arabian and Persian poets in bilingual editions. All in meticulous rows. On the desk, Doris Lessing's *Children of Violence*. Daquin whistled between his teeth. Took out a book, then another, opened them, leafed through, put them back. Hardly any dust. It was no dead library. Persian poets? Rare, even so. There were about thirty titles. He opened them one after another. And there on the flyleaf of a bilingual anthology of Court poetry, he read a date: 27 January 1958, and a dedication: 'An unforgettable meeting'. It was signed 'O'. He experienced a curious feeling. A sort of jealousy. He slipped the book into the inside pocket of his jacket. To bring him luck?

The last two shelves, as he did his complete tour of the room, were empty. Also empty, or almost, were the drawers of the desk. If there had been bookkeeping records here, there were no more. Lavorel would have to find something else. The apartment was arranged in a mad sort of way, and nowhere were there any photos. No mementoes of the past. No old letters, old keys, nothing whatever. The lady must have had a difficult relationship with her past.

Daquin walked around the apartment for a while longer. He didn't know exactly what he was looking for. In fact he couldn't bring himself to leave: night fell in the absent woman's apartment, and it was fascinating. Ashtrays everywhere, even on the edge of the bath: she was a heavy smoker. All were impeccably clean. Two large porcelain ashtrays with ads on them: Hostellerie du Bas-Bréau, at Barbizon.

In the kitchen, not much in the cupboards, nothing that suggested gourmet cooking. One thing however made him smile: she used the same coffee as he did. He must remember. He'd offer her a cup when he had her in front of him in his office. It was almost 7 o'clock, he must go. He wasn't tense enough any more, not on tenterhooks. It was becoming dangerous. He must close the door in the kitchen, listen carefully to all the noises from outside before going out, simply pull the door to behind him, go down the stairs, wait for the concierge to be distracted, that would never be for very long, and calmly walk out into the street. Then, once outside, a short walk in the fresh evening air as far as the Seine, and a stroll up to square de l'Alboni. What an exhilarating day.

10 a.m. Deauville

A spacious apartment on the seafront. Two policemen rang the bell. No answer. They rang again ... A man in his fifties came and opened the door in his dressing-gown. Obviously disturbed. And very surprised to find the policemen.

'Good morning, *monsieur*. The Paris Drugs Squad have asked us to check whether Mademoiselle Lamouroux is really here.'

The man turned to Virginie, who was wrapped in a bath towel and standing petrified in the middle of the sitting-room.

'Someone's asking for you, delightful girl.' Said with irony and a touch of malice.

Virginie came to the door.

'Mademoiselle, you should have notified the Drugs Squad of your change of address. Don't forget to report tomorrow at the 10th arrondissement police station, by nine a.m. at the latest. Thank you, *monsieur*. Excuse us for disturbing you. Have a nice Sunday.'

12 a.m. Villa des Artistes

Daquin went home to change, after a pleasant evening at the house of his friend, who was a TV producer, and a rather good night with a little blonde actress – the real works – who absolutely had to know how a superintendent – a real *commissaire* – made love. She was so tanked up that he wasn't certain she would remember who he was now.

Message on the answerphone. Soleiman's voice: 'I've been trying to get you. Call me.' No date, no time.

Daquin dialled the only number he had, the Committee one. Soleiman picked up the phone on the second ring. There was the hum of conversation – probably Turkish – in the background.

'I've phoned several times. You weren't at home all night.'

Daquin burst out laughing.

'Eh! You jealous?' A vexed silence. 'Ten, this evening, at my place. OK?'

'Fine.'   •

*

45

Daquin's asleep on the sofa in the living-room when Sol arrives. He opens one eye, grumbling. Sol signals he's going up to the bathroom. When he comes back down, wearing a brand-new white dressing-gown, that fits, and which was left for him on the edge of the bath, Daquin's awake and drinking coffee. He puts the full cafetière on the low table in front of him.

'I've made some lasagne for you. It's in the oven. I've already eaten.'

Soleiman goes to get his meal, and some cutlery, then sits beside Daquin on the sofa.

'What's happened to you? Have you been fighting with thugs?'

Daquin's upper lip is swollen and he has a bruise on his left cheek from a blow.

'Yes and no. I was playing rugby this afternoon. We were the weaker side and we suffered throughout the match. So you could say the other side were a bunch of thugs...'

'I've got some important things to show you.'

'Go on.'

From his dressing-gown pocket Soleiman takes out the four photos that Daquin gave him. On the back of each are names, initials, dates. The four men arrived in France almost at the same time – during the summer of 1979. All their papers are in order, residence permits, work permits. Three of them were members of the office of the Association of Lighting Technicians, when it was set up in September. Then, in January, when the workshops were opened, they left the association office to look after their management. But they can still be seen quite often where the association hangs out. There wasn't any falling out, more a specialization of duties.

'That confirms what we thought about the links between the extreme right and drugs. And that gives us a lead to follow up. How and why have these four got their papers?' Daquin leans back deeply into the sofa and draws Soleiman against himself. 'Move a bit closer. I'm very tired. I feel like being affectionate. Tell me, where are you living now, and what on?'

Soleiman suddenly stiffens and stands up.

'Why d'you ask me that. To fill up your police reports?'

Smile. 'Come here. Good God. There's no police report on you here in France. Sol, there never will be. I'd never write a word. You're mine, but mine alone. I asked you this question, simply because it interests me. And since you're mine, I've a certain amount of responsibility towards you.'

'You haven't made a report on me?'

'No.'

Soleiman sits down again.

'Not even one with a false name?'

Smile. 'No.'

'When this business is over, no one will know that I've given you information, and I shall be truly free again?'

'Of course. It's what I told you right from day one, isn't it?'

And even if it were true...? You couldn't trust cops, they're capable of anything, but, Soleiman thought, I really want to believe that.

Daquin's holding his neck and caressing him slowly.

Soleiman feels his whole body invaded by a sort of heat, drowsiness, relief. It reminds him exactly of the sensation he got from morphine – it was the day after ... The Istanbul press had published his photo on the front page: sought for a double murder. The fear and anguish were such that he'd only survived with morphine which his doctor friend had given him, until he managed to get out of Turkey with papers stolen from a French tourist. The same relief, that feeling of letting go. He feels it going to his head.

'Now, will you tell me how you're living nowadays?'

'I'd rather not talk about it.'

'Well, I'm going to tell you what my guess is. You don't have a sou, because you haven't the time to work to earn it. Your friends on the Committee have never thought of making you an advance.' He pauses. Daquin goes on looking Soleiman straight in the eye. 'Or, they may have suggested it to you, and you've refused it out of pride, so as not to appear beholden to them. You sleep under bridges and you're half dead with hunger.'

'Are you trying to humiliate me?'

'No. Of course not.'

Daquin slips his hand under the dressing-gown and slowly caresses the hollow of his thigh, then the buttocks, repeating the same movements, almost mechanically.

'Relax a bit and let yourself go, my boy. I'm only trying to help...' He carries on talking, very quietly.

Soleiman has his eyes closed. He mustn't move, mustn't feel

desire. I'm here, he thinks, because I'm powerless to do otherwise. But that isn't true, not completely, not any longer. Soleiman feels the heat, but has stopped listening, stopped understanding. Relaxing relief. He feels tears rising behind his closed eyelids. Tears ... When was the last time ... Never, not even when he was a child, in Anatolia. Daquin increases the pressure. Exquisite abandon.

7 a.m. Passage du Désir

Daquin spent some time working before his inspectors showed up. He looked at the mail on his desk: Ali Agça's file, which he'd requested from the Turkish police, had arrived. In it was a single murder, the assassination of Abdi Ipecki, editor-in-chief of *Milliyet*, Turkey's most important newspaper, in February 1979. Nothing on Ali Agça's *modus operandi* or previous record. Arrested *in flagrante delicto*, admitted to the murder. Imprisoned in Istanbul's central gaol, escaped November 1979; no other details. On the wanted list ever since. Photo attached, very poor quality, difficult to identify. Daquin wrote out an envelope, slid Ali Agça's photo inside, along with the one taken in rue du Faubourg-Saint-Martin. 'Can you let me know if these two are the same person?' Addressed it to the lab at the Palais de Justice.

His Turkish colleagues had been peculiarly laconic this time. If Soleiman's file hadn't been so much more complete, he'd never have been able to compromise him.

Then an alert scan of the newspapers.

'French Connection's impossible resurrection' ran a headline in *Libération*. The journalist had done quite a lot of homework, mentioned the role of the Americans in digging up the Marseilles lead again and concluded: 'No one has yet found a smidgen of heroin from Marseilles in New York.' So the Drugs Squad's special check on Marseilles was now public knowledge. But the real question that *Libération* did not ask was: why had the Americans systematically moved in on Marseilles? And what or who precisely was concealed under the vague term 'Americans'?

8 a.m.

When Attali and Romero arrived, Daquin was already making the coffee. They exchanged information as they sat round the table. Anna Beric, important for sure, Lavorel was on to that. Thomas and Santoni were continuing to look for a lead connected with the Aratoff Ballets, and their telephone was being tapped. VL had been staying in New York. That had to be investigated. Sobesky? Should they question him? Daquin adamant: not immediately. Find out the lie of the land first. That would be Attali's job for the day.

'And Romero, I've something else for you. Here are four names of Turks, with their photos. Recognize them? These are photos you took. My snout's identified them. These Turks arrived recently, around July 1979. They had their papers sorted with no problems. Why? Go and see the National Immigration Office, see if they can throw some light on these files, find some irregularity or other. But be wary, on two counts: one, don't mention it to any of your colleagues, not even Thomas and Santoni. They work in this neighbourhood all the time, my snout lives here and I want to protect him as much as I can, and that includes from my colleagues. Two, I don't want anyone at the Immigration Office to know what you're working on. When it comes to drugs, you must be more than careful. Use the rogatory letters* for the Thai girl's murder and make up some story or other.

9 a.m. 10th Arrondissement Police Station

Attali and Virginie Lamouroux at a desk in a crowded, cluttered room.

'What were you doing in New York from Saturday to Wednesday last?'

'How d'you know I was there?' She was shaken.

'Answer my question.'

'It was just a tourist trip.'

'A bit brief.'

'Well, that's what it was. I had some emotional problems with my boyfriend, and I felt I needed a change of air.'

'Sobesky's son?'

'You know that as well? Yes. Sobesky's son.'

'And the father?'

'I work for him. That's all.'

'Be a bit more specific.'

'Well, he employs me on a regular basis, as a model.'

'Why, in your opinion, did he tell the police you'd disappeared last Tuesday?'

'I didn't know he had. Could be I'd left his son and missed an

---

* In French law, these letters empower the police to carry out investigations.

appointment with him at work, and hadn't let him know. Perhaps he thought I'd had an accident.'

'Why didn't you tell him?'

'I'm getting pissed off with these questions...'

Attali didn't give her time to finish her sentence: in one move, he rose, leant over the top of the desk and gave her a resounding smack. Modelling himself on Daquin, but he didn't quite have the self-assurance. In headquarters all conversation stopped dead. Everyone was looking at them. Virginie Lamouroux squirmed in her chair. She clearly didn't know what attitude to adopt.

'I didn't tell him because I didn't want to tell him ... because, since I've been living with his son, I wasn't supposed to go on sleeping with the clients, and I wanted to ... for the money, and for the fun. So there.'

She'd half shouted her reply, like an insult, but she had replied. Attali thought he'd made the point. He insisted, stressing his professional approach.

'Tell me how and where I can get in touch with people in New York who could confirm that you were there from 1 to 5 March.'

Virginie Lamouroux took out her diary. Gave him five names.

'I'll be checking these. Till Wednesday at 9 a.m. here.'

11 a.m. Rue des Petites-Ecuries

Thomas rang the second floor of the building. A frail old woman came and opened the door.

'Madame, I'm a new neighbour of yours. I'm renting a flat on the fourth floor, I came to say hallo and ask a favour.'

'Come in, *monsieur*.' A sharp look. 'And sit down a minute.' She walked with difficulty, supporting herself on the furniture. 'Would you like some tea, or a coffee? I suppose at this hour it's not too early for an aperitif?'

'No, I won't have anything. Very nice of you though.'

'So, what's this favour?' She sat down opposite him.

'Well, it's this: the flat I'm renting doesn't have a cellar. The agents told me you might perhaps rent me yours.'

'That's not possible. I've already let it to people in the building, the Bernachons, I can't go down there any more myself, you understand, so it's of no use to me.'

'Well, in that case, please excuse me for disturbing you.' He stood up.

'Is that all you'd like to know, *monsieur le policier*?' Thomas was taken aback. 'You hadn't noticed you're built just like a cop? And, then, how d'you suppose the tenancy on the fourth floor would change without me knowing? Oh, don't worry. I won't say anything to the Bernachons, I don't really like them. But now, you can't refuse a coffee.'

Thomas took off his mack and sat down again.

'Well, since you're not all that fond of them, let's have a chat.'

11.30 a.m. Rue de la Procession

The Immigration Office's files were in perfect order. You could access them through the surname, nationality or date of arrival in France. Romero had no difficulty finding his four Turks. They'd been invited to come by the same employer, Monsieur Franco Moreira, of Morora Ltd, a rat extermination business in Nanterre. Quite a joker, this Moreira. And their files had been dealt with by the same civil servant at Immigration, Dominique Martens. It was just as easy to find all the files of Turks processed during the year and to discover that, out of a total of a hundred, twenty-two were dealt with through Martens, and of those twenty-two, all were working at Moreira's in Nanterre. All he had to do now was carefully note all the names, and the address of the business.

Then he went to say hallo to the director. All along the corridor, he could hear a buzz of conversation, punctuated by the clink of coffee spoons against cups. The deafening sound of inactivity.

1 p.m. Place Gaillon

As soon as he entered Chez Pierre in place Gaillon, Daquin noticed Lenglet sitting at a table at the back, with a man. They were talking and drinking champagne. There was about them that certain undeniable, calm familiarity – of old lovers. He went over to them. The two men rose to their feet. Lenglet did the introductions.

'May I introduce Superintendent Daquin. We did political science together. We shared everything in those three years, except our bed. Théo, Charles Lespinois, an old friend, an adviser to the France-Méditerranée Bank.'

Tall, thin, with a distinguished, refined air about him. An extreme reserve. A grey three-piece suit, grey like his hair and eyes: a man of steel. Daquin thought of Sol, warm, wild, alive. Lenglet and I have stayed friends because we never hunted the same patch, he thought. All three sat down. The sommelier filled Daquin's glass with champagne.

'I ordered for you, Théo.'

'You've always liked doing that.'

'That's true. Now let's get down to business. Charles is a great fan of Turkey. And, in fact, the greatest connoisseur of Turkish political life I know.'

'What would you like to know, *commissaire*?' The calm, steady voice of a man accustomed to the reality of power.

The maître d'hôtel brought in the entrées.

Daquin was tense and barely noticed what he was eating. These complex triangular relationships. Lespinois didn't exactly give the impression of being a well-disposed helpmate. And Lenglet, who was the most intelligent man he knew, had multiple interests in the Near East. He turned to Lespinois.

'Quite by chance, as the result of an inquiry in Paris, I've fallen on a whole bunch of extreme right-wing Turks, linked, it seems to me, to the Grey Wolves. I know nothing about Turkey. I've a hard job to place them. I'm looking for someone who can give me some pointers.'

'Why don't you go directly to the Quai?'

Lenglet butted in: 'Because Théo's like me: he knows the men at the Quai too well to confide in them. They'd only tell him what fits in with whatever their interests are at that particular moment.'

'So will I. I shall tell you what my interests allow me to tell you, as you know very well.'

'Well, naturally, but it's so much easier to suss your interests than those of the Quai!' And Lenglet turned to Daquin. 'In the 1960s, France-Méditerranée made a mess-up in a big way in that part of the world, and Parillaud Bank ditched them. Nowadays, they have to rely on political upsets there in order to get another foothold. To Parillaud's disadvantage, if need be.'

Lespinois was of the same mind. Daquin relaxed a little. He could see a few signposts now, more or less. Lespinois went into gear.

'The Turkish extreme right is organized into a legitimate party, The Turkès Nationalist Party, with a cluster of clandestine armed groups surrounding it, of which the Grey Wolves is the most important. It appears very powerful nowadays, since it's succeeded in imposing a situation of civil war, with twenty shot and killed every day. And it's infiltrated great sections of the State hierarchy.'

'I've already seen that for myself – in the police force.'

'But it's already beaten, because it doesn't have any coherence. It's an amalgam of the Nationalist civilian extreme right, more or less influenced by the Nazis and by anti-Kemalist Islamic movements. So it offers a superb field of manoeuver to every political force that counts, on the one hand, and the Turkish mafia on the other. Which one do you want me to start with?'

'The political forces. In any case, we'll come across the mafia along the way, I should imagine.'

'A fraction of the army encourages extreme right-wing terrorism, because it's using it to prepare the ground for its full return to power. The Russians play the extreme right as a destabilizing factor in a zone that's under American influence. And the Americans...' He made a gesture of disillusionment with his two slender hands.

Daquin recalled his year working with the FBI.

'As usual? Everything and its opposite?'

'The CIA's a real can of worms there.' He sighed. 'One part tends towards the so-called democratic parties who're all rotten to the core. And another part plots against them with the generals. And then some, more isolated, are acting off their own bat in some way, and infiltrate the terrorist extreme right. When you've the power the US has, there's no need to be intelligent, or coherent. You always end up on the winning side anyway.'

'Can you tell me about the ones in the CIA who're acting independently?'

The maître d'hôtel brought the main course and refilled the glasses. Lespinois, completely absorbed in his thoughts, ate in silence and drank a glass. Then he took up where he had left off, as though he hadn't heard the question.

'Lenglet's told me a bit about you, *commissaire*. It seems you enjoy cooking and eating well. The best food in Istanbul – and traditional Turkish cooking is very refined – you'll find at an

American's called John Erwin, who has a very beautiful timber-built house by the Bosphorus. He entertains Istanbul society there once a month. He's in his early sixties now. In 1943, he was twenty, was Turkish and called Mehmet Ervin. When Hitler attacked the Soviet Union, he enlisted in the Turkestan Legion and fought with the Nazis against Communism, for which he had a deep-seated and completely irrational hatred. An insane hatred. He just managed to escape the Soviets, fled to the States, became an American citizen in the middle of the cold war and returned to Turkey in the 1950s under the name of John Erwin. Officially, he deals in hides and leather. But his main job is as a CIA agent, and he's carrying on that same fight of 1943–5, by other means. Obviously, he's on friendly terms with everyone in the Turkish anti-Communist extreme right, But his world view is an original one. He doesn't believe in direct military confrontation between the US and Soviets. He dreams that the Soviets will disintegrate from within, a sort of implosion that would spread from the south northwards, a gangrene that would begin in the Central Asian republics. And this gangrene is called Islam. So this man, who's a complete atheist, supports every Islamic movement going.'

'He seems to show some foresight with the war beginning in Afghanistan. But how does he support those Islamic movements? The CIA doesn't have this as a general policy.'

'This is the crux of the matter. I'll tell you a couple of things first about the links between the Turkish extreme right and the Turkish mafia. At the present time – it hasn't always been so – the two work almost in symbiosis. It used to be the case that the mafia provided arms for the extreme right. You've no idea, *commissaire*, of the quantity of arms the Grey Wolves have stockpiled, well beyond their needs, even if there were to be an open civil war. Probably there's some deep psychological reason, a sort of violent collective therapy. The arms come from a zone under Soviet influence, via Bulgaria. In fact, in this region of the world, all the contraband between East and West passes through Bulgaria, whose principal source of currency it is, and through Western Turkey's mafia. It's therefore quite natural that Bulgaria's become the behind-the-scenes base of the Turkish mafia, its sanctuary. As the Grey Wolves are an excellent customer of the mafia, Bulgaria welcomes them too. With one thing leading to another, the bonds are woven and that explains in part why the Soviets rely on the Turkish extreme right. Erwin finds this situation politically dangerous. He'd like to emancipate the Turkish extreme right and, more broadly, the different Islamic movements, from all dependence with regard to the suppliers of Soviet arms. For that, there's only one way, in his opinion: drug trafficking. Not a very original solution. Lebanon and Syria have already tried it in that part of the world. On a personal level, it doesn't bother him. He's fond of opium himself and sees its use as part of his cultural heritage. He dreams of a powerful zone of production in Central Asia, controlled by the Islamic movements, which would finance the war against Communism. And he's counting on the Turks to form the framework for the project – let's say the technical cadres of the refining plants and distribution network – relying on the historical role played by the Ottoman Empire in this part of the world, the spread of the Turkish language, that sort of thing.'

Again, a silent pause. Lespinois seemed completely absorbed in his memories, or his projects. Then he went on.

'As you can imagine, Erwin's irreconcilably opposed to Turkey's entry into Europe. On that line, he'll find numerous supporters within the CIA, for a number of reasons – anti-Communism, hostility to Europe, and God knows what else... And also with those who've already played this game in the Golden Triangle regions, and still harbour a nostalgia for it.'

No dessert, coffees. Daquin studied the swirls his spoon made in his coffee. Once the coffee was drunk, Lespinois went on.

'No Western enterprise can get off the ground today in the Middle East, on a large scale, without participating in one way or another in the black economy of arms and drugs, *commissaire*. The delicate question is how to choose your back up, your alliances.'

2 p.m. Tax office, IIIrd Arrondissement

Having done a tour of Sobesky's showroom and admired the very distinctive style of his gear, jeans, embroidery, then checked he had no police record, Attali plunged into the voluminous file on his tax inspection, which dated from last year. He scanned it as well as he could and noticed a re-entry of significant new funds for the last two years: the sale of licensing contracts in the States, to someone called John D. Baker, a manufacturer in New York. New York? Attali noted it down, just on the off-chance.

Then he glanced at the conclusion: it all seemed to be in order, except for a few bits and pieces. Activity during the last few months before the inspection: for more than half of its trade, the business worked with factories. The rest was with workrooms in the Sentier district. Workrooms that were widely scattered, with various, short-lived names. There was a more important partner: SEB. Manager: Anna Beric.

4 p.m. Passage du Désir

Santoni was battling with the tapes from the telephone tapping of the Aratoff Ballets. A few uninteresting conversations. The fat woman had phoned her mother. Madame Bernachon had had a natter to a woman friend. Monsieur Bernachon had organized a bridge party for the weekend. And then three telephone calls by Monsieur Bernachon to Thailand, in English. And a long, seemingly stormy, conversation between Madame and a caller from Munich. In German. Santoni understood neither English nor German. Finding translators would take time.

Lavorel, looking drawn and in a rather worn three-piece suit, seemed happy. Daquin looked up from the report that he was writing, watched him come in and sit down, without a word.

'I've some news, *commissaire*. Can we start with the simplest: the shops. These are leased on a normal basis – through a lawyer – to a man called Darmon. A man of straw of course, but for the moment we have nothing on him. On the other hand, payment is by certified cheque from the Société Générale, guaranteed by a deposit of funds made the day before via the Bank of Cyprus and the East's authorized representative in France, someone called Assadi, a Lebanese resident in France.' He paused for a moment.

'Would you mind translating that for me?'

'The Bank of Cyprus and the East is at the centre of arms' trafficking to the Middle East. The fact that it's made an appearance as part of this circuitous route makes these two shops really significant.'

'OK. I hear what you say. Do me some notes on this bank, will you. What next?'

'Anna Beric.' Lavorel looked as though he was positively

savouring this bit. 'We began by looking at the manufacturers; the workrooms were too ephemeral: we would have lost too much time on them. So, all the manufacturers, all those we could get any details on who've worked with Anna Beric. We estimate she controls at least fifty or so workrooms, and has done so for at least five or six years. So it's a rip-off that must involve tens of billions' worth of centimes. D'you hear: tens of billions' worth. But apparently the manufacturers are in it up to their necks. They can't work over a period of years with a company that changes its name every three months and is perpetually "being registered" without asking themselves questions. And here's where it hurts. They've certainly shared the profits with Anna Beric. She's set up an enormous money-producing mechanism for the black economy which has infiltrated the whole of the Sentier district, but I've no proof. The manufacturers' accounts are in order. I need her collaboration to scare the shit out of them for certain. So, this morning we carried out a search of her home.'

Daquin raised his eyebrows. 'You could have talked about it to me first.'

'But in the context of the investigation into this woman's finances...'

'Anna Beric's one of our main leads for checking drugs coming from Turkey into France. Don't start again, Lavorel, or I'll chuck you out here and now. So, what about this search?'

'We got nothing out of it. There wasn't a single document left. And she's gone, left without a forwarding address.'

Daquin leaned back in his chair, folded his arms, and let silence reign. Lavorel chose to wait.

'This woman, I must have her. You'll have to do some research and find out first who she is. A woman who can set up a fiddle that's as profitable and lasting as this, and in an area like the Sentier, she can't be just anyone. She has a past. A weighty one, I don't doubt. Did you notice, at her place, if there were any photos or keepsakes of any sort?'

Daquin had said that in a perfectly normal tone. Lavorel hesitated.

'No. Nothing struck me.'

'Find out her past, Lavorel. That, perhaps, will give you a clue as to where to look for her now.'

58

Everyone has gone. Soleiman's alone in his small windowless office that reeks of stale tobacco. Dog-tired, anxious, lonely. Yet another night. Having to go out, walk, find a bed.

Or sleep here perhaps, on a table in the committee room? He sits down. There's the phone, with a direct line to Daquin's office. He won't be there at this hour. It rings once.

'Daquin speaking.'

A moment's silence.

'Can I spend tonight at your place?'

*

Next morning Soleiman opens his eyes. Daquin's already dressed, ready to leave. He kisses him on the neck.

'I'll leave you the key on the bedside table. It's simpler. Do you eat pork?'

9 a.m. At the Customs

Is there legitimate commercial trading with Turkey or Bulgaria which could be used as a channel for drug trafficking? Daquin had a whole morning's work with pleasant, competent customs officers, who were somewhat disconcerted by his questions. And nothing of interest.

No leads found. It would be taken up again when there was more concrete information.

10 a.m. In the Cité

Santoni listened to the Bernachons' recordings, in the company of two inspectors: bargain interpreters.

In English, M. Bernachon was preparing a trip to Thailand in a fortnight's time. He was making appointments with the people he spoke to.

'I don't think I'll need photos this time ... I've still got some stock ... I'd like to bring back two parcels.' A pause. 'Male ... Yes, I know. I haven't done it yet. But I have an order. I want two. Is that possible? ... Oh, no. Not at that price. We'll have to talk about it again when I'm out there with you. And of course I must see them.'

In German, Mme Bernachon answered someone calling from Munich.

'Yes, I know the ballet's incomplete. We're missing a dancer. I already discussed it with your manager last Tuesday. I'm not shirking my responsibilities, I'm refusing to accept sole responsibility for the entire loss. You know perfectly well, I'm just an intermediary. I think I'm right in this matter. In fact, you can't fault me. Yes, *monsieur*, you can't fault me.'

11 a.m. Passage du Désir

Daquin pushed open the glass door. Attali was sitting at the small desk writing up report from notes taken on a very small block of squared paper. Romero was working at the conference table. Both looked up at him and waited. On his own desk was a message from the lab: 'Re the two photos. There's absolutely no doubt it's the same man.' So Ali Agça had been in Paris, and perhaps still was.

'Coffee?' Without waiting for a reply, Daquin started the machine. 'So, VL?'

'She was very surprised and noticeably put out that we knew she'd been to New York. I asked her for the names of people who could verify her visit there, and she gave me some.' Attali pushed his note block over to Daquin. 'But I've something that's more interesting, perhaps. First of all, Sobesky works with Anna Beric. And he has an associate, in New York to be precise. A man called Baker. VL didn't mention him, but one never knows.'

'So, in fact, we've something we need to think hard about.' He thought for a moment. 'Track down Baker's full name and address. We'll phone him and see if that yields anything. And what about you Romero?'

Romero gave Daquin the list of Turks who'd entered France using the Morora company as sponsors.

'You've made a copy for me, obviously? This looks like an excellent lead. Carry on with it. By the way, Drugs are doing a stakeout of the two shops in rue du Faubourg-Saint-Martin. I'm also going to ask them to do one of Sobesky and tap his phone. Once it's set up, one of you'll have to go through the recordings on a daily basis. And arrange for him to come here for Thursday so that we can see what he looks like. Use his notification of a missing person at the 10th arrondissement police station as an excuse.'

*

Thomas telephoned his colleagues in Munich.

'We're sorting out a procurement case here in Paris. Can you give us a bit of help? Who does this Munich phone number belong to?'

Munich rang back a few minutes later: one of the smartest nightclubs in town. Dance shows. And rooms on the first floor. All perfectly legal and controlled. An Eroscenter above the nightclub in fact.

'Are there Thai dancers?'

'Yes, some of them are. It's quite exotic.'

'Minors?'

'Certainly not. I repeat – it's all legal.' A pause for a moment.

'The right kind of people go there. Know what I mean?'
'Perfectly. And thanks.'

4 p.m. The Grands Boulevards

Virginie Lamouroux felt strained and tired. She'd worked all morning and still hadn't eaten. But she wasn't hungry. She'd had no
drugs of any sort, ever since she'd got tangled up in these police
restrictions. It would have been too dangerous. But she needed
them, she just had to admit. She walked back up as far as the
Grands Boulevards, went into a cinema at random, and sat in the
fourth row. She was alone in front of the screen. She stretched out
in the seat: she needed to relax, regain her sense of calm. Could
she still get out of this tight spot or was it already the right moment
to disappear? There was someone in the fifth row, two seats to her
right. A sidelong glance. It was the cop who'd raped her. She was
sure of it. How was that possible? No one can have followed me
here, she thought. Her heart thumped, her hands were trembling.
The man didn't budge and said nothing. He was simply there, a
monstrous presence that filled the whole auditorium behind her.
She swayed as she stood up and rushed to the toilets. When she
came out, several minutes later, she looked around. He wasn't
there any more. At least, she couldn't see him any more. She sat
down again in the back row. And now, she thought, I need to think
about running away. How many days do I still have?

4 p.m. Passage du Désir

Attali was on the phone, speaking English with a heavy but passable French accent. Daquin picked up the receiver.

'Mr Baker, please. Inspector Attali. French police ... Good morning, sir, Inspector Attali of the Drugs Squad in Paris. I hope I'm
not disturbing you. You're obviously in no way obliged to give me
an answer. We have arrested a young woman in the act of selling
small quantities of drugs. She's a Virginie Lamouroux. We've
checked her whereabouts in the last fortnight. She's told us that
she was in New York from Saturday the first until Wednesday 5
March, on a tourist trip, and met you there. Can you confirm this?'

A marked silence. 'Yes, that is so.'

Once he'd hung up, Attali asked: 'Is he in the running too?'
Daquin shrugged his shoulders.

*

It was only towards eight in the evening that Lavorel returned to
passage du Désir, tense and excited.

'Anna Beric was accused in March 1958 of murdering her boss, a
Yugoslav by the name of Yavitch, and charged.' He consulted his
notes. 'The investigating judge, a man by the name of Parent, now
retired to Meung-sur-Loire, dismissed the case for lack of evidence,
after hearing the testimony of her clients, Scalfari and Rigault, two
stallholders on boulevard de la Villette, and an Iranian student,
Osman Kashguri.'

Daquin shivered, The Persian poetry, 'January 1958. An unforgettable meeting. O.' Could it be the same person?

'The police inspector who led the inquiry was called Pierre
Meillant.'

Pierre Meillant. Daquin closed his eyes and rocked in his chair.
Pierre Meillant, superintendent of the 10th arrondissement. They
were together at the Police Academy in 1971 and Meillant had
taken an immediate dislike to him. A labourer's son, and a former
member of the Resistance, entered the police as a patrolman in
1945, and climbed the ladder through internal promotions and
competition. First inspector, then superintendent when he was ap-
proaching his fifties; an exceptional career, clawing his way up.

He couldn't bear Daquin's sense of ease as a young man of
means, his brilliant academic career, superintendent at twenty-six.
And his taste for boys, one freedom too many and a permanent
provocation. Daquin had needed a great deal of sang-froid to avoid
a fight. That and his admiration he had for Meillant – he was a
very good cop. The real boss in his station and his district, where
he'd worked for more than twenty years. A man of power: a con-
cept of the police which gave him one more good reason to detest
Daquin, who liked the recreational side to his job. Daquin opened
his eyes and took a deep breath. Lavorel was still there, motionless,
with a suggestion of a smile.

'And, obviously, the next question is: is there still a connection
between Meillant and Anna Beric?'

'Obviously.'

63

A long heavy day. Daquin's worn out. So's Soleiman apparently. He's lingering in the bath, listening to the radio. He looks at his feet resting on the rim of the tub and remembers his first meeting with Daquin, in this house. Half dead with fear. His upper lip still stinging from the razor. And Daquin, surprising. In bed, he hadn't said a word. Authoritarian and attentive. Not hurried. A sensualist. At this precise moment Soleiman feels an unusual sense of well being.

'Hurry up, Sol. The pasta won't wait.'

It's spaghetti carbonara. Doesn't take long to make. Delicious. He hasn't wanted to cook for a long while.

Daquin has prepared a duplicate list of the twenty-two names Romero gave him and left them on the low table, along with a whole pack of photos taken by Attali and Romero.

'I'm leaving you all that. It's for you. The list has been made up using the four names you gave me to start with. They all obtained their papers under the same terms at the National Immigration Office, and they're all supposed to be working in the same business, which is probably a cover. Identify them, try to establish what links there can be between them that we know already, and find them. Sol, I've total confidence in you. We ourselves are working on the international links and French collusion. I'm giving you the whole of the Turkish side of this case in Paris. D'you think you can do this in a fortnight?'

A groan.

'And what does that mean?'

'It means "OK".'

7 a.m. Nanterre

Romero yawned. Not yet fully awake. It was a crappy suburb, amidst small villas built at the end of the nineteenth century, modern tower blocks and industrial warehouses. In this area it was mostly industrial warehouses and cul-de-sacs, with lots of potholes. But it was full of life at this time of day. Quite a few workmen and van drivers coming in to have a coffee or a glass of red wine before setting out. The café was just opposite Morora's premises. It would be hard to find a better observation point.

'A coffee, with cream, and a croissant please.'

'No croissants.'

'Bread and butter then?'

'Right, a coffee, with cream, and a slice of bread and butter.'

Buzz of conversation. Romero took his coffee, sat at a table near the window, took out *Le Parisien* from his pocket and a pencil to do the crossword. Renault vans began coming out of Morora's. He jotted down their departure times in the margin of his paper. In the van's driver's seat, as in the passenger seat, were immigrants. Romero could bet on it they weren't Turkish. North African, possibly, but not Turkish.

At around eight, the gate appeared to close finally. The café had emptied. Still feeling sleepy, Romero stood up and dragged himself to the counter. The owner was the thin alcoholic type, in his forties and already burnt out.

'*Patron*, get me a white wine. I need a bit of consoling. My mate's not turned up. Will you have one? Keep me company?'

The owner filled two glasses.

'I'm a driver/delivery-man,' Romero went on. 'Just lost my job.' The owner remained silent. 'D'you think it's worth my trying across the street? I've seen a load of vans come out this morning.'

The owner glanced vaguely across the street.

'At Morora's? No way. They only employ North Africans, and then, they don't make deliveries.'

Romero pushed his glass in his direction.

'Let's fill up again. It says "Rat Extermination" on the vans. What's that involve, job-wise?'

'They clean the waste chutes, sewers, abandoned cellars, all the places where there's trouble with mice and rats. It's a filthy job by all accounts. As it's very dirty, they can't find enough French people to do it, so they have to import North Africans. There're only two foremen who're French.'

'I shouldn't think that lot are very nice customers. They don't drink and they're always spoiling for a fight.'

Romero pushed his glass towards the owner again, who poured out the third round.

'No. I wouldn't say that. They slave their guts out, that lot, very quiet too. They never go out you know. Live on the premises. But Moreira, who owns the joint, has done a deal with me and I provide them with dinner every night. Which is good for my business, because without them this place'd be pretty dead in the evenings.'

'So it must be a really long day then, from six in the morning till late at night?'

'It's all finished by eight. And in the afternoon I have a siesta.'

'And these blokes pay up all right?'

'That's the good thing about it.' An evil smile. 'It's Moreira who pays, in a lump sum, every week. A bit like a canteen, you see. I'm not saying it doesn't mean I can't make a bit on the side.'

Fourth round.

'Are they Algerians?'

'No. Moroccans. And all from the same village what's more. They all arrived together.'

'So, nothing for me there then. Can you think of any leads?'

'Try the industrial baker's. Go out of the cul-de-sac, turn left, and it's the third on the right. I know they've got a big delivery service there.'

Romero thanked him, paid and left. With four dry white wines before nine in the morning, he could anticipate some heartburn.

9 a.m. 10th Arrondissement Police Station

Attali was waiting in a porch opposite the 10th arrondissement police station. He saw Virginie Lamouroux go in and come out again a few minutes later. He went up to her, took her familiarly by the elbow and said: 'Why didn't you mention Baker to me?'

She jumped, paled, brusquely withdrew her arm and hurried on. Attali let her go.

9 a.m. Rue des Petits Hôtels

The fat woman looked at her watch as she opened the agency office, not noticing the police vehicle parked twenty metres away. Daquin, Thomas and Santoni crossed the street, entered hot on her heels and took out their warrant cards and letters rogatory.

'Police. We've come to carry out a search.' They grabbed the fat woman. 'Are you on your own?'

'Yes, *messieurs*. The director and his wife aren't here.'

'At this time of day they're usually here. Call them on the phone. They can't take long, they live just upstairs.'

Overawed, the fat woman went to telephone without a word.

Less than five minutes later, the couple who directed the company came into the office. The three cops were sitting around the low table and looked hard at the new arrivals, without getting up. He was sly – that was the word that came into Daquin's mind. Small, rat-faced, very pale, with a pointed nose, grey eyes and thin hair. Like a sort of albino rat. As for her, Russian, big, solidly built, blonde with a thick plait round her head, a strawberries and cream complexion, blue eyes.

They introduced themselves. M. Bernachon, manager of the company, and Mme Irina Aratoff, his wife, choreographer (it was she after whom the ballets were named) and Mme Lilette Balland, secretary. Could they know what this was about?

'But of course, *monsieur*,' Daquin said, still sitting down. 'We're making enquiries about the murder of a young Thai girl. You might know her perhaps?'

Daquin drew a photo of the dead girl from his jacket.

Irina Aratoff, breasts thrust forward and with a slight accent, said very quickly: 'No. We don't know her at all.'

'We thought she could be one of your young dancers, the one who disappeared between Paris and Munich. So we're going to search your offices.'

The three cops rose. Thomas moved towards the secretary's office, Santoni and Daquin towards those at the back. They began a systematic, meticulous search. In the secretary's office: diaries, appointments, lists of telephone numbers. Files filed away, letters to and from airline companies, a voluminous correspondence with the nightclubs of Zurich and Munich about dancers, shows, contracts.

'Don't your dancers ever go back to Thailand?'

'Yes, of course, but it's not our job any more to take care of that part of the journey. Once in Germany or Switzerland, it's down to the other impresarii.'

Mme Aratoff pronounced *impresarii*, exaggerating the 'i's. Daquin laughed.

In Irina Aratoff's office: scripts, music, costume designs, orders for accessories. She was the artist of the troupe. Bernachon had reserved Thailand for himself: lists of addresses, files on every trip. The list of dancers, with a photocopy of the passport or visa for each one. And the choreography of each show. Everything seemed in order. According to their passports, the girls were all more than eighteen.

The most recent correspondence with Munich related to the fact that only five dancers had arrived at their destination, instead of the six expected. The settlement of the account with the Aratoff Ballets was therefore reduced by one sixth. Copy of the letter protesting sent by the said ballet company, who had expenses, and proposed that their loss be split equally.

'In the file for the last trip, there are only five names. Why?'

'We sent the records of the sixth to Munich, as proof of our good faith.'

Now to the apartment. Five rooms, very comfortable, big TV, video-recorder, numerous household gadgets. Fairly bad taste: the large bookless bookcase filled with *objets d'art*, and cocktail bar concealed behind a row of false books. But nothing, nothing.

'You've two maid's rooms, I believe.'

'Yes, if you'd like to follow me...'

Everyone went up to the sixth floor. Two tiny rooms. Three bunk beds in each. It was here that the dancers stayed during their time in Paris.

'We shall be taking fingerprints,' Daquin said.

But the meticulous cleanliness of the place left small chance of finding anything at all.

'Would you like to show us the cellar now?'

Everyone went down to the cellars. The group stopped outside the door numbered 29. Bernachon opened it. Bottles of wine, a few old bits of furniture, two paintings in a bad state, suitcases. Thomas busied himself with the contents of the suitcases. Ski clothes in one, the other empty. Then he turned to Bernachon.

'We've finished here.'

And he waited. Bernachon closed the cellar door and walked towards the exit.

'Hey. What about the other cellar?'

'What other cellar?'

'The one sublet to you by your neighbour, no. 39. Open it, please.'

The artists looked shocked.

'We haven't got the key to this cellar, we don't use it.'

'Perhaps the concierge has one?'

'You can ask. We know nothing about it.'

The concierge did not have the cellar keys. She seized the opportunity to ask what was going on. Absolutely nothing, Santoni told her, who was going to look out a crowbar from the police vehicle parked outside the door. He returned with a uniformed policeman who'd suggested he do the work, for the sake of something to do.

Cellar no. 39. Three locks. Easy. A heavy push on each lock was enough, the door gave way. The cellar was full of books. The ones which weren't on the bookshelves, Daquin thought. He picked up one and leafed through. It was a catalogue of Thai children. Each double page was devoted to a different child. On the one Daquin was looking at – on the left was a full-page photo, a boy of between ten and twelve, naked, slim, with golden skin and black hair, heavy fringe, kneeling, his hands tied behind his back, in the act of sucking off a corpulent blond male with a tache, a guy of about thirty, sitting in front of him, with another blond guy of the same build crouched behind the child buggering him and laughing. The whole against the background of a luxurious swimming pool. Both men were suntanned, you could see the white outline of their swimming trunks and the beginnings of a roll of fat around their midriffs. On the page opposite, two photos of the same boy, both naked again. On one, he was facing his 'objective', a bit lopsided, teasing. On the other, blindfolded, attached to the trunk of a palm tree, in the process of being whipped across the buttocks and back by one of the two blond guys, while the other one was getting a handsome hard-on. At the bottom of the page, a name, an address in Bangkok. A phone number and a price.

Daquin closed the brochure and passed it to the inspectors. His face was closed: these images were, for him, those of real suffering. He had to continue the inventory. There was a whole range of different publications, all based on the same photos. In some series, the addresses and price had disappeared. No longer were these catalogues for the preparation of a trip, but collections of pornographic photos, plain and simple. There were publications where boys and girls were mixed, others which featured only girls, or only boys. In all there were about 1,000 books, all intended for a specialist clientele of fickle sado-masochistic paedophiles. There was a public for that.

In the corridor there was consternation among the artists. The secretary half whispered: 'Any parent has only to keep an eye on their children.' Daquin hit her hard across the face, forehand and backhand, no holds barred. She fell on her bottom and let out a piercing shriek. The concierge hurtled down the cellar stairs to offer assistance to the unfortunate lady.

'You,' Daquin shouted at her, 'you get back up those stairs at top speed and shut yourself up in your goddamn cubbyhole and don't come out again, or I'll involve you in complicity to murder and rape minors!'

A dignified half-turn and disappearance by the concierge. The secretary shut up immediately. Daquin turned to Thomas and Santoni.

'I know it doesn't serve any useful purpose, but it makes me feel better.'

Thomas continued his search of the cellar. On the stacks on the right as you entered was a box of files. He opened it. There were various papers. He rapidly skimmed through a handwritten letter, in which the correspondent congratulated Bernachon on the quality of the photos he'd obtained for him and offered him 60,000 francs for a young boy, aged twelve maximum. He then went on to give a self-indulgent list of the physical characteristics he was looking for, and the uses he intended to put the boy to. There were other letters in the same vein. So the more official papers were in the offices, while in the cellar, away from prying eyes, was current business, deemed more compromising. And there, in the midst of the letters and receipts, he came across a passport. With a photo. It was the passport of the dead girl.

Age: 20. Forensics had said twelve maximum.

'Take these three bastards down to the local nick. Bang them up separately so there's absolutely no communication between them from this moment on. Load up the copies of their literature, and all their papers. Put someone on guard here till it can be sealed off. I'll see you later. I'm walking back. I need some air.'

Out in the street again, Daquin walked briskly. Tight, aching temples. All he wanted to do was lie beside Soleiman and not think about anything any more.

1 p.m. Nanterre – La Défense

After spending the end of the morning in the Social Security Contribution Collection Agency and the Tax office, Attali met up with Romero for a hot dog and a glass of beer. The Morora Company seemed clean: twenty-two workers all declared, and the names corresponding to the Turks found at the National Immigration Office. Wages declared in toto and taxes paid. Nothing to say.

'Just one small point, the workers I saw this morning aren't Turks, they're Moroccans. No doubt about that. I spent the whole morning in the area, it's what I've seen with my own eyes and witnesses agree. Moroccans.' A few minutes' reflection. 'We could go to the Factory Inspectorate and ask them.'

'You don't know what they're like. As a general rule, the Factory Inspectorate wouldn't even shake a cop's hand. The sad truth is they don't like us.'

'What? There are people like that?'

'There are.'

2 p.m. Passage du Désir

'Go for the two women, we'll see the man afterwards. Try to be quick. I've got a migraine.'

Irina Aratoff didn't yield a centimetre of ground in her interview with Thomas. Head erect and shoulders back: the bearing of a ballerina. Seated in the corner of the office, Daquin observed, rubbing his chin.

'I'm telling you. I don't know anything at all about this girl's death.'

'We'll see. You can explain first what it is exactly that you do in your husband's business. He acts as an intermediary with the brothels in Munich and Zurich. What about you?'

'The nightclubs we work with aren't brothels. They put on very high quality dance shows. It's me who chooses the music, writes the choreography and rehearses the girls while they're in Paris. The German clientele much appreciate my ballets.' And from then on it was impossible to staunch the profusion of details. 'I've references. I've worked in Carolyn Carlson's dance troupe.'

Slightly overwhelmed, Inspector Thomas asked her to spell the name and jotted it down. Daquin discreetly left the office.

On the floor below, Lilette Balland was fighting for breath. Santoni had asked her if Bernachon fucked the girls.

'How could you suggest such a thing? M. Bernachon is a man of impeccable behaviour. He loves his wife. There's never a gesture or remark out of place in his behaviour towards me.' An incredulous glance from Santoni in Daquin's direction. 'The girls are very carefully supervised, you know. Mme Aratoff even goes to the airport to collect them. Afterwards they live in the two maid's rooms, while they're in Paris. They eat and work and dance with Mme Aratoff, in the apartment . . . They never entertain anyone and never go out.'

'A veritable girls' convent. So, from what you've just told me, it can only be your dear boss who could have had the opportunity to strangle the girl.'

*

Accompanied by Thomas, Daquin had just sat down in front of Bernachon, who was perfectly aware of the gravity of the situation. Daquin gave him a smile.

'We've called the Vice Squad. They're coming to take care of you. Aggravated procurement. Abduction and rape of minors. All that sort of thing isn't in our line. On the other hand, we're indicting you for murder of and sexual violence on a minor. Didn't I tell you? She was raped during or just after her murder?'

'I didn't kill her.'

'Quite possibly. But, to tell you the truth, I couldn't give a damn.

Her passport was on your premises. Her friends whom we'll be questioning in Munich will confirm that she lived with you. And your secretary, a gem of devotion, has explained to us that these young Thai girls see no one in Paris other than yourself and your wife. Your wife, now she's an artist! She claims to know nothing, not even the meaning of the word prostitution. Furthermore, the girl was raped by a man: we've found his sperm. It's much more plausible that you rather than your wife is guilty.'

'I didn't kill her.'

'You can explain that to the Court of Assizes.'

Daquin stood up. Bernachon said nothing. Thomas intervened.

'Monsieur Bernachon. You'd better start thinking right away. There's only one way you can avoid an indictment for murder and that's to tell us who it was with the victim on the evening of the twenty-ninth.'

Bernachon, it seemed, could not manage to make up his mind. Daquin gathered together the file spread over the desk. Thomas went on: 'If you sold her to someone, you'll not make your case any worse by saying so, and that'll give you a chance of avoiding the indictment for murder.' Daquin walked towards the door. 'Say something. Say what you have to say before the Superintendent leaves this room.'

'Monsieur Simon.'

Daquin half-turned.

'Go on.'

'From time to time, I entrust my young dancers to trustworthy clients. For the evening.'

Daquin sat down, reopened the file.

'On the evening of the twenty-ninth, I took her to Monsieur Simon's – he directs a company called Simon Video on Boulevard de Strasbourg.'

'What does he do in this company? Does he show skinflicks?'

'I don't know, I've never asked him. I accompanied the girl to his place on Friday evening at eight. I went back to pick her up as agreed, on Saturday at eight in the morning.'

'And?'

'She wasn't there. Simon told me he didn't know where she was. We both thought she'd run away. Simon compensated me for the loss.'

'How much?'

'Twenty thousand francs – in cash.'

'Why did you keep the passport at your place?'

'At her age and without papers, in Paris, I thought I'd stand a chance of getting her back. And the Germans wouldn't have accepted her without her papers being in order. It costs a lot to get those papers in order.'

Daquin's head was now gripped in a vice. He calculated he had scarcely an hour of clear-headedness left before it would vanish.

'Can you take care of organizing a raid on Simon Video for tomorrow morning? We'll meet at eight here. I'm going home.'

9 p.m. Villa des Artistes

Soleiman has just squatted beside Daquin who's stretched out on the sofa in the half-dark, eyes closed, face livid.

'What's happened to you?'

'Migraine.' Daquin doesn't open his eyes, speaks very softly, hesitantly. 'It'll be over in a few hours.'

'Would you like me to go and get you some medicine?'

'No. Nothing. I never take any medication.'

'Would you like me to go away?'

'No. Please don't go. Make yourself some dinner, don't bother about me. I'll go up to bed when this is finished – at about one in the morning.'

Behind his closed eyelids, in blood red darkness, and beating to the rhythm of his pulse are those images of guys with 'taches and the children in Bernachon's catalogues.

Very late in the night, Daquin slips exhausted into bed, kisses Soleiman's shoulder and instantly falls asleep, his lips on his skin.

9 a.m. Boulevard de Strasbourg

Daquin was first to go into Simon Video. The receptionist walked towards him: a tall brunette, curves in all the right places, a fairly conventional beauty, and all smiles. It didn't last long. Daquin had decided they'd act tough, at least to start with, in that they were also going in 'blind'.

Inspectors Thomas and Santoni came in behind him and drew their guns. The secretary, dumbfounded, turned to stone.

'Police. Call your boss.'

Two very correct executives in dark suit and tie, sitting in a corner chatting, immediately shut up. A heavy silence followed as the inspectors still had their revolvers in their hands. The receptionist returned behind her desk and picked up the intercom.

'Monsieur Simon. You're wanted in reception – it's the police.'

Daquin moved quickly towards the office door marked 'Director' and threw it open.

'Come out of there.'

One gesture from the two inspectors and the executives took the opportunity to scarper.

Simon came out, dynamic, in his thirties, very self-assured. Yellow jacket over a black silk shirt, black trousers. Daquin thought Lavorel would love to be here. Simon defended himself for all he was worth.

'What on earth's this interruption about, and those revolvers? . . . this is a respectable business . . . you're frightening off my clients . . . my reputation . . .'

Bluff? Anger? Daquin took on a very official tone.

'We have letters rogatory to investigate a murder which occurred on the night of 29 February to 1 March, and we are acting within our bounds. We have good reason to think this murder was committed here. And we are taking precautions.'

Daquin signalled to Thomas, who pushed his revolver into Simon's back. The latter quietened down immediately.

'Sit down. Simon Video, what is it exactly?'

'We make video films for businesses, but mostly we train executives in public speaking and in front of the camera.'

'You make porn films?'

'Absolutely not.'

'D'you know this girl?' Photo of the dead Thai girl.

'No.' Simon crossed his hands.

'Be that as it may, Bernachon claims that he brought her here on Friday 29 February in the evening. And she was murdered during the night...'

Simon spread his hands, shrugged his shoulders.

'I don't know Bernachon.'

'Would you take us round your premises?'

Thomas pushed him with the end of his revolver. A tour of the offices was rapidly made – there were only three: Simon's, another for the secretarial staff. Where was the secretary? The receptionist said: 'It's me who does the secretarial work. I use this office when there aren't any customers to deal with.' Third office, practically empty.

'We allow it to be used by clients who're borrowing our equipment for the day and who come with their own staff.'

'And you, don't you have a cameraman or animator in your business?'

'No. I do everything myself. And when there's too much work I call in outside contributors, paid per performance.'

And now the studios. Daquin turned to the receptionist.

'Lock the front door and follow us.'

They went down a spiral staircase into a sort of square windowless lobby. On each side of the square was a cabin with a window in which you could see a video camera, attached to a stand. Control screen, projectors, numerous plugs and switches, small pieces of equipment etc. At the back of each cabin was a door. Daquin opened one: it led to a small studio, lined throughout, walls and ceiling, with white material, broad black beading framed each section of the wall, like a cinema screen, thick white carpet, two projectors fixed on the walls, And in the centre, a table and some chairs. The four studios were equipped in the same way.

'Is this all?' Daquin asked.

'That's all.' Simon was on the defensive.

Thomas knew a bit about videos. He went into a cabin, ferreted about, looked into the camera's viewfinder.

'How d'you switch it on?'

'From the table in the studio.'

Daquin switched it on. The picture was out of focus. The purr of an electric motor in the camera, and it automatically focused on the table. Thomas carefully inspected the camera. It seemed there were two possible positions to focus on, both pre-set, but the camera itself was fixed. He asked Daquin to turn the current off and on again. This time there was no noise from the motor and the focus remained on the table. Good. So where was the second focal point, and where did you release it from?

Thomas went back into the studio, and walked up to the back wall, tapped it. Pushed at the beading on the left, which moved, for there was a complete panel which slid to one side. The studio tripled its size. There was a big white bed in the centre of the new space, a fridge, an armchair. On the ceiling over the bed and on the three walls were large mirrors. A switch by the bedhead released the camera, automatically focusing it on the bed. The four studios were all built to the same plan. Daquin turned to Simon.

'It's a very clever system. Explain to me what it's used for.'

Simon was suddenly less at ease. The brilliant communicator had faded away.

'During the day, we work in the first part of the studio.'

'I doubt that. Then?'

'In the evening, I hire out the studios to people who want to keep a souvenir of their fucking parties. It's not against the law. We've the right to have it off whatever way we want. There are people in your neck of the woods who share that view. And who won't necessarily appreciate your pantomime performance.'

'We'll be the judge of that later. Don't forget that in one of these studios a young Thai girl of twelve was murdered. Our laboratories are going to go over them with a fine-tooth comb and even if you've done all your housework, I can guarantee that we're going to find traces of what went on and the murder. And that, you see, hasn't yet been gone through.'

Daquin sensed a shiver passing through Simon and his receptionist. 'Hurry up and take them away for questioning, they're ready for it.' They went back upstairs. The receptionist unlocked the entrance door. Daquin signalled to a cop who was waiting outside.

'From now on, I only want our lot going into this basement. Santoni, stay here and collect whatever you think merits it from the offices. Thomas, with me, to the Squad.'

In the police vehicle which took them back to the Local Squad headquarters, Daquin felt the tension between the girl and the young man. It was almost tangible.

11 a.m. Passage du Désir

Daquin handed over Simon to Thomas.

'Question him hard, but no knocking about. You understand, he's undoubtedly got protectors. I'll take the girl.'

'Your first name?'

'Christine.'

'How old are you?'

'Twenty-two.'

'You're Simon's mistress?'

'Yes.' Said in a weak, uncertain voice. Obvious unease.

'You're going to listen very carefully to what I say. You can interrupt me when you don't understand, but not to give me answers, not now. Then I shall leave you alone to reflect for a quarter of an hour. I'll begin. You're a mediocre girl, fairly pretty, fairly intelligent, no real education, and your family probably don't have the means to keep you at home doing nothing. You look for work and it's very hard to find. You have a bit of a hassle, and you sleep around. And then you come across Simon. He has the gift of the gab, he's affluent. He gives you work and is a passable lover. You trust him. You soon learn about his wheeling and dealing in sex parties, but in spite of or because of that, you've the impression that he's capable of doing better and making a load of money. You perhaps are dreaming of marriage. As you're hooked on novelettes, you imagine you're in love with him, and at this moment you're thinking yourself some sort of film heroine, and that you can save him from the clutches of the police, and then marry and have lots of children. Except that things aren't like that at all ... First, it's not sex parties we're talking about, but the murder of a child. I've brought along photos of the corpse. I'm going to leave them with you. I'll also leave you a report of the autopsy. You possibly won't understand everything. But you'll be able to check the age of the girl, and you'll see that she was sodomized after she died. In a case of this type, all Simon's good mates, his well-placed acquaintances, in short, everyone who profited from his little schemes, are going to drop him. They'll want to hush up those just-about-legal rumpy-pumpy parties, but no way will they be compromised in stories of prostitution and child murder. You follow me?'

She nodded.

'And you, who've no doubt had nothing to do with this, you, with your mind full of romantic notions, are going to get dragged into this business and find yourself doing time for complicity to murder. When you come out, you'll never even find Simon. And on top of all that, you won't find yourself another job either. And always for the same reason. People don't like hearing of sexual involvement with children, even Thai children. You get the picture?'

She nodded again.

'I'm going to have a coffee. You have exactly fifteen minutes not to ruin the rest of your life.'

*

When Daquin returned, Christine was as white as a sheet. He settled in a corner behind his typewriter and asked her surname, first name, address, status...

'How did Simon's system of hiring out studios work?'

'I didn't have anything to do with it. But I know he had membership of some kind. They had a key to the entrance door and the studios.'

'Did they come at any time?'

'No. I think they always rang first to make an appointment. On the phone they'd say: "It's about the members' evenings", so I wouldn't ask anything and passed them directly to Raphael.'

'Raphael. Is that Simon's first name?'

'Yes.'

'In the evening, what time did you leave the office?'

'I waited for Raphael, we'd leave together, practically every evening. About six or seven, depending on the workload.'

'You didn't wait for the members?'

'No, I've never seen even one of them.'

'And on Friday the 29th in the evening ... tell me what you did.'

The typewriter click-clacked away in bursts interspersed by long periods of silence.

'We waited for Bernachon.'

'Did he come often?'

'Not very, but, well . . . let's say, fairly regularly. I must have seen him four or five times.'

'Then?'

'He arrived with the girl at about eight. She didn't look as though she were twelve.'

'Go on.'

'He went away and the girl stayed. Raphael went down to the basement with her. He came up again after, I don't know, perhaps ten minutes, and we left for the cinema.'

'Can you be more precise about the time he stayed downstairs?'

'I did my hair, put my lipstick on, looked in the mirror, and he was back again. I wasn't conscious of waiting.'

'I see how you spend your time. It's not important. How did Bernachon come to pick up the girl?'

'That I don't know. The next day was a Saturday, and I never go into the office on Saturdays.'

'And did Simon go?'

'Yes.'

'At what time?'

'At eight.'

'Did Bernachon only come on Fridays?'

'No, I don't think so.'

'So in the mornings, what would happen?'

'I don't know. I never went to the office before nine. At that time of day, I've never seen any Thai girl.'

'And Simon? Did he go to the office earlier?'

'Yes, often. He had a lot of work to do before clients arrived.'

'So I imagine . . . And you didn't ever ask him any questions about his activities?'

'No. At the beginning I didn't know anything. And then he explained to me that he rented out the studios and that I should pass on certain calls to him direct. That's all. It's just that I'm not a busybody who asks all sorts of questions.'

Daquin finished typing his report.

'Reread it quietly. And if it concurs with what you've just told me, sign it. If there's something not right, tell me at once and we'll correct it.'

She read it concentrating hard for a while.

'It's OK. I'll sign it.'

'And now, young lady, let me say something to you: get out of here at the double, look for a new job, a new boyfriend and forget Simon. He's not worth it.'

*

With Bernachon's statement, and Christine's, Simon soon cracked. And from what he said, it was a funny business. He'd begun by fitting out a studio as a bedroom and hiring it occasionally to film X-rated videos. But very soon he'd had requests, coming first from his business clientele as a venue for their private orgies that the participants wanted to film. He soon saw there was a very profitable business here. As he was a very resourceful, imaginative man, he had not only fitted up the four studios along the same lines, but he'd also set up a club of a very special kind. Fifty members at 2,500 francs a month. Each member, when he joined for the first time, drew out a pseudonym at random from an urn, which had contained fifty of them, and received a key to the entrance door and studios. Simon explained to them how the cameras worked. It was extremely simple: it was automatic. Then, each member of the club telephoned using his pseudonym – they had complete anonymity. He kept a studio for a chosen weekday evening, or a half day at the weekend. He could come with the friends he wanted on condition that he said nothing about how the studios operated, the discretion of each individual guaranteeing everyone's else's security. He could also order girls, or boys, but there, Simon was only an intermediary and did not touch any additional money, the services being paid for directly to the prostitutes, except in the case of Thai girls, where it was paid to Bernachon.

'Let's go back to the Thais. How's that arranged?'

Bernachon would bring one (or several) girls, Simon accompanied her to the studio, she would undress and wait for the client. Simon locked her clothes in the camera-room. The clients, when they left, would lock the studio behind them and the girl would spend the night there. The following morning at eight, Bernachon would come to collect the girl, to whom Simon had returned her clothes. On that particular morning, when Simon arrived, he had found neither the girl nor her clothes and the studio was apparently in order. He thought the client had let the girl run away. And he'd compensated Bernachon for the loss.

'How much?'

'Twenty thousand francs.' Which had seemed reasonable to him. Not for an instant had he thought of a murder: all the members were gentlemen from 'very good backgrounds'. Simon didn't accept any Tom, Dick or Harry, they had to be recommended.

'And so, on Friday evening, you didn't know who was with the Thai?'

'No.' Simon knew simply that that evening, in that particular studio, was a member called Icarus. But who Icarus was he couldn't say.

Daquin stood up.

'Take Simon's statement. We must have the list of pseudonyms, the list of members and the list of the "service providers" whom he usually dealt with. Also his bank accounts and all his club accounts. If not we don't accept a single word of his devious tale and we indict him for murder. After all, he had all the time to do it. I'm leaving you – I've things to do upstairs.'

*

Sobesky was more than an hour late but didn't seem to notice. He went up to Attali sitting behind the big desk. He was small, thick-set, with muscles and a belly. Square mouth, light blue eyes, brush-cut hair and a necklet of grey beard. Open, warm. Attali and Romero stood up to greet him, introduced themselves and sat down. Daquin, behind the small desk, was deep in a pile of files.

Attali began: 'We asked you here for four,' he made a point of looking at his watch, 'to ask you some questions about your notification of the disappearance of Mademoiselle Lamouroux that you made on Tuesday 4 March at the 10th arrondissement police station. Can you tell us what motivated this move?'

'Virginie's been my star model for the last three years.' Sobesky, embarrassed, hesitated a little. 'She's also been my son's girlfriend for the last six months. She lived with him. On Friday 29 February, we had a family dinner, with some friends. After the meal, my son and Virginie had quite a violent row, so Virginie left on her own, I don't know why, Xavier didn't want to tell me. The following morning, I went to spend the weekend with friends at Deauville. On Monday morning I had a fashion show with a big client. It was Virginie who should have been doing it. Come 11 o'clock, no one. It was the first time in three years she'd let me down. My wife stood in for her at a moment's notice. She used to do that once ... a long time ago. The client left, the deal fell through, what's more I phoned my son at the hospital where he was on duty – he's a medical student – and he told me he hadn't seen Virginie since Friday evening. So, frankly, I was worried. On Monday I phoned all the friends we knew, no one had any news. So on Tuesday morning I decided to go to the police station.'

'Did you know that Virginie Lamouroux was back in Paris? Since 5 March to be precise?'

'I heard it from one of my friends who's a manufacturer.'

'She hasn't contacted you again since her return?'

'No.'

'You don't find that curious?'

'Of course I do, but what do you want me to say?'

'Did you know that Virginie Lamouroux went to New York from the first to the fifth of March, where she met your colleague Mr Baker?'

'No. I knew nothing about it.' Sobesky looked genuinely astonished.

'Why? In your opinion?'

'How d'you expect me to know?'

'Has she known Mr Baker for a long time?'

'It wasn't apparent to me that she knew him.'

'How long has Mr Baker been a colleague of yours?'

'What've these questions got to do with my visit to the police station?'

Romero took up the relay: 'Since she came back from New York, we've arrested Virginie Lamouroux. She was in possession of a certain quantity of heroin.'

'Virginie?' His voice broke on the high notes.

'You didn't know that she was trafficking in drugs?'

'No, absolutely not. I really like Virginie. She works as a model only now and then, like a lot of others, to finance her studies. She wants to become a museum curator.'

Attali and Romero tried, for an instant, to imagine VL as a museum curator. It was difficult to take on board.

'She's certainly had her share of affairs, that's normal for a girl nowadays. But to go from there to thinking that she's selling drugs...'

'That's why we're trying to clarify her relationship with Mr Baker.'

'Well, I've been working with Baker for a year and a half. We met at the ready-to-wear Salon. He suggested a licenced contract for the States. Obviously, I accepted. And it's working well. I've never seen Baker and Virginie together.'

Without moving from his desk, Daquin asked: 'Do you work with Anna Beric?'

Sobesky turned to him, frowning.

'Of course. What are you implying, asking that?'

'Mme Beric disappeared at the same time as Virginie Lamouroux, but she still hasn't reappeared.'

'What connection d'you think there is between these two women?'

'I don't know. It's you I'm asking. Is there a professional connection?'

'No. They each carry on in their own very different sectors. In my opinion, they don't even know each other. Anna's a very old friend. She started in the rag trade at the same time as me, as a dressmaker supervising alterations, nearly twenty years ago. Then, still with my setup, she did everything: she was a mannequin, a saleswoman, representative, secretary. I taught her everything. And she left to start her own business about twelve years after that. Since then I've gone on working with her. And don't tell me that she's into drugs too, because I'd laugh in your face.'

'How did she come to begin with you?'

'It was Superintendent Meillant who brought her to me. He was an inspector at the time. She was in a mess, and she needed help. And she came out of it remarkably well.'

'You know Superintendent Meillant?'

'Don't tell me he's disappeared too?' Smile.

'No. Not as far as I know.' Daquin returned his smile. 'It's simply curiosity on my part.'

Sobesky looked serious for a moment. Then: 'I've no reason not to give you an answer. Yes, I've known Meillant for a long time. Since the spring of 1943 to be precise. I was a child. A Jew. He wasn't much older than me. He saved my life. We've stayed great friends. Now I want you to explain to me what I'm really doing here.'

Attali took over: 'Quite simply, Monsieur Sobesky, we're inform-ing you officially that Virginie Lamouroux has not disappeared, that we're therefore filing your statement, and we thank you for being so co-operative in answering our questions.'

Sobesky got up, shook hands with the two inspectors, glanced at Daquin who was once more immersed in his files and went out.

Daquin rose to make a coffee.

'Where are we now, *patron*?'

'I'm not too sure, to tell you the truth. One thing's certain. VL knows Baker. So ask her how it is that Sobesky isn't up to date on the fact.'

*

Before leaving, Daquin took a large brown envelope from a drawer in his desk. Inside were two big black and white photos, doubtless taken at a cocktail party. On one of them was a woman outlined in crayon and a post-it from Lavorel: 'This is Anna Beric.' She was still very beautiful. Tall, dark. A brief reminder of the red dress in the wardrobe. And two smaller photos of Meillant coming out of the police station.

Meillant and Anna Beric had not just crossed paths once. He'd also taken the trouble to find her a job. It was hardly likely that he'd completely lost sight of her. She was too beautiful, too fasci-nating. And they both worked in the Sentier.

9 a.m. 10th Arrondissement Police Station

Attali was waiting for Virginie Lamouroux. She walked into the big waiting room, and went up to him, with a small nod and a smile.

'So where's this register I have to sign?'

Attali pushed it over to her. She signed.

'Mademoiselle. May I say you look ravishing this morning.'

'Thank you, *monsieur l'inspecteur*. Your compliment goes straight to my heart.'

'I've just one question to ask you.' He stood up, took her arm, in a move that was to be half gallant, and half to stop her running away. 'How is it Sobesky hasn't a clue you know Baker well enough to pay him a visit in New York?'

Virginie looked a bit perturbed by the question, but not enough to affect the good mood she had arrived in. She smiled at Attali.

'Because Sobesky's the sort of person who thinks he's cunning, when in fact he's a vain, naïve cunt. I'm pissed off with him, and his little schemes, and the way he puts his hand on my bottom. Pissed off with him and his son. Sod them. D'you understand, *monsieur l'inspecteur*?'

Attali was taken aback.

'I understand very well.'

She left with her dancing step.

Romero, hiding by the police station exit, followed her from a distance. She went in through the entrance of a building in rue des Vinaigriers. Romero could have sworn she gave him a little farewell wave. He hurried after her through the entrance. Several staircases, three courtyards in a row, two other exits out into a passageway that led to the street ... It took only a few minutes to ascertain that Virginie Lamouroux had abruptly and of her own free will left without saying goodbye.

10 a.m. Autoroute to the South

After a very peaceful beginning to the morning, a fuck with Soleiman and breakfast in bed (blinis, crème fraîche, taramasalata and coffee), Daquin drove towards Fontainebleau. It was a fairly nice day, and quite pleasant to get away for a time from all that Bernachon-Simon filth. How much did Simon actually make? Fifty memberships at 2,500 francs, 125,000 francs a month, tax-free, shit! And that, in addition to his official income. Obviously you had to deduct what he had to pay out to his protectors – about whom they knew nothing as yet. Daquin was not driving fast, which gave him time to think about a whole load of things. And to pay some attention to an alarm signal – completely instinctive – which told him that, when you're driving at 110 kilometres an hour, it wasn't normal to have that Citroën CX behind you the whole time. He checked ... filled the tank. The Citroën continued on its way. But two kilometres further on, it was behind him again. Daquin took the turn to Barbizon, stopped on the verge, spread out a map, which he pretended to consult, The Citroën overtook him. He set off again. He was now certain. But why have a superintendent followed – this is what was strange. And who would do it? Traffickers? Or other police services? People in cahoots with the Marseilles traffickers, for example. How should he react? Until he knew more, prudence was advisable. I'll wait and see what happens, he told himself. I'll still go on to Barbizon.

11 a.m. The Auberge of Bas-Bréau

The auberge was beautiful. The façade was very old and behind it stood low buildings of a more recent date, but discreet, with a garden full of flowers and colour. It was, no doubt about it, a marvellous spot for an amorous assignation. Daquin could readily imagine Anna Beric in this setting. Meillant, less so. But perhaps, after all, he didn't know him that well. He went into the bar. The décor was three-quarters English. No customers, the barman was alone: it was still rather early in the morning.

'A coffee, please.' He took out his warrant card. 'Don't worry. Nothing serious, just a routine inquiry about two people we've reason to believe are customers here.'

He showed the photos. The barman's face lit up with a big smile.

'Of course, it's Mme Beric. A delightful, beautiful woman, very polite, and not like some of those old cows, know what I mean?'

'I know what you mean very well. Does she come here often?'

'Yes, she's a regular. I couldn't say exactly how often she comes, but we see her at least once a month.'

'And him?'

'I don't know what his name is. He's always with her. Most times, they arrive separately and meet up in the bar, at about eight in the evening, then they have dinner and spend the night here. Next day they each go their separate ways. But it's always she who pays. Funny, isn't it? He doesn't look like a gigolo exactly.'

'No, not exactly. When was the last time you saw them? Roughly?'

'Three weeks ago? Tell me, I hope there's nothing serious bugging her?'

'For our part, no. She's only on the fringe of a very complicated case, and I need to hear from her as a witness. Thank you very much for your co-operation.'

And Daquin paid for his coffee, despite the barman's protests.

An idle stroll down Barbizon's main street: artists' studios and galleries showing piles of lousy paintings, and here, there was no trouble in tracking down the Citroën, parked in a small adjacent street. He memorized the registration number, lunched peacefully on the terrace of a little café and read the papers. Then an uneventful trip back to passage du Désir.

3.30 p.m. Passage du Désir

He had to check the Citroën CX's number. None was registered with this number, which belonged to a small Renault: a teacher, MAIF:[*] no report of it being stolen. So, false plates. Then he had to call Soleiman. He phoned from another office, you never knew.

'Sol. I've been followed, and I'm not sure by whom. I have to take precautions right away. Don't come to see me and don't try to meet me, either at my place or the office. I'll get in touch as soon as the situation becomes clearer. Be very careful Sol. Don't go out alone. These are probably drug traffickers and they've a pretty crude approach to things.'

Now he had to see Lavorel.

*

---

[*] Mutuel d'Assurance Automobile des Instituteurs de France – a large French insurance company with wide interests, including insuring teachers' cars.

'What are you up to?'

'I've almost pieced the network of Anna Beric's manufacturers together. When you bring her in to me, if you bring her in, I'll be able to launch the biggest operation in tax recovery the Sentier's ever known. I can't guarantee any link with drugs, but dirty money and white powder often go hand in hand.'

'Meillant's still Anna Beric's boyfriend. And they both conceal their relationship very carefully.' Lavorel was looking at Daquin and waiting for what came next. 'You're going to ask for a meeting with Meillant. And question him about the Sentier. He's been in this neighbourhood for twenty years, and knows everything. Nothing could be more natural than you asking his opinion.' Daquin thought for a moment. 'You can even mention Anna Beric. After all, we'd be pathetic cops if we hadn't traced things back to her.'

'What is it you want to know, *patron*?'

'I'd like to know what Meillant was up to today. Behaving like a Samurai, or taking early retirement?'

*

Thomas and Santoni hovered between triumphalism and despondency. Simon had given them everything: the lists, his accounts. Fifty members. About twenty highly-placed executives in very large businesses, six deputies, two senators, three well-known lawyers, two TV journalists and a superintendent from the Vice Squad who'd retired six months ago. And the hassle had only just started.

They also had the pseudonyms of the members who'd rented studios on Friday 29 February. Icarus, then, for the young Thai girl. Achilles, Prometheus and Theseus for the three other studios. Daquin felt like laughing. This is what the Ancient Greeks were used for these days. Prometheus so you can have a bang and smoke a joint.

And on the list of regular 'service providers' was Virginie Lamouroux.

Silence.

'A cover for dealing?'

Thomas shrugged his shoulders. Daquin was thinking aloud.

'We'll get Vice officially involved right away and leave them to sort it out with their old superintendent and Simon's theoretical, but probable protection. We're only interested in the murder ourselves. And in Virginie Lamouroux. And this time we're going to lock her up and examine what she has to say to us a bit more closely. As for the rest, the most logical course is to take the list of fifty members – after all, it's not enormous – question everybody, check their pseudonyms, alibis, habits as regards drugs and girls and what they know about Virginie Lamouroux. But with the clientele we're inheriting, three-quarters are going to refuse to acknowledge belonging to this network. If we shake them up, at the least we'll have the European Commission for Human Rights up our asses and if we insist even further, the United Nations. Not even mentioning our direct superiors. Leave these papers with me, I'm going to read them, write a report and see my chief.'

*

Peace and quiet, armchair, coffee, feet on desk: Daquin read the list of members attentively. The names were typed one below the other. Opposite each, the date they joined, the dates they settled their monthly instalments, by cheque or cash. Everyone was up to date. In the margin, Thomas and Santoni had noted a few bits of information in pencil: deputy... superintendent Vice Squad since 1979 ... journalist on *Le Monde* and, among the rest, were three names which meant something. Osman Kashguri, banker; Franco Moreira, businessman; Themistocles Lestiboudois, businessman.

So, Kashguri had cropped up yet again. An old customer of Anna Beric, who'd given her an alibi for the murder of her pimp. An Iranian. 'Iranians taught me to smoke heroin,' VL had said. The Turkish drugs came from Iran. It was time to phone Lenglet, get some leads on this Kashguri.

6 p.m. Nanterre

It was rush hour at Morora's warehouses, the time when almost all the vans came back to base.

'Factory inspection.' Attali briefly flashed his tricolour card at a foreman snowed-under with work. 'Is the boss around?'

'No. M. Moreira isn't here. He's not often here on a Friday evening.'

'Could you come around with me? I'm inspecting your company's business. Monsieur...?'

'Janvier. But you must realize I, I'm just a nobody here, just a wage-earner.'

'I quite understand, Monsieur Janvier. I'm asking you your name so I can enter it on the report. First of all I'd like to see the workmen.'

The men were parking the vans and taking out the equipment. Once the rumour had got round that the stranger there was the factory inspector, there was deathly silence. No one moved. The immigrants didn't know what a factory inspector was, but they perceived him as dangerous. Janvier introduced the workmen by name, one after the other. Attali made a note of all their identities and asked their country of origin. All originated in the same village, in the Moroccan Rif. He also asked for their work permits. There was a moment's hesitation.

'You'll have to ask the boss about that. We're not kept in the know about that.'

'They don't have their work permits on them?'

'No.'

'And their residence permits? While we're here . . .'

'No, nor those.'

A heavy atmosphere. Attali, looking grave, made a note of the absence of papers, and to ask the employer, then undertook a visit of the site.

'Where's the policy and procedures manual displayed?'

There was frank surprise on Janvier's face. 'Do we need one?'

Attali noted on the report: no policy and procedures manual. In the first half of the warehouse the vans were neatly parked and tools and machinery carefully stowed away. Against the walls were three benches for makeshift repairs. Attali went through the doorway set in the back wall to the second half of the warehouse. Beaten earth floor, walls of galvanized iron. On the left side, bunk beds, six rows of four. Five naked bulbs swung at the end of very long flexes, giving a gloomy light. In the corner was a row of cupboards, and along the back wall, five washbasins, two chemical WCs with no partitions, a fridge, two Butagaz burners, a big table, and some large cans which served as stools. It was simultaneously sordid and immaculately clean and tidy.

In the right-hand part of the warehouse, with no kind of partition, chemicals used in the business were stocked. Barrels, carboys, boxes, carefully stacked away and labelled. Attali conscientiously wrote down all the names of the products in his notebooks. A row of carboys a little apart from the rest had no labels. He went up to them.

'What's this?'

'No idea. We never use them.'

Janvier hadn't hesitated, so it seemed. Attali opened a carboy, which released a violent smell he knew by heart: acetic anhydride. He'd never hoped for such a find.

'And has this been here a long time?'

'Couldn't tell you. I have a feeling it hasn't.'

Attali went back through the first part of the warehouse. The Moroccans were gathered round a bench, with the other foreman. Visibly filled with misery and shame, they already saw themselves banged up.

Attali made his farewells to the foremen, informed them that he would call the boss on Monday and left in a dignified manner. Behind him he could hear the confused burble of people suddenly talking again. He sat at the steering wheel of his unmarked car which he'd parked in front of the café opposite. He sounded the horn to alert Romero, leaning on the counter, who said goodbye to the *patron* and jumped into the car beside his colleague.

'So, you managed to persuade him we were journalists?'

'Yes, but it was a long, difficult job. He'd never seen a journalist in his life.'

'Just as well.'

8.30 p.m. Passage du Désir

'Chief, it's a brilliant scam. Moreira declares twenty-two workers he doesn't actually employ: that's the Turks. And he has twenty-two workers he doesn't declare, and doesn't pay either: that's the Moroccans.'

Attali was euphoric, like some schoolboy who might have said it as a good joke, and for him that was a surprise.

'How d'you mean? He doesn't pay them?'

'No, I'm sure he doesn't. He gives them lodgings, you should see what they're like, he feeds them, but he doesn't pay them. They all come from the same village. Moreira must be in cahoots with a big Moroccan landlord who's probably organized their trip here, making them pay dearly ... The families have all stayed behind in their village. Like that, if a worker gets it into his head to protest, what would happen to his family back home would soon make him change his mind. His business has the appearance of being in order, nobody bothers them, not the tax people nor the factory inspectorate. The Turks in the network appear as innocent workers, and the boss makes an enormous profit out of the real workers, for he's only paying their national insurance, not wages. Which makes a change from the Sentier, where bosses pay them wages but no national insurance.'

'There's a lot of conjecture in all this. And we don't have time to dig deeper.'

'But that's not all. In the workshops I found acetic anhydride stacked up among other chemicals. The business's activities are ideal for buying chemical products the Turks need for refining heroin, without attracting attention, and they probably use the same methods to bring it back home as they do to bring the drug here.'

'Now, that's more solid. We'll tap Moreira's phone calls, business and home. You'll follow them with the others. There's something brand new as regards VL. She's dabbling in a complicated game of prostitution in which she's fooling the middlemen. And, what's more, Moreira and Lestiboudois feature in the list of clients. There's every possibility we've chanced on a network of dealers for our drug. Or some other one. But, this time, we've enough facts to make her spill the beans. Attali, find her as quick as you can, arrest her and bring her here for questioning.'

*

Night has fallen. In passage du Désir there's absolute calm. Time for reflection. I'm still in a complete fog, but at least I've several leads. Moreira and the setting up of the network? VL, Lestiboudois, the Club Simon and dealing? But, as far as I can see, nothing links it to the Mafia or the Turkish extreme right. Except, perhaps, one thing: the presence of the Bank of Cyprus and the East. Keep the report modest.

First, we have Attali and Romero's concrete results: a few words on Moreira and Martens to add weight to a request for tapping their line, and soonest possible. Nothing on the methods used, obviously.

Then Bernachon-Aratoff, that's already done. Everything on the

Simon scam. The list of clients – for which we're most grateful. Reactions in high places won't be long in coming. The two cases must remain our group's responsibility, the fact that Virginie Lamouroux is involved, just like Moreira, shows they're linked to drug trafficking. Nothing on the Citroën and the possible tailing. Let's wait. As for Anna Beric and Meillant, I'm keeping that to myself.

Finished. It's after 11 p.m. I'm tired. I'll file the report on my way home.

A real feeling of regret at not being able to meet Soleiman. A memory of his sleeping form under the orange duvet. His tanned skin and his darker, almost black, penis. Not worth going home for dinner. Some sauerkraut in a brasserie on the way will do.

10 a.m. Passage du Désir

'We'll begin rather at random with some of the businessmen, and some politicians.'

Thomas and Santoni listened and scribbled notes, relieved that Daquin was taking matters in hand.

'We've nothing against a man who frequents whores, of whatever persuasion. So, *a priori*, we must go softly-softly. But our aim is to throw light on the murder of a Thai child, committed on 29 February last by a certain Icarus. So they must give us their pseudonym, tell us what they were doing on the evening of the 29th, what they could see, if they went into the Club Simon that evening... if they wouldn't mind. And as we're obstinate creatures, we'd also like to know if they know Virginie Lamouroux, in what circumstances they've kept her company, if they've used her to procure girls or drugs ... We're going to contact them by phone. Obviously, they're not obliged to agree to meet us. But we can say to them that we're making inquiries about the murder and rape of a child, and if it comes to having to obtain rogatory letters in order to get them to talk to us as witnesses, we'll be considerably less discreet. Here are the lists of names to phone. Is everything clear? Get to work.'

*

Once he was on his own, Daquin began with Lestiboudois. Not at home. He was playing golf at the International Club du Lys at Chantilly. Telephone call to the clubhouse.

'M. Lestiboudois has just arrived.'

'Put him on to me. Superintendent Daquin here.' All it needed was a mention of the Club Simon to obtain an appointment. At 1 p.m. in the Lys club house.

'I shall be coming with one of my inspectors.'

'I'll wait for you in the hall. Obviously, I shall make you stay for lunch. I'll book a table right away.'

*

And now, Kashguri. Why resist his curiosity to get to know him? Kashguri was in the directory, and answered the phone after the first ring.

'Monsieur Kashguri? Superintendent Daquin of the Drugs Squad here. I hope I'm not disturbing you?'

'I'm working. What d'you want from me?'

'We've just arrested M. Simon for aggravated procurement. You appear on the list of his regular clients.'

'It's not illegal.'

'I know that as well as you do. But I'd like to ask you a few questions on the running of this private club.'

'And if I refuse?'

'I shall ask for letters rogatory from the judge and obtain them and demand your presence in, shall we say, a more official manner.'

'Very well, I'm looking at my appointments diary. I can come to see you on Wednesday next at 10. I'd prefer it if I came to you. Where should I go?'

'I'd rather see you at an earlier date.'

'That won't be possible. And, even if you go through the judge, it won't be any quicker.'

Daquin allowed some time to elapse.

'Wednesday at 10, at the 10th arrondissement Local Squad police station, passage du Désir, Paris 10th, Commissaire Daquin's office.'

He hung up, and sat motionless for a while, staring fixedly at the phone. It wasn't going to be easy.

1 p.m. Rue Piat

A whole morning waiting in a police Renault 5 in front of Martens' place: an old building, with little renovation done, just above Belleville Park. Undoubtedly, one of the prettiest views in Paris. Radio, crossword, a whole morning was a bloody long time. Martens came out of his place, on foot, sober and classically elegant in suit and tie. A few dozen metres on he went into a restaurant on the corner of rue Piat and rue des Envierges. Greeted like an old customer. Table reserved by the window. He ordered a bottle of champagne. A ravishing young woman arrived, with raven hair and very dark eyes. A warm vivacious face. She took off her long grey coat and underneath was an extremely clinging, extremely orange dress. Romero whistled in admiration. Lunch was washed down with a fair amount of booze, and apparently very happy. Outside it was chilly and miserable, nothing to eat. Romero asked himself, was this really the job I should have taken up?

They went back. Arm in arm to Martens'. This guy was a bastard – a lucky bastard. Romero took advantage of the slack period to have a sandwich.

1 p.m. Chantilly

With Santoni, unmarked car, destination Chantilly. Daquin didn't take long to spot the car following them. It wasn't a Citroën this time but a Peugeot 405. The tailing was well done, more discreet than the day before. The traffic was thicker though.

Daquin stopped outside a tobacconist's, noted the 405's number when it passed by him. Then he continued to the Club du Lys, without bothering about it any more. Santoni hadn't noticed anything.

They arrived at the Club du Lys. Daquin hated golf clubs. His childhood came back to him sickeningly. All those weekends when he'd been left on his own in luxurious, pseudo-English venues. Stop, now. Think of something else. One migraine a week was enough.

Lestiboudois spotted them and walked towards them. A small, good-natured man with white hair, amiable and rotund, in a beige wool and doeskin jacket over a dark brown sports shirt and matching velour trousers. He guided them towards the dining-room. A reserved table, a little apart, near a big bay window. White table-cloths, muted service. Aperitifs? Daquin ordered a margarita, Santoni a whisky, like Lestiboudois.

Daquin sat down, his back to the bay window, so that he wouldn't have to look at the artificially green golf links and the meticulously shaped yellow bunkers. He remembered a Sunday when he was a child, at the golf club bar in St Cloud, his father in an immense leather armchair, drinking whisky and going over the match he'd just played, blow by blow, with a human warmth he reserved exclusively for this sport.

He'd scored eight above par, as a Sunday amateur, who normally reached a score of between fifteen and eighteen. The match of his life. And all this while his mother was dying from the effects of a clever cocktail of medicines. When they returned home she was dead. And little Théo always thought his father knew. That's why he'd played so well that day. And I was used as his alibi, Daquin thought.

Lestiboudois placed his hand on Daquin's forearm.

'Everything OK?'

'Everything's fine, Monsieur Lestiboudois. To be perfectly frank with you, I have a bit of trouble imagining you romping in front of the cameras at the Club Simon.'

'You're quite right. I've never lain on one of those beds.'

The maître d'hôtel arrived. 'Mixed grills. With a chilled Saumur.'

'Explain to me then, why pay out all this money every month?'

'I run the export department in a big French firm which sells cosmetics and beauty products.'

'We know.'

'As such, I have to entertain foreign customers who come from the whole world over to sign very big contracts with us. Paris has a certain reputation. When they get here, they want...' hesitations, shame? 'Let's be clear, they want ass. Places like the Folies Bergère, the Crazy Horse, don't match up to our customers' expectations any more. They may be OK for a Chrysler dealer from Iowa or Danish peasants, but not for the type of person we're dealing with. The specialized networks of call-girls for businessmen, who provide very pretty girls, multilingual, able to accompany other clients to dinners or the theatre and sleep with them afterwards, they're quite good. We use some of them. But the Club Simon, believe me, is an inspired idea. We found some superb models there, models our clients have sometimes already seen as photos in magazines, who can give the illusion of being a bit amateur. And then, this kind of secret, members only, pseudonyms, a key, it's exciting. And the video ... they leave with it and they're enchanted. A really personalized souvenir – and not corny – of Gay Paree. Some, who've come several times before, arrive with their own video tape recording, with a list of credits already prepared. I think the Club Simon has helped us clinch several enormous international contracts. A good investment.'

'Was it your company who paid?'

'Of course. Included in general expenses. I accompany our clients, check that everything's going well, and then leave.'

'What pseudonym do you use?'

'Homer. I believe more or less all the pseudonyms are taken from Ancient Greece.'

'Good. Now, let's go on to the girls you've used. In fact, were there only girls?'

'No. Not always.' Lestiboudois was pink with confusion.

'Let's dwell on the girls. Who acted as the go-between?'

'Simon gave us the name and address of a Virginie Lamouroux. I'd phone her several days in advance. I'd say to her more or less what we needed, and she'd look after everything. That arrangement's always been perfect. And a lot cheaper than the classic call-girl networks.'

'How were payments made?'

'In our case, we came to an agreement that the girls shouldn't ask for anything direct from the clients. They'd send their invoices straight to our company the following day. I'd check everything. If there were any disputes, I'd settle it with Virginie. A marvellous girl, *commissaire*. So, these are rather specialized activities for her so she can finance her studies, you know.'

'Yes, I do know. She wants to be a museum curator. So, how d'you contact her?'

'By phone. I would leave a message on an answering machine. She'd always call me back during the day. As for paying, she'd send me her invoice and I'd send the payment to her postal address.'

'And would that also come under general business expenses in your company?'

'Of course.'

'A few supplementary questions: who put you in touch with the Club Simon?'

'M. Hershel, an industrialist, a whizz-kid in microcomputing. A sector which is also very open to international competition.'

'Have you sometime used the services of young Thai girls?'

'I don't think so. Our requirement is to make it a "Parisian" experience.'

'Did you rent a studio on the evening of Friday 29 February?'

'No, *commissaire*. We always rent on weekdays. Our clients return home at weekends.'

'To their family – ?'

'Precisely, to their family.'

'Were drugs being used at these get-togethers?'

'Not that I know of.' Lestiboudois had turned pink again. 'But it's not impossible. I wasn't there.'

'Come on. You don't have to pussyfoot. This is a private conversation.'

'Some clients have hinted about it to me. They simply told me that the girls procured all the substances they could possibly want. All you had to do was ask. I pretended not to understand.'

'And on the invoices?'

'It never appeared.'

'Not as such, but in another form perhaps?'

'Well, yes. Some invoices were larger than others, and I once asked Virginie Lamouroux why. She gave me a list of products that our clients had been provided with that evening. After that I never asked any more questions.'

'And what were those products?'

'Pot and LSD, on that day. Listen, *commissaire*, I'm aware that all this isn't exactly legal or very moral. But we're fighting a real economic war. We can't allow our business ventures to fade away in the face of foreign competition. It'd be like weakening France herself.'

'Don't worry about it, Monsieur Lestiboudois. If I wanted, I might take the same tack in your shoes.'

'An ice-cream? A coffee?'

'Thank you for everything, Monsieur Lestiboudois.'

*

Back to the office. Santoni driving. Daquin in the passenger seat. Silence.

'Lavorel will get a real kick out of that when I tell him.' And a few kilometres further on. 'People who play golf are capable of anything.'

Santoni looked puzzled.

4.15 p.m. Passage du Désir

'I've some good news and some bad news, *patron*. Which shall I begin with?'

'You can begin by making me a coffee, Attali. And you can then tell me the bad.'

'It seems VL is nowhere to be found. She hasn't slept at her girlfriend's, hasn't left any message, and Sobesky's son hasn't seen her again. None of her employers have heard from her since midday yesterday.'

'We'll see tomorrow morning. What next?'

'The Drugs team who've been watching the shops since Monday last have left a big batch of photos. I've been working on them, and I've compared them with ours. I've made up a file of about thirty faces, let's say, the hard core of people using the shops regularly. All we have to do is identify them. We can begin by comparing them with the twenty-two names found at the National Immigration Office. It may take a long time and need quite a few people on it.'

'I wouldn't think so. I'll take charge of that. Next?'

'Our colleagues in Drugs have told us that none of the regulars, except for the owner, turned up on Friday.'

'Yesterday? Now, that does interest me. Ask them, even so, to keep their surveillance going till Monday.'

'D'you think the traffickers can have closed down using the shops, after VL was arrested?'

'It's possible. Anything else?'

'Yes. Sobesky's American associate is in Paris.'

'Go on. Tell me.' Daquin was suddenly very tense.

'Sobesky phoned a manufacturer yesterday evening with whom he had an appointment at Deauville during the weekend, to put him off, as his associate had turned up unexpectedly from New York. He's dining with him today.'

'Baker never called him?'

'No. I've listened to everything again. No trace.'

'Thursday or Friday, Baker's in Paris. Friday, VL disappears. The shops are put out of bounds. Coincidence?'

'Wait. That's not all. On Friday Sobesky was giving his agents a rocket all day. They didn't want to sell his new collection of raincoats, the prices are too low, the margins aren't big enough.'

'Rivetting.'

'These raincoats are going to be delivered at the end of the month. They're coming from Romania.'

Romania? Which has six hundred kilometres of shared border with Bulgaria.

Returning home by taxi to change, have a bath, read a bit before meeting Lenglet, Daquin felt tired suddenly. His thoughts were that he was probably being followed and that he was going back to a house where Soleiman no longer was, and it was a shame. He opened his front door and, closing it behind him, stopped abruptly, without switching on the light. It smelled of stale tobacco. Not strong enough to alert a smoker, but there was no possible doubt as far as he was concerned, for he didn't allow cigarettes in the house. Some unknown person had been in here, and had stayed long enough to smoke one or more cigarettes. To do what? Look through his papers? There weren't any here. Bug the place? Plant a bomb? If I switch on the light, he thought, it could set it off. But if I don't put the light on and go out again straight away, the man following me could be outside, most probably under the porch at this very moment and will know that I know. And if these people are traffickers, my chances of catching them will diminish. Daquin crouched down, turned his back on the room and, stretching up his arm, switched on the light.

Nothing happened. So far so good. He sat on the floor, breathed again, relaxed. Now was a time to reflect. Someone was tailing him. Was it to find out how far the investigation had progressed? There were simpler, more discreet methods for the concerted services of the police, just as there were for traffickers. Was it to find a way of putting him under pressure to make him sing one way or another? Was it people who knew he was gay? That could mean a great many people. It was possible. They would have placed a lot of bugs in his house. That was the most likely. It was therefore unproductive to take risks. I simply won't move, he thought, and tomorrow I'll get the house examined by specialists. Still two hours to go before the meeting with Lenglet. He propped himself up as comfortably as he could. Nothing at hand to read.

He sat thinking about his father, as he had at midday, playing golf. Authoritarian and cold. He'd never touched his son. Never a kiss, not even a handshake. He used to put gloves on to make love to his wife – my mother. My mother who got plastered on booze and medicines to forget her husband – my father. The happiest moments of my childhood were those endless walks in the forest in the holidays at Grandmother's. And then, in that same forest, the year he was thirteen – the rape. The year his mother died. Suddenly, an obsessive thought came into his head: I've no way of protecting Soleiman. And then the flash of an image: his tanned body, under the orange duvet. Asleep. Inanimate. I don't want you to die, he thought.

5 p.m. Vincennes racecourse

At the wheel of his Renault 5 Martens drove into the car-park reserved for owners and trainers. Romero let him go on a little ahead, then introduced himself with his warrant card. The man at the gate raised his eyebrows, but allowed him through. But, just in the time it took to park, Martens had vanished. Romero entered the racecourse enclosure and bought a programme for the evening's races, which were to begin in two hours' time. In the second: Rheingold, owner D. Martens. He went along to the stable area, found where the horses in the second race were stabled. And there, inside the maze of looseboxes, he saw Martens, feverishly walking around a very pretty trotting horse, small build, burnt chestnut in colour. Just as Romero was passing them, the jockey's stable lad pushed Martens gently but firmly out of the box.

'Scram! You're making the horse nervous. Go and have a drink, we'll see you after the race.'

Inspiration. Romero caught Martens by the arm, gave him a big smile, and began: 'Oh well, that's that. I'll take you away. Let's go and have a drink.'

Martens leaned on his arm and followed him. Martens didn't want to go up to the Panorama restaurant, he preferred to stay in the great hall where all the punters were, he felt more anonymous like that, he would have liked the ground to swallow him up. They went to the bar on the ground floor to drink a pastis together. It was crowded, but there was no risk of losing one another. Martens clung to Romero as if he were suddenly all the family he had.

'You know, it's the first time one of my horses is running at Vincennes.'

'Do you have many?'

'No, only two. They are trained in the Orne, 200 kilometres from

Paris. I've had to put up with a lot of disruption to see them run, but I've never missed one of their races. And you?'

He would have to remain evasive, otherwise how could he explain his presence within the confines of the looseboxes. But the question and the reply were of no importance. Martens was only interested in his horses and himself. Romero ordered another round of pastis.

'Have you placed your bets on the first?'

'No. Not yet.'

'Go and do it, quickly. I'll wait for you here and then we'll go and find seats in the stand.'

Romero had never gambled, not at a racecourse, or a betting shop, or at the corner tobacconist's. He observed what others were doing in front of him and put two lots of ten francs to win on two horses, chosen at random, nos. 4 and 11. And for the second, 500 francs to win on Rheingold. I can't do less, he thought. Whether it would be accepted as justifiable expenses would be another matter.

He climbed up to the stand. Martens was ashen, tense, and more and more silent. Romero was caught up in the spectacle. Projectors produced an unreal light in the dusk. The sulkys passed back and forth in front of the stands: horses like automatons, horses that flew, astonishing bursts of speed. And the roar from the stands began to mount. It was cold. The horses were under orders. They were off. Romero tried to find nos. 4 and 11. He never succeeded. Happily the loudspeaker was there, accompanying the race with a sort of recitative. The roar grew louder. No. 4 took the lead, the stands shouted, no. 4 had won, the stands emptied. Romero turned to Martens, astounded: I've won. A weak smile from Martens: Congratulations.

'You seem pretty down in the dumps. I won't desert you though. I'll pick up my winnings a bit later.'

'You know, to see my horse run at Vincennes is really important to me. I'd never have believed it possible. My colours on this course. But you've seen the odds aren't good.'

'Have you owned horses for a long time?'

'Five years. Five years I've sacrificed all my money to them and every one of my weekends.'

Five years at least since his scam's been in operation, Romero thought. The horses for the second race had entered the course.

Rheingold, no. 5, grey vest with two orange stripes, orange cap. Romero had a flashback: the girl's dress at the lunch had had the same orange and the coat had been grey. Was it a present from Martens?

The horses were under orders. They were lining up at the starting gates. Martens clasped Romero's arm. The loudspeaker took up its chant again. No. 5 made a mess of his start, vanished into the depths of the cluster. Romero was surprised with himself: at the tight feeling in his chest. Martens was swaying and muttering, talking to his horse like a mother to her sick baby. The horses passed in front of the stand. Thunder of hooves, roar from the stands. No. 5 in the anonymous mass. Romero couldn't manage to track it down. Then in the line opposite, he saw no. 5 moving to the outside. The last lap: no. 5 was getting under way with a superior speed, all alone on the outside. Last straight, the speaker overexcited, no. 5 was passing the pack, and with a superb effort, a final burst of speed, it reached the finishing line, and crossed it in the lead. Romero was panting, and so hypnotized by no. 5's race that he hadn't even heard the stands this time. He turned to Martens, sitting as white as a sheet, tears in his eyes.

'Excuse me. My head's spinning.'

Romero looked at him: he had to stick to him like a leech now, he was going to crack. Instinct of the hunt. He caught him under his arms and put him back on his feet.

'We must go and congratulate the winners.'

He held him up as he walked.

Jostling, laughter, kisses, congratulations. Officials. Cup. All that flew past. The jockey was running in the fourth. He hardly had any time to spend with Martens. Martens accompanied his horse to the loosebox. Romero took the opportunity to collect his winnings while the third race was starting. His winnings were more than he earned in a month. The evening was becoming surreal. He ran towards the looseboxes. Found Martens again, who was gazing at his horse, punch drunk and full of love. It really had been beautiful: now, after the race, it had become a trotting horse, as though it had disintegrated through the effort. The stable lad was busy washing him, rubbing him down, protecting his legs.

'Come on. It's over. We're going to celebrate now.'

Martens woke up.

'OK.' To the lad. 'Tell your boss we'll be at the Rendezvous des Trotteurs, if he wants to join us after the races.'

10 p.m. Closerie des Lilas

The pianist was beginning a jazz piece. Daquin sat down at Lenglet's table in the brasserie where he was waiting for him on a red banquette, in suit and tie, very strict.

'How did it go at the Quai today?'

'So-so. At the moment, I'm fed up with the confined atmosphere of the motherhouse. I'd love to go back to the Middle East to be in one of the boxes in the dress circle for the start of the world war Giscard's announced for the new year.'

'You don't believe it will happen?'

'No, of course not. No more than you, I imagine. I remember we often had similar analyses and similar reactions at the Sciences Po.'[*]

'Yes, but that was more than ten years ago. I've lost my touch perhaps.'

'Steak tartare. Two, and a chilled Beaujolais.'

'You find anything on my man?'

'Yes. More than that even. I've found a lot. Don't trust that one. Be prudent. Don't touch him unless you're perfectly sure of your move; if not, he'll have your hide.'

'Does it bother you if I take notes?'

'Not at all, but, as usual, nothing's come from me. Let's begin at the beginning. He belongs to an important Iranian family, ultra-rich landowners, friends of the Shah. He studied at the Polytechnic as a foreign student, and passed in 1959. Then he moved on to the US, then back to Iran. From 1970 he worked as an intermediary in negotiations for all the important contracts between France and Iran, in particular Eurodif. It was he who swept the Iranian decision along. I can't check the exact amount, but I remember even so that that involved several billions' worth of francs. In January 1979, he left Tehran, around the same time as the Shah, but he himself came to France. There was a welcoming committee of government representatives at the airport, you get the picture? Apparently, he still had a number of contacts back in Iran, where the political

[*] French School of Political Science.

struggles are quite complex, since the Central Bank of Iran used him as an expert in the court case that they took out against the Bank of America, in Paris. There the stakes could be counted in billions of dollars. He's also a consultant to the parliamentary study group on Iran and a French government expert on Iranian questions in European workers groups. At the moment, with the hostage crises, American blackmail, threats of war and all the rest, there's no need to spell it out ... Alongside his more or less official activities – which must be generously rewarded – he's also an authorized European representative for the Bank of Cyprus and the East, little known here, but it's the linchpin in all the arms traffic to the Middle East. I leave you to imagine what all that represents. He's a very powerful man.'

Daquin leaned back in his chair. The pianist attacked the *Blue Monk* theme. He wasn't up to it, but it didn't matter, it made one think of the greats. It was a moment of intense happiness. Here was an adversary, a real one. It was a challenge, it had a sense of danger. This guy, one of these four, I shall hold in the palm of my hand, Daquin thought.

Lenglet looked at him, smiling.

'Théo, one day you're going to get your teeth knocked out.'

'Possibly. If I avoid it, I'll join you in the Middle East, and you can employ me as a mercenary.'

'While we're waiting, shall we go for a bit of hunting tonight?'

'I'd rather get drunk, but I'll keep you company all the way.'

11 p.m. Vincennes

A popular bistro on the other side of avenue de Joinville. Stable lads, jockeys, trainers, owners, punters, various conmen, everyone here lived for racing and talked about it. Martens entered, followed by Romero. A murmur. He was already known to the regulars.

He reached the bar and announced: 'Drinks all round. I'm christening my horse. Rheingold, in the second.'

Martens had found all his old aplomb, but he was already slightly drunk. Romero knew how to direct succeeding events. Hit the sauce as little as possible, make Martens drink the maximum and hold himself in readiness to pick him up. Two hours to keep it up, in the midst of incessant comings and goings, in the perpetually jam-packed bistro. He felt vaguely nauseous, he hadn't eaten enough.

And then, suddenly, Martens passed out. Emotion, alcohol. Romero caught him in mid-flight. I'll take him home, he thought. No one seems concerned about him. I'll carry him as far as the Renault 5. Fresh air, a few smacks. Martens came to, Romero helped him be sick. He went through his pockets, found his car keys and his house keys, then loaded him into the Renault. He was asleep. They were on their way.

1 a.m. Rue Piat

Romero dragged Martens, now asleep, out of the vehicle. No code needed to enter the building, just an entryphone. Elevator to the fifth floor. Open up – it worked. He laid the guy down in the hallway. Switched on the light and made a tour of the apartment. Spacious, well laid-out, kitchen, big dining-room, guest-room, perhaps a bit cold. In the entrance hall was a spiral staircase. Romero went up it, and – amazingly – there was a huge, completely open space, with immense bay windows which gave on to a flowery terrace and, beyond, the whole of Paris from Montmartre to Montparnasse. At this hour the city was dimly lit, it was quite moving. To the right of the staircase was an immense bed and behind it a double bath built into a platform. Along the walls, cupboards and a washbasin. To the left of the staircase, looking across Paris, a desk full of drawers, a coffee-table and sofas. Romero opened several drawers. Files were carefully stored in folders, each bearing a name and number. He leafed through. Unhoped for: all the funny business was there, filed away, just as they taught you to do in the Civil Service.

Romero went downstairs, loaded Martens, who was snoring, on to his back and hoisted him, with difficulty, up to the bedroom. Still snoring. He laid him on the bed, carefully removed his shoes. Then he rushed to the desk, keeping an eye on the sleeping form at the same time. Martens supplied blank, but already stamped, residence permits and work permits to a whole network of distributors: foreign embassies and the French police mainly. No businesses. Nothing on Moreira. At the Turkish embassy there was someone called Turgut Sener who bought a hundred cards a year. Martens sold them at 2,000 francs apiece. At this precise moment, Martens raised himself on his bed and muttered. Romero went swiftly to him – no way must he hesitate – took out his revolver and hit him sharply behind the ear with the grip. Martens fell back in a heap. He took the time to check he wasn't dead, then rushed back to the desk. Tomorrow Martens would probably be incapable of remembering anything whatsoever.

He examined the file systematically and took notes. Put everything back in its exact place, left as few traces as possible. It was 5 a.m. when Romero left, having gazed one last time on the lights of Paris. Martens was sleeping peacefully. He put out all the lights. Left the keys on the floor in the entrance.

Romero went home. His apartment was ... mediocre. Two tiny rooms, a kitchen, a bathroom. Overlooking a yard. There was calm and sun above the salting factory: good morning smells, summer. He took a long shower, shaved, changed his clothes ... and found the packet of notes in his trouser pocket. He'd forgotten about them. He put them away carefully in his kitchen drawer and downed an enormous breakfast of bread, eggs, cheese, orange juice and a half-litre of coffee. His boss would be a happy man and he was, frankly, enjoying himself.

1 a.m. Quartier de l'Opéra

A bar, deep armchairs, dimmed lights, a piano, encounters.

In the basement contacts were more intensive. Lenglet hurried downstairs. But Daquin had no desire to follow him. Sunk in an armchair in a quiet corner, he sipped cognacs, with eyes half-closed. He was going to drink till the night ended. Boozing alongside the memory of his mother. From time to time he looked around. Who was there watching him? Perhaps that rather uptight fortyish guy, on a high stool by the bar. Or one of these very delightful adolescents passing to and fro in front of him all night? One of them, in the early hours, came and sat on his knee.

'So, handsome, you drinking on your own?'

Daquin ruffled his hair, kissed him on the forehead. Another day perhaps. Then he got up. Rushed down to the basement, into the toilets. A route he knew and had already taken. A door marked PRIVATE, a dark corridor, several closed doors and at the end, another door, a staircase, a yard, then another yard. And finally a street, parallel to that of the bar.

It was daylight. Always a bit of a shock to find it light after a night spent drinking in the dark. He couldn't allow his drunken state to set in. He walked quickly, as far as Les Halles, very nearby. He called the boss from a phonebox. It was a respectable hour to call. Seven o'clock.

'Come right away.'

He took a taxi to the plush building on boulevard Malesherbes, a gloomy area. A large apartment on the second floor, all in silence. The family must be asleep. The Chief led him into the kitchen and a big surprise: a solid breakfast lay prepared on the table. Coffee, rolls, butter and jam, orange juice, yoghurt. Just what he needed to sponge up the night's drinking. Daquin talked. The tail – followed at least twice – and yesterday, his house visited. Was it our people or traffickers?

The Chief pulled a face. The smell of stale tobacco, a real old woman's tale. Who was he going to make swallow that? But he couldn't take risks, mustn't allow anything to happen, whatever it might be, to one of his most brilliant superintendents.

'I'll take personal charge of this business. Leave me your keys. And let's meet this evening in my office.'

If Daquin hadn't gone mad, if he were truly being followed, who was it pulling the strings? Impossible to be certain.

10 a.m. *Passage du Désir*

Daquin smiled at Attali and Romero. He felt less and less drunk.

'Who's going to start? Attali?'

'VL didn't turn up at the station this morning.'

'Good. Attali, to work. A notification of a missing person to all police. And find everything out about this girl, her family, her friends, her clients.'

Daquin turned to Romero, who told him about his evening and his night. He could feel Daquin's interest and amusement and became scintillating. Attali envied him.

'Martens sells his correspondents blank documents, but they're authentic – at 2,000 francs apiece. The illegal immigrants are going to pay 5,000 to 7,000 francs with their name on them. It's lucrative. But I don't think he's directly implicated in drug trafficking. His clients are a very mixed collection of people.'

'Does Martens have any way of finding you again?'

'A way of meeting me again, of course. But of finding me, no. He knows absolutely nothing about me, not even my name.'

'He's going to find out pretty soon that his desk's been rifled.'

'Not necessarily. I took the files out one by one and put all the pages back in their exact order. I took a great deal of care. I only took one original.'

And Romero placed on the table a piece of paper covered in figures and dates. Every month, ten blank residence permits and work permits. Unit cost: 2,000 francs. Dates of deliveries and payments. Destination: Pierre Meillant. Daquin made no attempt to hide his surprise and excitement.

'Romero, you really have the luck it takes to make a good cop. Not a word to Thomas and Santoni, obviously, they're close to Meillant. And on the Turkish side, what does that give us?'

'Martens' correspondent at the embassy, the one who buys papers regularly, is someone called Turgut Sener. That's all I know. The real papers for the Turks who put us on to Martens and Moreira's trail don't seem to be have been bought. At least, I didn't find any trace of them. It could be a trade-off of processed vouchers.'

'We must look into what could connect this Sener to the Sentier and drugs. If my memory serves me well, you've already established a contact at the embassy?'

'Yes, *commissaire*.'

'Good, well, just the right time to activate it, as our Secret Service boffins would say.'

Romero felt somewhat miffed. But there was nothing he could say. Two months ago, when he'd come to work with Daquin, a cousin had phoned him – a distant cousin ('She's the granddaughter of the sister of one of our great-grandmother's . . .' 'Stop, I can't take any more!') who'd just arrived in France as a secretary at the Turkish embassy ('Well, that sounds really interesting.'). She wanted to meet some French people, go out a bit. ('To be honest with you, I got the impression she'd really wanted to marry a Frenchman and leave Turkey – she never wanted to go back there, she said.') Romero immediately imagined a sour-tempered, desiccated prune. Since then he'd telephoned the distant relative twice – professional conscience obliged – without ever meeting her. It was a teaser: how could he strengthen the telephone link, yet avoid a clinging relationship? He'd get there in the end.

*

New meetings with the Club Simon members. The first admitted his participation without any reticence – the pseudonym he used was Minos (which would have been very suitable for a child killer) and came up with a more or less similar version to Lestiboudois.

His particular interest was in petroleum by-products. His Arab clients loved the evenings at the Club Simon. Afterwards they'd take everyone, girls and boys, to finish off the night in the most expensive nightclubs in Paris, and when they were happy with their performance, would show the videos they'd just recorded quite openly.

'Were you there?'

'Me? Oh, no. Never. People would tell me about it.'

'What about Thai girls?'

He'd never tried them: they weren't 'Parisian' enough. He didn't know Virginie Lamouroux.

The second was more interesting. A man called Lamergie, who worked in food-processing. His pseudonym was Theseus (oh, really!) and he acknowledged that he'd always taken part in the evenings his company offered to foreign clients. And on several occasions he'd used the services of Thai girls. When Daquin spelled out to him that these girls were between the ages of ten and fourteen, were slaves, bought, sold and locked up with no clothes in their studios so that they couldn't escape, he didn't seem too shocked and said simply that he hadn't known. He knew Virginie Lamouroux well and he'd used her on numerous occasions.

And what had he been doing on the evening of Friday 29 February? He took out his diary. Yes, he was at the club with two clients, with girls provided by Virginie Lamouroux.

What were the girls' names? Estelle, Maud and Véronique. He knew nothing further about them, but could recognize them.

Had he noticed anything that evening? No, it finished quite early, about midnight, difficult to be more precise. He'd passed Virginie Lamouroux in the small lobby in the basement, coming out of one of the projection cabins.

'You're sure of that?'

'Absolutely.' He flipped through his diary. 'It was the last time I visited the club. I said hallo to Virginie, she seemed to be on very good form. I suggested she join us for dinner, but she turned me down.'

'Was she on her own?'

'Yes.'

'And can you recall which projection cabin she came out of?'

Lamergie pictured the scene.

'I was coming from the studio at the back.' Daquin rapidly

checked on the page of notes in front of him. 'Virginie was coming out of the cabin immediately to the left, at the foot of the stairs.'

Daquin glanced at his plan again, but he already knew the answer. It was the studio hired by Icarus, the one where, in all probability, the murder had taken place.

When Lamergie had gone, Daquin swore aloud two or three times and thumped the partition, the table and the chairs in quick succession. How could I have let this girl go, he thought. Lamouroux's now involved in the Thai girl's murder ... I've behaved like an imbecilic misogynist. I always underestimate women.

*

This was a good time to phone New York on a Sunday morning. It must have been ten or eleven there, people were already up and about and still at home. Daquin went into an empty office, called New York and on the first ring found Frank Steiger at home. He was a very good friend, in the FBI. They'd worked together for a year on a very delicate case and the American owed him one.

'Steiger? Daquin here ... I've a real favour to ask you. Do you know a man called Baker? He's currently directing a big ready-to-wear operation in New York and has quite a lot of business dealings in foreign parts.'

Silence from the other side of the Atlantic. Then Steiger said: 'Daquin. I'm not going to ask you why you're interested in him, but you mustn't mention this conversation to anyone.'

'Understood.'

'He's seen as an upright citizen, above suspicion. He's old CIA. And what's more he's consulted regularly by this section and others.'

'What d'you mean by "He's seen as"?'

'I'm not meaning anything in particular.'

'One last question: when did he leave the CIA, and what were his last posts?'

'I don't know. Can I phone you back and tell you this evening? Well, for you it'll be in the night.'

'I'd rather you sent me a telex at the Drugs Squad.'

'I'll be in France in two or three months' time. I'll drop in to see you.'

'I'll give you the address of my present office.'

'Passage du Désir. Wow! An address like that sets you dreaming...'

2 p.m. Somewhere in Paris

First general assembly of all the Turkish members from the Sentier. Order of the day: what was to be done about the Ministry's decision. After ten days of negotiation, they'd taken the initiative of opening an office for legalizing residence and work permits, using critieria which didn't take the committee's proposals into account. Everyone knew the discussions were going to be stormy. The government's proposed legalization programme would, at best, only cover ten to twenty per cent of Turkish workers. So in order to discuss this calmly, away from the indiscreet ears of Police Security, a confederation of trade unionists had hired a quiet, well managed assembly room with seating arrangements for 250, equipped with armchairs with writing flaps. And always free on a Sunday.

The hall filled rapidly: 500 people, all men with moustaches, arrived. The atmosphere was overheated . Bedlam. You had to shout to make yourself heard. And soon you could hardly see anything any more for the thick cigarette smoke. Everywhere were NO SMOKING notices and burn marks of stubbed-out cigarette ends on the carpet and seats. In the polished stone entrance hall was a coffee machine; dirty paper cups overflowed from the rubbish bins spilling into the hall and assembly room.

Soleiman was on the platform, with three Frenchmen supporting the committee and participating in the negotiations, along with a Turkish student who'd agreed to come and translate for the French. Soleiman opened the general assembly by asking members to confirm his appointment as Secretary General. Unanimity, public acclaim. A surge of intense happiness. That I, in my lifetime, should have known this, at least once, he thought. He began by recalling the positions the committee defended during the negotiations: that papers were to be provided for all Turks who had work. The logical conclusion was therefore to reject the government's 'legalization'. Enthusiastic shouts of support. The student faithfully translated.

And, now, what do we do? The general assembly exploded into a jumble of vehement, confused proposals.

Start another strike? No agreement, we'd lose money and the government doesn't give a damn.

A demo? We've already had several, which weren't very effective, we must find another way.

The student was still translating.

A bomb at the ministry? Not very interesting, we'd be unleashing police operations and losing public sympathy. The student was still translating.

At that moment, a moustachioed man stood up and made a long proposal. Silence was gradually established. Around him, one, two, three, then ten people stood up. There was a thunder of applause. Soleiman was as white as a sheet. The student refused purely and simply to translate. The French were getting anxious. Soleiman suggested the meeting be adjourned and left to discuss things with several friends. The French managed to have what had just been said translated: that the committee should write a memorandum of their position in a letter to the Press, then a Turkish volunteer should jump from the first storey of the Eiffel Tower every two hours. Beginning tomorrow, Monday, at midday and continuing until the government gives in . . . The boys who had stood up were volunteering to commit suicide. At this point there was straightforward panic among the French, who were convinced that the Turks were truly capable of doing it.

Soleiman returned, the general assembly continued. He had another proposal: tomorrow morning, let's boycott the legalization office set up by the ministry. No Turks will turn up, and none are going to as long as the committee's positions don't form the basis of the legalization. And Soleiman defended his position in an impassioned tone: it was less heroic, perhaps, but more realistic, and would involve everyone's participation. The working class exists because of its collective solidarity, not because of its martyrs. The student translated everything he could. The general assembly was swung over, Soleiman was given an ovation and the decision taken. He was sweating, his hands moist. A Frenchman shivered nervously.

And now the boycott had to be organized. Small groups were formed and these would immediately spread out to cover all the bistros in the Sentier. A meeting was set up for fifty or so militants, including the French, who would gather tomorrow morning in front of the legalization office and use dissuasion tactics, should the need be felt.

All over. It was 6 p.m. The general assembly broke up slowly, as though with regret. Soleiman and the French were the last to leave the room. A vague glance at the battlefield, littered with papers, rubbish, paper cups, cigarette ends overflowing everywhere. It reeked of stale tobacco. Their anxiety created solidarity: if the boycott were to fail (and was it possible for a boycott of this sort to succeed?), all that would be left for them to do would be to go and pick up the corpses on the Champs-de-Mars, watched by gawping tourists. At least the first one, before the cops locked everyone up.

7 p.m. Drugs Squad

In the office, the atmosphere was smoky and tense. Quite a few people: the chief, his sidekick, one of the men in charge of the Organized Crime Squad, a member from the office of the Police Director, a technician from Drugs, a specialist in electronics. Daquin arrived last. He was at first surprised, then amused.

The technician gave a summary of the 'inventory of fixtures'. On the ground floor were three microphones hidden in a cupboard and connected to a recording machine buried outside, a device which was practically impossible to detect unless one were looking for it. On the first floor, a camera had been hidden in the bedroom, behind one of the spotlight fittings in the ceiling. It was directed on to the bed, of which it had complete coverage. The work of a pro, and very sophisticated materials: extra-flat, silent, the camera turned itself on to infra-red, that's to say, whenever there was human activity in its field of vision. The technician was silent.

'What have you done with the matériel?'

'We've left it all in working order and removed any trace of our being there.'

'What services do we have who have use of this matériel?'

'Well, they all have microphones. As for the camera, no one to my knowledge has it. And in my case it's the first time I've seen that type of apparatus.'

'Daquin, what's your view?'

'I have a possible theory: traffickers know that I'm on their trail.

They have to react. By having me followed, installing the microphones, they're trying to get information on the state of the investigation. The camera's something else. They must have heard it said I like boys,' a glance around the room, 'and they probably imagine they can make me squeal, or else put pressure elsewhere to get me off the case. There's another theory, apparently: one of our services wants to be in the know about the investigation into the Turkish network. Or practise blackmail for its own ends.'

'That theory's rejected, for the moment.' The Chief looked piqued. 'Leave everything in its present state. We'll watch your house from tomorrow morning onwards, and we'll tail the "plumbers" when they come to read the meters.'

After a few practical details of how the work would be set in motion, everyone left. Daquin remained alone with his chief.

'If it is one of our services, which I don't exclude, I could quite well see they might have connections with the Marseilles trail and its American end, from whence the hyper-sophisticated materiél. We can determine that very quickly. One way or another, they'll know that we know, and no one will come to read the meters. If they're traffickers, there's a bit more of a chance they'll fall into our trap.'

*

Under the camera's eye, Daquin was in bed, all alone under the orange duvet. Longing to savour the acid taste of Soleiman's skin once more, telling himself: don't forget – it's impossible to fall in love. What a shame.

7 a.m. Sentier Metro station

A small group of militants, a mix of Turks and French were standing around Soleiman, just as they had a fortnight ago. Coffee and
croissants. Tense and tired. No one had slept. Since the general
assembly had ended, they'd been covering every part of the Sentier
to explain why the legalization office opened by the government
had to be boycotted, this Monday, 17 March. But wasn't it too much
to ask those who might have benefited from this measure to let
such an opportunity pass them by?

Soleiman was risking everything in this venture. If the boycott
went through, he'd establish his leadership in the Sentier once and
for all, and keep a chance of satisfying Daquin's demands. If the
boycott didn't go through, he'd be wiped out and Daquin could
continue to play with him as he pleased. But he sensed that the
idea had had a response in the Sentier. *Ya hip Ya hop.* Everyone or
no one. By about 2 a.m. everyone who was a regular at the Café
Gymnase was already in the know. That was a good sign. If the
boycott hadn't met with an intense response, the order wouldn't
have spread like that.

Ever since Friday night, when he couldn't go back to Daquin's
any more, Soleiman hadn't been able to sleep. He lived to the
rhythm of the committee, and the cafés in the boulevard, snatched
a few moments' sleep on a table, in a corner, and swallowed the
pills that his friends gave him. Everyone in the Sentier used them
to keep going during the Fashion Shows when they're sometimes
working at the sewing-machine for more than twenty-four hours at
a stretch. They were good because they also stopped you feeling
hungry and so reduced anxiety.

8 a.m. Passage du Désir

First 'interview' with a politician: a Breton deputy called Caron,
from the Catholic right, a member of the club practically from the
start. He has a different patter from the businessmen. He's agreed
on an informal interview with the police out of a sense of public
duty. But can't you see it can only be a crude conspiracy, with the

end goal of compromising the people's representatives, and, beyond that, democracy as a whole? You've no proof. There's no trace of any payment by cheque or any means of identifying the member. I believe, then, in my duty, to protect the institution to which I belong. I believe in using parliamentary immunity and what's more I don't intend to respond to any notification to attend further interviews.

A small office meeting with Thomas, Santoni and their colleagues from Vice. There was still an 'interview' to do that afternoon with Paternaud, a radical deputy from the south-west, but 'I'm ready to bet that he's going to come out with exactly the same old patter. It smacks of something learned by heart. It's time to change tack. One can conjecture that certain clients regularly use Thai children and that the murder's committed by one of them. Let's make a photofile of all the members, and go and show it to the Thai girls in Munich and Zurich and see what that produces. With a bit of luck we'll find five or six regular customers and we can then turn the pressure on them.'

8.30 a.m. Rue de la Procession

Dirty, grey weather, A fine drizzle. A day in mourning at the start of a luminous spring. A bad sign? The group took up their positions on the pavement in front of the Immigration Offices, unrolled a banner, *Ya hip Ya hop*, and waited, soaked through, ill at ease. The offices opened at nine a.m. At a quarter to nine, some policemen arrived and pushed the little group and their banners back on to the pavement opposite. No resistance. At nine, the office doors opened. Nobody, nobody! It was hardly credible. At ten, a Turk came up rue de la Procession, on the Immigration Offices' side. When he noticed the banner, he crossed over to Soleiman, who explained to him why they had to boycott. The man approved, apologized for coming: he hadn't known, he hadn't been in the Sentier yesterday. He greeted everyone and set off for the Metro. On the pavement, there was an explosion of joy. The French kissed one another, a Turk had tears in his eyes. It didn't matter that it was raining any more.

During the whole course of the day, only five Turks would come through rue de la Procession. Not a single one would go into the legalization office. The minister had to negotiate, the minister would negotiate. We would return tomorrow.

10 a.m. *Passage du Désir*

A telephone call to Customs.

'So, Sobesky and Romania? Have you been able to find anything for me, since last Friday?'

'Yes, it's about some raincoats manufactured in Romania. A request for transit for 500,000 articles, to be loaded at Le Havre, to be shipped to New York to the Blue and Stripes Co. manager: John D. Baker. Scheduled for the end of March. Exact date to be confirmed later. And, as an addendum, the importation of 20,000 raincoats by Francimper, a new trademark created for the occasion by Sobesky. You must excuse us, the file had escaped our notice last week. It had been filed with the transit applications ... And then we were looking for Bulgaria.'

'Nothing lost. When will you have the exact date?'

'We should have it any day now.'

'You'll let me know immediately. And have you anything else in this file?'

'Transport insured by Euroriencar Company, registered in Munich, branch at Gennevilliers.'

10 a.m. *Avenue Jean-Jaurès*

Romero was lying on his bed. He was leafing through a strip cartoon book without reading it, to pass the time, waiting for a reasonable moment to phone his distant cousin at the Turkish embassy. A glass of whisky to give himself courage and then, time to make a move! The phone was ringing.

'Hallo.'

He recognized the voice.

'*Bonjour*, Yildiz.' Romero spoke into the phone.

'Oh, I'm so glad to hear you, Romeo. I thought you'd never call me.'

Her voice was serious, and the accent could pass for charming, but the lady had the nasty habit of calling him 'Romeo'.

'Are you alone in your office?'

'At this moment I am.' With a laugh. 'Why? Want to join me here?'

'Don't laugh at me, Yildiz. Do you know Turgut Sener?'

'Yes, very well. He's the Social Affairs attaché at the embassy. And we work in the same place, in the annex at boulevard Malesherbes. Would you like me to introduce you?'

'No, not really, I've come across him in the course of my work.' A moment's silence. 'It might be embarrassing if he knew I've been asking questions about him.' Romero felt bogged down. 'Yildiz, would you like it if we had dinner together? It would be much easier to talk about all this in a normal voice.'

'Yes. I'd be delighted.'

'What about this evening, at eight-thirty at the Hippopotamus in boulevard des Italiens?'

'I'll be there, Romeo.'

Romero hung up, very ill at ease.

11 a.m. Orléans

Attali, who'd only ever known Algiers when he was a little kid, then Marseilles and Paris, didn't feel at home in the unhurried half silence of the real provinces. Monsieur Lamouroux was a chemist in rue Jeanne d'Arc, Orleans' main street. He'd perhaps go and see him in a while. But for now he had an appointment with Madame Lamouroux, waiting for him at home in boulevard de Verdun, a short step from the station. A broad tree-lined boulevard, almost deserted at this end of a rainy morning. A large, affluent-looking, turn of the century house, surrounded by a small garden. No buzzer, a real bell instead. A charming woman opened the door and waited for him at the top of the steps. In her fifties, smiling, permed grey hair, little dark brown suit, pink blouse. Attali would have liked to protect her from her wayward daughter. She took him into the *salon*, obviously anxious behind her smile. She'd had no news for several days, but this wasn't out of the ordinary, so why the police?

'As I said on the phone, we're looking for your daughter as a witness in an important and dangerous case. She's no longer living at her usual address in Paris and hasn't shown any sign of life to anyone since Friday. It's possible that she would have tried to disappear when she understood the kind of business she's become involved in. It would be better for her if we're the ones who find her first.'

'And what sort of case is it?' A very small voice.

'Drugs and procuring. Minors are involved.'

'Virginie! She's such a serious, gentle girl. Our only daughter. She writes to us every week. And comes to see us once, even twice a month.'

'When was the last time she came?'

'On 6 March. She came for dinner and left the following morning.'

'Did she mention a trip abroad she'd just made?'

'No. Not at all. She told us about her studies. Everything was going very smoothly. She seemed certain of finishing soon.'

Her room had flowery wallpaper with bunches of roses, pink curtains at the window, a pink flounced bedspread, a single bed, fluffy animals. A small veneered desk and shelves full of books: *Stories and Legends*, a collection of Classics on one side; Balzac in the Pléiade edition, Stendhal, Flaubert, on the other. Attali gazed, transfixed. He remembered what Sobesky had said: so it was no pure and simple lie. VL was simultaneously a well-mannered student from the provinces in this pink bedroom and a drug-ridden procuress in the Club Simon. He had a flash of intuition: if she had a secret, it was here he was going to find it, in this young girl's bedroom, to which she'd come on 6 March, when she returned from New York.

'Madame, would you give me permission to have a bit of a look through your daughter's room?'

'Certainly, *inspecteur*. But don't make it untidy. I shall leave you. I'm going to prepare lunch. Will you stay and have some with me, *inspecteur*?'

He began with the desk. Bank statements. Orléans branch. Her income from modelling apparently, between 6,000 and 7,000 francs a month, in several payments. 'She poses for fashion shots, she pays for all her studies, you know. She never asks us for a sou.' Nothing else. The expenses of a young girl in Paris. A few fairly old letters. Attali made a note of the correspondents' names. A small address book: all in Orléans and surrounding districts. Attali took it even so. Leave nothing to chance. School photos, holiday snaps of course, her first date perhaps. Nothing which seemed to have any bearing on her life in Paris.

He returned to the desk drawers, nothing was stuck underneath. The fluffy animals he examined one by one, felt them, found nothing. He lifted the mattress, gently tapped the walls, feeling faintly ridiculous, opened the windows, shook the curtains, opened books, searched the bedside table – it was empty.

Discouraged, he sat on the bed. Lay down, as if taking a nap, did some hard thinking. Imagined VL, sleeping here. Stretching out her arm, switching on the bedside light. It had a deep pink shade, a very beautiful light. He looked at the pedestal of the lamp: a cylinder of translucent glass filled with different coloured marbles. He turned off the light, unscrewed the fitting on which the bulb was mounted, tipped up the glass marbles on to the bed. And there, hidden amongst all the marbles, were cut diamonds. About twenty of them. He couldn't possibly have got it wrong. With his heart beating, he sat for a moment thinking. Then he left the room, leaned over the banister of the stairs, listened to the sounds of cooking and crockery coming from the ground floor, and called Madame Lamouroux.

She came upstairs quickly, looking anxious. He placed a hand on her shoulder and asked her to come in. She took a diamond in her hand, looked at it, gave it back.

'Is this my daughter's?'

'Yes, and, what's more, I found them inside the bedside lamp.' She was completely thrown.

'Madame Lamouroux, I don't understand any more than you do what these diamonds are doing here. If I go through the normal legal procedure to have them valued, not only is that going to take time, but everybody's going to know about them. That would do your daughter no good when she returns.'

'I really don't want my husband to know anything about this.'

'Bring the diamonds, and come with me to Paris. We're going to question a number of people. As soon as we know what these stones have to say, you can come back here with them, and I'll continue my investigation. It's quicker and more discreet. Don't you agree?'

'How many days will it take?'

'I really don't know. Say two at the most.'

'Leave me a bit of time to get ready. We'll go in my car after lunch...'

The instructions were clear. Today, tomorrow or later, a stranger would introduce himself into Commissaire Daquin's house, stay for ten minutes or so and leave. He would be left to do what he wanted and would then be followed. Absolute discretion was required. It was, in principle, an easy job, at the beginning at least. The estate had only one entrance, through the porch of the building on avenue Jean-Moulin. Daquin's house was being watched from the stairs of the building by Inspector Conrad, two other inspectors were waiting for his signal in the avenue to start the tail.

The estate was very quiet, seemed deserted. A smallish man, very broad shouldered, black hair cut short, went through the porch, down the pathway between the houses, stopped in front of Daquin's door. It was obvious he had the keys. Conrad sauntered out into avenue Jean-Moulin, that being the agreed signal which would put Inspectors Allard and Zanetta on alert, a few dozen metres away, and came back into the estate. Hardly was he under the porch when he heard a woman screaming. It seemed to come from Daquin's house. His initial reaction was to pull out his revolver. But that was absolutely not on. The instructions were clear: whatever happened, the 'target' must not suspect he's being followed by cops. He began to run, heard windows opening behind him in the building which overlooked the estate. The door of the house was half open now. Without slowing down Conrad pushed it. Carried in by his thrust, he knocked against a body, slipped and went head first. And was given a thwack by a perfectly tailored cuff at the base of his skull, without him ever even seeing his aggressor. He crumpled, lights flashing before his eyes.

When he was at last able to stand on his feet again, he was alone beside a woman's body stretched out full-length, face down. A puddle of blood, as deep as a pool, was slowly and steadily spreading around her. A pile of clean laundry had fallen to the ground. A white towelling dressing-gown was slowly soaking up the blood. Conrad ran out. There was no one on the estate, and in the avenue, Allard and Zanetta were still waiting for his signal.

On Daquin's desk was Steiger's telex: B. officially dropped out in 1975. Before 1970, he was in Islamabad, and from 70 to 75 in Tehran. His name then was Edward Thompson.

*

The photo team came by at about five: there was no one at the sandwich bar any more. The surveillance was stopped. A good job that no one had tried to retrace the network from there ...

*

'Lavorel. Time for coffee. Tell me, are your bosses at Finance still waiting for your first written report? Aren't they getting impatient?'

'I'm working relentlessly. I'm accumulating the files. Bring me Anna Beric and you'll have one of the most colourful trials in the annals of Finance.'

'I need you.'

'I don't doubt it. You only ever offer me a coffee when you need me.'

Daquin smiled.

'What's that, Lavorel? You starting a protest movement?'

'No, no, *monsieur le commissaire*, just stating a fact.'

'The Euroriencar business, with its registered offices in Munich, branch in France, at Gennevilliers. What can you find out about it? Fast, obviously.'

'I've made a note of it, *patron*.'

'And now, what about Meillant? Have you seen him?'

'Last Friday, at length. He knows the Sentier like nobody's business. But he won't give me any real help, most probably because he's up to his neck in it, or because he's protecting others who are.'

'I know all that ... another coffee?'

Lavorel pushed his empty cup over to Daquin, who rose and made two more coffees.

'And he already knows that he mustn't delay to be still in the running.'

'Explain more.'

'He's taking a gamble on the success of the fight in progress in favour of giving the Turks permits. That's going to make quite a big change to the networks and circuits put in place in the 1960s.

And now the Chinese are beginning to move in. Meillant doesn't want a brush with them.'

'Lavorel, you see what I'm driving at?'

'Of course. You're going to lean on Meillant to get Anna Beric back. A lot depends on what you have up your sleeve, but it could work.'

*

Telephone.

'Théo?'

'Yes, chief.'

'You must return to your house, urgently. The concierge of the estate has just been stabbed at your place, in your entrance hall.'

7 p.m. Villa des Artistes

The concierge died on arrival at the hospital. Daquin, seated on his sofa, was exasperated and ill at ease. He would have to go and see the family. He didn't even know if she had one. To be truly honest, he couldn't even remember exactly what she looked like any more. It was far from satisfactory. Cops and various specialists were milling in all directions, in his home, in his house. Unbearable. A scent of haste and mess. He drank one coffee after another. Gradually the house emptied. Till only the Drugs chief, Conrad and the two inspectors from Crime who were responsible for the case remained. Daquin offered them a drink. Everyone sat down. The chief explained very succinctly to the two inspectors from Crime the reasons why Daquin's house was under surveillance, and asked them to omit all this aspect in their written reports. Daquin explained: 'The concierge had my keys. She came to work every morning, she did everything, housework, laundry. She didn't usually come in the afternoon, she worked somewhere else, and the murderers probably knew that. But today she most probably stopped by to drop off the clean laundry.' Flashback to Soleiman's dressing-gown, dripping with blood.

Conrad had seen nothing. Just the man from behind. Thickset. They must systematically question the whole neighbourhood, apartments and houses. Windows had been opened when the concierge screamed. Perhaps someone had seen the man running away? It was their only lead. Fingerprints would show nothing. The man would have been wearing gloves for certain. They would have to wait for the autopsy report. Essentially, it would confirm that the woman had died from being stabbed by a knife which had ripped her open from the base of the abdomen right up to the sternum. But they would possibly also learn things about the nature of the weapon and the assassin's technique.

*

Daquin and his chief were alone. Daquin, still in a bad mood.

'You could send Inspector Conrad to work with the group in Marseilles. I don't want to see him any more. I agree with what the press says. The system for training police officers must be changed completely.'

'Théo, give me a whisky and when you've finished blowing your top, tell me how we're going to proceed.'

'I think that we can now dismiss the theory of a set-up by colleagues...'

'I really hope so.'

Daquin groaned, without specifying what he was thinking at that moment.

'In any case, after a cock-up like this, the traffickers, if it is them, won't continue putting the pressure directly on me. That would be a bit too risky for them. And, to encourage them along this route, I'd like to be given constant visible protection, an armed policeman at my door, a surveillance vehicle nearby. I hope that that isn't going to last long. And they should check my phone isn't being tapped, at my office and at home.'

*

As soon as his boss had left, Daquin went out to call Soleiman from a phone box. It was ten in the evening. No reply. He went home and to bed, without eating.

8.30 p.m. At the Hippopotamus

Romero drank a whisky standing at the bar, and munched some crisps. Ever since that morning he hadn't been able to shake off an uneasy feeling every time he thought of Yildiz. A strange mixture of curiosity, anxiety and guilt. At eight-thirty precisely a woman came into the restaurant. Medium height, but the impression of being tall because her shoulders were strong, her hips slim and legs long. Very pale, triangular face, broad forehead, high cheek-bones, immense golden eyes. All crowned with a great mass of naturally curly, coppery red hair, which this evening was arranged in a large 1900s-style chignon. Romero was transfixed. For an instant, he looked round to see what lucky man she was smiling at.

'Are you Romeo?'

The serious voice, the accent...

'Yes, well, I'd like to...'

'I'm Yildiz.'

His breath was taken away. Fortunately, the receptionist came looking for them to take them to their table. A house cocktail for Yildiz, another whisky for Romero. Their grills arrived. Yildiz spoke first, about Istanbul, and how difficult life was for Turkish women, about her family. And her shyness, her loneliness during the four months she'd been in France...

Romero thought she laid it on a bit thick there. He would have to stay on his guard. He launched into his job: he was a police inspector, in the Finance Squad, a difficult investigation into the trafficking of black labour ... in the course of which the name of Turgut Sener had cropped up.

'I remembered that you worked at the embassy, and I thought you might be able to save me a lot of time and save me from making a few blunders if you could tell me what sort of man Turgut Sener is, what they say about him at the embassy...'

Yildiz took time to look at him, her chin resting on her hand. 'Turgut Sener isn't liked, or valued at the embassy. He belongs to the Turkès party, he's been put there to watch the ambassador, who's considered too moderate. He has a reputation for trafficking in everything, and extorting money under every kind of pretext from Turkish workers who need his services.' She smiled at him. 'Does that satisfy you?'

'If you don't mind me saying ... Pardon my indiscretion, but why would an ambassador keep such a corrupt attaché?'

'You perhaps aren't all that familiar with the situation in Turkey at this moment. Turgut Sener will stay at the embassy as long as the Turkès party deems it necessary. The ambassador has no choice.'

Romero digested the information. Daquin would know what to do about it.

'One more thing, Yildiz. If he's corrupt and if everyone knows it at the embassy, it wouldn't be all that inconvenient for you if the French police take an interest in him?'

'You could see it like that.'

'And you could give me some information on how he spends his time? In exchange, I'll tell you all the little villainies he gets up to, if I find any.'

'It could be fun.'

And she held out her hand to seal the deal. Romero took it and raised it to his lips.

This woman's dangerous, he thought, and I'm in love.

8 a.m. Passage du Désir

'As predicted, the meeting with Deputy Paternaud turned up nothing. He gave us the same spiel as Caron. On the other hand, we're making rapid progress on the photofile of club members: the majority of them are well known, and we're finding their photos at press agencies. We'll have a complete file by Wednesday evening.'

'Very good. Santoni can then leave for Munich on Thursday. I'll see about contacting the Swiss and German police. While you're waiting to go, Santoni, try to find out what these deputies have in common. They're not in the same parties, nor elected from the same regions, so what's the link between them?'

10 a.m. Rue Cadet

Madame Lamouroux led the way up the dark stairs, with Attali at her heels. This was the third diamond merchant they'd visited that morning. First floor, hefty old reinforced door. They rang. A young man in his thirties came to open up for them. Attali presented his card, explained: a woman had disappeared leaving her diamonds behind. The family and police were trying to identify them. They walked into a narrow, ill-lit, terribly old-fashioned office. There was a long wait. Madame Lamouroux no longer understood what she was doing there.

Enter a stooped old man with a limp. Madame Lamouroux took out an envelope from her bag, tipped it up on the little table covered in black velvet. The man turned on a lamp, put a magnifying glass to his eye, rolled the stones, then straightened up.

'You're from the police, they tell me?'

Attali held out his card.

'Madame is the mother of the young woman we're looking for.'

'I know these stones very well. I was the one who sold them. All of them.'

Photo of Virginie Lamouroux.

'Yes. To her. There're about two million francs' worth here.'

Madame Lamouroux felt tears welling in her eyes. The old man fondled the stones.

'This one here's the last I sold her. Two hundred thousand francs.' (He opened the drawer of his desk, consulted an enormous register.) 'The sixth of March. She brought me the money in cash.'

2 p.m. Boulevard Saint-Denis

On the Grands Boulevards, it was a fine day, there were lots of people about: coming out after lunch, returning to work, strolling around. A tall man, almost six foot, tanned, well-built, in his fifties, with a big moustache, came out of a café on Boulevard Saint-Denis and walked unhurriedly towards Faubourg-Saint-Martin. He stopped at a newspaper kiosk, bought *Hürriyet* and read the front page as he walked on. A thin young man in a grey wool bomber jacket, leaning against the kiosk, watched him pass, let him walk ahead a little, then followed him, hands in jacket pockets. He measured his step exactly in time with his, increased his stride without changing the rhythm, caught up with him. There was a bulge in his jacket. The other man felt something touch his back, just under the shoulder blade. He wanted to turn round. Heard a champagne cork pop. A luminous bloody explosion in his head. He crumpled to the pavement, stone dead. The thin young man overtook him, continued walking with the same measured step, until the next entrance to the Metro.

3 p.m. Passage du Désir

Daquin dealt with his current business. Contacted his Swiss and German colleagues. Agreed. Mail to follow. Wrote a report on Euroriencar in order to get permission for Drugs to tap the telephone and do a surveillance.

Called Soleiman. 'This evening at the house. No danger any more. A cop at the door. I'll explain to you. Just make sure he doesn't see your face.'

*

Telephone.

'Commissaire Daquin?'

'Speaking.'

'Jurandeau here, superintendent at the 2nd arrondissement. There's been a murder right on the street, corner of boulevards

Saint-Denis and Sébastapol. I'm letting you know because the victim is a Turk, a workroom manager. And you're working in the Sentier at the moment, so they tell me.'

'Yes. Absolutely. I'm on my way. Thanks.'

'We'll meet down there.'

3.30 p.m. Boulevard Saint-Denis

The uniformed cops had blocked off a large rectangle on the wide boulevard pavement and were directing the crowd around it. In the centre, clusters of men in civvies were to-ing and fro-ing. Flashlights. Daquin showed his papers and stepped over the barrier. He introduced himself to Jurandeau, said hello to Crime, explained his presence. The photo service had finished. Daquin crouched beside the body, spread face-down. A tall, broad-shouldered man. A black hole under his left shoulder-blade. A rivulet of blood had trickled on to the pavement, beside his head. In his right hand, the man held a Turkish newspaper. Daquin looked at the title. A clean murder. Nothing to do with the butchery yesterday at his house. More like a setting for a tasteful *film noir*.

He stood up and went to see the inspectors from Crime, busily looking for witnesses among those nearby, but no one had seen anything. And that is undoubtedly true, thought Daquin. One of the inspectors took the time to tell him that the corpse was of someone called Osman Celik, boss of a tailoring workroom in passage Brady. He had papers on him, which were apparently in order. Killed at about 2 p.m. with a bullet from a revolver, at close range, in the back. The weapon was probably armed with a silencer. The bullet must have burst the heart and death would have been instantaneous, pending the autopsy report. As for anything else, they didn't know where he came from, or why he'd had a bullet put in him.

'You think this death can have any link with your investigation?'

'I don't know. The only thing I can tell you is that I've not come across the name of Osman Celik yet. A complete stranger to me. That puts your case in a more difficult light.'

'To be honest, we were really hoping you'd take it on.'

'No, keep it, keep it. But keep me posted, obviously, if you come across an enormous packet of heroin in his workroom...'

The body was taken away, the various police services left, one after the other, and the pavement was again free for pedestrians. A team from Crime pursued their systematic questioning of people in the nearby shops, while another went to visit Celik's workroom. Daquin retraced the last few metres the victim had strolled. He walked with his nose in the air, in a state of alert. A hundred metres or so away was a newsagent's kiosk, with several Turkish newspapers on a rack. Daquin showed his warrant card.

'Just now, at about two, did you sell *Hürriyet* to a tall Turk of about fifty?'

'Yes. Is that the man who's been killed up the road?'

'News travels fast. So, this man?'

'He comes by almost every day, at the same time.'

'You know him?'

'Yes and no. *Bonjour*, thank you, that's all. He always comes from further down the boulevard and continues up that way.'

'Anything special today?'

'No. Nothing.'

Daquin continued down the boulevard, towards the Opéra. On his left, a big café, the Gymnase. A name Soleiman often mentioned. 'I dropped in at the Gymnase... They said at the Gymnase...' The Gymnase was the general meeting place for Turks in the Sentier. It was plausible that Celik went there on a regular basis. Daquin went in and drank a coffee at the counter. It had a special atmosphere. Only Turkish customers. Conversations were animated, sometimes violent, punctuated with frankly hostile looks directed towards the intruder. Obviously everyone was talking of the murder, but no one said anything to him. Daquin refrained from asking questions, and went out on to the terrace. He sat down, ordered another coffee and looked at the sea of pedestrians on the boulevard. Around the café, on the trees and posts were waste-paper baskets and on a fence to a worksite a bit further off was a small very crudely made poster; Turks were stopping to read it and hold even more discussions. Daquin stood up, paid and went to take a look. It was in Turkish obviously, but there, very clearly, on the second line, he saw the name of Celik Osman. Daquin touched it with his finger, the glue was still fresh. He went back into the Gymnase, asked for a knife – the proprietor gave him one with undisguised ill grace, but without asking for an explanation.

Daquin carefully eased a poster off, folded it and put it in his pocket, and went back into the café to return the knife to the proprietor. You could have heard a pin drop.

5 p.m. Passage du Désir

Attali, Romero and Lavorel looked through the file which had just arrived on the murder of Mme Buisson, the concierge at the Villa des Artistes. There was an identikit picture of the murderer. Short, five foot two or five foot four. Very broad shoulders, swarthy, short black hair. Square face, very developed jawbones, hook nose, thick black eyebrows. There was the list of witnesses who'd been questioned to make the identikit. It was astonishing how many there were: five people had seen the killer. First autopsy report: a single stab wound, very violent, and with an upward thrust. The work of a specialist. Commando training? The weapon: a long, curved, thin-bladed dagger, rare, very difficult to handle, but which generally made a fatal wound.

When Daquin arrived he also looked at the file. A speedy job by the look of it, but well done. Signed Conrad. The nerd was trying to make amends.

'You look knackered, boss. Sit down. For once, I'll make the coffee.'

Daquin sat down, and let them get on with it. It was true that he was tired. He glanced at his watch: in three or four hours he'd be fucking Soleiman.

Lavorel began.

'Euroriencar belongs to someone called Kutluer, who directs a vast assortment of Turkish companies in Germany. He himself lives in Istanbul. And in that business capital also happens to be the Bank of Cyprus and the East. The French branch was opened in 1979.'

Romero took over: 'Euroriencar was the company that Moreira called on the phone yesterday. He talked to someone called Mehmet. He told him about the visit from a man posing as a work inspector. He's still under the impression it was a journalist hard-up for copy and isn't too bothered by it, but, even so, he wants to offload some chemical products, he says. Mehmet's agreed to stock them until they can be despatched.'

'With Moreira and Euroriencar, we've got the first definite staging post in the network in France. There'll be others. Drugs are going to take over their surveillance. But Romero will continue to supervise the phone tap. And what about Sener?'

'I've arranged it with two inspectors from Drugs. We start tomorrow.'

Daquin gave a quick rundown on the body in boulevard Saint-Denis. 'Not necessarily any connection with our case but ... This coffee's red-hot, too weak.'

Attali talked about VL's family and the diamonds.

'Why stones?'

'Because she wanted to be able to get out quietly and quickly. According to the diamond merchant, in situations like that, people buy diamonds. More interestingly, VL made her last purchase on the morning of Thursday 6 March. She bought more than 200,000 francs' worth of stones.'

'That's dear for a screw with an anonymous model, even in New York.'

'That's what I think. If you add up everything you know about VL's activities around 1 March, this is what you get. She was present at the scene of the crime on Friday night. She went off to New York. She came back with a load of cash. It looks as though either she saw something, or more likely, she salvaged the video of the murder. There must have been a video, and we've hardly taken much interest in it till now. And she's blackmailing the murderer.'

'Baker?'

'If Baker was in Paris on 29 February, but then VL wouldn't have needed to go to New York. More likely someone Baker and VL knew, and they joined forces to blackmail the murderer.'

'An interesting theory. Attali, you must find VL for me. But stake out her parents' house in case, improbable now, but one never knows, she might go back there to look for her diamonds. Read the statements that have been made again, go back to see the models, the friends and perhaps Sobesky's son as well. Show them the photos we have, all the photos, of the Turks as well as the members of the Club Simon, in fact everybody, and try to get a lead for me, just a tiny lead, to look for VL.'

Daquin's lying on the sofa in a long silk dressing-gown, and reading a novel by Yaschar Kemal. When Soleiman comes in, he gets up and walks towards him, his eyes impenetrable. Stops in front of him. Soleiman closes his eyes. Shivers. Daquin begins undressing him: first the jacket, then the shirt. He kneels down: the trousers, shoes. He stands up, puts him over his shoulder and mounts the stairs to his bedroom, lays him under the orange duvet. And rediscovers on this body those unerring memories that have at times overwhelmed him in these last five days. The smoothest of skins, the tuft of blond curly hair in the small of his back. The lean, firm buttocks. The contours of his thigh, shoulder, neck. The silky black penis. The familiarity. He has to know it's there, like that, he has to check every remembered detail. He has to find his pleasure again.

'Let me see your eyes, Sol.'

Soleiman, with his eyes wide open, no longer resists the pleasure invading him.

Later, with Soleiman lying full length on his stomach on the orange duvet, Daquin sits leaning against the wall. There's a tray laden with shrimps, smoked salmon, taramasalata, various breads, cheeses. White wine. A thermos of coffee.

'A lot's been going on in the last five days. Tell me, what have you been up to?'

And Soleiman tells him about the general assembly, the suicide threats. Would they really have jumped? Who knows? Then there's the boycott, the negotiations that have started up again with the minister's office.

'You've won your case. The minister's trapped.'

'Yes. We've won. Almost.'

Daquin places his hand lightly on the small of Soleiman's back. And Soleiman rubs himself slowly against the hand. My turn. Network. Camera. Murders.

'I've some supplementary photos to give you. But nothing really new. Will your list be ready for the end of the month?'

'Yes.'

'And now, something to please you.' His hand begins to press more insistently. 'The boss of the network may well be an American, a CIA man.'

137

'Yes, I'd really enjoy that. You'll have him?'

'I hope so. Sol, what're your friends saying about the murder of Celik Osman?'

'It's Agça who killed him.'

'I thought so. Do'you have any proof?'

'No.'

'And why did he kill him?'

'I really don't know.' Soleiman hesitates. 'Celik Osman had nothing to do with the traffickers. In Turkey, he'd already fallen foul of the Grey Wolves, who'd set fire to his workplace because he'd given money to left-wing organizations. Here, he was a good employer. He paid his workers properly and always helped out any of our people who needed it.'

Daquin took up a piece of paper from the floor beside the bed.

'What does it say on this poster?'

'So it's you, you're the cop who thought of taking away this tract? That's all they talk about at the Gymnase. I didn't recognize you from the description the bar owner gave me.'

'What does it say on it?'

'"Turks must not collaborate with the French police. Celik Osman collaborated. He's dead. The same thing will happen to any Turk who approaches the French police." And it's signed by the Grey Wolves.'

'Was he a grass?'

'Absolutely not.'

Soleiman says this with shocked conviction. Daquin laughs.

'You are of course well placed to know that no one can be sure of anything as regards that particular area.'

Soleiman, in a toneless voice: 'Daquin, one day I'll kill you.'

For a long moment, Daquin looks at Soleiman, still lying on his stomach. His brown buttocks, surprisingly round for this tall slender body. You have, he thought, the most beautiful pair of buttocks I've ever seen, all categories included.

7 a.m. Villa des Artistes

Breakfast over, Daquin stretched out on the sofa with his feet up and the sound of Europe 1 in the background. Two hours' thinking time in front of him. Soleiman was still moving about in the house before leaving but Daquin no longer saw nor heard him.

Kashguri. An interview ... Too soon for formal questioning. Was it a fight already? No, just a matter of getting acquainted. I've too little information yet to challenge him.

I've got five people: Sobesky, VL, Kashguri, Anna Beric and Baker. They're all in the race. I don't know in what order. And I don't even know what their relationships are to each other. Sobesky knows VL, Anna Beric and Baker. But what about Kashguri? Anna Beric knows Sobesky and Kashguri. But what about Baker? VL knows Sobesky, Baker, Kashguri (very probably), but what about Anna Beric? Is there a link between Kashguri and Baker?

Daquin moved slightly. He realized that Soleiman had left, he drank a cup of coffee and returned to his thoughts.

Of all the people involved, Kashguri is the most difficult to figure out. He holds an important post at the Bank of Cyprus and the East which finances Kutluer's enterprises and therefore the network, more or less directly. But it's impossible to know if he's personally implicated. And the subject's too dangerous for me to approach it just now. I'm sure he's a member of the Club Simon. Just a few points on which I can hope to go further: does he know VL, and was it through him that she learnt to smoke heroin? Did he have sex with young Thai girls and what was he doing on the evening of 29 February? Lastly, what was his relationship with Anna Beric twenty years ago and does he still see her nowadays? I'll keep this last question safely in reserve. I don't know how to handle it.

And what about Meillant? No reason to leave him out. I can't see him as a gang leader, but why not? He's very involved with Sobesky and Anna Beric.

I might as well admit it, I'm completely in the dark. Who does what in this business? One thing's certain, we've entered a new phase, and this is how I see it: the network bosses, whoever they are, know we're getting close to them. Most likely they've found out through VL, while Baker and Sobesky are in it too, one way or another. We put the shops in Faubourg-Saint-Martin under surveillance. VL disappears, they've been trying to set a trap for me since Friday. And on Tuesday Celik was shot. The reason's obvious: they want to scare the Turks and stop them from talking to us. The way I see it, Celik was a snout. But who for? And who knows? That doesn't seem to be public knowledge. Must see Meillant. And in the end this murder's good news in its way. It means they're not after Sol. Not yet.

Another piece of good news, the delivery of the Romanian raincoats. If I set my mind to it I see that they're coming through Bulgaria, by means of Euroriencar, the Bank of Cyprus and the East. And finally there's Baker and the CIA. More or less all the strands that Lespinois mentioned to us. And when they get here there's Sobesky, one of my prime suspects. That's a lot for a harmless delivery of raincoats. I've every right to think it's not harmless and that it's either a delivery of drugs or else they're setting up an infrastructure that can be used regularly afterwards. My job is to stop everything involved with this delivery and take a gamble that the henchmen will deliver the leaders into my hands. All I've got to do now is convince the chief.

Nine o'clock signal on Europe 1. Time to get dressed and go.

9.30 a.m. Passage du Désir

Just time to telephone Istanbul before Kashguri arrives. Kutluer's well known at the French consulate. He's a rich businessman and everyone's aware of his links with the Turkish mafia, which doesn't prevent him from being received into the highest society, including, it must be said, the consulate.

He spoke to the wife of the director of the French Institute for Anatolian studies.

'Madame, I'm really sorry to bother you. I'm Superintendent Daquin of the Paris Drugs Squad, I'm telephoning you on the advice of Monsieur Dumas, an attaché at the French consulate.'

'What can I do for you?'

It was a very young voice, full of smiles, with a faint Slav accent. Daquin imagined her a chubby blonde.

'Monsieur Dumas tells me you know John Erwin very well.'

'That depends on what you call well. I go to dinner parties at his house quite often, along with fifty or so other people.'

'That's precisely what I'm interested in. Would you be able to supply me with a list of his guests?'

'I'd do it for you gladly, but I don't know the names of all the people.'

'Couldn't you possibly ask him for his lists? Pretend you're preparing a reception for the French Institute?'

She hesitated for a moment.

'Yes, I could. Certainly.'

'I'm only interested in the last year.'

'Very well, I'll try.'

As he hung up Daquin dreamt about making love to a little curvaceous blonde, all smiles. That would make a change for him.

*

Kashguri arrived dead on 10 o'clock. Tall, same height as Daquin, slim, black hair, black eyes, light complexion, smooth face with very regular features. A very good-looking man, of his type. Not my type, more Lenglet's. A classic suit, cut in the English style, blue-grey. A tie in darker grey, a very pale blue shirt. He sat down in the armchair Daquin had put ready for him. Placed his arms on the armrests. Hands clasped in front of him, well-manicured hands, long-fingered and muscular, giving an impression of brittle strength.

'Thank you for coming, Monsieur Kashguri. I wanted to meet you to talk about a murder committed at the Club Simon on 29 February. You're a member, we're seeing all the members.'

Kashguri slowly opened and closed his hands, looking at Daquin. He leant forward slightly.

'Superintendent, I've no intention of playing cat and mouse with you.' Not the slightest trace of an accent. Perfect French. 'I play an important part in Franco-Iranian relationships, which at the present time are particularly complex, as you know...'

'Which doesn't place you above the laws of our country.' Daquin was keeping a low profile.

A smile from Kashguri. 'Clearly, but it gives me a lot of work, and so I've no time to waste. Yes, I'm very partial to hired women, which is legal in France. But I'm not prepared to tell you in what circumstances I enjoy that pleasure.'

'And that's not what I intend to talk to you about. My first question: do you confirm you were a member of the Club Simon?'

'Yes, I was.'

'What alias did you use?'

'I shan't tell you that. You're encroaching on my private life.'

'A murder was committed...'

'That's not a reason.'

'...on 29 February in the evening.'

'On the other hand I'm quite willing to tell you what I was doing on the evening of 29 February.' He leafed through his diary and showed the page to Daquin. 'At four o'clock I attended a meeting of the Franco-Iranian parliamentary group. After which I had dinner with the chairman of the group, Deputy Bertrand.'

Daquin looked at the page: 4 p.m. *FI group*. And 8 p.m.: *Bertrand*.

'Do you remember where you went to have dinner? And at about what time?'

'Yes, we went to the Brasserie Lipp, where we usually go.'

'I'll have it checked.'

'Be discreet.'

'Of course. I also wanted to tell you that in France the use of certain substances is illegal.'

Kashguri showed great self-control, smiled and still kept his hands folded.

'On that point you could certainly catch me out fairly easily. It's a habit I acquired in my own country where such things are widely tolerated. But you know as well as I do that a charge of that sort would cause you many problems, involving many people over what is really a minor offence.'

He's pleased with himself, thought Daquin, he's convinced he's won a point. It was the right moment to try something on.

'Do you know Virginie Lamouroux?'

'No, I don't know that person.'

Kashguri had not reacted. Daquin showed him the photograph of Virginie that Madame Lamouroux had given to Attali.

'You've never met her?'

'No, never.'

'Yet Virginie Lamouroux has told us that she learnt to smoke heroin in your company.'

At those words Daquin was sure he noticed a reaction. Kashguri sat bolt upright in his chair.

'Listen,' he said in a very dry voice, 'I'm not intimately acquainted with all the people in whose company I spend somewhat hectic evenings. I don't know this lady and I don't wish to discuss my favourite pastime any further.'

'Very well, Monsieur Kashguri. Thank you for attending this interview.'

Kashguri was surprised that Daquin had brought it to an end so quickly.

They both stood up. Daquin accompanied him back to the door and returned to his desk.

He wants to send me towards Bertrand. Very well. Attali will go. I must find out why he wants us to go in that direction. I think he knows VL. But I have to prove it. If I manage that, he's in it up to his neck. But in what? Drug trafficking? The murder of the Thai girl? Both? Is it him VL's blackmailing?

Noon. Chez Mado

Daquin was meeting Meillant for lunch. He went to pick him up at the police station in the 10th arrondissement. The two men shook hands. They'd hardly seen each other since the Police Academy. That was nearly ten years ago already. Meillant hadn't changed. Short, thickset rather than fat. Three-piece suit, white shirt, dark tie. Grey hair, carefully combed back. Was he wearing Brylcreem? He looked fearfully old-fashioned. Whatever can Anna Beric see in him? Daquin still felt the animosity that had kept them apart at the Academy.

'I'm taking you out to lunch. I've booked a table at Chez Mado. Do you know it?'

'No.'

'It's a local curiosity, just two steps away.'

They reached Chez Mado, didn't linger at the bar and went through the red curtains. Mado came over rapidly to meet them, embraced Meillant and shook hands with Daquin, looking him over for a moment with the eye of a connoisseur, and seated them at a table in a quiet area right at the back of the room.

'It's cassoulet day today.'

'Perfect, two cassoulets, Cahors wine, and bring us the best hors-d'œuvres you've got to make us wait patiently.'

As he spoke Meillant tapped the owner's impressive pair of buttocks, she thanked him with a smile and swayed off towards the kitchen.

Meillant described Mado's career to Daquin in minute detail.

'You see all that hardware that Mado carries around?' he said finally. 'Well, it's all real gold and precious stones. Even her spectacles aren't made of rubbish: they're diamonds and platinum. She doesn't trust banks and prefers to carry her fortune about on her person. And she keeps all her jewellery on when she's having sex, apart from her spectacles.'

Meillant really made a meal of it.

'You know that it was here that Thomas found the trail leading to the Ballets Aratoff?'

No, Daquin didn't know that. It was Meillant who had sent me Thomas and Santoni in order to keep himself informed about an investigation that was taking place on his patch. How could I have been so naïve as not to realize that earlier? Continue acting as if all was in order. Fortunately the cassoulet was superb.

'Meillant, did you know Osman Celik?'

'Yes, I knew him well.'

'I thought you did. Can you tell me a bit more about him?'

'I helped him to get his papers in order, about two years ago that was, and to open his workroom. We kept in touch ever since.'

'You knew of course that he was assassinated yesterday?'

'Yes, I've read the report from the Crime Squad.'

'Have you got a theory?'

'Settlement of political accounts. Osman Celik was a man of the left. He'd already had problems with the Grey Wolves in Istanbul.'

'He wasn't involved with drugs at any level?'

'No, really not. Not his scene at all. The usual little carry-ons in the Sentier, yes. But people don't kill each other over those, not so far, in my district.'

On his way back Daquin mused a little. So, Celik had been a snout for Meillant. Should he tell Sol or not? And who knew about it?

3 p.m. *Passage du Désir*

Two hours given over to questioning, one after the other, two young mannequins who had worked with Virginie Lamouroux.

Thomas led the interrogation, assisted by an inspector from the Vice Squad. Daquin sat behind them in an armchair, observing without intervening. They didn't learn much. Virginie Lamouroux used to work through an answering machine. Attali had already found it, installed in the apartment owned by Sobesky's son. She took a very reasonable commission. The girls liked her, there were never any dirty tricks or arguments. As for the drugs business, that was more difficult. The girls had to be hustled along a bit, but they had no experience of police tactics and were soon caught out. It was the clients who took drugs. The fashion at the moment was for LSD. Did they smoke too? Yes, perhaps, in a very small way, and they preferred heroin. Did everything go via Virginie Lamouroux? No, not necessarily. And what about Kashguri? They had both had him as a client, the appointments were made through Virginie, like the others. He was a rather unusual client. He would come with friends and sit apart through the whole performance, smoking, watching, drinking, but he never even took his clothes off.

*

Santoni had had good hunting. The six deputies and two senators who had belonged to the Club Simon were all members of the parliamentary group for Franco-Iranian Friendship, which comprised about thirty people. He had a complete list of the names. The chairman was Gérard Bertrand. He could be found at the Assembly or at home, 57 avenue Bosquet. Daquin showed his appreciation.

'And I've found a good photo of Bertrand at a press agency. Shall I add it to the file I'm taking to Munich tomorrow?'

'It's an idea, but keep it out of the reports.'

*

Romero reported late in the afternoon. No developments anywhere. Except with Moreira. He'd telephoned to a certain Paulette asking her to supply false papers. His men had been so scared since the visit by the fraudulent works inspector that they would have to be replaced. Since this was happening rather sooner than expected the usual supplier had run out. Could she manage to arrange it? She would try.

Paulette's telephone number was that of a Sentier workroom in the passage de l'Industrie.

8.a.m. Passage du Désir

Everyone in the office was studying something. Daquin was reading the papers. *Libération* led on the boycott of the ministerial regu-
larization of Turks without papers.

There was some admiration for Soleiman.

Romero was drafting a report on the shadowing of Sener.

The telephone rang.

'Théo?'

'Yes, chief.'

'Rouen have just called us. They've got a nameless corpse on
their hands which might belong to you. Can you send someone to
take a look?'

'Why did they think of us?'

'He looks like a half-breed and his clothes come from Istanbul.
Contact Inspector Petitjean at the Central Police Station in Rouen.'

Daquin hung up.

'Romero, that's for you. Take the file of photos with you. It could
be useful.'

9.30 a.m. Brasserie Lipp

The swing doors to the Brasserie Lipp were propped open and a
deliveryman in blue overalls was bringing out crates of empty bottles and taking in full ones. Attali sat down on the terrace and
glanced at the interior, endless mirrors, light-coloured ceramics
and dark wood. A woman arranging a huge bunch of orange lilies.
No customers. There was one waiter, all in black and wearing a
vast white apron that reached down to his feet. He came up to
Attali. Sounds of crockery and voices in the kitchens. Attali showed
his identity card. The waiter went to find the person in charge, a
respectable man wearing a grey suit, white shirt, dark tie.

'I need to ask you a few questions about two customers, just
routine.'

The two men sat down on the terrace, where the doors were still
open.

'Do you know Monsieur Bertrand and Monsieur Kashguri?'

'Yes, they're regulars.'

'Were they here on Friday 29 February in the evening?'

The man went to fetch two thick registers from behind the till, beside the orange flowers. The first one listed the names of the waiters, by teams, along with their hours of duty. Each man had added his signature beside his name.

'29 February. I was here that evening. I might as well tell you at once that I don't have any very clear recollections.'

The second register contained the reservations.

'29 February, Monsieur Bertrand had reserved a table for two at 9 o'clock.'

'Why are all those reservations crossed out?'

'We cross them out as and when the clients arrive.'

'So if Monsieur Bertrand hadn't come, his name wouldn't be crossed out?'

'Unless he'd cancelled by telephone. If a client cancels, we also cross out the name, since we don't have to keep the table any longer.'

'And do clients take the trouble to telephone if they want to cancel?'

'Yes, our *habitués* here are careful not to let us down without warning.'

'If Monsieur Bertrand had cancelled, would that have gone through you?'

'Yes.'

'And you don't remember if he did?'

'No. It's three weeks ago now. Monsieur Bertrand comes several times a week. We have a hundred or so reservations a day. Three or four of them are cancelled. So . . .'

'Could you ask the waiters who were on duty that evening to contact me on this number if anyone remembers anything?'

'Certainly, Inspector.'

Attali left. He already knew there would be no follow-up.

10 *a.m. Passage du Désir*

The interrogation of the mannequins began again. It was becoming routine. Thomas was working together with the same inspector from the Vice Squad. Daquin remained to one side, observing without saying anything. Maud Mathieu. The interrogation was dull but confirmed the statements made by Lamergie.

Daquin was bored. The presence of VL at the Club Simon on the evening of the 29th could be considered as established. Apart from that nobody knew anything about her. Everyone was marking time. I'll stay for the last interview of the morning. Then I'll go on to something else.

Enter Dorothée Marty, a tall, slim, dark girl. Hair cut square, dark and full, a huge fringe covering her entire forehead. Framed by this black helmet her face looked childlike and small. She's graceful, thought Daquin, who had remained slightly absent-minded. The interrogation began. Like the others. Daquin had to make an effort to concentrate. Then suddenly, at the question 'Do you know Kashguri, have you had him as a client?' her whole body became rigid. Her attitude and her expression froze.

'Yes.'

'Who found him for you?'

'Virginie Lamouroux, like the others.'

'Do you know if she was a personal friend of his?'

'No, I never discussed that with her.'

Thomas went on to something else. Dorothée Marty relaxed and her attitude became normal again. The interrogation continued. Incredible that neither Thomas nor the Vice Squad inspector had noticed anything. Not good cops. Or else they didn't care.

End of the interrogation. Dorothée Marty stood up, signed her statement and prepared to leave. Daquin stood up also. The two inspectors saw him open the door for the young woman and take hold of her elbow.

'Does your superintendent try to pick up girls?' the Vice Squad inspector asked Thomas. The latter shrugged his shoulders, indicating that he didn't know and didn't understand.

'Mademoiselle, may I invite you to lunch? It's the right time now and I'd like to talk to you a little in a completely informal way, obviously.' Dorothée Marty looked surprised and hesitant. 'Say yes. You've not much to lose, you have a Superintendent's word for it.'

'You know, I don't usually eat lunch.'

'I'll take you to an Italian place that you'll like. If you want, you need only have a cup of coffee.'

Cold, tiled floor, smells. The body on a trolley. The face was uncovered. White complexion, swellings more or less everywhere. Unreal. Not a dead man, more like a mask.

'Those are burns caused by the lime,' explained Petitjean. 'But we've had his face made up, identification will be easier that way.'

Romero put his briefcase down on a table, took out the set of photographs, leafed through them, picked out one of them and showed it to Petitjean.

'OK. It's him.'

'Let's get out of here.'

They walked up and down in front of the morgue. Romero had brought some little cigars, Italian ones from Tuscany, which he always took when he went to a morgue: they smelt worse than the corpses. He offered one to Petitjean, who refused it.

'Do you mind if I smoke?'

'Not at all. Well?'

'He's a little Turkish dealer whom we've been on to for a couple of weeks, a certain Celebi.'

12.30 p.m. Da Mimo

Neapolitan atmosphere. Daquin was obviously an *habitué*. A small table at the end, with a red and white checked tablecloth. Daquin installed the young woman with her back to the room. For her he chose *hors d'œuvres variés* on a bed of vegetables dressed with oil and vinegar and for himself a pizza alla rughetta. Followed by grilled fish, chilled Orvieto as usual and for Madame, a mineral water.

He had to take advantage of the fact that the girl was destabilized, he mustn't let her recover her self-control.

'Tell me about your relationship with Kashguri.'

She retreated into her shell again. Tried to hide her feelings with a smile.

'I've nothing more to say.'

'That's not true. Whenever that name is mentioned your whole body goes on the defensive. Did it turn out badly?'

'Maybe. So what?'

'Tell me about it. We aren't on police premises here. You want to talk about it and there's no better listener than me.'

Dorothée hid her face in her hands to escape Daquin's gaze.

'How do you know that?'

'I listen to you, I look at you, I pay attention to you, that's all.'

'He got me raped under appalling conditions.'

Her voice was low, all on one note, her hands still over her face. Daquin allowed silence to set in. For her the worst was over, she certainly had the right to fix her own speed. Dorothée retreated into her memories. She then fixed her eyes on her plate. Her voice didn't change.

'He offered me a lot of money to spend an evening at his apartment, with some friends, he said. I'd had him as a client two or three times at the Club Simon, he used to come with friends and he'd watch us make love. That was all. I thought it would be the same sort of thing at his place. I accepted.'

Silence again, a very long silence.

'I arrived at his place. He seemed to be alone and thanked me for coming. We sat in the drawing-room and smoked a little heroin. I began to feel drowsy. He led me into a bedroom, somewhere in the apartment. There was hardly any furniture, just a big brass bed.' For the first time Dorothée looked up at Daquin. 'You know, old-fashioned, with high rails at the top and bottom.'

'Yes, there was one in my grandmother's house.'

Dorothée looked down at her plate again. 'There were two men in the room, his menservants. They caught hold of me, one held me, the other literally tore my clothes off. I began to scream and struggle. That made them laugh. Kashguri sat in an armchair and smiled. I was terrified, I thought they were going to kill me and that nobody would ever find me again. When I was completely naked they tied me to the bed with cords, I was stretched out on my back, with my arms and legs apart and they began to beat me with riding whips. I screamed as loudly as I could.'

A long silence. The memory of her suffering.

'When I stopped crying out they untied me. I couldn't move. I was bleeding all over, and they raped me, one after the other, and then both of them at once. I lost consciousness. I think Kashguri was masturbating during this time.' Silence again. 'Then one of the men looked after me, putting something on the wounds that smelt very strong. And then they wrapped me up in a kind of towelling sheet and carried me to a car, then they took me to my own apartment. They left me there in the middle of the night with a pile of money. I didn't make a complaint. I looked after myself. I'm not working any more, I don't go out any more, I'm living on Kashguri's money.' A pause. In the end she looked up from her plate. She smiled, a young smile. 'It's true, you're really a good listener.'

Daquin wanted to stroke her face gently, but thought it was surely the last thing to do. I'll get Kashguri. One way or another. I'll have him in my power.

2.30 p.m. Passage du Désir

A message from Romero on the desk: *The corpse is that of Celebi, the little Turkish dealer, the accomplice of the Yugoslav workroom boss. I'll be back at 8 o'clock this evening.*

Celebi had been liquidated: the news produced a reaction. Daquin prepared a note for Attali and Lavorel: *Be in the office at 8 o'clock this evening.* Then he went home. Gave himself coffee and cognac. Lay down on the sofa, closed his eyes, his mind wandering half-way between light sleep and conscious intellectual activity.

3 p.m. The National Assembly annexe

Bertrand had agreed to give Attali an appointment. 'Half an hour, not more, I've a lot of work on hand. And I'd be glad if you'd be discreet and not tell the usher or my secretary that you're a police officer.'

The building was modern: marble, steel, wood, thick carpets. Genuine luxury. At least one can see what happens to the money paid out in taxes. And it wasn't going into police stations.

Attali entered the office. Bertrand stood up, shook hands and indicated an armchair. He was fairly tall, heavily built, with red hair and white skin, well over forty. Attali immediately found him antipathetic.

'Well?'

'Monsieur, we're checking the movements of Monsieur Kashguri during the evening of 29 February. He's told us that he spent the evening with you.'

'What is Monsieur Kashguri accused of?'

'He's not been accused of anything. We're checking the movements of many people, it's to do with an investigation following a murder committed during the evening of 29 February.'

Bertrand stared at Attali, chewing his lower lip. A long silence. A feeling of unease. He opened his desk diary.

'On 29 February, from 4 o'clock onwards, I chaired a meeting of the parliamentary support group for Franco-Iranian relationships, to which Monsieur Kashguri had been invited as an expert. The meeting ended at about 8 o'clock or 8.30, and then we went to have dinner together at the Brasserie Lipp, as we do fairly often. My secretary had booked the table.'

'Fine, thank you, Monsieur Bertrand.'

'Inspector, the situation between the United States and Iran is very tense at the moment. France has considerable interests in Iran. It plays a leading role in efforts to make Europe adopt an attitude of mediation and dialogue. In order to avoid an irreparable break. Monsieur Kashguri is a valuable ally for French diplomacy. I won't say anything more on the subject. Obviously that doesn't mean that he's above the laws of this country. But it clearly means that we're asking you to proceed with the greatest caution.'

In the elevator Attali spoke loudly and clearly: I'm full of hate. And in the end it made him laugh.

3.30 p.m. On the Route Nationale between Paris and Rouen

The road ran alongside the Seine, at least thirty metres above it. Beneath was a vast platform where trucks came to discharge their loads of chalk into the hangars. Below was a lime factory with silos going down to the river. Barges tied up there, below the silos, as they took on their cargoes. Petitjean let Romero look at the layout of the place.

'According to the forensic surgeon, the man was probably killed on the platform by a bullet through the heart, fired at point-blank range. After 5 o'clock the trucks stop driving round and the place is deserted. The killer went through the factory fence here.' He pointed to a place where the wire had been pushed down. 'And he went on to the lime silos that way, dragging the corpse along.' He indicated the marks on the clayey soil. 'Then he slid the body into silo no. 3 and went off. If the body had remained in the lime for more than forty-eight hours inside the silos or in a barge it would have been impossible to identify it. But a barge came to take on a load beneath Silo no. 3 at 5 o'clock in the morning on 19 March. The bargee, who was going backwards and forwards several times a day at that time, took on the load by himself and didn't notice anything. We checked this out, it's quite possible that the body slipped through the loading shaft. Then the bargee left for the Rouen cement works, thirty kilometres from here, where unloading began at 8 o'clock. By 9 o'clock we had the corpse. No papers on it. Nothing in the pockets. The labels on his jacket, his trousers and shirt had been torn off. He was wearing socks. Identification seemed to be very difficult. Fortunately, when I came to make enquiries here I found a shoe that must have fallen off the body when it was being dragged away from the platform beneath the overhanging slope. The shoes were certainly expensive, since the name of the shop was marked inside the leather, with the address: Istiklal Caddesi, Istanbul. After that I worked my way up through the system until I came to you. Twenty-four hours, no longer. I don't think we've done too badly over this, considering we're just little country cops.'

Romero smiled at the notion that he'd become a Parisian.

8 p.m. Passage du Désir

Attali and Lavorel were playing draughts. Daquin was making himself coffee in silence.

Romero arrived. Very dirty, thought Daquin. His hair, his face, his hands and his clothes were covered in fine white dust. His shoes were completely white. He was so excited and pleased that he didn't seem to notice. The game of draughts stopped.

'We'll start with Attali,' said Daquin.

Attali explained the system for reserving and cancelling restaurant tables. So an alibi was possible but couldn't be guaranteed. Bertrand's little speech about the political importance of Kashguri.

'And then the sense of unease took over and the feeling that Bertrand knew more than I did about the progress of the investigation.'

'Was Bertrand pleased to fly to the aid of his friend?'

'He'd have given his shirt not to have to do it.'

'So, Kashguri's trying to drag Bertrand into it. What's he getting in exchange? We'll find out. Lavorel?'

'Nothing new, but one thing's been confirmed: the Frenchman who lent his name for the purchase of the two shops is on the Euroriencar payroll.'

Daquin seemed satisfied.

'And you, Romero, give us some details about your scoop.'

The identification of the body and the way in which it had been dumped in the lime. Killed point-blank range by a bullet through the heart, fired from the front. Transported after the murder. For the time being, that was all.

Daquin sank back into his armchair. He was tense.

'I want to draw your attention to two points about this murder. One: this assassination resembles the liquidation of Celik. I don't know if I'd told you already but Celik was one of the guys who acted as a snout for Meillant, and very few people knew it. Two: very few people were aware that we'd traced Celebi and were holding a witness who would testify against him. We're on to a big drugs case, which involves a lot of money. And a lot of money means murders, we've already got three, four or five, depending on how you look at them. And corruption. Corruption of politicians, perhaps, but it could happen to police officers too. Remember that.'

Point taken, deathly silence.

'Romero, tomorrow you'll start trailing your attaché from the embassy again, plus the telephone tapping and Paulette. Attali, go back to the VL case. At the end of the month there's going to be a delivery of raincoats from Romania to Sobesky's place. I'd like us to be as far ahead as possible by then.'

Silence again. Daquin stood up, put on his jacket, said good evening and left.

8 a.m. Avenue Jean-Jaurès

Romero was fast asleep. The telephone rang. He picked it up, grumbling. In a bad temper. Exhausting day yesterday, and he hadn't slept all night, because of Daquin's allusion to bent police officers. What had he meant? Impossible to say. He'd fallen into a deep sleep about 6 in the morning, barely two hours ago ... What a job.

The voice belonged to Yildiz...

'Did I wake you up, Romeo?'

'Yes.'

'All right, I'll be quick. Today Turgut Sener is going to collect the diplomatic bag at Roissy, as he does every month. He'll be leaving from boulevard Malesherbes about 10, in an embassy van.'

'When are we going to have dinner together, Yildiz? I miss you.'

She laughed.

'Ring me back when you're in a better mood.'

Romero got up. A nearly cold shower, a litre of coffee. The untidiness of his apartment disgusted him. A little pile of white dust under the chair where he'd left his clothes the day before. Dirty crockery all over the place. Must get organized.

A clean sweatshirt, the last but one, jeans, trainers, a leather jacket. Must join his colleagues in the Drugs Squad.

9.30 a.m. Shadowing

The two inspectors, Romero and Marinoni, were waiting in an unmarked Renault 5 fifty metres away from the annex to the Turkish Embassy in boulevard Haussmann. Marinoni was very cheerful and told one funny story after another. Romero relaxed a little.

A small white van drove out from the embassy buildings. It was easy to follow, the traffic was flowing freely and they knew where it was going.

10.30 a.m.

The van turned into the Customs transit car-park at Roissy airport.

Romero let it go ahead for a few moments and then followed it into the supervised area, showing his police card. Sener remained nearly an hour in the Customs office, then he returned, along with a packer and a large sealed crate, on a trolley. It was manoeuvred into the van, which then left, followed by the two inspectors in their Renault 5. They returned to Paris without incident.

12.15 p.m.

The van drove into the embassy garage in avenue de Lamballe.

Another wait. Marinoni went to have a drink in a café twenty metres away. Romero made notes about the various moves that had taken place in the morning, adding the exact times, then he started on the crosswords.

12.45 p.m.

Sener reappeared at the wheel of a dark blue 205 with a Paris registration. He drove towards the city centre. At that time of day it was still not difficult to follow a vehicle. Sener parked on a pedestrian crossing in rue du Faubourg-Saint-Denis, got out of the 205 and took from the back seat a plastic bag from FNAC which seemed to contain a rectangular box. Romero remained at the wheel and Marinoni followed Sener on foot.

1 p.m.

Marinoni came back.

'Sener's sitting at a table in the Brasserie Flo in cour des Petites-Ecuries, along with a woman of about fifty. They seem to know each other well. They've ordered lunch, they'll be there for some time. Let's go and have a bite to eat too, I'm really starving.'

It took twenty minutes to swallow some hot food in a brasserie in rue du Faubourg-Saint-Denis, while keeping an eye on the entrance to cour des Petites-Ecuries. Then they walked slowly towards the Brasserie Flo, talking as they did so.

Sener came out with the woman whom Marinoni had seen earlier. Fairly average, about fifty, tall and slightly plump, chestnut hair, permed and tinted, discreet make-up, classic suit. No time wasted on her appearance, but well groomed. Now she was carrying the FNAC bag. They separated in rue du Faubourg-Saint-Denis. He embraced her, kissing her lightly on the lips, then, in stylish fashion, kissed her hand, with meaningful implications.

'I assume that Sener's the old girl's lover.'

'Looks like it.'

She turned right, followed by Marinoni. Sener went back to his car, with Romero after him, absent-mindedly stuffed the parking ticket in his raincoat pocket and drove off. Romero followed without difficulty.

3.25 p.m.

Sener reached rue de la Procession, parked on a pedestrian crossing again and disappeared into the Immigration Office. Romero parked in his turn, just anywhere, and walked towards the 205. From the inside pocket of his jacket he took out a little file that he had modified for his personal use a few years ago when he was an adolescent in Marseilles. He glanced at the second hand on his watch, bent over the boot of the 205 with a very preoccupied air and tinkered with the lock, which gave way. He checked: forty-five seconds. Good. Despite lack of practice it could be done in less than a minute. He had one regret, however: his range was still very limited. French cars, Volkswagens ... He would have liked to try American or Japanese cars. He'd never had the opportunity. The boot was empty. Romero closed it again and went back to sit in his car once more. Another hour-long wait. He was really fed up.

4.35 p.m.

Sener came out of the Immigration Office with Martens. I could have taken a bet on it.

And they went off on foot. Romero followed them at a distance.

They turned right, then left, stopped at Martens' Renault 5, got in, drove off and left Romero behind.

7.30 p.m. Passage du Désir

When Romero came into the general office Santoni was beginning to describe his trip to Munich. He had found only ten or so young Thai girls who had been through Paris.

'In Switzerland and Germany there's a whole network of specialized cabarets and the girls don't usually stay longer than six months in the same town. They have no money, never go out into the street, always travel from one town to another with a minder who holds their identity papers. After three or four years, when they're "old", they join the "normal" prostitution network or else they're given an air ticket to fly back home. The police and the owners of the nightclubs pretend to believe they're twenty years old, as stated on their passports, but the clients don't get it wrong, and it's really paedophiles who frequent those clubs. It saves them the expense of travelling to Thailand ... The clubs are never empty. Enough said. Of the ten or so children who went through Paris seven had "worked" for the Club Simon and they identified five of the members. The retired Superintendent was the most assiduous. No comment. An entrepreneur, Lamergie, who's already admitted having made use of them. Two deputies. And Kashguri. But he never had sex with them. He watched while other men did. Obviously I took statements in the official way. But in a few months' time it will certainly be difficult to find those girls. There. It's all in my report and the statements are attached.'

'Good work, thank you. Here, as far as the mannequins are concerned, we're marking time. Thomas will tell you about it. Have your weekend off, you'll need at least two days to get over all that Swiss-German cleanliness.'

*

Daquin remained alone with Romero.

'I've already had a call from Marinoni. The woman he followed from the Brasserie Flo went up into the Berican workroom in passage de l'Industrie.'

Romero was very surprised.

'Could she be Paulette? Moreira's friend?'

'It's possible. Marinoni's still over there. And what about you?'

'Sener went to see Martens at the Immigration Office and I lost track of them when they left in Martens' car, after 4 o'clock. Before that I took a look, unofficially of course, into the boot of Sener's car. It was empty. Has Marinoni spoken to you about the FNAC plastic bag?'

'Yes.'

'I didn't go in to question the staff at the Brasserie Flo. I was waiting for the green light from you. If those two are good clients the owners could possibly warn them.'

'You did right. Forget Flo. We've better things to do. Romero, tomorrow it'll be the Berican workroom.'

*

In front of Daquin was a telex sent to him during the afternoon by the head of the Drugs Squad. The reply from the wife of the director of the French Institute for Anatolian Studies. Fifty or so names. Personal remarks against some of them. *Grumpy. Dirty. Good-looking.* The director's wife had enjoyed herself. Only one name meant anything to Daquin: Kutluer. *Already middle-aged. Pity.*

And then, right at the end:

'At the last Erwin dinner I had long discussions with a woman whose name isn't on the list, because she was only passing through, Erwin told me. Anna Beric. She's beautiful, intelligent and cultured. And I don't know her address.'

Madame, one day I'll go to Istanbul to thank you.

7.30 a.m. Passage de l'Industrie

The weather was cool and fine, a delightful spring. Romero stretched his legs. He was glad to be sitting outside a café with Lavorel, after an average night spent in the arms of an average blonde. Lavorel had brought the file on the Berican workroom which he had put together quickly the day before: records of trading, taxes, social security. Paulette was Paulette Dupin, manageress of the company for the last five years, living at no. 44 in rue Gallieni at Villemomble. The workroom was flourishing and seemed slightly more on the level than most of those in the Sentier. Berican, director of the workroom, had been in the passage de l'Industrie – a large three-room suite – for eight years and for the last five he had even owned it, which was highly unusual. He declared five salaried staff and paid regularly the social security contributions due on their behalf. In view of the size of the apartment this was many fewer than the numbers actually employed. He made a profit, paid a small amount of VAT and taxes. In what proportion, that was another story.

Romero went to telephone Daquin. No more was known yet about the woman they'd followed yesterday. She'd spent all after-noon in the workroom but Marinoni had lost sight of her about 8 o'clock. She had come out of the workroom and taken a taxi, leaving him behind. No more assignments than yesterday. He said so long to Lavorel.

He decided to take a look on the spot. No. 2 passage de l'Industrie. There was a plaque at the foot of the dark staircase: *Berican, second floor right*. A smell of leather all the way up. On the second floor right, from behind a standard nineteenth-century bourgeois apartment door came sounds of intense activity, voices, footsteps, the throbbing of machines, with a foreign language radio in the background. A glance through the staircase window seemed to show that the apartment ran along the side of the passage. Lavorel climbed the staircase at no. 4 passage de l'Industrie. On the second floor left there was probably another workroom. No plaque, no name, but the characteristic sound of machines. It surely communicated with the other, useful in the case of an unexpected visit by the works inspector.

What should he do now? Lavorel was a bit short of ideas. Two Pakistanis arrived with their hand-trucks. They climbed up to Berican's place and came down with bulky packages wrapped in white plastic and secured with broad strips of brown adhesive tape. After going up and down three times they had loaded their trucks to the limit. The Pakistanis forged ahead with remarkable skill along the crowded pavements, the two inspectors following. Delivery was made to Berelovitch, a garment manufacturer in rue du Vertbois and the two Pakistanis left again. Inside the shop two men had begun to undo the packages, taking out leather jackets and placing them on hangers. They were checking, counting. Lavorel went in.

'I'd like to try on that jacket.'

'Sorry, *monsieur*, but we don't do any retail selling at all.'

He came out again.

'They're Ted Lapidus jackets. High-class ready-to-wear. I imagine the customer at the end of the line pays about 5000 francs for one of those, and 10,000 for a coat. At those prices it's really worthwhile sorting out a few schemes.'

The two inspectors walked back to passage de l'Industrie. Romero sat down in a quiet café to read the newspaper. Lavorel went up to the Berican workroom, rang the bell and waited one or two minutes. The sound level behind the door fell noticeably. The door opened slightly. Strong smell of leather. A colossal man appeared in the half-open doorway. Nearly six feet tall, broad-shouldered, stout yet not too much so. Dressed in black. Swarthy complexion, shaven head, huge grey moustache. Striking.

'Monsieur Berican?'

'Yes, I am. What do you want from me?' Strong accent, fluent French.

'I'm a journalist. I'm preparing a series of articles about the legalization of Turkish workers in the Sentier district. I'd like to interview a workroom boss and Berelovitch, the manufacturer I've met, told me you'd certainly agree to answer my questions.'

Warm smile. 'Wait a moment.'

Berican turned towards the interior of the apartment, which was now more or less silent. A few sentences in Turkish. The sound of the machines and the conversations began again.

'Let's go and have a drink,' Berican said to Lavorel. 'But we mustn't be long, I've got a lot of work to do.'

A café in rue du Faubourg-Saint-Denis. A lot of men, swarthy and moustachioed. At the bar, more ouzo and raki than pastis. And cups of coffee. Very noisy conversations in totally strange languages. Groups standing round the pinball machines. You could hardly see through the cigarette smoke. Berican led Lavorel to a smoke-free table outside, it was a little easier to breathe there. Jovial type, Berican.

'It's my round, what will you have? One pastis. And a raki. What do you want to know?'

'Do you think the Turks will win the right to work legally?'

'For the last two or three days we've all begun to think so, yes.'

'You employ clandestine workers. If they're able to work legally that won't help you. They'll cost you more.'

Berican laughed. 'It doesn't happen like that. I was a clandestine worker once, like them. I fled Turkey in 1960. I worked here without papers for ten years. You can't possibly know what that means. I shaved off my moustache and dyed my hair light brown. I regretted being tall. I travelled in buses, never in the Metro. And I always walked about with a camera dangling over my stomach. But whatever I did, I couldn't manage to look like a German tourist. Every time I stepped into the street I felt afraid. It was a strange life, you know. It's the life my workers lead today. I've given money to support their Committee. As soon as I can I'll give work contracts to everyone.'

'And will you pay the social security contributions?'

He shrugged his shoulders.

'I want very good workers, and I want Turks. I only trust Turks. They've been working with leather for centuries, they know about it. But there are no legal Turkish workers. Today, I pay my workers well, in cash ... Tomorrow I'll write out payslips, the wages will be a little lower, that's all.'

'And what about your manager, does he see things the same way as you do?'

'My manager is a manageress. An old friend. I met her ten years or so ago. She does all the accounts for the workroom and most of the presentations for the manufacturers. She knows the Sentier as well as I do. I look after the quality of the work. She looks after the management.'

'Do you think I could interview her?'

'Not today. She's never here on Saturdays.'

'Could you describe her to me, so that I could write about her in my article, you know, to liven it up?'

He laughed.

'She's no longer all that young, a little over fifty, I believe. She's well built and sturdy, but she also has style. I don't know what else I can tell you. She looks reliable. I'm going back up to work. Do you want to look round the workroom?'

'Yes, I'd like to.'

Berican got up and collected a tray with twenty cups of coffee from the bar, without paying. He had an account and all his workers could charge their coffees to it.

In the passage he turned to Lavorel: 'You see, passages like this with workrooms everywhere are rather like certain places in Istanbul. But in Istanbul there would be a little stall at the entrance kept by an old man who would make tea and coffee and take it up to the workrooms all day long. We miss that here.'

They climbed the stairs and pushed open the door to the apartment. The smell of leather again, almost suffocating. A lot of noise, machines, talk, radio. Intense activity. The boss called out: 'Coffee'. All the machines stopped. The men went into the kitchen by the entrance to drink and chat. Berican introduced Lavorel, a journalist. Smiles, laughter. They were going to win. *Ya hip Ya hop*. Warm atmosphere.

A tour round the apartment. A very classic petit-bourgeois apartment. Three rooms along the side of the building, separated from the kitchen, bathroom and storeroom by a corridor. The principal rooms opened onto the passage. Nothing had been rearranged, just a thicket of cables hanging from the ceiling, and neon strip lighting in every room. In the first of these, the biggest, opposite the kitchen, was a huge cutting-out table equipped with four big, heavy and noisy sewing-machines. In the second room there were four long tables with rows of machines. In the third room, yet another table with machines and three small individual tables with lighter machines. The finishings, explained Berican, buttonholes, buttons, various accessories. And the labels. The labels are important for us: we work for the biggest names in the ready-to-wear business. As he goes along each worker marks on a sheet of paper the number of labels given to him and the number used. At the end of this room was the connecting door to the next apartment. It seemed to be permanently sealed off with bolts but ... In any case that doesn't interest me and I haven't got much information to work on, thought Lavorel. They went back along the corridor. The storeroom had been fitted out as a little office for the manageress with less than sparse furnishings: a metal desk, with drawers that locked, a few shelves, a big standard lamp and an armchair. On the desk, tidily arranged, were two notebooks and the plastic bag from FNAC, described by Romero, with the box inside it. Berican caught sight of it at the same time as Lavorel. He looked slightly annoyed. He took out his bunch of keys, picked up the bag and locked it up in one of the desk drawers. They went back into the corridor. Kitchen and bathroom, littered with leftover food, coffee pots, cups and glasses. The tour was over. Berican returned to his work with the cutters.

Lavorel said goodbye to everyone, pulled the door to behind him and joined Romero in his quiet café a little way up the street. They took stock.

'Paulette and the woman we saw yesterday are probably one and the same person. The descriptions seem to tally. If there's some dealing going on Paulette's playing an important part in it. But what sort of dealing? I can't answer that. The box in the FNAC bag is there, I know where it is but I don't know what's in it. I'd like to go round the place during the night. But what would the chief say?'

Romero laughed.

'He'd say: "Don't get caught." Ask him all the same.'

After steak, chips and a beer they went to Villemomble. Saturday afternoon, an easy drive. Lavorel and Romero swapped childhood memories which were similar: from the Belle de Mai estate to the Courneuve. Romero drove, Lavorel studied the street plan ... 44 rue Gallieni. First they would drive past it, then they would come back, look and think about what to do. Villemomble was rather petit-bourgeois, but rue Gallieni was definitely ritzy. No more bungalows, but solid houses of several storeys with terraces, verandas and real gardens behind high gates. No. 44 was a very attractive white house, late nineteenth-century, with a little tower, well protected by a high stone wall and a black-painted iron door. The interior of the property was hardly visible.

'Things aren't looking too bad for Paulette Dupin, you might say. What'll we do now?'

The railway station was close by, they could stop for coffee. Two coffees with brandy, Romero went to have a look in the telephone kiosk down in the basement and came back up with the directory. No Dupin in Villemomble. The two inspectors looked quickly through the columns of subscribers to find out who lived at 44 in rue Gallieni. Romero swore and knocked over the rest of his coffee. With his fingernail he underlined a name: *Yves Thomas, 44 rue Gallieni.*

6 p.m. Passage du Désir

Daquin looked strained and exhausted. Romero and Lavorel very tense. Attali was fidgeting with impatience. Daquin smiled at him.

'You start, you're the only one who wants to.'

'I've got a few more little details about VL. After I saw her at the 10th arrondissement commissariat she went to see Julie La Tour, a manufacturer with whom she had an appointment to do a presentation. She was in a hurry, but she carried out her work correctly. She left quickly, saying she had a rendezvous.'

'That's already a step forward, Attali.'

'After that, nothing, no trace any more. She's a strange girl. Lots of people know her, but nobody's capable of saying anything worthwhile about her, or of telling me what sort of person she is.' He paused. 'But I've got something else.'

'We rather thought so.'

'You told me to show all the identikit portraits we have to as many people as possible. I did that. One mannequin, a certain Sophie Lambert, had attended evenings at Kashguri's place. She's formally identified the portrait of the man who killed your concierge. He's one of Kashguri's menservants-cum-henchmen.'

A long silence.

'Always stir the pot. You don't know what you're looking for, but in the end you find it. Well done, Attali, It's the first tangible clue we've got for implicating Kashguri. But it's a sizeable one. If his manservant acts on his orders, which is likely, then Kashguri's playing a direct part in the network in France. Romero?'

'Paulette Dupin is the wife of Inspector Thomas.'

Another silence.

'There couldn't be any mistake?'

'No, we checked at the registration office. No mistake possible.'

'Your turn, Lavorel.'

'And Paulette Dupin really is the woman who was having lunch with Sener. But I don't know yet what they're up to. The packet that Sener brought her yesterday is in the office at the Berican workroom. If you were to give me the authority it wouldn't take me more than a quarter of an hour tonight to know what it's all about.'

'How can I give you the authority? Do it without my knowing. And don't get caught.' Romero and Lavorel exchanged a smile. 'Romero will certainly help you. He loves picking locks, it reminds him of his adolescence.' Daquin took a deep breath. 'Now it's my turn. I wanted to talk to you a little again about some of the problems involving corruption among the police. I realize it's easier after the discoveries by Romero and Lavorel. I've been thinking about it since the identification of Celebi's body on Thursday afternoon. I've thought about the way the dealers have been conducting their counter-offensive during the last week. On one side I'll list what they've done. They've put the shops in the Faubourg-Saint-Martin out of action. Caused VL to disappear. Assassinated one of Meillant's snouts, and the only Turk we've positively identified as a dealer, with a witness for the prosecution. On the other side, what they haven't done. Sobesky, the enterprises of Martens and Kutluer, the guy from the Immigration Office, the embassy attaché, all that goes on as if nothing had happened, although we're on their track. I'm forced to ask myself the question: which cops know the first lot of facts and can pass them on to the dealers, and don't know the second lot?'

Total discomfort. Daquin seemed to expect a reply.

'You're the chief,' murmured Attali.

'Precisely. The answer is: Thomas and Santoni.'

'And what about Meillant? You've got proof that he's bent.'

'I don't agree. I don't see Meillant as bent. He's got power. He wants to run his district, not just maintain order on the surface. In order to govern, you have to compromise and do deals on the side. You always have to negotiate what you get. For Meillant, selling false papers is one way of checking the flow of illegal workers.' A silence. 'I can see that I'm not being understood. Besides, I might have boobed. I realize that he could be considered a suspect. In any case, what he knows about our work can only reach him through Thomas and Santoni. Unless you, Lavorel ...'

'That's ridiculous, guv.'

'I know. I was saying that to defuse the atmosphere. So on Thursday evening I took the responsibilty of asking the police disciplinary service to make enquiries about Thomas and Santoni. What we've learnt today may make it unnecessary. It's Thomas who's been informing the dealers through his wife and Sener, or Moreira. She knows both of them.'

'You haven't got a shred of evidence.'

'Quite right. And if we want to bring this affair to a conclusion, we've got to find some, and very quickly. Lavorel, when you know exactly what kind of trafficking Paulette Dupin is conducting, telephone me at home, at any time of the night. And then we'll see if we can organize a search on Monday. Can you take in all that? So let's go back to the entertaining part of our work. Customs tell me that the delivery date has been fixed. It'll take place on 4 April, no doubt very early in the morning. In thirteen days' time precisely. Before that we only have to find out who runs this bloody mess, implicate Kashguri, find VL, solve the murder of the Thai girl and unmask the bent cops. And get Anna Beric back home. Simple.'

2 a.m. *Villa des Artistes*

Daquin woke up with difficulty. Comatose.

'Guv...'

'It's you, Lavorel ... Where are you? Are you at home? Wait a minute then. I'm going to put my head under the cold tap.'

Daquin put the telephone down. Sol was there in the bed asleep. He hadn't heard him come back last night. He lifted the duvet and looked at him for a moment. The black dick. The face with its sharp features, so different when the pale blue eyes were closed. A disconcerting mixture of submission and revolt.

His head under the tap. Towel. Back to the bed.

'OK. Lavorel, I'm listening.'

Daquin was naked, his back against the wall, the telephone on his stomach, the receiver in his left hand, his right hand on the nape of Soleiman's neck.

'The box contains rolls of labels with the big names in the French ready-to-wear business, Ted Lapidus, Yves Saint-Laurent. The ones the workroom works for. That allows Berican to produce counterfeit garments on a big scale.'

'Is it illegal?'

'Totally.'

'And does it earn money?'

'Lots of it.'

'If we carry out a search on Monday morning, can we find evidence against Paulette?'

'If it's done early enough, yes. The rolls of labels are too big to allow any possible explanation. They're locked up in one of the desk drawers.'

'You're sure we can take her in when we leave?'

'Yes, sure.' He hesitated. 'There's something else that worries me.'

'Tell me.'

'We won't be arresting just Paulette. We'll have to take Berican too, and his workers will be out in the street. Without jobs. Just when they're all hoping to get their papers.'

'I warned you that you wouldn't find many suit-and-tie people in the Sentier.' Silence. 'I'll think about it. Tomorrow afternoon'... a look at his watch: 1 o'clock in the morning 'this afternoon rather, in my office, so that we can organize the search?'

'I'll be there.'

'And did you enjoy yourself?'

'Rather easy and rather quick.'

'We'll try to find you something better. Good-night.'

He hung up. Turned to Soleiman who had woken up.

'You look all in, my boy.'

'I am. On Monday it's the general assembly. We're going to propose that the new offers by the Ministry should be accepted. I don't know what will happen. Turks don't like compromise.'

Daquin moved Soleiman's head onto his shoulder and licked the back of his neck gently, almost biting it.

'You'll win your vote, my boy. I hear what people are saying these days in the workrooms. They see you as a winner. I've got a gift for you. On Monday morning we're going to arrest a workroom boss. Berican, 2 passage de l'Industrie. If the workers protest loudly enough we'll blame the manageress for everything and let them have their boss back.' He'd got down to the base of Soleiman's spine.

'Stop, Daquin. I don't understand a word of what you're saying.'

'I'll stop. For the time being. Go and make some coffee.'

Soleiman came back upstairs with the coffee-pot and two cups. He sat down at the end of the bed. Daquin told him about the Berican workroom.

'The Fraud Squad will arrest the manageress and the workroom boss, they can't do anything else. If the workers make enough fuss we'll blame the manageress for everything and you can have the boss back. As for you, you'll arrive at the general assembly. with him, the workroom will be reopened ... Do you know Berican?'

'Yes. He's sent money to the Committee. You're making me a real gift. What do you want in exchange?'

'Nothing. You've given me all I want in any case. I want everything you can find out about Sener. I'm convinced he's in the network, but I've no proof. And I want your ass. Now.'

7 a.m. Passage de l'Industrie

Berican went up the staircase to his workroom, as he did every day it opened. On the landing, four sinister individuals, three raincoats, one jacket. Panic. Was it the Grey Wolves, as with Celik Osman? No. They were not Turks. Were they French police officers? They showed him their identity cards and a document he didn't read. A search. He came out in a sweat. His vision was blurred. Paulette had sworn this would never happen...

Berican went in with the police officers. One of them stayed by the door. As the workers arrived they were sent into the kitchen. Morale was definitely low.

A rapid tour of the workrooms. The police officers seemed almost absent-minded. Tension increased when they reached the finishing machines. One officer carefully collected the checklists for the labels. But the place they really wanted to search was the manageress's office. Account books, orders, invoices, they took out everything. One cop sat down and began to leaf through it all. In a locked drawer were designer labels from the couturiers and a register of their issue and return. A quick check showed that the totals were correct. Bottom drawer on the left, the boss opened it. Plastic bag from FNAC. Inside, a cardboard box. In the box, two rolls of labels, Saint-Laurent and Ted Lapidus. About five hundred of each.

'And what's this?'

Berican didn't have to try very hard to look completely astonished.

'I've no idea. This is the manageress's office. I'm always in the workroom.'

'And when does the manageress arrive?'

'At 8.30, every day.'

'We'll wait for her. Sit down.'

One of the officers took statements from the workers. Hardly any of them had identity papers, the addresses were imaginary and nobody had ever seen that plastic bag.

Shortly after 8.30 Paulette Dupin arrived. When she saw the workroom empty and two unknown men coming out of her office she went pale. Flanked by the two men she was pushed into the office. She looked at Berican who was sitting on a chair. Salvation would not come from that quarter but he didn't seem to be in a state of collapse.

Account books, first irregularities identified.

Paulette shrugged her shoulders, suspecting that they hadn't come to look at those.

'And these labels? What are they used for?'

Paulette glanced sideways at Berican.

'I've never seen that box. I didn't bring it here.'

'In the bottom drawer of your desk, which was locked, and you've never seen it?'

'No.'

'That's a position you'll find rather difficult to maintain.'

The officers took Paulette and Berican into custody, the workers were asked to leave and the workroom was closed.

9.30 a.m. Passage du Désir

Paulette Dupin and Berican were locked up in two separate offices on the first floor. While the Fraud Squad team was preparing the interrogation Attali went to make his report to Daquin.

'She's tough. She denies ever having seen the plastic bag. In my opinion it's a ridiculous defence. We'll find the retailers who've been selling the counterfeit stuff. And perhaps too the producer of the labels in Turkey . . .'

'Perhaps, but that's how Fraud sees it. I want her to break down and quickly. I don't care a damn about the swindles, I want the truth about the information leaks. We must know before the end of the custody period. After that we'll never be able to manage it. You'll be taking part in the Berican interrogation. Only one thing interests us: he has to admit he saw the plastic bag in the hands of Paulette, but if I understand correctly, we've little chance of getting that. Nothing else matters to us. Charge Paulette, clear Berican, that way we can release him late in the morning. Got that?'

*

Paulette was interrogated in Daquin's office. The Fraud Squad superintendent and the inspector directed operations, Daquin observed.

Paulette was brought in by a cop in uniform, sat down in the chair indicated to her and tried not to panic. True, she hadn't expected this, not she, married to a cop, she wasn't prepared for it. Only one thought in her head: resistance, persistence, denial.

'You are the manageress of the Berican workroom?'

'Yes.'

'A quick look at your accounts has shown up several irregularities. The workroom declares five workers and employs more than twenty on a permanent basis.'

'That's true, but the entire Sentier works like that. Haven't you heard about the legalization of workers being negotiated with the government at the moment? We aren't the only people involved.'

'Let's move on to the search this morning. That bundle of labels . . .'

'I've never seen it.'

'So I understand. Then these are not the labels supplied to you by the manufacturers?'

'No.'

'What could such a bundle of labels be used for?'

'I've no idea.'

'You're not credible on that point, madame. After years of managing a workroom of this kind . . .'

'I've nothing to say about that.'

'Very well. Do you know a certain Turgut Sener?'

'Yes.'

'How did you come to meet him?'

'The embassy gave us an order for some furnishing work in leather. He was in charge of the arrangements. I met him on that occasion.'

'When?'

'Three years ago.'

'And do you continue to see him regularly?'

'Yes, he's a friend.'

'Did you have lunch with him at Chez Flo, last Friday?'

'Yes.' Surprise.

'And he gave you a plastic bag from FNAC?'

'No.'

'We have witnesses, madame.'

'They made a mistake.'

'We'll continue this interrogation tomorrow, madame. One last question: is your husband involved in your professional activities?'

Paulette Dupin sat up, as though electrified.

'Superintendent, when we married we both retained control over our personal property, and I am an adult. Leave my husband out of this.'

Paulette Dupin was led away for her first day in custody.

Daquin began to hope. She was acting the tough lady, perhaps that's what she was. But her defence was desperate and totally lacking in flexibility. We can make her crack up. We must concentrate on Sener. According to Romero there's a good chance they may be lovers. She's in her fifties, he's twenty years younger, she surely clings to him.

9.30 a.m. Passage de l'Industrie

Berican's workers were huddled together at the foot of the staircase. Smoking and arguing with Soleiman, who was passing through. At first, despair: no work, no papers. It was more difficult to find work in leather than in fabrics. Someone suggested going up to the second floor, breaking open the door, taking away the machines, selling them and sharing the money in order to keep going until they found new jobs.

'Gangster behaviour,' said Soleiman.

'In any case you know that if we don't take over the machines the cops will seize them.'

'No, there's no reason to let them do that. Those days are over. We'll fight, all of us together, we'll go to the police station to demand Berican's release and the reopening of the workroom.'

'It's impossible. They're going to bang up the lot of us and send us back to Turkey.'

'No, you'll see. The Committee will be there and they'll telephone the ministry. Other Turks will come and support us.'

Soleiman spoke with real conviction. In the end it was unanimously agreed to go in a group and demand Berican's release. A stop at the usual café, raki to give themselves courage. On Berican's account, naturally. In the mean time Soleiman telephoned the Committee. Round up all the French militants you can find, meet in half an hour's time or sooner at passage du Désir, yes, that's it, outside the police station. Bring stuff to make a banner. Is Omar there? Yes? Put him on. Omar, run over to the

Gymnase and send to passage du Désir all the Turks who want to go. It's important.

When the Berican workers reached the local police station they weren't reassured. A moment's hesitation. Ten or so French militants arrived at the other end of the passage. Three of them unrolled a broad strip of fabric and painted on it in white: *Berican's workers want to work*, Soleiman and a Frenchman undertook to negotiate with the cop on the door. They wanted to see the Superintendent.

'Which Superintendent?'

'The one who ordered the search at the Berican workroom this morning.'

'No idea who.'

'A woman lawyer, well known for her aggressive behaviour, bombarded the station with phone calls. She insisted on speaking to Monsieur Berican, who was her client. Why impossible? I'll call the minister's office.'

The banner was fixed to the wall opposite the station.

By 10.45 Turks began arriving in small groups. Soon a small crowd of two hundred and fifty or three hundred people were shouting slogans in Turkish and French. Lavorel watched from a third-floor window.

At 11.30 the minister's first secretary telephoned the station. Everyone should avoid making waves, just when the negotiations were about to be successful. Had Monsieur Berican been charged with particularly serious offences? No? Well then...

At noon Berican was freed and emerged to applause, whistles of approval and cheering, like a member of the Galatasaray football team after a win over a Greek club. Within five minutes the crowd had dispersed and calm returned to passage du Désir. Lavorel was still at the window, admiring and bewildered.

*

The news that Thomas's wife was in police custody spread like wildfire through the local squad. Thomas, taken completely by surprise, felt unwell and told the Fraud Squad superintendent he was going home. He would be interviewed as a witness the next day,

Tuesday, at 10 a.m. Santoni stopped work abruptly and rushed over to the 10th arrondissement commissariat to see Meillant, who telephoned at once: 'Daquin, I want to see you, this morning.'

'Come to my office about noon.'

Meillant arrived at the height of the demonstration. He had to push his way through the crowd, nobody seemed to recognize him or take any notice of him. To his fury and astonishment he saw Berican coming out. He went up to Daquin's office in total exasperation.

'What's all this carry-on? Have you decided to play Mister Clean in the Sentier all on your own?' He pointed to the window. 'Or are you trying to buy yourself a clientele on the cheap? And what for? On the way you're destroying one of the best inspectors I've ever known, with thirty years' service behind him. And with me. Is it me you're getting at?'

Daquin had decided to act friendly. For Meillant the worst was yet to come. Daquin described in great detail how his team had come across Paulette because of Sener (omitting everything about the tapping of Moreira's telephone) and without knowing she was Madame Thomas.

'Very well, I accept that. But why act so quickly? You surely can't believe this is the only case of label trafficking in the Sentier? You should have talked to me before getting Fraud involved.'

'The decision to intervene was taken for reasons that have nothing to do with Fraud, but I won't explain them to you today. Not for one or two days, the length of Paulette Thomas' custody, which will be extended.'

Meillant had completely failed to understand the situation, and he knew it.

6.30 p.m. At the Trades Union Centre

Once again the big hall in the old Trades Union Centre in rue du Château d'Eau was completely packed. Men everywhere, standing between the rows of seats, even along the promenade.

Very different now from the excitement of the early days, the thrill of being together, in the street or the Centre, free from clandestine life. Now people looked grave, there was a buzz of conversation in lowered voices, the tension of decision day. These men had restored something of the utopian atmosphere and nineteenth-century spirit to the old Trades Union Centre.

Soleiman reached the platform along with four Frenchmen and Turgut Sener, present for the first time as embassy representative in the negotiations. They sat down. Sener remained slightly apart, he looked uncomfortable. Soleiman stood up. He spoke briefly, in Turkish, in a loud, hoarse voice, without using the microphone or any rhetorical effects. When he'd finished he turned towards the platform and spoke in French, his voice even hoarser and his accent very strong.

'I've told how far we've got in the negotiations with the minister. We've made a lot of progress. Yesterday he proposed legalized status for Turks who had arrived here before 1976, barely 10 per cent of us. Today the crucial date has been brought forward to 1979. That involves 80 per cent of us now. Of course, it's not exactly what we proposed at the beginning. But we're convinced we won't get any further in global negotiating. So we have to accept. And afterwards we'll support each individual case step by step. Many points are still obscure: lodgings, conditions in the workrooms, work contracts. Let's have confidence in our collective strength. We'll fight on every front, we won't let anyone down. *Ya hip Ya hop,* but before we can carry on, we have to say yes to the minister.'

No reaction in the hall. Then came two or three angry objections to the proposed agreement. Soleiman translated for the platform in a low voice. The audience were extremely attentive but still did not react.

Berican stood up. He was in one of the front rows, surrounded by his workers. He told his story. How he'd acquired papers ten years earlier, by paying the embassy, paying the immigration services, paying the French police. His arrest that morning by the French police, then his release: 'This is the first time I've seen successful collective action by Turkish workers in France. It's a great day for me, I'm proud to be Turkish, here in Paris.' His voice trembled with emotion. 'And when Soleiman says he'll fight for every case, I believe him, for I've seen him take action this morning, and win.'

His workers rose to their feet and applauded. The entire hall stood up, applauding and whistling for a good five minutes.

The decision was taken *de facto* and everyone lost their anxiety.

On the platform Sener looked as though he was going to be ill.

When calm returned Soleiman arranged for a vote in due form with a show of hands and a teller for each row. Then all those who hadn't been able to find a seat voted too: 1,754 for ratifying the agreement proposed by the minister, 217 against. Adopted. Then Soleiman passed on to questions-and-answers with the audience, dealing with all the practical aspects of the first phase of legalization which would begin the following day. The general assembly. broke up into endless little groups. Soleiman omnipresent, patient, indispensable.

The general assembly ended. The Turks streamed out towards place de la République. Romero located Sener who went off alone, looking crushed. He went up rue du Château d'Eau, crossed Boulevard de Strasbourg and went into a building where the many front windows were painted over white up to a height of about two metres. The plate by the door: ASSOCIATION OF LIGHTING TECH-NICIANS. Romero went into a porch opposite, climbed up a boundary stone and craned his neck. There seemed to be quite a lot of people inside and the discussions were fairly agitated. Sener's head was visible occasionally. Romero got cramp. He climbed down from his boundary stone and waited in the dark. Sener didn't leave until two hours later. On his own and looking even more dejected. Romero followed him to his home and watched the apartment until lights out.

Nothing to report.

8 a.m. Passage du Désir

Daquin had been pacing about in his office for the last half-hour. The pressure was on and wouldn't stop rising until 3 April. He would have to cope with it.

Romero telephoned and told him about Sener and the Association of Lighting Technicians. Keep trailing Sener.

Then the two officers from the disciplinary inspectorate arrived. Dark clothes, sombre expressions. They had a slight tendency to overdo it.

'Madame Thomas has a Swiss bank account.'

'You haven't been hanging about...'

Smiles understood. 'We paid. We had something to bargain with. Madame Thomas's account is a joint account in the name of Monsieur and Madame Thomas.'

'That alters everything. It means that Thomas can be implicated in his wife's swindling.'

'We're going to do that. As of this morning. We wanted to tell you about it. Thomas will be in custody as from 10 o'clock.'

After they had gone Daquin spoke to the switchboard.

'Whatever happens, I don't want any calls from Meillant today, have you got that?'

The Drugs Squad chief on the line: Daquin, come and see me at once.

8 a.m. At the Committee

Soleiman had barely come through the door when the telephone rang. A Turk on the line.

'We were at the general assembly last night. We're on strike, the Committee must come.'

'Where?'

'24 rue des Maraîchers, 20th arrondissement.'

'I'll come as soon as I can.'

'Be quick. We've said we're on strike, we don't know what to do now.'

Attali, wearing a dark suit and tie, carrying a leather dispatch case in his right hand and a volume of the *Encyclopédie Universelle* tucked under his left arm, entered a building in avenue du Maréchal-Lyautey, walked to the elevator and pressed the button for the fifth floor, the top one. That was where Kashguri lived. The elevator didn't move. Attali was surprised and tried again. Still nothing.

A man's voice came down from somewhere and told him, in crude French: 'Give your name, please, and the reason for your visit.

Attali: 'My name is Lambert and I'm selling books, the *Encyclopédie Universelle.*'

The reply came quickly: 'We are not interested. No thank you.'

*

Less than half an hour later Attali found himself back in the main entrance hall, deeply discouraged, having experienced one rejection after another, on every floor, while learning nothing about the tenants of the apartment on the fifth. The concierge, a sturdy woman in her forties, wearing a tight grey woollen dress, came out of her lodge.

'What are you up to, young man? Door-to-door selling is prohibited in the building, there's a notice saying so.'

Attali assumed a dejected look. He didn't have to try very hard. He showed her the *Encyclopédie Universelle* catalogue: the culture and science of the whole world, nobody wanted it.

'That doesn't surprise me. Come and have a beer in my lodge. That'll cheer you up. I've no work at this time of day.'

The lodge was small: a table, four chairs, one armchair, a fridge. A television. The living-quarters must have been somewhere else. Attali sat down.

'I got off to a bad start. I tried the elevator, I pressed the button for the fifth floor.'

'Where the Iranians live.'

'Are they like the Iranians we see on TV, yelling and refusing to release the American hostages?'

'Just like that. Ours don't yell but they're the same sort of savages.'

She put the beers on the table and sat down beside Attali. She had rough hands and dyed hair. Why did she sit beside him and not opposite?

'Have they been here a long time?'

'Eight or ten months. The apartment's magnificent, you know. And that Kashguri, that's his name, lives there alone with four servants, two men and two women. I don't know what he gets up to with them.'

Am I dreaming or had she moved her chair closer? What shall I do, for God's sake, what shall I do?

'In any case, the women, they're Asian, never go out. Not once in eight months. And the menservants take things in turn. One does the shopping or drives Kashguri about, the other one stays up there, looking after the apartment and the girls. I think it's suspicious. What do you think about it?' And she placed one hand on his wrist.

'That's true, it's not normal. Doesn't anyone ever go up there?'

'I never go, neither do the delivery people. But there are often receptions in the evening. In the end the tenants on the fourth floor complained. Fashionable people too at those receptions.' She smiled at him and put her other hand on his thigh. 'Feeling better, dear?'

'I could drink another beer.' She went to get it out of the fridge. Attali was sweating. 'And when they have receptions, does the elevator work the same way?'

'Yes.' She sat down again and moved her chair closer to Attali. Her thigh was touching his now. 'The people give their names. The menservants check them from a list and let them come up. One wonders what they've got to hide.' Once again, her hand on his thigh, higher up, very near his dick.

Attali jumped to his feet, red-faced and tense.

'Sorry, *madame*, I'm homosexual.'

He caught hold of his dispatch case and fled as fast as he could.

9 *a.m. Rue des Maraîchers*

A shop at street level, its windows painted over. Soleiman pushed open the door and went directly into the workroom. Thicket of cables, machines, as everywhere else. Eight illegal Turks, four

French women workers and a little old man who was already elderly, in his seventies, quivering with rage. When he saw Soleiman come in he rushed to his desk at the back of the room, opened the drawer and brandished a revolver at him. The girls were terrified, the Turks ready to fight. Soleiman smiled. It was like a scene from vaudeville.

Half an hour later the boss put his pistol away and called the police station.

'I've been occupied.'

'Who by?'

'Ten or so workers.'

'Where from?'

'They're my workers.'

'So what's the problem?'

'There's a stranger with them.'

Soleiman, in a loud voice: 'I'm the official representative of the Defence Committee for Turks in France.'

Nobody at the commissariat was keen to rush over: Dispute over working conditions, negotiate. Phone down.

Soleiman smiled, they began to talk. The boss, by name Gribsky, admitted in the end that he was completely ruined; he'd lost everything at the races, his own money and the money for the workers' pay, and he'd been counting, he said, on the pile of finished garments at the back of the workroom for the workers' wages. But there now, the Turks were preventing delivery, twice already the people who'd ordered them had been stopped from collecting them ... The girls laughed: that old horror had been counting on the delivery to recoup what he'd lost at the races, fancy that! The Turks warned Soleiman that they would dismantle the machines that night and pay themselves out of the proceeds.

Soleiman to the boss: 'Sell your business, lease, machines and stock. You'll pay the wages and still have something left over. Otherwise, criminal bankruptcy, theft of machines, anything could happen ... and you'll be left with nothing.'

Gribsky went off in search of someone who could mount a rescue. The workers settled down to occupy the workroom. A meeting was arranged for the next morning at the Committee office.

'Théo, I've read your last two reports very carefully, as I did with the others in fact...'

Daquin waited.

'I've been thinking about this plan for a raid when the raincoats are delivered. We'll work together on the details. I agree we should play it that way. But you realize the dangerous nature of the operation, the many unknown factors...'

Still no reaction.

'This morning I had a phone call from the chief secretary at the minister's office. Yesterday one of your inspectors contacted two deputies, asking for interviews...'

'Yes, Inspector Attali, on my instructions.'

'OK. But the minister's actual orders are clear: we have to forget the deputies. You've got no firm evidence against them ... and that will free resources you can use to concentrate on the Turkish network.'

With a laugh. 'Agreed.'

'Aren't you going to protest? Aren't you going to tell me I'm not fulfilling my role, not protecting the work of my departments?'

'No, chief. I'd expected it. I'm even surprised you didn't say this earlier, and I'll deal with it. On the other hand I'd like to know if the minister has anything to say about Kashguri.'

'Yes, I was coming to that. We'll drop any action against him as well, as long as there's no formal evidence against him. Same treatment as for the deputies.'

'Very well. Your orders will be respected. No action as long as we have no firm evidence. By the way, and obviously there's no connection: I've got several people who've seen the identikit portrait of the man who killed my concierge and they've formally identified him as Kashguri's manservant. What shall I do about it?'

3 p.m. At the Committee

The little windowless office was crowded with people. Soleiman had just reached rue des Maraîchers. He was drinking coffee at the little stall further down the corridor. He was happy.

A Turkish worker came to see him.

'My name's Yavouz. The boss owes me 6,000 francs. He sacked me a few days ago and doesn't want to pay me. The Committee must help me.'

'Have you got proof?'

'Proof, what proof? I work illegally, I've never had a payslip.'

'Let's go. But not on our own.'

Fifteen or so Turks set off in a group and knocked discreetly on the workroom door. The boss, who wasn't suspicious, opened it. Peaceful invasion, led by Yavouz. The boss, who was a Yugoslav, shouted insults and tried to snatch a pair of scissors to defend himself. Two workers came close to stop him. The tension dropped a notch.

'You owe Yavouz 6,000 francs.'

'That man? I've never set eyes on him. I'll call the police.'

He grabbed the telephone and got the commissariat. He spoke French very badly. The man at the other end didn't understand a word of what he was saying.

'Isn't there someone around who can speak French better?'

'Yes.'

'Put him on to me.'

The boss handed the telephone to Soleiman, who explained: labour dispute, unpaid wages.

'Is there any fighting?'

'No, none.'

'Very well, sort it out,' said the duty officer finally, and hung up.

'The police won't come,' said Soleiman to the boss.

'Yes they will.'

'Very well, let's wait for them.'

Everyone settled down, they played draughts, someone went to get coffee. The boss drank some along with everyone else.

Two hours later the boss realized the police weren't coming. After all, maybe he did know Yavouz. He even remembered him. He'd worked there the week before. They began to negotiate. The boss offered 1,000 francs in cash at once. 3,000, no less. 2,000? OK for 2,000. Agreed. Yavouz was delighted. Everybody left. The boss watched them go downstairs. Goodbye, Monsieur Committee.

9 a.m. At the Committee

Soleiman was drinking coffee with four workers, two men and two girls, from rue des Maraîchers. The others had stayed behind to occupy the workroom.

Gribsky arrived accompanied by a flamboyant Lebanese, Hammad, who had parked his Mercedes on the pavement in front of the main door to the church. He stroked the girls' cheeks, called them darling, and took bundles of banknotes out of his black dispatch case.

The telephone rang. A Turk.

'Is that the Committee? Come quickly, rue d'Hauteville ... The boss wants to sack a Turk.'

'Impossible for me to come now, call back later.'

Hammad owned fashion boutiques in the Sentier and on the Mediterranean coast. He was tempted by the adventure of production. Intense discussions about the price of the machines, the stocks of finished garments, the back pay owing, the lease. No written document, no accountancy statements. In the end Gribsky, Hammad and the workers came to an agreement. A settlement was drawn up by Hammad, countersigned by Gribsky, the workers and Soleiman, on behalf of the Committee. Bundles of notes changed hands. Everyone went to celebrate at the local café, ogling the Mercedes on the way.

Soleiman went back to the office. Telephone.

'It's the Turk in rue d'Hauteville. OK, it's sorted out, no need to come.'

'And how was it sorted out?'

'Well, the boss had attacked the worker on the head with a pair of scissors, the worker then cut his hand, right through. The manageress called the police The boss said it was an accident, the cops left. Both men are in hospital and the boss has said that the worker would keep his job.'

12.30 p.m. Avenue des Champs-Elysées

Sener was going up the avenue from the Rond-Point towards the

Lido, accompanied by two members of the embassy staff. He was much too preoccupied to enjoy the good weather. He was in trouble on all fronts. On Monday Paulette had been arrested, the police asked the embassy for permission to question him and his political friends reproached him vehemently for compromising himself in various forms of trafficking which didn't serve the cause ... On Tuesday Paulette's husband, a senior police inspector, was also arrested. Today he himself had an appointment in a few moments' time in an attempt to negotiate his withdrawal from business affairs and his return to Turkey. It was going to be difficult.

Marinoni was also walking up the Champs-Elysées a short distance in front of Sener, while Romero was following him, his eyes fixed on Sener's back. A group of Italian youths were larking about in a kind of game, concealing Sener from him for a moment. Romero tried to get closer. When he saw Sener again he had collapsed on the pavement and his two companions were bending over him with a puzzled expression. Romero rushed forward. Sener was lying face down, with a bullet hole below his left shoulder blade, while a pool of blood was beginning to form in the gutter. Romero stood up, looked round everywhere, saw only people walking along and Marinoni running towards him. He asked Sener's two companions what had happened but they indicated that they didn't speak French.

Romero left Marinoni waiting for the police to arrive and ran to a telephone box.

'Hullo, Daquin speaking.'

'*Commissaire*, Sener has just been shot in front of me, in the street, and I didn't see a thing.'

'Where are you?'

'In the Champs-Elysées.'

'You'll have to cope, Romero. Find a press photographer quickly. There are newspaper offices in the area. I want touching photographs of the dead man. Paulette's custody has only got twenty-four hours to run. Don't waste any time.'

2 p.m. At the Committee

The first sets of papers requesting legalization were starting to come in and the little office was overcrowded. Each dossier was

185

examined. If it was complete it was photocopied, the Committee kept the copy and filed it. The worker only went to deposit the dossier at the Immigration Office after that had been done. In this way the Committee could really keep an eye on all the administrative decisions, case by case. A lot of work. But Soleiman took it on with enthusiasm. He felt useful and powerful. Not afraid at all. The telephone never stopped ringing. Two Turkish militants took it in turn to reply to the requests for information.

'Soleiman, for you. A new strike.'

It was Hassan, one of the pillars of the Committee, on the line. He'd been working for a few days at LVT, a big workroom with sixty or so workers, all clandestine, more or less. Yugoslavs, Africans, thirty or so Turks. A Yugoslav boss, Jencovich. That morning the Turks had asked him for work contracts to establish their legality. In reply the boss sacked them. The Turks remained sitting in front of their machines, doing nothing. If they got up they would be replaced by Yugoslavs.

'The foreigners are continuing to work as though nothing's happening,' said Hassan. 'You've got to come, it could turn violent.'

Soleiman looked for help from the people around him. Telephone, files, everyone was busy. There was a queue in the corridor outside the Committee's door. Too bad, I'll go on my own.

High up in rue du Faubourg-Saint-Denis, near the overhead railway, past the Bouffes du Nord theatre, Soleiman went up to the third floor and entered the workroom. He'd never seen such a big one, six rooms, all looking on to the street. Otherwise a tangle of cables, machines, neon lights like everywhere else. At the very moment he went in a fight broke out between Turks and Yugoslavs. One Yugoslav collapsed with a scissor wound in his thigh. Carnage was imminent. The boss, Soleiman and the Africans intervened. The scissors fell onto the tables again. Two Yugoslavs laid the injured man down in another room.

Jencovich telephoned the Superintendent of the 10th arrondissement and then turned to Soleiman: 'I warn you, I've called the police. I know the Superintendent. He'll be here any minute. He'll send all the Turks out of here. I employ the people I want to employ. And I don't want that lot any more. And as for you, you've no right to be here.'

Soleiman suggested a discussion. Useless.

Sirens. Soleiman looked through the window. Three police mini-buses, together with Police-Assistance, stopped outside the entrance to the building. Thirty or more cops in uniform got out as well as three men in plain clothes. They all rushed into the building and could be heard running up the stairs. Soleiman went pale.

The police came into the workroom. Three of them went to see to the injured Yugoslav and took him away on a stretcher to the hospital. The others spread out through the workroom and checked the distance between the two communities. A plainclothes cop, a short, thickset man, well over fifty, seemed to be in charge of the operations.

Soleiman spoke to him: 'I'm here on behalf of the Committee...'

'Shut up, you. I didn't speak to you.'

Then he took the boss by the arm and led him into the apartment on the other side of the landing.

Soleiman asked the Turks in the workroom to explain what was happening. They laughed. The apartment opposite belonged to the boss. The Superintendent knew him well because he came every Friday at noon to have sex with the boss's wife, a French blonde, precisely in the apartment opposite. The boss and the Superintendent were great buddies. The boss paid, on top of that the Superintendent fucked his wife, there were never any police checks in the workroom, the business flourished...

The Superintendent came back again, followed by the boss, who looked rather sheepish. A quick order, a sign to his cops who split up and stood along the three sections of the staircase. Only the plainclothes men and two in uniform remained in the workroom.

'This scrap is over now. Nobody's been sacked. Everyone back to work, at once. If anyone mentions a work contract I'll get him banged up immediately. Did you hear what I said? As for you, you bloody fool,' he caught hold of Soleiman by his hair before he realized what was happening, while the two plainclothes men twisted his arms behind his back, 'I recognize you. I saw you Monday morning in passage du Désir. You won't come back to my district playing Zorro again. You're going to go out of here on your hands and knees and we shan't see you again, got that?'

He dragged him over to the staircase and pushed him down, head first, while one of the cops tripped him up. Soleiman hit the banisters hard. A cut over his left eye blinded him with blood. He tried to get up by groping at the banisters. Two blows with a truncheon on his hands. A kick in the small of his back. He tumbled down to the second floor landing where a cop in uniform got him to his feet with a kick on his jaw. A blow on his right temple covered his eyes with a veil of blood, and blood filled his mouth. He was pushed down the staircase again, tried to roll into a ball and reached the first-floor landing. Someone pulled him up by the collar and kicked him in the crotch, he heard himself scream. Couldn't breathe any more. He was dropped onto the staircase and sent down by kicks in the ribs. A hellish noise inside his head. Heard a voice in the distance saying 'Don't kill him'.

The lower half of his body was crushed. I can't even crawl. He felt himself lifted and carried ... A door banged. He was put down on a platform, couldn't straighten his legs. Wet towels to wipe the blood from his face. A terrible pain in his chest. He still couldn't breathe but he made out two silhouettes bending over him.

'Who are you?' Barely a murmur.

'You're safe, you're in the theatre. We heard screaming. We rushed into the entrance, we picked you up. As soon as the cops have gone we'll take you to the hospital.'

Soleiman began to breathe gently in short gasps. Painful.

'Not to the hospital. My place.'

'But you need treatment.'

A pause while he got his breath back.

'There's someone at my place who can give it.'

'Where's your place?'

'Avenue Jean-Moulin, in the 14th.'

4 p.m. *Passage du Désir*

Daquin hadn't seen Paulette again since Monday. Found that she was cracking up. He rose to give her a chair.

'Romero, describe what happened in the Champs-Elysées a short time ago.'

Romero described it, clumsily. Paulette froze, white-faced. When Romero had finished Daquin pushed towards her two large photographs of Sener lying dead, one showing him as he had fallen, his face turned to the left, the other showing him from the front, stretched out on his back. Daquin let time pass. Paulette looked at the photographs for a long time. Without moving. Then she passed her hand gently over the dead man's face.

'Who killed him?'

'A hired killer from the Turkish gang of drug traffickers for whom he worked.'

'Why?'

'So that we couldn't question him. Paulette, did you know that he worked for that gang?'

'No.'

'So why did you repeat to him everything your husband told you?'

'I've no idea.' A long silence. Paulette remained motionless. 'No doubt I didn't realize what I was doing. I thought we could run our joint affairs better.' Another long silence. 'And then I loved him.' Pathetic.

'Will you agree now to answer a few precise questions?'

She removed her hand from the photographs and turned her head towards Daquin.

'Go on. I no longer have anyone or anything left to shield.'

In less than an hour everything was sorted out. The counterfeit labels: produced in Turkey, brought over in the diplomatic bag. Much less risky than having them done in France. The amount of the profits, the Swiss bank account, the retailers who sold things on. And the long confidences from her husband. (He doesn't like you, Daquin.) Everything that she passed on to Sener. Paulette seemed outside time. There was only one question that mattered, and she tried in vain to find the answer within her memory: had Sener loved her, or had he merely used her?

6 p.m. Villa des Artistes

There had to be an end to the stress. Cook things that needed a little time and attention. Veal in white sauce with leeks, and a walnut soufflé. And afterwards, love.

Daquin came back home, laden with plastic bags. He greeted the man on guard duty who gave him an odd look.

'What's the matter?'

'Well, your . . . young man came back in a very poor state.'

'Was that long ago?'

'Just over an hour ago.'

Daquin went in, put his bags down on the kitchen counter and went to the sofa. Soleiman, lying on his back, had dozed off. From time to time he trembled. He certainly looked in a very bad way, his face badly damaged, traces of blood, a cut over one eye, the bridge of his nose broken, his lips swollen to twice their normal size ... He'd be more comfortable in bed. Daquin lifted him up. Soleiman opened his eyes, saw Daquin and closed them again. Daquin carried him into the bedroom, laid him down on the bed, undressed him and covered him up again. Then he searched through the bathroom cabinet and returned to the bed with a whole assortment of things, thread, needles, syringes and bandages. First he had to clean up his face and disinfect the wounds. He sat down on the bed beside Soleiman. Orderly movements. Soleiman felt Daquin's thigh against his arm, his hands over his face, wouldn't move at all, go to sleep again. He heard Daquin speak to him: 'I'm going to put four stitches over your eye. I don't think you'll feel very much.'

Soleiman relaxed completely. Pain, torpor, warmth returning.

'Sol, two of your fingers are dislocated. I'm going to put them right. It'll hurt, but not for long. Are you ready?'

Soleiman opened his eyes, eyelashes flickered. He moaned. Elastoplast bandaging. Wonderful feeling of relief. Then, Daquin's hands all over his body, a light touch now from those hands, so authoritarian when he fucked him. Broken ribs. Nothing to be done, just wait. Balls swollen and painful. No sign of haemotome bruising, it won't last long. Daquin stroked the penis with the back of his hand. A big cut on one knee, it just had to be disinfected and bandaged, that was all.

'I'm going to give you three injections. No need to move, I'll manage. Did you hear me?' Eyelashes flickered. 'Anti-tetanus and antibiotic, plus one as a painkiller, for your comfort.'

'No, Daquin, not the third one.' Tired. Didn't want to talk, to explain, morphine, in Turkey, every day in the end. 'I'm afraid of addiction.'

'As you wish.'

The two injections. Covered him up with the duvet and stayed there, sitting beside him, stroking his hair. Soleiman opened his eyes, blue, exhaustion. Daquin's lips close to his ear. A whisper, a caress. Sol, do you want me to fuck you? Gently, very gently ... Eyelashes flickered.

6.30 a.m. Villa des Artistes

Soleiman opened his eyes. He was emerging from a very deep sleep. Heard Daquin downstairs, making coffee. Rapid check, he ached all over, but everything seemed to function, more or less. Sat up in bed. Groaned: had forgotten his broken ribs. Got up somehow, went as far as the bathroom. The big mirror: face almost unrecognizable, one hand bandaged, a dressing on his knee, bruises all over his body. Urine normal. I've got off lightly.

Daquin, in his dressing-gown, brought the breakfast up: scrambled eggs, fromage blanc, coffee. Soleiman got back into bed and began to eat. Had to be very careful about his jaw: cracking sounds, stabs of pain. Daquin still hadn't asked any questions.

'Do you already know what happened to me?'

'No, I don't know anything.'

'I was beaten up by some cops, your buddies.'

Soleiman seemed so shocked that Daquin laughed.

'You should have told them you belonged to me, and they needed my permission to touch you.'

Soleiman went silent. Daquin leant over towards him and kissed him on the neck.

'Sorry, I couldn't resist the temptation, you were funny when you said that. Go on, I'm listening.'

Soleiman gave a sober account of the whole incident.

'The superintendent knew me already,' he went on, 'he'd seen me on Monday at the demonstration in passage du Désir. I got the impression he hated me.'

'Do you know his name?'

'No.'

'Describe him to me.'

'Over fifty. Not tall. Thickset. Average upmarket Frenchman.'

'In the 10th arrondissement, highly possible it was Meillant.'

A long silence, both of them thoughtful. Soleiman, who was lying on his back in the bed, moved slightly closer to Daquin, rested his head on his thigh.

'Listen, Daquin. This wasn't the first beating up I've had. Each time I just tried to survive. I hid in a hole, and I came out when I hadn't any more marks on my body. Today it's different. For the first time I'm starting to exist in the eyes of others, I've got a past, I'm a man. Do you understand what I'm trying to say?' Daquin indicated that he did. 'And it's all being destroyed by that bastard. He humiliated me in front of my own people. I've no choice. Either I disappear again or I kill him.' Despair in the blue eyes.

Silence for a long moment. Daquin stroked Soleiman's left breast with its dark, hard nipple. I love this body. It suits me very well.

'Neither solution will get you out of it, my boy, and you know that already. Look at it differently. He humiliated you, do the same to him, in front of the same public. He roughed you up because he's a cop. Force him to resign from the police. Can you imagine the prestige you'll get out of that?'

'It's beyond my reach, you know that very well.'

'It's not certain. We'll operate together, you and I, to break Meillant.'

Soleiman sat up, pulled a face. His ribs were painful.

'Why would you do that?'

'I need to do it for my own purposes. And I can just see a way of doing it, with you. Are you game? I warn you, it'll be risky and difficult.'

'I'll do anything to get out of this.'

'We'll talk about it again tonight.'

Daquin got up, went into the bathroom, shaved and dressed.

'Stay here, in bed, today. You need to. But telephone the Committee, explain what happened and the way you look. A serious protest to the ministers, Interior and Labour, could be very helpful. Also, let the Turks at LVT know you're alive, that you'll need them, and that they must manage to stay with LVT until Monday evening. As for me, I'm going to look round the Bouffes du Nord area to see what can be done.' A kiss on the lips, a smile, another kiss. 'There's something to eat in the fridge. I'm entrusting the house to you. Be good.'

10 a.m. Turkish Embassy

The ambassador, a middle-aged man, very much the Quai d'Orsay type, stood up to welcome the two inspectors from the Fraud Squad responsible for the enquiry, accompanied by Romero. But his manner of receiving them at once established a dividing line: they belonged to a lower order. Romero tensed up.

'An extremely regrettable incident. Our staff will obviously collaborate with the French police. For us, the situation is clear: Monsieur Sener fell beneath the bullets of the same Armenian terrorists who struck down our ambassador to the Vatican in 1977, or our ambassador in Berne on 6 February last.'

He observed a moment's silence, then turned towards Romero: 'My staff have told me that you and one of your colleagues were present on the spot at the time of the murder. Might the French police be taking an interest in the activities of one of our diplomats without informing us? I'm not contemplating that hypothesis, which would be laden with future complications. I believe that your presence on the spot was accidental and I'm glad of it, for it will certainly allow the enquiry to lead very quickly to the arrest of the guilty parties.'

Romero acknowledged this with a slight bow from the waist.

*

An office was placed at the disposal of the inspectors for them to interview the two men who had accompanied Sener along the Champs-Elysées, Tahir Bodrum and Dogan Carim. They were both built on the same model: tall, heavy, thickset, moustachioed. They looked like henchman. Grey suits. Very well cut, essential for concealing their revolvers, white shirts, dark ties. Their function at the embassy: cultural attachés. Odd-looking lot, the Turkish intellectuals. They had both arrived at the embassy in 1979. Since then they had become very friendly with Sener. Yesterday they had gone out for a walk with no particular purpose. Taking advantage of the good weather in the most beautiful avenue in the world. Sener was no more preoccupied than usual. They heard a kind of 'plop', like the subdued sound of a balloon bursting, and Sener collapsed. They hadn't understood what was happening, they bent down over him. He was dead. Astonishment. As they stood up they saw Romero and Marinoni running towards them.

'How was it that the dead man had no diary on him, not even his keys, only his wallet and his identity papers?'

'We weren't on our way to a professional appointment. Perhaps he had left everything in his office?'

'Your addresses, gentlemen?'

'The embassy, naturally, inspector.'

Noon. Boulevard Haussmann

Systematic search of Sener's office in the presence of an embassy man. Nothing. Nothing to an astonishing degree. It was an office without files, without correspondence, without a diary, without an address book. The inspectors talked to the secretaries who had worked with Sener, and to the colleagues closest to him: he was irreproachable, meticulous and calm.

'Did he have a diary, any files?'

'Yes, certainly.'

'Where are they?'

Wide-eyed looks of surprise, a pretence at goodwill that remained helpless.

'Didn't his secretary keep his appointments book?'

'No, Monsieur Sener worked in a highly personal way.'

Noon. Passage du Désir

Daquin arrived at his office whistling. A lengthy examination of the building at the Bouffes du Nord: he was full of ideas. Attali was completing a report on the two days he had just spent on the surveillance of Kashguri. He was in a foul mood.

'Do you want to know what's happening in the office? The custody of Paulette and her husband is over. They've both been charged. Can you imagine what it was like when they met again? Thomas is resigning from the police and Santoni has asked for leave. Lavorel is following up the Paulette Dupin case. So there are only the three of us left to work on a massive case, and we're swamped. What's more, here in the office, nobody says good-morning to us any more.'

'What's making you so pessimistic today?'

Attali was considering the best reply to this apparently simple question when the telephone rang. At a sign from Daquin he picked it up.

'Superintendent Daquin's office, Inspector Attali speaking.'

Gradually his face brightened. He took a sheet of paper and a pencil.

'Noted. I'm informing the Super at once.' He hung up and turned to Daquin. 'The cops at Mantes have fished up a corpse from the river, it could be that of VL. They're expecting us at the morgue for the identification.'

2 p.m. Square Nicolay

After Sener's office, his apartment. And always the inevitable observer from the embassy. Attractive apartment, on the fifth floor of a nineteenth-century building looking onto a private square, green and quiet. Air, silence, space. A small entrance hall, a large room alongside the outside wall, two bedrooms. Old-style kitchen and bathroom. The furniture was modern, comfortable and unostentatious. The concierge for the building did Sener's housework. At the inspectors' request she went up with them. Everything was impeccably tidy.

'When did you come here last?'

'Yesterday morning.'

One of the two bedrooms served as an office. Not a single paper on the table, nothing.

'Was it usually like this?'

'No. Here, by the telephone, there was a kind of black notebook, with a list of telephone numbers, and a pad of paper for writing down notes.'

The inspectors burrowed everywhere. A large collection of clothes. Few books. No papers.

'Any files? No, he didn't have many here. Sometimes he brought one or two back in the evening but he took them away again the next morning.'

*

As soon as the search was over, the seals put in place, and the embassy man gone, the concierge invited the three inspectors to have coffee in her lodge.

'Tell us something about this Monsieur Sener. How did he live?'

'He was a good tenant. He'd been here just over a year. Never late with the rent. I collect it. If only all the tenants were like that... He paid me regularly too. There was work to do in his place but it was never totally filthy. If you knew what some places are like...'

'Women?'

'One. Much older than him. Not all that beautiful. More the businesswoman type. She spent the night there two or three times a week.'

Paulette. Whenever images of Paulette or Thomas cropped up again Romero felt uneasy.

'No others?'

'What can I tell you? No other regulars, that's all.'

'And on the other evenings?'

'Either he came back very late or he entertained friends. Practically all of them men. Turks, no doubt. Many with moustaches. They had dinner, they talked, they drank, they smoked like chimneys. And they gambled heavily.'

'At what?'

'I've no idea. Dice, cards...'

'For money?'

'Yes, I think so, lots of it. But that's only an impression.'

3 p.m. Mantes

The Crime Squad inspectors were waiting for Daquin and Attali outside the hospital in Mantes.

'A rather alarming corpse, as you'll see.'

They entered the small room where the forensic surgeon worked, with its white tiling, metal trolleys, phials, scalpels and the mingled smells of decomposition and disinfectant.

The doctor straightened up. Daquin and Attali came close. Attali exclaimed with shock. It was certainly her, but she was unrecognizable. The beautiful face was not only white and swollen, decomposed through its time in the water, it was also frozen in a near-unbearable grimace of suffering, the eyes rolled back, the mouth wide open, the features deformed, the neck twisted in a desperate attempt to escape. From what? A glance at the body. The flesh was lacerated, split open, rotting, from the chest to the knees. The breasts had gone, there was only a yawning white wound.

Attali went out, swaying dizzily.

Daquin turned to the doctor, who threw a sheet over the body.

'Would you be able to give me some information about her death now, or must I wait for the report?'

'I can tell you two or three things. Death took place about two weeks ago, difficult to be more precise for the moment. The victim died before being thrown into the water, perhaps even much earlier. Death was caused by the lacerations you've seen, possibly whip strokes. She was tied down by the wrists and ankles, whipped to death, raped by two different men while she was still alive. Then the body was placed in a wickerwork trunk immediately after death and thrown into the water later. There are pleasanter ways of dying.'

'Thank you, doctor.'

Daquin rejoined the Crime Squad inspectors and Attali who were walking up and down outside the hospital.

'It's her, there's no doubt about that.'

'The face seemed to match the missing person notice. According to the doctor her age and the date of disappearance apparently matched too, so we called you. Do we transfer the papers to you?'

*

Police station in Mantes. Small office. The two inspectors gave Daquin and Attali the report on the discovery of the body. A bargee who was tying up at a factory quay in Mantes saw that he'd left a rope trailing in the water. He pulled it up and found a large wickerwork trunk, in a rather damaged state, attached to it. He hauled it up on deck, forced it open and found the body. He fainted and his wife telephoned the police station. The bargee's name, his statement, how to contact him, the description of the body in the trunk, everything was there. Let's go and see the trunk.

In the police station basement, Daquin suddenly came to a halt. I know that trunk. The pattern of the wickerwork, the leather corners, the brass clasp, even though half torn off. It was the trunk that had been in Anna Beric's bedroom ... Administrative formalities, then Daquin and Attali loaded the trunk into the boot of their car and returned to Paris. Attali, who was driving, didn't utter a word.

'What's got into you?'

'I think I was beginning to understand that girl. She wanted to get away from her family, who were stifling her, and from bastards like Sobesky and Romero who only thought of stroking her bottom. She wanted to be someone different, somewhere else. And I wasn't good enough. That tortured face, what a horrible sight! It'll haunt me for a long time.'

'Find the killer, that'll help you forget.'

Attali literally exploded.

'*Commissaire*, what a lousy thing to say! I've tried to do that by all methods, with all my conviction. I've questioned people, I've listened. I don't think I've neglected anything. And no result, nothing, nothing, nothing. I can't do anything.'

'Calm down, Attali, I think I've got an idea.'

Attali gave him a sceptical look and put his foot down hard on the accelerator. They were going at nearly 180 kilometres an hour.

'Slow down. I'm scared in cars, and I'm expected home this evening. Does my idea interest you or not?'

'Of course it does.'

Daquin settled back into his seat and tried not to look at the speedometer.

'All the statements we've got from the mannequins and the Thai girls, all say the same thing. Kashguri's a voyeur. I know from one of the mannequins through a private conversation, that he organized rather unusual sessions in his apartment. The girls were tied down by their ankles and wrists, flagellated then fucked or raped – I don't know what term the law might prefer – by his menservants, while he masturbated close by. The girls were not killed: they were taken back to their homes with a load of money and so far none of them have made a complaint. That seems to be rather like what happened to VL. But she died from it. Two possibly hypotheses. VL took part in one of the special soirées, it went wrong. Kashguri got rid of the corpse. Or else Kashguri had good reasons for liquidating VL. Perhaps she tried to blackmail him with the video cassette from the Club Simon, or else she represented a danger for the network because the police were closing in on it. Or other reasons that we don't even suspect. The fact remains that he had her killed while providing himself with a little sexual pleasure on the way. There's no hard evidence to support all that, I agree. But perhaps you could see the people again who met VL on the morning of her disappearance and try to see if we can't find a trace of Kashguri somewhere close to her. Sometimes it's easier to locate two people rather than one.'

'Chief,' said Attali, a few kilometres farther on, 'Mantes is on the way to Rouen.'

'That's certainly true.'

'In the Seine, in a barge, the same sort of thing.'

'But she didn't die from a bullet through the heart.'

4 p.m. Crime Squad Headquarters

The Superintendent in charge of the case heard the report by his
two inspectors without a word. Then he passed over to them a
despatch from Agence France Presse. They read it in silence and
then gave it to Romero.

Paris, 27 March. 3.30 p.m.

*Agence France Presse has just received the following communiqué,
delivered by hand to their Paris office:*

*A Turkish diplomat has just been shot in the centre of Paris, in
exactly the same way as another diplomat in Rome. We shall
avenge with arms the extermination of our people, until the
Turkish government acknowledges its crimes.*

Commando of the Armenian Avengers

'Now,' the Superintendent went on, 'we shall quietly explore the
Armenian trail.'

Romero was surprised.

'Do you think the communiqué is genuine?'

'Perhaps it isn't. But the embassy have locked us out, that's obvious. This business involves only Turks who are all members of
the embassy staff. And we're not being asked to clean things up for
them.'

8 p.m. Rue des Pyrenées

Romero was hovering about in the apartment that his cousin had
lent him. A very small three-room place behind Père Lachaise. Lace
covers over the television set, lace mats on the tables ... He had a
date with Yildiz. A last look round, everything was ready, the aperitifs, the dinner ... The bell rang, he opened the door. Yildiz, her
hair held back simply with a slide. A plain cotton dress, with long
sleeves, turquoise blue. White sandals. Once again he felt a stab in
the stomach. He kissed her hand. She stopped in the hall. Nervous.

'Where is your cousin? She'd told me...' A pause.

'Do you really think I would make a crude pass at you?' Sudden recollection of VL at the foot of a dark staircase ... Soon gone. Be careful, a difficult evening to manage, no interference from the outside. 'You've hurt me.'

'No, of course I don't think that.'

She still hesitated, put down her handbag, went into the sitting-room and sat down on the sofa.

'Well then?'

'First, what will you drink?'

'Vodka with orange.'

Romero took a whisky, sat down in an armchair on the other side of the table, smiled at her. She drank a mouthful, still looking anxious.

'What do you want, Romeo?'

'To talk to you in peace. Things have been happening ... And I think I may be under surveillance by the embassy. So, no public places. I don't want to compromise you.'

'Answer me honestly. Am I, in some way or another, responsible for Sener's death?' She looked anguished.

'Certainly not.'

'I should have told the ambassador about our conversation.'

'Definitely not.'

'Did you kill him?'

'What makes you think that?'

'You were in the Champs-Elysées.'

'I was following him.'

'Yes.' She was not convinced.

It was the right moment. Don't play the scene wrong.

'I'll tell you what I think about Sener's murder. I certainly owe you that. First, I'm not a member of the Fraud Squad. I belong to an anti-drug unit...'

Yildiz, her eyes lowered, finished her drink. He refilled her glass.

'We've been working for nearly three months in the Paris area. And we've found practically nothing, apart from a few small dealers. But on the way we've come across the networks. I won't mention prostitution. And in the ready-to-wear business, in the Sentier.' At this point, described Berican, Paulette and Sener in detail. A brilliant account. Yildiz laughed, she was moved. 'That's where you come in, Yildiz, and you helped me to follow Sener.'

'You still haven't explained to me who killed him, and why.'

'I'm not at all sure. But we think the Berican workroom isn't an isolated case. There's probably a much wider network in which Sener was the kingpin. His associates liquidated him before we could interview him.'

'All over selling a few clothes?'

'But it all adds up to a lot of money.' Yildiz looked sceptical.

'And I need you for something else.'

'Why?' She was on her guard.

'The embassy is concealing all the leads, to prevent a possible scandal. But two people know a lot about it, and they are Dogan Carim and Tahar Bodrum, who were with Sener in the Champs-Elysées. We think they were on their way to a business appointment linked to the dealing in the Sentier. We interviewed them but got nowhere.'

'They're attached to the embassy.'

'We suspected it. And that's why I need you. Who are those two men? Where were they living until yesterday? Who are their friends and acquaintances? Only you can supply me with a starting point from where I can go forward. Without you I'm stuck, I've come to a halt.'

'I feel remorse, Romeo. I feel I acted wrongly. And it came to a bad end.'

'I beg you to believe me, you didn't act wrongly. Sener was always on the fiddle, all for money, and he was liquidated by his own buddies. Yildiz, help me.'

Silence. Yildiz stared fixedly at her glass and twiddled it round in her fingers.

'I'll do what I can, Romeo. Tomorrow.'

Romero stood up. Went towards the kitchen. Came back with a bouquet of red roses, knelt at Yildiz' feet and placed the bouquet on her knees.

'Yildiz, will you marry me?'

She was astonished.

*

When the cousin came back at midnight, as arranged, she found all the lights on, the dinner untouched in the kitchen. Romero and Yildiz, fast asleep, in her bed. The auburn hair spread out over the pillows and Romero buried beneath it.

8 a.m. Passage du Désir

Daquin was making coffee.

'Well, Romero, where have you got to?'

'Nothing very positive. The embassy's blocking everything to do with our investigation, and they're not bothering to be discreet about it. Because of that the Crime Squad drops it and pretends to believe in the attack by the Armenians. My contact at the embassy will bring me nothing.' He paused. Bright image of Yildiz' breasts, pale ringed nipples and endless freckles. 'I think she's been playing a double game from the start. She gave me a few clues while the ambassador was hoping we were going to get rid of Sener quietly for him. Now the scandal threatens to be too big and so it's blackout.'

'And you didn't take any risks with her?'

'No, none.' A moment's hesitation. 'Still, that depends on what you call risk. I've asked her to marry me.' Daquin waited for the follow-up. 'And if she accepts, I'll go through with it.'

'When it's all over, will you explain it to me?'

'When it's all over, I'll introduce her to you. To come back to what I'm doing, I think the only way to go further is with Paulette or Martens.'

'Paulette has committed suicide. She hanged herself at her home yesterday afternoon. Thomas wasn't there and didn't come back all night. He found her this morning when he returned.'

Once again Romero had to take in bad news. Why was this story so moving? Daquin went on: 'There remains Martens. You can go and interrogate him if you're sure he's not in the network. Otherwise it's too dangerous.'

'In my opinion he's not. Moreira doesn't know him directly, his clients are very varied. He has his own business. Sener was the only member of the network whom he knew.'

'Well, let's play it like that. Your two acolytes in Drugs, Marinoni and Rimbot, will do the interview, which the three of you will prepare together. Try to sort it by the end of the day.'

Daquin took Lavorel with him for a second search at Anna Beric's place. They entered the apartment, Daquin went straight to the bedroom and opened one of the cupboards. The wickerwork trunk was still there, in the same place. Relief or disappointment?

'Take a good look at that trunk, Lavorel. It's the only thing I came here to see. Have you taken it in? The wickerwork, the corners, the clasp, the dimensions?'

*

Return in silence to passage du Désir. Daquin and Lavorel went straight down to the basement where a few objects involved in current investigations were kept.

'There's the trunk in which VL's body was found.'

'It's the same as the one we've just seen at Anna Beric's place. No possible doubt about it.'

'When I saw it yesterday I thought it was Anna's. It's not hers, but it's identical with it. We're going to have a great many subjects of conversation with that lady.'

10 a.m. Rue des Jeûneurs

Attali went to Julie La Tour's, the manufacturer where Virginie Lamouroux had been working on the morning of Friday 14 March and approached the boss.

'I'm extremely sorry to disturb you again but yesterday we found the body of Virginie Lamouroux. She was killed on 14 March in the afternoon. As far as we know you were the last people to see her alive. So all the details are important, you understand?'

'Certainly. How was she killed?'

'She was whipped to death.'

'No!!! Some sadist?'

'No doubt.'

The manager called out to everyone: 'We're closing for half an hour, everyone in my office!'

The accountant, the secretary, two salesgirls, the cutter, the retoucher, the accessorist and the manager were all there.

Attali repeated the information for everybody. A weighty silence. Then the manager made an announcement: 'I'll try to describe that Friday morning. If anyone remembers the slightest detail, then tell us. Virginie arrived at 10 o'clock. She was always on time. She went up to the showroom with the retoucher. The models were already up there. I went up in my turn, I told her in which order to present the models and then I came down again.'

Attali to the retoucher: 'Did she say anything to you?'

'I think we exchanged a few words about the models, the ones she liked, the ones she didn't like. That was all.'

'At 10.30 the clients arrived, they were Japanese.'

'Did Virginie know them?'

'No, apparently not. The presentation began. Virginie was good, as usual. She wasn't a very great mannequin, but in private presentations like this one she was excellent, for she was very ... how shall I put it? ... she made people want to touch things and take them away.'

Attali remembered Romero raping her at the foot of a staircase, while he ... 'I understand very well what you mean.'

'By 11.30 or thereabouts she had presented everything. The Japanese asked to see several models a second time. Towards noon she began to be slightly impatient. She told me she had a lunch appointment at half-past twelve. And she always hated being late.'

'"For lunch", are you sure?'

'Yes, that's what I remember. At about the same time the Japanese had seen enough. Virginie changed at high speed and went down to the shop. I stayed upstairs with the Japanese.'

The secretary continued the story: 'She came downstairs saying "I'm going to be late". I suggested calling a taxi for her. She replied "It'll be quicker for me to walk". I looked at my watch. It was 12.20, more or less.'

The cutter added: 'I saw her going out through the door. She was walking quickly in the Opéra direction.'

11 a.m. Le Capucin café, La Chapelle Metro

Daquin went towards a small table at the back of the café. A big guy stood up to greet him. The thirty-year-old man looked like a fighter, he was squarely built, sturdy with close-cropped hair. They had met on rugby pitches. Beside him on the banquette was a whole collection of photographic equipment.

'Another cup of coffee, please,' he asked the owner.

'Well, what's it about this time, mystery man?'

'I'm going to take you onto the balcony of an empty flat in a block near here. I'll manage to get you in somehow, and you'll manage not to be seen. From there you have the unrestricted view of a bed on the floor below, where there should be a leg-show between 12 and 1 o'clock. You will take a few photographs for me, suggestive ones, as the phrase goes...'

'That you'll use to blackmail the protagonists.'

'No way. At the most I'll use them to apply pressure in the cause of truth and justice.'

'And in exchange?'

'I'll see you're informed when we arrest the biggest network of drug traffickers ever dismantled to date. It'll be exclusive to you.'

'Have you got confidence in yourself?'

'As far as I can have in this kind of business. That's to say not much.'

'I'm on. Let's go. Pay for my coffee, *commissaire*.'

1 p.m. *Passage du Désir*

Daquin listened, Attali talked: 'VL had a lunch date on Friday 14 March at 12.30. I don't know where, I don't know who with. But it was in an area a quarter of an hour's walk away from rue des Jeûneurs, going towards the Opéra. I've got one possibility: I'll get a map of the district, I'll mark off the area I can reach in twenty minutes or so walking time from the Julie La Tour boutique, and I'll go into all the restaurants in that area with photos of VL and Kashguri. It's dangerous. Because, even if VL had lunched somewhere in the district, there's not much chance that anyone would remember her. But I can't think of anything else.'

'Agreed. In particular you must target the chic expensive restaurants. And you must find some backup. But for that...'

*

A jubilant Romero came back.

'Martens is devastated by Sener's murder. He hadn't heard about it. Marinoni had told him that his name and address had been found in Sener's diary and that they'd spent the last weekend together. He confirmed it. He knows the two Turkish intellectuals.

About three months ago he went to the races at Enghien with Sener. They met the two in question at the racecourse, spent the afternoon with them and since they were dead drunk by the end of it they drove them back to Enghien, to the door of a luxury villa in a location which Martens has described in fairly precise detail. It's the only trail left to us for my contact at the embassy, as I'd foreseen, brought me nothing. Shall we continue further in that direction?'

'Certainly.'

*

Telephone. The duty man at the entrance.

'A Monsieur Alain to see you, *commissaire*.'

'Yes, I'm expecting him, send him up.'

Alain entered in a rush and threw a large brown envelope onto the desk.

'You'll have a good laugh. Good luck, and don't forget the reward, as you promised.'

He left immediately.

Daquin opened the envelope. Three large photos. Not works of art, but clear enough. In the first one Meillant, standing, seen in profile, perfectly recognizable, was taking part in fellatio with a big peroxide blonde who was kneeling in front of him, her face buried between her legs. Next photo: the big blonde, with her hair in her eyes and her breasts thrust forward, was sitting astride Meillant who was lying on his back. The identification in this one was less obvious. In the last photo the woman was kneeling while Meillant was fucking her from behind. She was clutching the foot of the bed and her features were very distinct, she was facing the camera. All that within an hour, the guy was in good form. I couldn't have imagined anything better.

The image of Soleiman flashed before his eyes, his shattered body beneath the duvet. A stab of desire. I'm going home.

9 a.m. Enghien-les-Bains

Not very difficult to find the villa. Martens had said: 'They had come to the racecourse on foot, as neighbours. To get them back home we drove about one or two kilometres. They live in a house beside the lake, in a cul-de-sac that runs alongside a big lycée built of brick.'

Romero and Marinoni easily found the lycée on a map and went straight there. They entered the cul-de-sac, Martens had said: 'A very big house, well hidden, a black gate, very high, with gilding, very flashy.' The house was there at the corner of avenue Regina and avenue Château-Léon, pompous names for two deserted culs-de-sac. Closely protected in fact. Railings covered with ivy, more than two metres high, and above it, carefully pruned chestnut trees. It was just possible to make out a large garden and a large house, millstones, brick and cement, tasteless. The shutters were open, the house seemed to be inhabited, but that was all that could be said. Access to the lake was also closed off by railings. No shops or concierges nearby. Impossible too to stay there too long without attracting attention. Go round the lake to see if the house was visible from the opposite bank.

A few hundred metres away the estate agents Gay, announcing that they specialized in high-class property. Let's give them a try.

The two inspectors went in and introduced themselves to a charming young blonde woman, wearing a grey suit, serious efficiency. The villa at the corner of the avenue Regina and the avenue Château-Léon? The villa Léon. Yes indeed, she knew it very well. The Gay Agency manage it. It had been let for two years to Monsieur Oumourzarov, a Turkish businessman. Very high rent, paid without difficulty. The villa was very handsome, the entire raised ground floor was given over to reception-rooms, drawing-rooms, a dining-room, a smoking-room. On the first and second floors, ten or so bedrooms, five bathrooms. View over the lake...

'What do you know about Monsieur Oumourzarov?'

'Well ... not very much.' She searched through her files and took out the one dealing with the villa Léon. 'On his form he had described himself as director of a commercial firm. Payslips from the Turkimport company, registered office in Istanbul. And the Parillaud Bank had guaranteed his credit-worthiness. Would you like the address of Turkimport?'

'Certainly.'

She wrote it out on one of the agency cards and held it out to them.

'What's he like physically?'

'About forty, medium height, slim, Brown hair, fairly average in fact. Typical businessman of today.'

The two inspectors left.

'We'll have a drink by the lake, then back to passage du Désir. I don't think we've wasted our time.'

11 a.m. In Paris

Attali and Rimbot had decided to work systematically through the entire area marked out the day before as the one where Virginie Lamouroux probably had a lunch date. Daquin had said 'the smart expensive restaurants'. But what was a really smart and expensive restaurant like? Not always easy to identify. Better to spread the net a little too wide rather than too narrow. In each restaurant the inspectors showed first the photo of Virginie, then that of Kashguri, then the two together. Do you know either of them? You've never seen either of them? Nor both of them together? Which ones of you were there on Friday 14 March at lunchtime? These two faces don't mean anything to you?

It was difficult on Saturday, in this area. Most of the restaurants were closed. They had to note carefully those that had been visited and those they would have to come back to. Mark on the map which streets had been explored. And continue to believe in what they were doing.

6 p.m. Passage du Désir

The atmosphere in Daquin's office was that of a council of war. Everyone was there, Romero, Marinoni, Rimbot, Attali and Lavorel, surrounding the chief.

Lavorel had worked well. In less than six hours, and on a Saturday, he had produced a solid report on the Turkimport company: 'Turkimport is a very big Turkish import-export company, the second largest in this sector, specializing in the import of machine tools and agricultural machinery and in the export of processed agricultural products. A limited company, quoted on the Bourse. The chairman is a former general, now retired. The Parillaud Bank supplies part of their capital through its subsidiary branch in Turkey. This latter also has agreements with the Bank of Cyprus and the East in a number of very big operations in Turkey and the Lebanon.'

Silence, Lavorel considered his achievement, it was a success.

'The French office was opened two years ago. It has been run by Oumourzarov from the start. The registered office is at La Défense, in the Atlantic Tower. We have the list of the principal customers, import and export. Some of them are linked to the Parillaud Bank. It will be very difficult for us to find out more. About the prices charged, for example. Turkimport is considered at high levels as a support for the French presence in the Near East.'

'Can we establish a link with Kutluer?'

'Not at the moment. And it's not at all certain that such a link exists. Kutluer and Moreira are family concerns, small-time operators in one sense. With Turkimport we're entering the world of large-scale international trade and high finance. A change of scale.'

'Where does the merchandise come in?'

'Partly through Roissy, partly through Marseilles.'

'Romero and Marinoni, tomorrow you'll go to the customs at Roissy. Get out of them all you can. I shan't tell the magistrate or my chief before Monday. In fact I'll try to do it as late as possible. We've been obstructed over the murder of the Thai girl. Let's see how far we can get this time.'

10 a.m. Villa des Artistes

Daquin was still in bed. Barely awake. Sounds in the kitchen. Soleiman was making the breakfast. A flood of light through the glass panel in the roof. Soleiman brought the tray up. Naked. Great blue and green bruises on his body. His face still badly marked. He put the tray down on the bed.

'Come and say good morning to me, my boy.'

*

Both down on their knees, by the low table in the downstairs room. A large map of the Paris area. Photographs. Soleiman spoke, Daquin wrote. For each name, a photo and a record card: address, known activities, descriptions of all habits or individual characteristics that it had been possible to discover, possible links with the Association of Lighting Technicians or the shops in Faubourg Saint-Martin. For each card, a cross on the map. Soleiman had added a few names to the list, without photographs. Thirty or so people in all. Sometimes Daquin asked questions. It took three hours to complete everything.

'Now, let's tackle Operation Meillant.'

Daquin got up, went to the bookcase and produced a brown envelope from between two big volumes. He took out the photos of Meillant making love with the wife of Jencovitch, the boss of the workshop at the Bouffes du Nord, and put them down on the table.

'Not bad, quite a feat.'

'Do you also have a laugh when you show photos of me to your buddies?'

Daquin, suddenly serious, sat down on the sofa.

'What I'm suggesting to you is a big risk for me. If you continue to persist with your victim mentality, you're going to feel sorry about the fate of the guy you're in process of destroying, because you'll be thinking of yourself, and you'll feel sorry about your own fate. And inevitably you'll do stupid things. If you're incapable of thinking of yourself as anything but a victim you might as well tell me now, Sol, and I'll stop bothering.'

Subdued activity in the commercial transactions section.

Romero and Marinoni introduced themselves: working on the drugs traffic between Turkey and Iran. Had come to have a chat with specialists, on the spot, in a totally unofficial way. In your opinion is it possible or not that drugs are getting through on a regular basis thanks to big companies officially carrying out large-scale international trade?

Some activity in the office. Men coming in, others going out. The customs officers offered coffee. The discussion became general.

'You know, we only work efficiently through denunciation. Everything happens higher up along the line. When the companies are well known, and the flow of goods is regular, only a minute part of the delivery is checked.'

'And can the companies know in advance which part?'

Laughter.

'Yes and no, that depends. And then we have orders to speed up the transactions in the case of some French companies or those very close to them. And besides, we may receive orders that work the other way, when we're told to be really meticulous with awkward foreign companies in order to make them lose a few days, or even a few months, which has happened.'

It was aperitif time. The customs office was fully manned. The name of Turkimport cropped up in conversation. A man of about forty, silent so far, was following their enquiries. He still didn't say anything, but a little later he announced that he was going off-duty at 1 o'clock. The two inspectors came across him again, as though by accident, in the car-park. He addressed them first: 'Where can we go for some peace and quiet?'

'You're the one who knows the area.'

'There's nothing here. Follow me, I'll take you to the place where I live.'

Ezanville. A few kilometres from the airport. Once a little Ile-de-France village, now lost among bungalows and dormitory-style estates. A café crammed with people in a deserted street. They sat down at a little table right at the back. The atmosphere was suffocating. The customs officer introduced himself: 'I'm Pascal Dumont. Why are you interested in Turkimport?'

Romero hardly knew what to say.

'We're not only interested in Turkimport. It's just one of the names.'

'Stop. I'm not stupid. You've given up a whole Sunday morning just to pick up something about Turkimport. Now that you've got something, take it further. I started work very early this morning, I want to get back home as soon as possible.'

'Why do you want to talk to cops about Turkimport, outside duty hours?'

Smile. 'Suspicious, it's normal. But you'll have to take risks.' He was silent for a moment. 'I'm over forty, I have a family, I lead a conventional life. It's just that sometimes I get fed up with being told to be quick, not to try too hard. Customs officers are treated like half-wits. My brother and one of his friends were working on the flight of French capital to Switzerland. With not very orthodox methods, no doubt, but with the green light from their superiors. As long as they discovered accounts held by ordinary French people, all was well, they were heroes. Two weeks ago they brought back a print-out which included the names of members of the government. Three days later they fell into a trap set by the Swiss. They've been in prison over there in Basle, for over a week, and everyone's been letting them down. Not even a word in the papers. There's a rumour that they've been "exchanged" in return for information about bent coppers who have bank accounts in Switzerland. I'm helping you about Turkimport because it's both personal vendetta and professional revenge.'

A pause. Romero and Marinoni didn't react. Dumont went on: 'I can tell you how the Turkimport business is carried out, at least for the export side. The papers are always in order. Deliveries every week, twenty or so packing-cases. We always check the first one, not the others. For the last two years I've been waiting to know what's inside them.'

'Why not open them?'

'Because we have orders. Turkimport is protected.'

'Who by?'

'I don't know exactly. It comes from government departments, probably going through our secret services. Are you really looking for drugs?'

'Let's say we are.'

'I'd be tempted to imagine something else. Illegal transfers of technology, things of that sort. In view of the type of protection.'

'How are the Turkimport operations carried out?'

'Every Monday morning twenty cases arrive. Customs inspection. Then they go to the transit area and despatch takes place over a week, depending on the space available in the planes leaving for Istanbul. Turkimport doesn't have its own airlines. Let's get some fresh air out on the pavement.'

They stood by the cars.

'We'll make a date for tomorrow evening. About 10 o'clock. I'll take you into the transit zone warehouse area, I'll manage to leave you alone somewhere and I'll come back for you about 2 o'clock in the morning. OK with you?'

'OK with us.'

6 p.m. At the Bouffes du Nord

At 6 p.m. precisely Soleiman, along with two Turkish friends from the Committee, entered the building where Jencovitch had his workroom. The Turkish workers were waiting for them upstairs. Three minutes after Soleiman, Romero, in the uniform of a Telecom worker, came through the door in his turn and went to a dark corner under the main staircase where there was a tangled mass of cables, quite different from the normal security systems in modern blocks. He'd examined them in advance with an expert. He cut the cable which he'd marked with red. From that moment the Jencovitch workroom no longer had a telephone.

Three floors up, Soleiman had just come in. Daquin had warned him: 'This is the most delicate part of the operation. Don't let your arrival go wrong.' The Turks stood up.

'I don't mean any harm to anyone. But I've got the right to have a man-to-man discussion with that bastard who gets workers roughed up by the cops.'

Stake everything on surprise and speed. The Turks went round the tables and collected anything lying about that could be used as weapons, such as scissors or craft knives.

'All right then, everyone leave, it's time.'

Glances at the boss, who was frozen with astonishment. The Africans began the walkout, the Yugoslavs followed, with some encouragement from the Turks. Romero heard them coming down the stairs above his head, looked at his watch and began to time the operation. Daquin had said ten minutes.

Upstairs there was no one left, only Soleiman and the boss, facing each other. The latter began to recover.

'I'll call the police.'

'Try, your phone's cut off.'

The boss rushed over and picked up the receiver: no dialling tone. He went towards the door.

'No point, the Turks have locked it and you haven't got your keys any more.'

The boss searched his pockets: no keys.

'You see, stop worrying and look at these photos.'

And Soleiman put down on a table three large photos and moved one step away.

The boss looked. His wife, his wife totally naked, making love with Meillant. On his own bed. He was livid.

'Haven't you ever seen them at it? He's quite gifted, the Superintendent, even if he looks a quiet fatherly type. I'd be surprised if you did all that with your wife.'

Daquin had said: 'Destroy him utterly before you come to blows, it's safer.'

The boss, mad with panic and anger, came towards Soleiman.

'What do you want of me, then? What do you want of me?'

This was the moment. Soleiman wasn't a fighter. But Daquin had rehearsed him: 'When he comes close to you, threaten him in the neck, as though you were going to catch hold of him and strangle him. Knock him down flat with a kick in the crotch. Knock him down with a single blow.' The man collapsed, screaming, clutching his crotch. Incredibly easy. Anger and bitterness were satisfied. As the man lay on the floor Soleiman kicked him in the ribs, although he hardly knew why. He caught hold of his shirt and dragged him over to the wall, propped him up, held him with his left hand and struck him hard, three times, with his right. A trace of blood on his hand.

At the bottom of the stairs Romero had reconnected the telephone and removed his Telecom worker's overall. He went out and sat in the unmarked police car which was parked on the other side of the crossroads, by the taxi rank. From there he watched the entrance to the building.

Jencovitch was ready now. He had difficulty in breathing, stabs of pain, blood in his mouth, the image of his wife before his eyes. He didn't understand anything that was happening to him, he was afraid of dying. Soleiman began to speak: 'You don't interest me, it's Meillant I want. You're going to tell me now what you've been paying Meillant, for how long and what he's been doing for you in exchange. If you refuse to talk I'll show the photos tomorrow morning to all your workers and in all the Yugoslav cafés. Your wife could always take up a career as a tart, but as for you, you could just pack your bags.'

'It's been going on for five years.' He spat, there was blood in his saliva, he kept his eyes closed. 'I pay a 1,000 francs a month. I get a warning in advance if there's to be a work inspection. And if a worker causes me trouble Meillant arrests him. After that the man behaves. Since I've been paying I've never had any trouble.'

Daquin had told Soleiman: 'Keep the pressure up all the time, don't allow him a single moment to recover. He mustn't stop being frightened.' Soleiman stood up, caught hold of a wooden chair and smashed it hard against the cutters' table. Then he took the firmest strut out of it and came up to the man on the floor.

'Do you realize I could break your limbs without any trouble? You're on your own. Your wife's been called in by the police. And she'll stay there as long as I'm here. There's nobody in the flat opposite. Do you understand what that means?' The boss looked at him. 'You'll pick up the telephone and call Meillant.'

'The telephone's not working.'

'It is now.' Soleiman put the instrument down beside the boss and took off the receiver with his foot. The dialling tone could be heard. Soleiman put the receiver back. 'You see. And Meillant is in his office. In fact he's waiting for your call. You've got to manage somehow, but you must get him to come here. As for me, I'll leave a tape recorder here and I'll go into the next room. I want to hear Meillant talking about the money he receives. I want to hear him say he's a bastard.'

'I can't do that.'

No time to finish his sentence. Soleiman caught hold of his left hand, placed it on a corner of the table and brought down the strut from the chair on it. The hand cracked, the boss screamed. No movement in the building. The man sweated and wept.

'I'll call. Give me the phone.'

Soleiman handed him the instrument. Jencovitch got Meillant at once. Soleiman didn't take his eyes off him.

'I've been beaten up ... The militants from the Committee... Photos, and they know things ... I'm alone, I'm afraid, come, I can't move ... My wife's being questioned by the police about accounting problems ... Yes, please, quickly...'

*

At the station Meillant hung up, looking preoccupied. Opposite him sat Lavorel, who had come to ask his advice about how to stop the circulation of black money between manufacturers and workrooms.

'I can't stay, sorry, a very urgent call.'

'Not to worry, I understand very well, we'll meet again. Nothing urgent.'

Lavorel went back to passage du Désir to wait for Daquin.

*

Jencovitch had hung up.

'That's a good boy.'

With his finger Soleiman wiped the tears away from the man's face as he lay on the floor. Daquin had told him: 'Keep him occupied until Meillant comes. It'll take a long time. He mustn't be allowed to recover.'

'Tell me what you're going to say to Meillant when he arrives?'

The boss, who was sweating, didn't reply. Soleiman caught hold of his injured hand and squeezed it. Another yell.

'What are you going to say to him?'

'That I pay him, he must protect me.'

'What do I want to hear?'

'Yes, he's had money, yes, he's going to protect me.'

Soleiman quickly concealed a miniature tape recorder inside a sewing-machine. 'If I get the tape I'll give you the photo and you'll never see me again. If something goes wrong the photos will go all round the Sentier and my buddies will come back and beat you on the back with iron bars. Can you still manage to understand that?'

The boss signalled that he could.

Soleiman bent over him. A clear memory of an icy day in Istanbul during the winter of '78–'79, a mob of macho young men attacking gays and he was pushed along the ground against a wall. The assailant who was kicking him bent over, caught hold of him by his balls and yelled: 'Hey, he's still got some.' And then nothing, a black hole.

Soleiman smiled and put his hand between the boss's legs. A look of desperation. Don't be frightened, you're not going to die, not just yet. In a rapid movement his hand tightened over one of the balls, and the boss fainted.

Soleiman stood up again, went to the workroom door, took the bunch of keys out of the boss's jacket, unlocked the door, replaced the keys in the pocket and waited on the landing.

From the other side of the crossroads Romero saw Meillant enter the building. Amazing. The crazy plan seemed to be working.

Looking at his watch, he let two minutes go by, then walked calmly towards the building, went in and waited on the landing.

Soleiman heard Meillant coming up. He closed the door again, crossed the room and on the way stroked the boss's hair: he was still unconscious. 'Concentrate, it's the right moment now.' And he went into the next room. Daquin was there, leaning against a table. Smiled at him. They went to the back of the apartment, opened the service door, locked it again and waited on the landing. Be wary of Meillant, he's an old hand.

Meillant came in and went straight to Jencovitch, lying unconscious against the wall, the telephone on the floor beside him. He looked him over: some pink froth at the corner of his mouth, his left hand out of shape, a swelling between his legs, the guy was clearly in a bad way. Meillant checked that he wasn't dead and went rapidly round the apartment: one can never be too careful. Nobody there and the service door locked. Came back to Jencovitch who was beginning to come round. Meillant crouched down beside him.

'What's happened to you?' Jencovitch cast a terrified look round. 'We're alone, you can talk.'

'The guy from the other day, the one you threw down the stairs. He came back, with some of his buddies, after the workroom had closed.' He had difficulty in getting his breath back. 'They beat me up.' Meillant waited for the rest. 'They've got photos of you, with my wife, in my bed.' A series of little sobs.

'What do they want to do with them?'

'They want to show them all round the district if I don't pay. *Commissaire*, if those photos are circulated, I'm a dead man.' Meillant thought he wouldn't be too lively, either. '*Commissaire*, I've paid you 1,000 francs every month for five years.' Jencovitch clutched Meillant's jacket with one hand. 'You know that, don't you? You haven't suddenly forgotten?'

'Yes, I know that.'

'You're not going to let me down now?'

'Let go of me and calm down. No, I'm not going to let you down. When do you have to pay?'

'Tomorrow morning, here, at 7 o'clock.'

'And how much?'

'30,000 francs.'

'Not too greedy, that means they intend to come back. Tomorrow morning I'll be there with a few men. We'll arrest the others, get the photos back by force and we'll have them deported from France quickly. It won't be said that anyone can get away with blackmailing the people I protect and not be punished for it. Now, I'll help you get home and your wife will look after you when she comes back.'

There was a sound in the next room. Meillant raised his head and saw Daquin standing I the doorway. He stood up, without a word. Daquin called Romero, who came in.

'Pick up this guy, get him as far as the local station and record his statement. After that, off to the hospital.'

Romero led Jencovitch away while Daquin took the tape recorder out of the sewing-machine and slipped it into his pocket. Meillant sat down on the corner of the table.

'I was afraid of some underhand blow but I didn't think it would come from you. What do you want?'

'Don't you want to know first what cards I'm holding?' Meillant was silent. 'Nothing very serious in one sense, but they all add up to something that will go down very badly just when the legalization of clandestine Turkish workers is being negotiated.'

Daquin put down on the table beside Meillant a photocopy of the accounts page taken from Martens and the photos of Meillant with Madame Jencovitch.

'You've been regularly selling false papers, and some genuine ones as well, to the illegal workers in the Sentier. You make some workroom bosses pay for your protection. You're very close to Thomas and his late wife, who don't have a good press in the police force at the moment. I won't mention how a member of the team negotiating with the ministry was beaten up last Wednesday, right here. As for the activities of your mistress, Anna Beric ...' Meillant reacted to that, 'she's a key person in the system of false invoices and black money that the Sentier lives on today. Without going back to the murder of her pimp. And she's the woman in your life. It's a rather heavy casebook, don't you think?'

'That's enough, Daquin. What do you want?'

'Two things. Your resignation. And the return of Anna Beric.'

A long pause for reflection.

'Why my resignation?'

'To protect those behind me.' What would he have said if I'd replied: To please my lover?

Another silence.

'And what will you give me in exchange?'

'An honourable reputation, a happy and ... prosperous retirement. I'll keep all I know to myself.'

'What about Anna?'

'Anna will spend a few months in jail, a year at the very most, before rejoining you. I don't think that sort of thing will frighten her.' Meillant shot him a suspicious glance: does he know her? 'The Sentier's changing, Meillant. A lot. It's time to go.'

Meillant looked at his watch: 7 p.m. He picked up the telephone. The director of the urban police forces. He's left, but would you like his chief secretary? Very well, the chief secretary. Meillant speaking ... He had just seen his cardiologist. Serious health problems. Very upset by the Thomas incident. Requests early retirement and would like to take some leave while waiting for the formalities to be worked out. Call tomorrow at the director's office? Certainly, he'd be there.

'As for Anna, it's for her to decide. I'll give you her reply in an hour's time at your office.'

And Meillant left. Daquin marvelled.

*

Soleiman left the Jencovitch workroom by the back staircase while Daquin was finishing off Meillant. He felt deeply uneasy. Mustn't think about it, that was important. Tomorrow, we'll see. Impossible to join Daquin that evening. He went down the rue du Faubourg-Saint-Denis as far as the Boulevards. Spend the night with a girl, any girl.

10 p.m. Roissy

The warehouses were piled up with merchandise, but deserted. Dim bluish light. Romero and Marinoni, wearing packers' overalls, both with badges perfectly in order, carrying a large toolbox. Dumont had accompanied them as far as the Turkimport packing-cases. 'The security people do a round every hour. They've just done the last one. Check your watches. You've got to stop working before you hear them coming and hide right here, between these four cases. They won't have their dogs tonight. Be brave. Good luck!'

It wasn't difficult to open the cases, nor to burrow through the first layer of merchandise. It would be much more difficult to go further down. And closing them was tricky. It was no good hammering gently, the noise seemed deafening. Three cases during the first hour. The hiding-place. Romero and Marinoni were sweating. And if Dumont ... The round went through. Work began again. The fourth case. The cover came off. The inner packing pushed aside. A range of firing-pins for sub-machine-guns, apparently.

Marinoni hugged Romero.

'Shall we look further down?'

'Not worth it. And no more cases. That's enough.'

Closed it again. Marked it discreetly, collect all the tools and put them away. Wait in the hiding-place. Dumont would come at 2 a.m. Romero fell asleep.

9 a.m. At the Gymnase

Soleiman emerged slowly from sleep. The girl had gone. Good. She'd left a note on the floor beside the bed: 'Coffee on the stove to be reheated. Pull the door to behind you when you leave. See you again soon?'

He got up. A kind of hangover. Converted maid's bedroom, rue du Faubourg-Poissonnière, quite nice. Sunshine and light through the two little windows. He reheated the coffee and drank it, stretched out naked in a patch of sunlight. It felt good. Looked at the time. Nine o'clock, he had to leave. Don't think, let time pass. Got dressed, pulled the door to behind him. The Boulevards. A little further on, the Gymnase. Why not? A moment of warmth in the Turkish cocoon, that could help.

Soleiman pushed the café door open. All talking stopped. The Turks rose to their feet. Applause, whistling, cheerful shouts, slogans. Soleiman hesitated. News got round quickly in the Sentier. After the beating up he'd suffered a week before Soleiman had put Jencovitch in hospital and sacked the Superintendent of the 10th arrondissement. He was a hero. Everyone wanted to tap him on the shoulder, offer him a coffee or a raki. And belong to the Committee. Soleiman sat down. His head was swimming.

9 a.m. Passage du Désir

Romero was alone in the office with Daquin. Spares for weapons. Clandestine traffic. Protected at a high level.

'We've got into another splendid wasp's nest. Does your customs man know where the hardware ends up?'

'Nothing's very certain. Istanbul first. Then ... The stuff's pretty classic. Iran perhaps, one way of getting round the international blockade? We need a specialist to tell us more about these problems.'

Daquin made two coffees which they drank in silence.

'How can we organize that? In any case the arms traffic will elude us. There may be financial links with drugs, but they may be complicated to expose. On the other hand the link with Sener's murder is fairly direct. We'll have to pin down this man Oumourzarov. We'll see what can be got out of them. How do you see the next move?'

'Accidents can happen quickly. When the contents of a packing case spill out over the floor it's hard not to know what's inside it.'

'When can that happen?'

'Tomorrow if necessary, in the afternoon at the latest.'

The telephone rang.

'Good morning, *commissaire*, Lespinois here. How are you?'

'Very well, Monsieur Lespinois.'

'I'm with Lenglet and we're talking about the Middle East. I'm going there tonight. He tells me you're taking a close interest in the Iranian drug scene.'

'I am interested in it, yes. As for closely, that's another matter...'

'Things are changing out there. The Islamic Revolutionary Party is launching a great campaign against drugs and drug-takers. It's rather new in the cultural profile of that country. Under the Shah, you know, people aged over sixty had the right to their free supply of opium, distributed by the State. I think it's principally a means of liquidating those who run the traffic, mostly pro-Westerners. The Islamists will certainly take over the traffic again on their own account later. But it's certain that the current traffickers, and their contacts overseas, won't be there much longer. I thought this information might interest you, it's not in circulation yet.'

'Certainly, Monsieur Lespinois. And thank you for calling me. Best wishes to Lenglet, since he's with you, and *bon voyage*.'

He hung up.

'Congratulations, Romero. You've become a pawn in the struggle between the big international banks. Few people acquire that honour.' Romero didn't understand a word. 'The France-Mediterranean Bank is trying to destroy the position held by the Parillaud Bank in the Middle East, a position probably due to the alliance between the bank and the traffickers in drugs and arms. What we're doing can weaken Parillaud out there and France-Mediterranean will be very grateful to us. What can we do in all this? Let's go back to our own affairs. I'm sending a report today to my chief and to the investigating magistrate about the links between our two strong-arm guys from the embassy and Oumourzarov. I'm asking permission to use the letters rogatory available to me for carrying out a search at the company's headquarters and at Oumourzarov's house. I'll be turned down. But when the packing-case falls over we might just be able to stay on the case. By the way, when you go to supervise the falling packing-case take a press photographer with you. Here are the details of a friend of mine who helps me sometimes. The soul of discretion. Telephone him on my behalf.'

11 a.m. The Opéra district

Attali and Rimbot were starting their third day of enquiries at the restaurants. First restaurant, Le Petit Riche, rue Le Peletier. The waiters were about to finish laying the tables, the dining-room was still very dark. A waiter called the *maître d'hotel*, who did not invite them to sit down; his lack of goodwill was obvious. First photo, VL. Never seen her. Second photo, Kashguri. Attali did not possess Daquin's experience yet, but he could have sworn that the man was lying when he replied that he didn't know him.

'Who was on duty on Friday 14 March, at lunchtime?'

'I don't remember.'

Attali raised his voice, the waiters began to listen: 'Pay attention, if you take us for half-wits we might get angry and even accuse you of complicity. Let me remind you that we're investigating a murder. This girl was assassinated just after lunching with this man. Give me a list of all the waiters who were present that day.'

The *maître d'hotel* grumbled a bit, disappeared for a short time and came back with the required list. Attali took it and checked with the waiters present. Three of them had been there on March 14 at midday.

'I'll interview them one at a time. Where can I sit? That table will suit me very well.'

He had a table at the back of the room cleared.

'Inspector, you're going to disrupt my entire service.'

'No way. I'll have finished very quickly.'

It was the third waiter, a certain Judicelli, who formally identified Virginie Lamouroux.

'It was I who served them. They were at that table.' He indicated one of the tables at the back, not far from where they were at the moment. 'They looked like a normal couple. I wouldn't have noticed them if the woman hadn't spilt a glass of wine over the man's trousers. I don't know how it happened, I didn't see it. I myself had just knocked over a dish in the kitchen.' He glanced at the *maître d'hotel*, not to worry, he was a long way off. 'I remember thinking: "But it's Friday 14 and not Friday 13." I rushed over to try and repair the damage. What struck me was the man's attitude. He was very good-mannered, so he said nothing, but he was overtaken by a kind of suppressed fury, it was remarkable. He was trembling. It seemed a bit over the top for a wine stain on a pair of trousers. Do you think that's why he killed her?'

6 p.m. Villa des Artistes

Daquin had just come out of the shower, he had almost finished shaving in front of the wash-basin mirror. Soleiman appeared at the bathroom door. A sideways glance from Daquin. Soleiman looked relaxed, almost happy, he'd never seen him like that before.

'I didn't hear you come in. You look pleased with life this evening...'

'Daquin, if you knew ...' Soleiman described his triumph at the Gymnase that morning. 'And it's been like that all day. I went round the workrooms. In the street people said good-morning to me, walked along with me, bought me coffees...' He had begun to undress.

'Only coffees?'

A smile from Soleiman. 'Not only coffees, today. Quite a lot of rakis too. In the workrooms they shouted and applauded ... Last night I didn't know what to think. It was the first time I'd beaten up a guy. It made me feel sick, I was disgusted, and I hated you.'

He climbed into the bath and turned on the shower.

Daquin went to the kitchen for some coffee and drank it in the bathroom, leaning against the wash-basin, watching Soleiman as he stood still under the stream of water which he'd turned on full. He's shot two men but hitting a man twice while he was down on the floor made him feel sick ... So what?

'Come out, Sol.'

Daquin took him in his arms, holding the damp body, leaning it against the washbasin. The two men were facing the mirror. They were both the same height, but Daquin was much heavier. He put his hand in Soleiman's hair and pulled his head up.

225

'Look at yourself, Sol, while I fuck you.'

*

Soleiman was already half-asleep under the duvet, while Daquin dressed. Collarless shirt, dark red, grey Hollington suit in a wool and cotton mixture. A glance at the mirror. OK. He leant over the bed, 'I shan't be back tonight.'

Kissed him on the neck. Today he's submissive. When will rebellion set in?

9 p.m. Roissy

The plane from Marrakesh via Casablanca, with Anna Beric on board, landed on time at 3 minutes past 8. Daquin was waiting for her at the airport police window. The passengers arrived in groups. Daquin recognized her. Tall and slim, with shoulder-length hair. She was wearing a beige safari jacket and a matching linen skirt. A brown shirt blouse, apparently silk, brown leather sandals, and carrying a matching handbag.

'Madame Beric.'

She turned towards him. Deep blue eyes, sunburnt skin, no make-up. He went up to her, kissed her hand and introduced himself.

'I'm Superintendent Daquin.' A faint smile, she was surprised. 'Have you any luggage?'

'Yes, one suitcase.'

'I'll come with you.'

He took her case from her. They went through the airport police offices and walked in silence towards the unmarked car that was parked just in front of the entrance. Daquin put the suitcase in the boot, opened the door for her, sat down at the wheel and drove off.

'Where are you taking me, *commissaire*?'

'To have dinner first of all. I've booked a table at the Pouilly Reuilly, a very good bistro in Pré-Saint-Gervais. You must have missed French cooking during that long month.' Anna Beric looked at him without a word. 'Afterwards I'll take you home. We have an appointment tomorrow morning at 8 o'clock with Inspector Lavorel who's dealing with your case in more detail.'

'Am I under arrest or not?'

'Yes, you are. Would you prefer me to take you to the local police station now?'

No reply. She looked at Daquin who was driving along calmly. Not more than 80 kilometres an hour in the outskirts of Paris. Meillant had told me he was 'an out-and-out homo'. And I find a handsome man, a seducer.

'I don't understand. You blackmail Meillant to make me come back and stick me in prison. I arrive and you try to pick me up ... for you really are trying to pick me up, aren't you?'

'I'm not trying to pick you up, I'm behaving like a man in love.'

'You're in love with me?'

'Yes.'

'I've a right to a few explanations.'

'When I went to search your apartment I already knew you were a strong woman, which for me is very attractive. And then I loved your lingerie, its delicacy, its scent. Your coffee. Your red dress, fabulous. Last summer I saw one very like it, in Venice, in a shop window in Campo Santo Stefano. Displayed on an incredible wooden mannequin with the head of a doge.'

They arrived at the Pouilly Reuilly, a bistro in a narrow deserted street in Pré-Saint-Gervais. A long narrow room, bright yellow table-cloths, waiters in black and white, the proprietress relaxed and smiling. They sat down at a table near the door and ordered two glasses of champagne.

Anna Beric leant against the banquette. Closed her eyes for a moment. I knew I was playing a dangerous game. But I hadn't reckoned with this Daquin man. Pierre, help. She opened her eyes again.

'That's where I bought that dress. In Venice. In Campo Santo Stefano.'

Huge eyes. Daquin looked at her, then studied the menu. A violent urge to possess her. Don't be led astray. Remain in command of the evening.

'Eggs in wine sauce, then tripoux, twice, and a chilled Brouilly. Starting with that dress I imagined what you were like, and at the airport I recognized you. But your eyes surprised me. I hadn't imagined them as blue. Your drawing-room had intrigued me through its negative quality, but I loved your office. And I was madly jealous of this O ... '

He took the anthology of Persian poetry out of his jacket pocket and opened it at the fly-leaf: 27 January 1958, an unforgettable *encounter.* Signed: O. Anna Beric placed her hand on the book. She was moved. Daquin took her hand, turned it over and kissed the throbbing veins at the wrist.

'Forgive me for borrowing it, I'm returning it to you. But tell me how you met Osman Kashguri.'

Anna Beric leant back against the banquette. Felt she was definitely getting out of her depth and how pleasant that was. The eggs in wine sauce were sublime.

'What do you know about my life, Daquin?'

'A certain number of things. How you crossed war-time Europe on foot, at the age of ten. The aunt who slept with the Germans and took you over in Belleville. Her pimp who put you into prostitution on the streets when you were thirteen. And who was assassinated when you were twenty-three.'

'In fact, you know a lot about me.' She reflected briefly. 'It was work I didn't like. One day I was waiting for clients outside the café, supervised by my aunt. A young man stopped, he was about eighteen or twenty, he was good-looking. He had good manners, as my aunt used to say. He asked me if he could watch me when I was making love with another client. I said no, it wasn't my sort of thing. And what is your sort of thing? I don't know what got into me but I replied: Greek tragedies. He then began to recite to me the first lines of Cassandra's prophecy in *Agamemnon*. I continued with those that followed. At that period I would recite the Greek tragedians to myself during the assignations. We would go upstairs together and spend an hour reciting poetry. He moved over very quickly to the Persian poets, whom I didn't know at all. In Persian and in French. I liked that a lot. He came back often...'

She had never told this story to anyone, not even to Meillant. The tripoux came. And suddenly she was overcome with anxiety. Would it be prison tomorrow, and for how long?

'Give me something to drink, Daquin.'

'And then your wickerwork trunk, at the bottom of your wardrobe, also made me think long and hard. The workmanship of the weave, the beauty of the clasp, the leather corners. It expresses an atmosphere of other times, or other lands. Another gift from Kashguri?'

'What are you trying to make me say? That I still see him? Well, I'll tell you: he's remained one of my best friends. He's a rather flamboyant personality.'

'And the trunk?'

Anna drank her glass of wine very slowly, her eyes on Daquin.

'When he returned from Iran, in 1979, everything he brought with him, linen, books and small things were in trunks like that. I had gone to greet him when he arrived. I found those trunks superb. He gave me one. Now, it's your turn, tell me how you . . . found me.'

Daquin described the police file, the old investigating magistrate, the ashtrays, the inn at Le Bas-Bréau. Anna was impressed. For desert there were prunes in Armagnac.

'And the body in my workroom, which was the start of it all for me, have you found the murderer?'

'No, not yet. Why did you go away? That body was there by accident, apparently.'

'I'm not in the habit of underestimating the police. I thought there was a strong possibility that my setup would be discovered during the investigation. I wanted to find shelter. That seems logical to me.'

'In Marrakesh?'

'The weather is very fine there at this time of year.'

'Certainly it is. But why not Istanbul?' No reply. 'Shall I take you home?'

*

In the car:

'One more question, Daquin. Meillant told me you liked boys.'

A broad smile. 'I like boys too. Why?'

No answer.

The car stopped in rue Raynouard, by the block where Anna Beric lived. Daquin didn't move. Anna Beric looked at him.

'What's going to happen now?'

'You're going to go up to your apartment.'

'And you?'

'If you like, I'll come up with you. Otherwise I'll wait for you here. In any case tomorrow we're going together to the local squad office in passage du Désir.'

Her hand on Daquin's arm.

'Come along. I'd like to offer you coffee, since you appreciate the brand I use.'

7.30 a.m. In the car, on the way to the local squad office

'Do you know what we're expecting from you?'

'More or less.'

'We want to know how the profits between the manufacturers and yourself were divided up. With proof. And to get some idea about what they do with the dirty money. Will you tell us?'

'Yes.'

A silence. The car was held up in the underpass along the quais.

'Who are you protecting, Anna?'

'Meillant, as you well know.'

'Not only him.'

Anna turned her head away and said nothing. Daquin went on: 'I'm going to ask for, and get, a period of preventive detention for you. Until my investigation into the Turkish network is over.' Silence. 'If you co-operate with the Fraud Squad as arranged I'll do nothing special to find out more than I already know about your part in the drugs business that I'm investigating. But I don't want to look a fool if I come across some material proofs that you have inadvertently left somewhere behind you.'

They drove in silence to passage du Désir through the morning traffic blocks. As they reached Boulevard de Strasbourg Anna turned to Daquin, her eyes creased into a smile.

'You remind me of someone, Daquin. But I was younger. And available.'

Noon. Daquin's office

'Let's go over it again. The trucks will arrive at the French frontier tomorrow, Thursday. The Customs officers will arrange for them to arrive at Sobesky's place at about 4 a.m. The raincoats will be unloaded. That should take about two hours, more or less. A group from Drugs will be there, and will play it by ear. But they'll certainly wait a little before going into the boutique. Once empty, the trucks will set off for their garage, Euroriencar, at Gennevilliers. There, the chief will direct operations. He'll arrest everything that moves and he'll have the trucks searched. From 6 a.m. about thirty

Turks, whose names I've listed, will be arrested, and Moreira too. I hope also to arrest Oumourzarov, but it's far from certain. Another group will follow the trucks going towards Le Havre, and what they do will depend on what's happened in Paris. Altogether two hundred and fifty police officers will be mobilized. I'm going to spend the time I've got left preparing notes about the people we're going to arrest. I'll use the information I already have plus whatever we learn from the groups responsible for the surveillance of Moreira and Kutluer. I'll settle the details with the chief. In emergency you can contact me through his office. But I advise you to take a day's leave, you'll be needing it.'

'And what do we do on Friday morning?'

'That's why I've called you together today. Attali will be attached to the Sobesky surveillance group, Romero to Moreira's. I will arrest Kashguri. Lavorel, you'll come with me.'

Very early in the morning

The early evening had been terrible. Waiting. Impossible to touch Sol. Nerves too tense. Daquin wasn't available. Now it was just after 1 o'clock in the morning. Time to get dressed. He looked for his service revolver, in a kitchen drawer, among utensils he didn't use often, such as the hand-operated liquidizer or the ice-cream scoop. That made Soleiman laugh, after which he went to sleep.

Daquin went out onto the avenue Jean-Moulin pavement. He could feel his pistol under his jacket and didn't like it. Being armed always made him aware of possible failure. That was very much on the cards tonight. A large unmarked car, with radio, two inspectors in front. Daquin got in behind. They set off to avenue du Maréchal-Lyautey. They arrived quietly outside Kashguri's place. Stopped twenty metres away from it, by the pavement. The radio was permanently switched on and spluttered quietly. The wait began.

3.24 a.m.

'Bosphorus 4 to all Bosphorus groups: The convoy of trucks divided into two on reaching Brie-Comte-Robert. Two went off towards Paris. As agreed we're following the convoy going north.'

3.30 a.m.

There were four of them in the car, Attali driving. They stopped quietly in the driveway entrance, exactly opposite the Sobesky boutique. Parisot got out, opened the iron carriage entrance door. The car drove in and stopped at the back of the courtyard. Superintendent Raymond, who was in charge of the group, and Attali closed the carriage entrance door and hid behind it. At eye level there was a frieze of little openwork flowers cut in the metal. The ideal hiding-place, provided you didn't move.

*

A strange place, between town and woods. To the right the last row of Parisian buildings, to the left the first trees of the Bois de Boulogne, planted in a straight line, unnatural trees. At the top floor of the block six big windows, brilliantly lit, some of them open. Music could be heard, almost continuous. Music unknown to Daquin, probably Iranian, and then jazz.

'Keith Jarrett.'

'What did you say, *commissaire*?'

'It's a Keith Jarrett record up there. Don't you recognize the sound of the piano?'

The inspectors exchanged a glance.

Silhouettes near the Bois. Teenagers came soliciting the three men in the parked car. One of them, very thin, a mixture of provocation and anxiety. Daquin interested. Sol must have looked like that, in Istanbul. The two inspectors were uncomfortable.

'Beat it, you silly lot.'

They watched the door to the building and the car-park exit. Daquin drank some coffee from the thermos flask he had brought. From time to time a couple, dark suit, long dress, came out, probably from Kashghuri's place and walked away. In the avenue cars with solitary male drivers signalled by flashing their headlights, stopped, the men looked, waved, the cops sat motionless, the cars drove off again slowly. One inspector dozed off. Second coffee.

At 3.30 a girl in a long black dress, with a short white jacket, came out of the building. She looked right and left, then crossed the road. Daquin signalled to her. She came towards the police car and climbed in at the back, next to Daquin. Dorothée Marty, very pale beneath her helmet of black hair. The inspectors watched in the driving mirror.

'Is he still up there?'

'Yes, he waved to me from the door to the apartment a moment ago.'

'What's he doing?'

'He's chatting, going from one person to another. He's putting on the records.'

'Is he smoking, drinking?'

'No, he's not doing very much.' Hesitation. 'He seems to be waiting. Waiting for you?'

4.13 a.m.

'Bosphorus 2 to all Bosphorus groups: The two trucks have reached their destination. The unloading's about to begin.'

4.30 a.m.

'Bosphorus 1 to all Bosphorus groups: Warehouses under control. Dead calm.'

4.32 a.m.

Attali signalled to the Superintendent, they both went without a sound into the car-parked in the garage forecourt.

'There's an unexpected problem. I recognize most of the men who are unloading. They're Turks whom we've got listed. So they won't be at home when our men arrive at 6 o'clock. What should we do?'

5 a.m.

'Bosphorus 1 to Bosphorus groups 6 to 32: Those who don't find their targets soon should make contact with Bosphorus 2, and follow instructions.'

5.45 a.m.

Superintendent Nanteuil and Romero reached Boulevard Suchet outside Moreira's home. Very modern luxury apartment block. Moreira lived on the ground floor in the rear building that looked onto the garden. Nanteuil and Romero paced up and down, waiting for the fateful hour of 6 a.m. A glance at the inspector who remained in the car, listening to the radio. Nothing to report. We're going in.

House phone. Repeated ringing to wake up the caretaker.

'Police. Open up. Quickly.'

The caretaker opened the door, looking terrified. The Superintendent showed his identity card. And they ran to the rear building. Ground floor left. Rang the bell. Nothing. Rang again.

'What is it?' said a sleepy woman's voice.

'Open up, madame. Police.'

A deathly silence behind the door. Romero listened, desperately tense. He heard the faint but distinct sound of a sliding glass door. Signed to the Superintendent: he's getting away at the back.

'Open up or I'll shoot through the door.'

She opened the door. The cops pushed past her, ran through the apartment at the double, went through the sliding doors and raced across the garden. At the far end, a wall surmounted with a railing. Climbed over it. On the other side, in a deep cutting, a disused railway line. Recent traces of footprints over the slippery soil and to the right, the silhouette of Moreira, in a dressing-gown, running along the track in the darkness.

'Is it him?'

'Yes.'

They both slid down the bank. Hard landing.

'Stop, police.'

Moreira went on running. In front of him, about fifty metres ahead, was a tunnel. The two cops rushed after him as fast as they could. Moreira kept ahead. The entrance to the tunnel came closer.

'Stop or I'll fire!'

A shot in the air. And then the Superintendent stopped, his knees bent, his arms stretched forward. Romero did the same. Three shots. Moreira collapsed, falling face down. Nanteuil and Romero, standing, sober now, revolvers in their hands, beside the body. Above the cutting, the silhouette of a woman, clutching the railing.

5.50 a.m.

It was still dark. The operation got under way. One inspector stayed by the radio, in the car. A small group watched the entrance to the car-park. Sixteen of them went into the building. Two inspectors entered through the back door, down a long corridor and out into the main courtyard. One never knows. Daquin remained by the elevator with two inspectors aged about forty, experienced in fighting, and the electronics expert who had already worked for him a fortnight earlier when he came to repair a convenient elevator breakdown. For more than an hour he carefully prepared new connections for the electrical circuits in the cabin, enabling it to go directly up to the fifth floor without the help of a key. All the other cops, about ten of them, went up the staircase, led by Lavorel.

Daquin and the two fighters exchanged a few words to pass the time and discovered that they all three of them played rugby. The walkie-talkie crackled.

'We're outside the door.'

'OK.'

Daquin's team blocked the entrance to the elevator. The expert got to work. He dismantled the cover protecting the electrical circuits. The conversation was still about rugby. One man was a forward, the other a half-back and Daquin a three-quarter. The expert made the connection and signalled to Daquin: OK. And came out of the elevator.

Walkie-talkie: 'Ready down here, over to you up there.'

Lavorel rang the bell and knocked on the door.

'Open up. Police.'

Hard to hear what was happening on the other side of the door, it was very thick. First a voice with a strong accent: 'What do you want?'

'Police. It's a search. Open up.'

Walkie-talkie, quietly: 'The elevator's all yours.'

Daquin looked at his two helpers – go for it, scrum – and pressed the button for the fifth floor. The elevator began to go up. No door on the landing side. The two Iranians were probably armed. The tricky moment: the arrival of the elevator at Kashguri's floor.

The group of inspectors outside the door went on ringing the bell, talking very loudly, knocking on the door more violently. They announced they were going to shoot through the lock. One of them took out a revolver...

Daquin and the half-back dived out of the elevator together, the forward covering them. The two Iranians turned round, then collapsed after a leg tackle.

'Perfect tackle,' said the forward, as though he was at a training session.

Daquin pulled up his Iranian roughly, twisting one arm behind his back, 'Police. Open that door. Be quick.'

It was true that he looked like the identikit portrait. But so did the other one.

6 a.m.

Rue des Vinaigriers, a rather dilapidated building. Inspector Danièle Ribout, an energetic red-haired little woman, went up the stairs in silence with her chum Inspector Saval. They'd been a team for a long time, they didn't need to speak in order to understand each other. She signalled to him: as usual. He nodded in agreement. They reached the third floor. A solid door equipped with a spyhole. Saval stood against the wall at the side. Danièle Ribout stood just opposite the spyhole and rang the bell twice, as though in a hurry... The sound of bare feet could be heard behind the door. She pretended to be upset and feeble.

'Help me, please. I'm on my own, I live just above and there's a leak, I don't know what to do.'

The door opened a little. The two inspectors rushed into the apartment, their revolvers in their hands.

'Police. Don't move.'

Each time the same feeling of satisfaction. Revenge on the machos.

*

The door was open. The entrance hall was invaded by cops. Four inspectors took charge of the two Iranians. Daquin indicated the two doors and the interior staircase which opened into the entrance hall.

'Hurry. Three groups. Find Kashguri in particular.'

Not many people left in the huge drawing-room. At a gaming-table five men were feverishly collecting the crumpled banknotes that littered the surface. Three pretty young women tried to escape down the corridor. No use. And Bertrand was asleep on a sofa. Two Asian girls in black dresses and lace aprons were standing by a half-empty buffet. Terrified. They were going to start crying any moment.

'Police. Nobody move.'

Daquin and three inspectors went through the smoking-room. Nobody. At the double, into the first bedroom. There, men and women, six in all, dressing in a hurry. Clothes scattered about, make-up ruined, half-clad bodies, surprise, anxiety, nobody really at their best. The cops laughed openly. But still no Kashguri. All the rest of the apartment was deserted.

6.38 a.m.

'Bosphorus 2 to Bosphorus 1: The unloading's almost complete.'

6.41 a.m.

Attali was startled: he'd recognized the Turk who'd just taken the wheel of one of the trucks. Another Turk got in beside him and the trucks drove off.

'We've got to follow them.' Attali said it almost instinctively.

Near panic starting in the yard. The Superintendent co-ordinated by radio the smoothly conducted arrest of the Turks who were dispersing over the area. Intercept them as far as possible from Sobesky's place.

Attali left the building, followed the pavement, turned left two streets further on and found an unmarked police car with a colleague listening to the radio. Sat beside him.

'Step on it, we may be lucky enough to meet the trucks again.'

7.30 a.m.

'Bosphorus 2 to Bosphorus 1: We've rejoined the trucks at porte de la Chapelle. We're starting to follow them.'

7.17 a.m.

'Bosphorus 2 to Bosphorus 1: One of the trucks is going via Gennevilliers, towards Euroriencar, presumably. The other's continuing on the A86, we're following it.'

7.20 a.m.

'Bosphorus 2 to Boshorus 1: The truck's going via Nanterre.'

7.28 a.m.

'Bosphorus 2 to Bosphorus 1: The truck's gone into a garage forecourt in rue de l'Avenir, Nanterre. We await instructions.'

The Drugs Squad chief walked past the Réveil Social café. Attali had been sitting by the window, he paid for his coffee with cream and went out. They discussed things as they walked up the street.

'I've sent half the men I had at Gennevilliers to Nanterre. What do you think about that?'

'I've really no idea.'

They walked alongside the garage. The front looked rather dirty, vaguely dilapidated, with a passage alongside, and behind it a huge yard where old broken-down cars could be seen. They went on until they reached the police car-parked at the other end of the street. A young inspector sent off on reconnaissance. Came back.

'I got in without difficulty. The truck's in the yard, the cabin's tipped up and the garage owner, an old grandfather, is tinkering with the engine. I didn't see what he was doing. The two Turks are sitting a little further off in the yard, smoking. I made an appointment for tomorrow to bring in my car for repair. No sign of any nerves.'

'That's rather depressing.'

'We have to go and see all the same. Three inspectors along with Attali. Check the identities. If the Turks are on our list, arrest them. And take a good look at the truck. The rest of our men will come closer ready to intervene as support. Keep your revolvers and walkie-talkies ready, you never know.'

The inspectors came in through the passage and approached the old man just as he was unscrewing a rectangular metal plate.

'Police, we've got a few questions to ask you.'

The old man threw the metal plate at Attali's head, the inspector fell down, the Turks jumped to their feet and fired through their jackets. Attali, who'd been hit in one arm, dragged himself over to the shelter of the truck wheels. Shooting went on round him.

Walkie-talkie: 'Everyone to the garage, weapons at the ready.'

At this precise moment the Morora company lorries arrived slowly and began to park in the garage forecourt, followed by fifteen or so inspectors at the double. Indescribable chaos.

When the chief finally got the operations under control all the lorry drivers, innocent Moroccans who were visibly upset, were handcuffed and parked in the garage. The Turks and the elderly garage-owner had disappeared. Attali got back on his feet, clutching his left arm, which was covered in blood. In front of him the reservoir of the dismantled truck: a gaping hole, access to the false bottom and there, neatly stacked, packets of white powder.

8.01 a.m.

'Bosphorus 1 to all Bosphorus groups: We've found the white stuff. Lots of it. Green light to all groups.'

'Sunday saw publication of the first results in the second round of elections to the Iranian Parliament, in which the Party of the Islamic Republic, led by the Ayatollah Béhechti, is certain to be victorious...'

Libération, 13 May 1980

Thursday 15 May, 7 p.m. Rue du Château-d'Eau

For two days student demonstrations had been going on near rue Jussieu. Heavy police presence round the Faculté. Rumour had it that there had been one death. The area round the Gare de l'Est was much calmer. Rue du Château-d'Eau was almost deserted when a motorcycle rode into it at high speed. Two men wearing crash helmets. They stopped, with the engine still running, outside the Association of Lighting Technicians, full of people at this hour of the day. The pillion passenger dismounted, reached into the carrier at the back and took out a sub-machine-gun. He stood up and fired a volley towards the top of the façade, which collapsed with a deafening noise of breaking glass. Everyone inside threw themselves flat on the floor. The man with the gun raised the visor of his helmet and shouted two or three sentences in Turkish. Another volley. Then he jumped onto the pillion seat of the motorcycle which rode off and disappeared. The police would arrive at the spot a few minutes later.

Friday 16 May, 8 a.m. Passage du Désir

Daquin was in a very bad mood. He'd been at a standstill for more than a month now. True, he'd brought off a splendid coup, the entire network had collapsed, along with its connections in France and a few financial links. But Kashguri had vanished without trace. The investigation had proved that he owned a Renault 5, kept in the second car-park at his apartment block, which led to Boulevard Suchet, and he had probably used it to get away, at about 4 a.m. on the morning of 4 April. Was he going to supervise the arrival of the delivery? The registration number of the car had been circulated to all police forces without success. The man had purely and simply disappeared during the night of 3–4 April. Oumourzarov, who had been present at Kashgour's soirée, had been released the same afternoon. Almost with apologies. Nothing had been proved against Sobesky. The murder of the Thai girl had still not been solved. And, last night, Soleiman hadn't returned to sleep with him. He missed him, even if he found it hard to admit the fact.

Daquin skimmed rapidly through the various notes scattered over his desk and came across one from the local squad inspectors – the office of the Association of Lighting Technicians had been machine-gunned the previous night. Shots at the ceiling. Two people slightly hurt by flying glass. According to witnesses the man responsible for firing the shots was a certain Soleiman Keyser, a militant from a Turkish group of the extreme left. People present at the Association office alleged they had definitely recognized him when he raised the visor on his helmet and shouted: 'No place for Fascists in this district! Get out, or next time we'll fire at your height.' Search warrant issued.

Daquin's first reaction: Tonight I'll get hold of him by the scruff of his neck and spank him. Second reaction: If I want to do that I'll have to send two cops to find him. That sounds very much like goodbye.

Friday 16 May, 9 a.m. Parish of Saint-Bernard

Soleiman walked there, his head high, taking his time. The weather was fine, the Turks had appreciated the shooting of the previous day. Two hundred metres away from the church a Frenchman who had been looking out for him took him by the arm and pushed him into the nearest café.

'The cops are looking for you. There's already been a search at 6 o'clock this morning at Thévenard's place, where your mail's delivered. And two cops are waiting for you opposite the church. The Fascists are alleging that it was you who carried out the shooting at their Association's office.'

'So what?'

'We're not asking anything of you. We see all this as provocation by the cops or the Fascists, that's all. We're taking you to the country for a few days, long enough for it all to blow over. Don't argue, Soleiman. We can't risk trouble now, when legalization's just about to be achieved.'

'But I'm not arguing.'

The telephone rang. Ten minutes later a car arrived. Two French chums from the Committee sitting in front. Soleiman got in at the back. Rather odd route across Paris: somebody had already been killed in the rue Jussieu area and things were hotting up in the Latin Quarter. There had been endless detours to avoid the police roadblocks now set up at all the main crossing points. Soleiman, who was sitting low down at the back, was suddenly upset at the idea of being taken before Daquin between two cops.

*

At 11.30 the journey came to an end in front of an attractive stone-built house in the Vexin area. A big wooden door. Behind the house, sheltered from view, a very large garden, full of fruit-trees, some of them in flower. A plump woman came out of the kitchen, a Mauritian, with yellow skin, all smiles.

'Maria, here's the young man we're entrusting to you.'

'He's sweet. No problem, I'll take good care of him.'

'Don't go. I've no clothes, no money...'

How can he say that he feels lost? And that Maria scares him?

'We told you we'd look after everything. Maria will do the shopping and the cooking. As for you, you can go out in the garden, but not into the village. We've brought clothes, you'll find everything in your room.'

Soleiman watched the car go. Maria closed the door. Things were moving rather too quickly for him, he couldn't really understand.

'In an hour,' said Maria, 'lunch will be ready.'

Soleiman smiled at her. From that point of view at least, I shan't feel like a fish out of water. It was a lovely day. He took a few steps in the garden, stretched out on the grass in the sunshine and went to sleep.

Saturday 17 May, 10 p.m. At Le Sancerre.

Not many people were left in the bistro. Daquin and Steiger were alone on the small, enclosed terrace, with its panelling in light coloured wood and its intimate atmosphere. They were eating a splendid stuffed shoulder of lamb. With chilled Brouilly. Their conversation travelled all round the Middle East and then came back to the dismantling of the Turkish network.

'Your friends aren't co-operative. It's frustrating. I wasn't even able to interrogate Baker in person.'

'You must know that he's been assassinated.'

'That's what they tell me, yes. Assassinated in the shower by a junkie. Did you help him to die? Or is he starting a new career under another name in South America?'

Steiger hesitated for a moment. 'You don't realize what a storm you've unleashed in the microcosmos of the American secret services.'

'Yes, I do, I've some idea. It could be said, for example, that Baker had always worked for the CIA. He apparently belonged to a faction that had decided to use drugs against communism and the Soviet Union. When that comes out into the open it always creates a stir, and the others, those who are against the use of drug trafficking and favour more traditional methods, can take advantage of it. All things considered, I think he must have been liquidated.'

'That's not the most embarrassing thing in the Baker case. This type of conflict between rival factions is traditional in the CIA, and they know how to manage it. No, Baker did something much worse for the image of the CIA. While continuing to work for them from time to time, he'd set up a personal business in video cassettes awash with blood and porn, torture and murders filmed live, guaranteed authentic: it was extremely lucrative for him. And the funds for starting it up had been supplied by the live recordings of the tortures that the Savak inflicted on anyone opposing the Shah's regime in Tehran, while Baker was employed there. It's said that Baker himself did the filming. Apparently there were men burnt alive on heated metal plates, others whose bones were cut out while they were still alive. I won't mention the mass rapes of women and children, in front of their husbands and fathers. The Americans apparently tolerate collaboration by civil servants with torturers in faraway places but transforming all that into porn videos is more difficult to admit. In short, the CIA didn't want to take the risk.'

Daquin was astounded.

'And I knew nothing about all that. Do you think that's normal? Now I know what Virginie Lamouroux went to do in New York. Frank, I must see those casssettes as soon as possible.'

'I didn't know you had a taste for that sort of thing.'

Daquin smiled at him.

'Waiter, two glasses of champagne. What will you have for dessert?'

Sunday 18 May, 1 a.m. Villa des Artistes

Daquin was fast asleep when the telephone rang. He picked it up and glanced at his watch. Quarter to 1. He sat up, his bare back against the wall and the duvet pulled up to his waist.

'Yes.'

'It's Soleiman.'

Daquin looked automatically at the chubby little blonde who was slowly waking up beside him, crumpled and delightful.

'Daquin, I know what Ali Agça has come to do in France.'

'Go on.'

'He's come to assassinate the Pope.'

'Explain, slowly. It's late, I was asleep.'

'I'm in the country. I've nothing to do. I spend my evenings dozing in front of the telly. I don't really listen, but that's the only thing they talk about, the Pope in Paris, at the end of the month. And suddenly, this evening, it reminded me of something. Agça escaped from prison in November 1979, when the Pope was visiting Turkey. And he wrote to the *Milliyet* to explain that he'd escaped because he wanted to assassinate the Pope, a symbol of the West, or something like that. I don't remember exactly because I was on the run at the time, and then it seemed to me to be crazy, but you can check. Maybe it's a coincidence, but maybe not. Are you still listening?'

'Of course.'

'Goodbye, Daquin.'

Monday 19 May, 8 a.m. Passage du Désir

Lavorel, in a dark suit, wearing a tie, carrying an attaché case, accompanied by a Superintendent from the Finance Squad, came to hand over to Daquin his report on the papers seized in Kashguri's apartment. He was terribly serious and, following all the rules, Daquin played the game and sat up straight in his chair.

'*Monsieur le commissaire*, you'll see that the Kashguri papers allow us to form a precise notion of how the Bank of Cyprus and the East functions. It finances the arms traffic directed towards Turkey and the Lebanon and also the setting-up of the Turkish network. It's also the deposit bank for well-known drug traffickers in Syria and the Lebanon. This black money finances in part the bribes and various commissions paid by the European enterprises which work with the bank in the Near and Middle East, of which the most important is the Parillaud Bank. You've got all the details in the report. But nothing in those papers supplies any proof that Kashguri was implicated in any other way in the Turkish network. He financed it, yes, but nothing allows us to say that he was the mastermind.'

'Thank you for the quality and clarity of your work. What kind of follow-up will there be to this report?'

Lavorel said nothing and looked at his superintendent, who went on: 'Since we're on our own, I might as well tell you: probably nothing. The law doesn't allow us to take action against banks that launder dirty money. And who would dare touch Parillaud?'

'One more thing, Lavorel. Where have you got to with Anna Beric?'

'She told me everything, as planned. We're now arranging to call in the different manufacturers involved. It's going to take a long time, but we'll arrive at some staggering tax adjustments.'

'Do you confirm that there's nothing in the Kashguri papers that could link Anna Beric to the Turkish network?'

'No, nothing. Anna Beric only comes into it through her use of the Bank of Cyprus and the East for sending money out of France, as several other manufacturers do, in fact.'

'I think we'll have to agree to her release. What do you think about it?'

'I think we'll find it difficult to avoid. Her lawyers asked the investigating magistrate to allow it, two days ago. I reserved my opinion until today.'

'No objections on my side. However, I must tell you that I'll have her followed and that the magistrate has already given permission for her telephone to be tapped.'

Monday 19 May, 11 a.m. Office of the Drugs Squad

Summit meeting, Chief of the Drugs Squad, Ministry of the Interior, Crime Squad, Official Travel Service. Daquin presented a report on Ali Agça. He had decided in favour of a strictly chronological exposé: surveillance of the sandwich shop, photos, identification, and therefore his presence in France and his links with the network all proved. Report by the Turkish police. The three murders ordered by the traffickers had, he was convinced, been carried out by Ali Agça, for the method employed was his.

After 4 April, nothing more. Daquin explained the work he had had to do in order to establish a solid case against the traffickers and the French people who sold the stuff on, sixty or so altogether, the killers of Virginie Lamouroux and Madame Buisson, his concierge, Kashguri's henchmen. The difficulties of bringing to light the financial procedures based on Kashguri's papers. The vain search for Kashguri himself, all over France, many people questioned without any results. The setback experienced over the Turkimport company, which was exonerated in the end. And finally the two inspectors who had been working with him since the beginning, and who were therefore perfectly up-to-date with the case, were out of action for a time: Attali, who had been slightly hurt, and Romero, subjected to an enquiry by the police disciplinary service following the murder of Moreira. Fortunately he was a bad shot! All in all, he, Daquin, had not had time to deal with Ali Agça. He had taken up the case again a few days earlier. The first stage was to enlarge the report by the Turkish police, which was extremely brief. Work on the Turkish press. And at that point Daquin read out a translation of Ali Agça's letter to the *Milliyet*, dated November 1979, in which he explained why he would certainly kill the Pope, who had commanded the Crusades. A long, impassioned document, nationalist, Islamist, anti-Western. Just a little crazy. All in all, plausible.

Consternation. The Pope was due to arrive in Paris on 31 May. There were twelve days left to find Ali Agça or else learn that he had definitely left French territory.

NARCOTICS EXECUTIONER

'The Ayatollah Sadegh Khalkahli stated over Radio Tehran on
Monday that he had resumed his work as head of the Iranian
narcotics bureau. On 14 May the Ayatollah had resigned from
his post as leader of the fight against drugs, four days after his
appointment, since he considered his powers were limited.
The Iranian president, Monsieur Abolhassan Bani Sadr, had
asked him to reconsider his position. The Ayatollah has stated
that his first big success was the seizure by his staff of 900
kilos of opium and the arrest of the traffickers.'

Libération, 20 May

Tuesday 20 May, 8 a.m. Roissy

Attali flew to New York. The FBI were trying to identify the killers
and the victims filmed live on more than three hundred cassettes.
Those that had been recorded in Tehran had been classified as
'secret defence', but Attali would have free access to all the others,
and an FBI agent would help him to make the selection.

Daquin left for two days in Istanbul. His first meeting with the
Turkish police, which had been long postponed due to the diver-
gences of understanding between France and Turkey concerning
the murder of Sener. But finally made possible from 14 May last,
when the French government had officially recognized the responsibility of the Armenian terrorists. Two days to hand over to the
Turkish government all the additional information it could hope
for about the Turkish network. And to obtain everything possible
about Ali Agça.

Romero drove him to Roissy.

'Manage things any way you want, Romero. When I come back I
want the Turks to have handed over Agça. We've let Kashguri get
away. One, not two.'

There were ten or so inspectors along with Romero in the Drugs
Squad. Results essential, all possible methods permissible.

The top brass in the Official Travel Service and the Ministry of
the Interior were taking a second look at the security arrangements
planned for the Pope's visit.

Romero, unshaven, exhausted, his clothes creased, came to meet Daquin. The airport was almost deserted. Daquin glanced critically at Romero's appearance but seemed in a better temper than the day before.

'Was Istanbul OK?'

'Beautiful, beautiful town.' A heartfelt thought for the wife of the director for Anatolian Studies, the little wooden hotel below Saint Sophia, the seagulls in the pinnacles, the dark shape of the basilica against the clear sky, the radiophonic tone of the muez-zins. 'I met police officers who knew Agça. According to them he's crazy enough to plot the assassination of the Pope and lucid enough to have a chance of success. On the other hand, according to the Turkish cops, he's a rather bad shot, which explains why he always shoots at point-blank range. That gives us a chance. After his escape, last November, he settled in Germany. They thought he was still there. As for the rest, no real clues. What about you?'

'We've begun all the interrogations again. We've had no sleep since yesterday morning. Results: on Wednesday 5 March, the day when the photo was taken, Agça arrived in Paris, coming from Germany, apparently. Since then he's completely disappeared. The Turks think he wasn't living in Paris. One detail, interesting, per-haps: he doesn't speak a word of French. We identified the two men who put up the leaflets round the Gymnase about the assassi-nation of Osman Celik, and we got them to talk. It really was Agça who assassinated Celik. They were there to create a diversion and cover his flight. He didn't even need it. He left again that same evening by car, with Celebi, the little dealer whose corpse I identi-fied in Rouen. The decisions to kill Celik and Sener were taken by the leader of the network in France, whom no Turk has ever met. He was the only man to have had contact with Agça. He issued his orders by post to the two Turkish leaders in the shops, poste re-stante, written in Turkish. When they had to say or to ask for some-thing, it went through Moreira and Kutluer.'

'Well protected.'

'So it seems. The Turks didn't know that Celebi had been killed and they don't understand why. That's it. That's all we've been able to get in two days of uninterrupted interrogations. They're not kind-hearted. We're tired, but so are they.'

'From the little I was able to see over there, they must have acquired a certain resistance to tough interrogations, they've got used to them. Do you think there's anything more to be got out of them?'

'I don't think so.'

Thursday 22 May, 8 a.m. Passage du Désir

Attali, the first to arrive, had acquired a television from another office, with some difficulty, together with a video recorder, and prepared the cassette. He waited for the others. Tense, exhausted, somewhat confused by what he had seen during the last few days. Romero, Lavorel, and then Daquin came in and sat down round the table.

Attali switched on the television and inserted the cassette.

*

The girl was there, sitting naked on the edge of the vast white bed in the middle of the room, with mirrors all round. She's childlike yet already world-weary. In a corner is a Louis XV armchair, at the far end, a table-height fridge. On it are tumblers, flutes, goblets, an assortment of glasses. She's gently swinging her legs and singing to herself. A man comes in. He's also naked. She studies him, gives him the once-over. Around forty-five, bullneck, fat, small bum, thin legs, balding, but a real mat of ginger hair on his chest. She smiles and beckons, and he, with gluttonous face, sidles slowly towards the icebox, opens it, pours himself a very generous whisky. 'Want a drink, baby girl?' – he raises his glass to her. The gesture is rather too expansive: he sloshes the whisky on the thick white carpet. She shakes her head, says nothing, but has a constant smile. He drinks, lets the glass fall on the carpet, goes over to her, collapses on the bed, laughing.

She makes him lie face down, sits on the small of his back. Next to him, she's incredibly fragile. She begins massaging him, mewing softly to get herself into the rhythm. He lets her do it, groans with pleasure, encourages her. 'Give your little daddy a cuddle.' She lies on top of him, nibbles his neck, his ears. He stirs slowly, emits a few inaudible sounds, snatches at the carpet with his fingers. She

turns him over on to his back. He looks pleased. She gently massages his dick. The man leans up on his elbows. He looks at this
tiny body barely able to balance on his, turns towards the mirrors
and smiles at them. He's humming. She solemnly applies herself
to her task. Her face is more attentive, her smile fixed, her eyes
watching the other person's reaction.

All at once the man senses he's being watched. He seems to be
waking from a long sleep, but his eyes are glazed. The girl slowly
raises her hands towards the man's nipples and starts pinching
them gently. The humming transmutes to a long moan. He sits up
and she falls on the bed. He's overcome with panicky fear. His eyes
are dilated. He screams 'She's going to kill me'. He curls up, hands
over eyes, and starts kicking out at the girl. 'Is it a game?' she asks,
still smiling, but seems a little anxious. She avoids the kicks and
tries to calm him by drawing him down on the bed, caressing his
shoulders and nipples. 'Remember, I'm your baby.' But he screams
again. 'Don't grow up, don't grow up.' Then he grabs her by the
throat, shakes her, throws her down on the bed and squeezes,
squeezes. 'You won't have me.' She struggles a bit, not much, she's
completely crushed by the man's massive weight. She can't cry out
any more. After one, two minutes she stops struggling altogether.

*

The cassette came to an end.

'So, it was Bertrand.' Romero and Daquin looked at each other.

'That fat pig had had a bad trip.'

'I'd expected it to be Kashguri.'

'He must have been in a corner, full of heroin, masturbating.
Then the two of them came out of it. Picked up the body, which
they wrapped up in just anything. The girl was very small. They
left Simon Video by the back alleys, completely deserted at night, to
dump the body as far away as possible, but without crossing rue du
Faubourg-Saint-Martin, which was busier. They went into the last
building, found the door to Bostic's workroom inadequately locked,
hid the body beneath the gypsy pants and slammed the door behind them. They threw away the clothes somewhere else, or gave
them to the Salvation Army. And, since they'd barely got over the
trip, they forgot the video cassette. VL came by and found it.
Things must have happened more or less like that.'

'Can Bertrand lead us to Kashguri and Ali Agça?'

'Wait. That's not all. I must tell you where I found the cassette. Baker's video cassettes were divided up into three series by the FBI. First series, the cassettes filmed in Tehran, "secret defence". I was spared those. Second series, the commercial stock. I worked with an agent from the FBI who helped me sort them out. Everything showing boys was eliminated, since I was looking for the murder of a young girl. I viewed a hundred speeded up cassettes. I didn't know such things were possible. A young girl whose sex and anus had been slashed with a razor . . . I'll skip that. In the end, nothing. Then the FBI guy told me there was a third series, Baker's private cassettes, those he hadn't had reproduced for commercial distribution, and the FBI thought that he used them for applying pressure or blackmail. Twenty or so altogether, usually scenes that were much more "soft", classic adultery or homosexual love scenes.'

Daquin laughed.

'No doubt that's the collection in which I might almost have ended up myself.'

'You'd have been in very good company. Apparently there's one cassette with the wife of a French cabinet minister. I wasn't allowed to see it. And it was in that series that I found the Bertrand cassette.'

For the last few moments everyone had been waiting for the finale. There was a short pause, while they digested the news.

'If Bertrand was important enough in Baker's eyes for the latter to find a means of pressurizing him, then it might mean that he could have a direct role in the network.'

'The outcome may have been like this: VL went to the Club Simon, where she had a date with Kashguri. The studio was empty. She had a quick look at the cassette that had remained there and took it to Baker, whose little business she knew about, but she didn't know who Bertrand was. Baker bought the cassette and had VL killed in order to protect Bertrand.'

'What worries me about this version is that too much in it happens by accident.'

'And for the time being we're not even sure that Kashguri was present at the Club Simon during the murder.'

'We're not sure but it's more than likely. He's the member. And also he's the one that the Thais recognized.'

'There could be a quite different version. VL had been working

with Baker for a long time. It was she who'd told him that Sobesky
was the ideal sucker, and it was she who stayed in the house to
observe him. On instructions from Baker she set a trap for
Bertrand and made an appointment with him at the Club Simon.
Remember: she left Sobesky for an important appointment. She
arranged for Bertrand to swallow something nasty which would
definitely give him a bad trip. If it went as far as murder, then all
the better. While Bertrand was dealing with the corpse she dashed
off to New York with the cassette.'

'And was it Bertrand who had her assassinated by Kashguri?'

'Or had her assassinated by the Kashguri method? Kashguri has
a hold over Bertrand because he knows about the murder of the
Thai girl. That's the message he sent him when he gave us his alibi
for the evening of 29 February. Bertrand's reply: he has a hold
over Kashguri by making him responsible for the murder of VL.'

'How do you fit the 14 March lunch into that scenario?'

'Baker had his faithful collaborator assassinated by Kashguri
when he learnt, through Attali's phone call, that the police were on
to him.'

'In any case we haven't done enough work on Bertrand.'

'We were ordered not to do it.'

'That's not a sufficient reason, as you well know. I've rather concentrated on Kashguri. We should have investigated Bertrand's
past. I'm sure we're going to come across him somewhere between
Tehran and Istanbul during the 70s, and involved with the CIA
trafficking. Perhaps he's a member of our own secret services.
We'll have time now to go into all that. We'll start by arresting him
for murder. But he's a Deputy, protected by parliamentary immunity. It'll certainly be complicated.'

Daquin telephoned the Drugs chief while Romero made coffee
for everyone.

*

It was after 5 p.m. when Daquin and his team went to Bertrand's
home. The day had been spent in various telephone calls. Various
procedures had to be followed before Daquin could obtain author-
ization to interrogate the Deputy immediately, before he could be
charged and arrested. In the end contact was made with the secretary in Bertrand's office at the Assembly. After receiving a telephone call at about 3 p.m. Bertrand had immediately gone home,

leaving orders that he was not to be disturbed for any reason whatever.

'Who was this telephone call from?'

'I couldn't tell you. A man, with a foreign accent.'

Elevator. The door to the apartment was locked. They rang the bell. Nothing. Daquin sent for the concierge. She opened the door. They found Bertrand in his office, lying over the big leather arm-chair, a bullet in his head, the pistol on the floor. The enquiry would conclude it was suicide.

Who had telephoned, or got someone to telephone? A friend in political life? A cop? Anna Beric? Erwin?

Friday 23 May, 3 p.m. Passage du Désir

Noted with half an eye in *Libération* ...

> ... It would be reasonable to assume that Sheikh Khalkhali would carry out with obvious awareness an apparently modest task for the man who had decided to exterminate the enemies of Islam ... Twenty executions on Wednesday, nine on Thursday: the Sheikh has not disappointed his admirers ... The thirty condemned men were accused of belonging to an international group who sold drugs throughout Iran and had connections with counter-revolutionaries abroad.

*

Attali, who had been somewhat tested by his New York trip, had asked for a few days' leave, which he was spending with his family at Antony. Romero had taken a day off too. The Official Travel Service had grilled Kashguri's two menservants, in vain. Daquin, alone in his office, was working on photocopies of Bertrand's personal papers. Without much conviction. The ending of any affair is always bitter, but he felt totally apathetic. Kashguri and Ağça had disappeared, and for the time being there wasn't the slightest sign of a clue. Baker had died in New York and he hadn't even seen him once. Bertrand had committed suicide or his suicide had been arranged before he could arrest him. Frustration and more frustration.

Romero appeared at the door of his office.

'Chief, may I disturb you for a few moments?'

Daquin indicated that he could.

Romero stepped back and showed in a woman, a bunch of curly red hair, white skin, golden eyes. Daquin stood up, fascinated.

'Chief, let me introduce Yildiz, we're going to get married, and I should like you to be my witness.'

Once they had left Daquin closed his files and decided to start his weekend at once.

Monday 26 May, 10 a.m. Passage du Désir

The Official Travel people were tensed up.

'All security measures have been reviewed and strengthened. We have two facts on our side. The first is that Agça doesn't speak French and will find himself very isolated, because you've arrested most of the people he knew in Paris. We've arranged surveillance of all the remaining militants and extreme right Turkish areas in Paris, so far without results. Second fact: Agça is a bad shot. If we succeed in always keeping the Pope away from contact with the crowds, we can avoid catastrophe. We've planned to use helicopters and cars for his journeys: access will be carefully controlled: invitation only or passes. Twenty thousand volunteer lookout men have been taken on, plus three thousand state security police and five hundred plainclothes inspectors. There will be two very delicate moments because it will be difficult to keep the Pope at a distance: the meeting with the Polish community at the Champ-de-Mars, and the visit to Saint-Denis where the Pope is meeting the immigrants . . . you can see the sort of thing . . .'

'It's all the better that Agça, on the whole, looks very like an immigrant . . . Less like a Pole.'

'For Saint-Denis we've informed the local council who are calling in the disciplinary services of the Communist Party.'

'Well, then, everything's going well.'

'Every police force in France has received a photo of Agça. But we've still had no response. And about your side?'

'On my side, nothing. I must tell you that since the death of Bertrand I've had no ideas. And I'm somewhat unmotivated.'

*

Telephone call from the chief of Drugs. He'd just been informed that Iran was asking officially for the extradition of Kashguri on charges of drug trafficking. Daquin made himself coffee and, in his armchair thought vaguely about Lespinois, who must be negotiating hard at this moment. With the Islamists, against Parillaud. Like the CIA in Afghanistan, against the Soviets ... The drug traffic forming an element not to be neglected in confused strategies. And suddenly he had an idea. He searched through his files, found the address and telephone number of Oumourzarov and called his office at La Défense. The secretary. A wait.

'Oumourzarov here. What do you want of me, *commissaire*?' Slightly aggressive.

'I should like to meet you and have a talk. There's nothing official about this, and frankly, I haven't told my superiors about it. They would certainly not have authorized me to telephone you.'

A long silence.

'Tomorrow, for an aperitif, 7 o'clock, at my place. You know the address.'

Tuesday 27 May, 7 p.m. Enghien-les-Bains

Daquin rang the bell. A click, the impressive black metal door opened, he went in. A servant wearing black trousers and a white jacket came to meet him. 'Monsieur is waiting for you in the garden,' and led him to the edge of the lake. There, beneath a chestnut tree, a garden table and armchairs on the lawn. Grey-blue lake beyond the tree-trunks. The water lapped against the stone wall. Oumazarov stood up to greet him and shook his hand. Very much the traditional businessman, young and dynamic. Daquin remembered having seen him on 4 April, in Kashguri's apartment, then in the Drugs Squad offices, before he was released after a firm intervention by the Minister of Defence.

'*Commissaire*, delighted to make your acquaintance in circumstances, let us say, acceptable for me. You've given me a few problems lately but you've given your government even more. Are you behind the Anglo-Saxon press campaign denouncing the violation by the French government of the embargo on weapons destined for Iran?'

'No, I've got nothing to do with that. My government does what it considers right in that field. I only crossed your path when Carim and Bodrum, whom you know well, might possibly have taken part in the murder of Sener.'

He was irritated. 'Since then the French police have officially admitted the responsibility of the Armenian terrorists and the question is closed. Therefore you didn't come to talk to me about that.'

'True.' At the mention of Sener it was the sumptuous Yildiz whom he saw in his mind's eye. Double game, Romero had said. Could it have been triple? 'I came to give you two items of news, which I'd like to discuss with you. First, Iran has just officially requested the extradition of Kashguri. Do you see what that means?'

The footman arrived, carrying a tray with glasses and an ice-bucket.

'Put all that down and leave us. What can I offer you?'

'Vodka with ice, thank you.'

'So, what does this mean, in your opinion?'

'That the Islamists are definitely rejecting the pro-Westerners and the moderates, and in future it will be necessary to go through them in order to conduct business in Iran. It will soon be a disadvantage to be linked to Parillaud or the Bank of Cyprus and the East.'

Oumourzarov prepared the glasses. They began to drink in silence.

'And your second item of news?'

'Kashguri has used the services of a Turkish extremist who had assassinated two of his compatriots here in France, and I think he had also executed Sener. His name is Ali Agça.' Oumourzarov did not react. 'We think that the said Ali Agça intends to assassinate the Pope during his visit to Paris.'

Oumourzarov put down his glass in surprise.

'Are you serious?'

'I fear I am.'

And Daquin gave a rapid description of the letter to the *Milliyet* and his recent visit to the Turkish police.

'I agree that it's hard to believe. But admit that if this did happen it would deal a very severe blow to certain Turkish interests in France. In plain words that makes two good reasons why you might risk finding yourself in the uncomfortable role of scapegoat.'

'*Commissaire*, I don't regret meeting you, I'm not bored for one moment in your company. Tell me now why you're here, apart from the passionate interest you feel for the Turks living in France.'

'Good question.' Awareness of absence and emptiness. 'My request is very simple. In the discussions you may have had with Kashguri can you remember anything, even apparently harmless, which could help me in finding Kashguri or Agça? An allusion, a joke, anything at all?'

A long silence. The two men finished their drinks, sipping slowly while looking at the lake, luminous, without a ripple. A very beautiful spring evening.

'Kashguri never spoke to me about Agça. For the good reason that he didn't know him. Only one person spoke to me about Agça, and that was Bertrand.'

Oumourzarov let Daquin absorb the news and then went on: 'It was right here, he was sitting in your place. He described him to me as a very strange fanatic.' Detached tone of voice. 'And he told me that here in France his only acquaintances were the Catholic fundamentalists. That made me laugh, for I'm totally secular. But there may be some connection with your story about the assassination of the Pope.' A pause. 'Would you like to stay to dinner with us, *commissaire*? My wife would be delighted to make your acquaintance.'

Wednesday 28 May, 9 a.m. Passage du Désir

Daquin earned more scepticism than enthusiasm from the people in charge of Official Travel.

'Search among the Catholic fundamentalists? What are your sources?'

'No source I can quote.'

'We've got no files about the fundamentalists. And what can a nationalist Turk, an Islamist, possibly have in common with Catholic fundamentalists?'

'I've no idea, it's not my culture. Do what you like about it.'

Conviction that they would do nothing.

*

Soleiman went into the local squad office. He had come to settle once and for all the question of the machine-gun attack on the Association of Electrical Technicians, which had since been assimilated with provocation by the Turkish extreme right. An office on the second floor, an inspector with a typewriter, a statement. On that day, at that time, he was at the Committee office, surrounded with many witnesses. Signature. Soleiman went out. By the door a young cop in plain clothes looked at him with curiosity.

'Monsieur Keyder?'

'Yes, that's me.'

'Superintendent Daquin would like to make your acquaintance and asks if you would kindly go to his office.'

'After you.'

Third floor. He recognized the glass door. As though it were yesterday. He fingered his upper lip. Felt his moustache, now growing again, to give himself confidence. The young cop left him. Daquin, seated behind his desk, watched him come in. He doesn't belong to me any more. It's still my jacket. But he's got his moustache back already.

Soleiman sat down. Daquin took a file from a drawer in his desk and pushed it over to him.

'That's the original of the file about you kept by the Turkish police. If you want to go back to your own country one day, you can do so more or less safely.'

Soleiman didn't dare believe it. Placed his hand on the file.

'How did you manage it?'

'That's my business.'

Soleiman opened the file and leafed through it. A kind of mist before his eyes.

'There aren't any photos. I haven't kept them as a souvenir, there never were any.'

Soleiman was struck dumb. Got up, took the file, stuffed it inside his jacket and left almost at a run.

Wednesday 28 May, noon. Parish of Saint-Bernard

Press conference. The Committee officially announced the success of their action and the beginning of legalized status for the Sentier workers. The Trades Union Confederations had sent representatives, there were many journalists from the newspapers, the radio and the television. Soleiman presided from the platform. He was the hero of the day. The file, that was still there between his jacket and his shirt, gave him a sensation of liberty.

Exciting. Four months that have changed my life. Here, nobody knows me. For them I'm only a militant. A machine for thinking and speaking, and that's all. I'll keep the memory of the Sentier like that of a warm stomach, the atmosphere of the streets, the cafés, the workrooms. And the memory of Daquin. His hand. The weight of his body. His gaze.

Wednesday 28 May 3 p.m. Passage du Désir

Daquin on the telephone. He was looking for people who knew the French Catholic fundamentalists and were capable of talking about them in a language he could understand. In the end he came to the Jesuits. He made an appointment for the following morning with a senior member of the Order, the spokesman for the French bishops.

Thursday 29 May, noon Passage du Désir

Daquin had recalled his troops. In the absence of Lavorel they were reduced to Romero and Attali, both somewhat rested but lacking in punch. Daquin spoke to them quickly about the clue involving the Catholic fundamentalists, without giving his sources. Polite scepticism. He presented them with a summary of the various current fundamentalist attitudes, at least as far as he had understood them that morning. They took notes, they concentrated, without enthusiasm. Finally Daquin produced a map of France on which he had marked the location of fundamentalist groups with different colours indicating various shades of opinion. Pink for those closest to orthodoxy, dark red for those most hostile to the Vatican.

'Good. There are three of us. The other police departments are not interested in my idea. Neither are you, either, but I'm your superior within the hierarchy. We've only time for one operation. Where shall we go?'

Attali bent over the map, suddenly interested.

'To Rouen, obviously.'

'I agree, to Rouen. Father Juan Roth Gomez runs a fundamentalist parish there. He was consecrated priest by Monsignor Lefebvre but left Ecône because he found the community too moderate. He's close to the "Sedes Vacans" group who regard the Pope as heretic from the time of Vatican II. He's a Spaniard. He's travelled widely in Europe and has recently been staying in Germany from where his father came. On the way to Rouen, the corpses of Celebi and VL. Rouen, not far from Paris. If Agça is somewhere, he's there. And the Pope arrives in Paris tomorrow. Romero, telephone your chum Petitjean. We're going to call on him this afternoon. In the mean time I'm going to take you for a quick snack, to raise the morale of the troops.'

Thursday 29 May, 5.15 p.m. Rouen

Daquin and his team arrived in an unmarked car outside a modest little house in a very quiet deserted street. Petitjean had done what he could to provide them with some information but in fact nobody knew anything about this house and its occupants, a priest and his old housekeeper. True, there were fiery sermons on Sundays in the nearby parish. It appeared that certain parishioners came from Paris every week to hear them. But the priest apparently led a blameless life and had a very good reputation among all the local tradespeople.

'We've got no choice. We're going in blind. Attalli, you've got fifteen minutes to find the ways out at the back and a point from which you can watch them. In a quarter of an hour we're going in. If nothing's happening after ten minutes, come and find us inside.'

Romero got out of the car to have a smoke.

*

Daquin rang the bell. An old woman who was rather stout and walked with difficulty, wearing a black smock and carpet slippers, opened the door.

'Madame, we're from the police, and we'd like to talk to Father Roth Gomez.'

'Come in, gentlemen. He's working in the dining-room, preparing his next sermon.'

She took them to the dining-room. Daquin signalled to Romero to make a quick tour of the house.

The small dining-room looked on to a garden, of which only part was visible, rough grass and three apple trees. The furniture was heavy, Henri II style, as sold by the Galeries Barbès. On the big table was a pile of books, two pads of paper and ten or so felt-tip pens of different colours. As they came in a man stood up.

Tall, sturdy, young, mop of black hair, very white complexion. And a gaze...fanatical, thought Daquin, He was wearing a worn cassock.

The old woman made the introductions.

'Father, some police officers who wish to speak to you.'

'Sit down, gentlemen. What can I do for you?' Spanish accent.

'Do you know Ali Agça?'

'Yes, indeed.' He folded his hands. 'He's more than a friend. Let us say a spiritual brother.'

'Is he here?'

'No, not at the moment. He's away for a few days. But he was here last Tuesday. Why these questions? Has some misfortune befallen him?'

Romero returned at that moment and indicated to Daquin that the house was empty.

'No, not as far as I know. Has he spoken to you of his wish to kill the Pope?'

'Monsieur, we no longer have a Pope. And it is truly our misfortune.'

'Let's not quibble. I mean Pope John-Paul II.'

'The man you call John-Paul II is a heretic, a secret agent in the pay of the communists. If someone were to kill him, it wouldn't be such a great misfortune. Since the so-called Vatican Council II the communists have infiltrated a whole section of the Catholic church. Fortunately...'

Attali came into the dining-room and leant over to Daquin: Kashguri's Renault 5 was parked in the garden.

'...some of us still embody the true faith, the church of former times will live again, you'll see. I myself am at God's disposal. I shall do what He commands me to do in order to restore the true church.'

'I'm sure of that, Father. I don't doubt it for a single moment. And do you also know Osman Kashguri, a friend of Agça?'

'I don't know his name. But someone came, about a month ago, who was sent by a friend of Ali. Unfortunately this man was a henchman of the devil.'

'What has happened to him?'

'I buried him in the garden.'

'What do you mean?'

262

'That's what I did. Where else would you want me to bury him? Not in consecrated ground, surely?'

'Of course not. But if you buried him, he must have been dead. How did he die?'

'God took pity on him.'

'Father, I don't doubt divine pity for one moment, but could you be a little more precise?'

'After a discussion with Ali, this man asked me for hospitality. I saw at once that evil was within him. And I was afraid that he would have a bad influence on Ali, who is a pure man. But the Church is a refuge. A man of God cannot refuse aid and succour when a sinner asks him for it. I arranged for him to have the bedroom next to mine. At first everything was more or less all right. And then he began to have trances. He sweated, he trembled. He seemed to be suffering deeply. It was the first time I had seen at close quarters a man possessed of the devil. I overcame him, I fastened him down to his bed, I brought him holy water and I blessed him several times a day. At one moment he began to shout. Ali and I gagged him. I didn't want the neighbours to know that in my house there was a man possessed of the devil. One morning I went in for the first blessing and I found him dead. I thanked God for having delivered him from his torment. Ali helped me and we buried him in the garden.'

'Did Agça know that he was fastened to his bed?'

'Of course. Sometimes he held conversations with him so that he would keep still.'

'Didn't Agça tell you that he was a heroin addict and didn't you want to call in a doctor?'

'A doctor for the body can do nothing when the soul is ill. And his soul was very ill. Drugs are an absolute evil. Believe me, if my prayers and my blessings were not able to help him, and my soul is very pure, then there was nothing to be done.'

'When was he delivered from his sufferings?'

'Last Sunday, just before the service, and I buried him before vespers.'

'Could you show us where you buried the body?'

'Why? I buried him very decently, and I performed all the necessary rites. And God is merciful.'

'I don't doubt that. But we must be able to identify the body, since you do not know his name. In order to inform the family, they too would like to pray for him, perhaps.'

'You are right. Follow me.'

*

Daquin, standing beneath an apple tree, gazed for a long moment at the dead body of Kashguri, stretched out on the grass. Clad in a strange white nightshirt, very full, fastened at the neck and the wrists, reaching down to his knees. Provided no doubt by the housekeeper. He had been wrapped in a white sheet and buried beneath a thin layer of earth, fifteen centimetres deep beneath an apple tree in blossom. Terribly thin, as though mummified, shoulder-length hair, black rings under his eyes, his skin streaked with green. Suffering. A drugged tramp in the midst of a withdrawal crisis. Only his hands had barely changed, long and thin, folded over his chest, they still gave an impression of strength, as they had done that day in the office. Daquin thrust his hands into his trouser pockets. He felt ferociously alive.

Romero, standing beside him, lit a small Tuscan cigar.

'It's the first time I've seen him.'

'He doesn't look much like the person he was when I met him. Handsome man, rather impressive. I must inform Anna of his death. She might want to arrange a funeral for him, a normal one, let us say. Romero, call the police in Rouen, let's have done with this mad priest as soon as possible. I feel very uncomfortable here.'

Friday 30 May, 5 p.m. Champs-Elysées

The crowd had gathered along the avenue, in order to get a glimpse of the Holy Father. A crowd, well ... not really a crowd. Two or three rows of spectators on each side, all along the avenue, behind the protective barriers. Unmarked police cars drove up and down the whole time, on the wide pavements where traffic and parking had been prohibited. State security police officers every twenty metres, facing the crowd. Scouts everywhere. The security machine was in place.

Waiting. A helicopter landed in the place de l'Etoile. The Pope stepped out. An hour and a half late. It had been an order from the Official Travel people. He got into an open car and began to go down the avenue, standing, waving to the crowd. Cheering, people crossed themselves. At the same time, at the Rond-Point, a police car braked suddenly. Two inspectors got out, revolvers in their hands. They had just seen a man who had been sitting on an electricity transformer stand up and hoist himself into a tree, a sports kit-bag over his shoulder. Whistles blew, plainclothes police and scouts converged from all sides. The man dropped down from the tree. An inspector fired into the air. Two other shots answered him. Scuffle. Two scouts and a spectator were very slightly injured. The man disappeared into the crowd. The kit-bag remaining in the tree contained an old German MP 44. Later the fingerprints of Ali Agça would be identified. His chances of killing the Pope with that type of weapon, and at that distance, said the experts, were very slim.

A reporter for Agence France Presse, alerted by the skirmish, asked some inspectors for information. It was a lone gunman, he had been dealt with.

Telegram from Agence France Presse: *A terrorist attempts to fire at the Pope.*

Astonishment and excitement in the editorial departments. The press office at police headquarters was overwhelmed with telephone calls. Categorical denial. It had been an unfortunate mistake. We arrested 'a man with a gun', that was to say a pickpocket and not a terrorist. Shots for a pickpocket? The press blamed the nervousness of the security services for the incident.

*

All the clandestine workers in the Sentier were given legal status. But at first the identity cards arrived in dribs and drabs. Then, when the legalization was well on the way, the military *coup d'état* in Turkey had just taken place. And everyone was obsessed by the violence of the repression there. In the end there was no great celebration to fête our victory. And that's my one remaining regret from the spring of 1980.

Ali Agça did not succeed in assassinating the Pope on 13 May 1981 in Rome. Neither did the fanatical priest who attacked him with a bayonet on 12 May 1982 at Fatima.

Daquin never saw Soleiman again.

Anna Beric and Meillant are living in the Bahamas, where they are bored.

The area of the Golden Crescent – Afghanistan, Pakistan, Iran – now produces 70 per cent of the heroin consumed in Europe, and 20 per cent of that destined for the North American market. It offers serious competition to the Golden Triangle, Burma and Thailand.